DURANGO

DURANGO

A Novel

JOHN B. KEANE

MERCIER PRESS

Mercier Press
PO Box No. 5, 5 French Church Street, Cork
24 Lower Abbey Street, Dublin 1

© John B. Keane 1992

ISBN 1 85635-001-0

First published March 1992
Reprinted April 1992, June 1992, September 1992, February
1993, August 1993

A CIP record for this book is available from the British Library.

To Noel Pearson

Printed in Ireland by Colour Books Ltd.

1

The idea was Mark Doran's and throughout the years that followed he never grew tired of reminding anybody who would listen that it occurred to him on his way homewards from the quarterly cattle and pig fair in the village of Tubberlick.

It was towards the end of March. Stars twinkled in the evening sky and there was a mild twinge of frost in the air.

He drew rein on his grey mare and slid to the roadway, staggering backwards as he did but managing to maintain his balance, albeit with some difficulty. He held firmly on to the mare's tail as he composed himself. Planting his feet firmly apart he shook his curly head to dispel the drunkenness. Well-knit, spare and classically handsome, not his but a general female estimation, he loosened the tweed tie to which he would never become accustomed. For several minutes he inhaled the sobering night air, each breath deeper than the one preceding as his grogginess receded.

'Too much porter girl,' he explained to the mare. For her part she moved inwards to the green margin of the roadway and sampled a mouthful of the fresh grass which had sprung up abundantly over the previous fine days. Mark Doran undid his flies and released his plentiful waters through the third and fourth bars of the rust-covered gate where he had stopped so often in the past. The mare, now in her tenth year, champed contentedly as she moved slowly along the narrow sward.

Mark Doran absently secured his flies and leaned on the uppermost bar of the gate. In the adjoining hills the smoke ascended in rakish plumes from the cottages and farmhouses whose lights dotted the landscape. There was no sound to be heard saving the mare's incisive cropping, now growing fainter as she moved further away from the gate. Mark Doran located his watch in a coat pocket. Six forty-five. Barring a calamity he should arrive home by seven. Then he would eat the boiled bacon, cabbage and potatoes which always confronted him on the kitchen table, steaming and savoury whenever he returned ravenous from the public houses of Tubberlick. The slobber trickled down the sides of his mouth at the prospect. He could see his mother sitting by the fire, a fork in her hand, alert to his every need, ready to coil the juicy cabbage in the skillet around the fork prongs or to impale a choice sliver of streaky bacon whenever the contents of his plate ran down. There wasn't a woman in the hills could prepare cabbage like his mother.

'Whoa girl!' he called gently to the mare as he turned her back towards the gate. Lodging a left hand on her withers he drew her close to the gate pier. Placing his right hand atop the pier he swung into the saddle and bent over her chest to retrieve the reins.

It was precisely at the moment when he turned her that the idea came to him. Privately he always regarded it as more than just an idea. In his considered opinion inspiration seemed to be a fairer assessment.

In Tubberlick that day the talk in the pubs had been of a Second World War. There had been no great sense of alarm. The local papers had carried a story that conscription was being introduced in Britain.

Czechoslovakia had already been annexed by Germany and a mutual assistance pact between Britain, France and Poland had been ratified in its wake. There were other ominous rumblings from Italy so that it was no trouble for the more astute observers in Tubberlick to deduce that a large scale war in Europe was inevitable.

'And if there's war in Europe,' the forecast came from the proprietor of McCarthy's public house in Tubberlick where Mark Doran had spent most of his day, 'the price of cattle and pigs will soar.'

Word of Vester McCarthy's widely respected prognostications may or may not have reached the ears of the five cattle buyers in attendance at the Tubberlick quarterly fair. Certainly they were not reflected in the inexplicably low prices being offered for the wide variety of cattle on offer from frisky calves to venerable Roscreas. The latter was the name given to old cows whose usefulness had been terminated by age and who ended their days in the cannery in the far-off town of Roscrea.

Mark Doran had long suspected the visiting buyers of being part of a ring and his suspicions were reinforced by the fact that cattle prices in Tubberlick were always a fraction behind those in other villages of the countryside. The trouble was that the villages in question were too far distant, the nearest ten and the furthest fifteen miles. Tubberlick on the other hand was only five miles from Mark Doran's farmstead. The nearest cattle wagons were at Trallock Station almost forty miles away.

'Cattle jobbers have to live too', his mother would say whenever he voiced his dissatisfaction after a frustrating day of haggling at the quarterly fair. She enjoyed in particular the calf dealers with their outsize horserails who called to the door. They brought news from faraway places as well as more intimate and often sensational disclosures from the less forthcoming of her immediate neighbours. Such revelations, false or true, had considerable trade value at mealtimes and even during sale negotiations. Mark himself showed little interest in these travellers' tales but he listened nevertheless.

'Whoa, whoa!' he called to the mare. Dutifully she drew to a leisurely halt. Sobering by the minute Mark sat alert in his saddle and waited. In the distance behind him there arose the sound of discordant singing. He smiled to himself. It could only be the Mullanney brothers Tom and Jay in the horse-rail. Their father would be fast asleep on a bag of hay on the floor of this rickety conveyance, senseless from the day-long session of drinking which had begun at noon, the precise time he had received payment for the five calves which they had transported to Tubberlick shortly after daybreak.

Mark also had calves but he had decided against offering them for sale in Tubberlick. He would try elsewhere later in the year, much later, if his freshly-born idea should materialise. He would keep it to himself for awhile, let it simmer, see how he might feel on the morrow or during the weeks ahead.

Mark had found, after his father's death two years before, that there were few places to turn when he wanted practical advice about holding or releasing his stock. He had found that it was wiser to wait, not always, but generally. Once he had waited too long and paid the price when the bottom fell out of the in-calf market because of over-supply. Things were always changing in the cattle world, sometimes imperceptibly, sometimes suddenly. Occasionally it was possible to make a fairly accurate prediction but there were no killings. The biggest bonus a producer might expect was a marginal increase on the market prices of the previous week.

He slackened the rein so that the mare might again address herself to the green margin. While she munched he waited. The singing had stopped. The brothers were arguing now, loud expletives shattering the benign silence of the bright March night. The stars still twinkled undismayed and the full moon, unaffected by cloud, shone serenely on blasphemous and pious alike as hair-raising threats, fiercely mouthed, erupted in turn from the approaching Mullanneys. To those who were not acquainted with their temperaments the Mullanneys represented extreme physical danger when their tempers ran high. Their acquaintances knew differently.

Nonie Doran, Mark's mother, summed it up accurately when she heard an account of one of the fiercest fights to have taken place in the Mullanney household. Mother, father, brothers and sisters had all been involved and such were the scars borne by the menfolk after the affray that no male member of the family attended Sunday Mass for several weeks. Only Tom, the oldest was possessed of the gumption to present himself at the creamery with the milk supply, morning after morning, while his father and brothers wilted under their self-imposed incarceration.

'They're like the tinkers,' Mark Doran's mother Nonie had commented. 'They'll only fight amongst themselves.'

This wasn't quite accurate. While it was true to say that they preferred to fight amongst themselves it would also be true to say that they were not above fighting with others. After their fights there were no recriminations for long periods but then a member of the clan would recall a particularly shifty blow or kick during a previous engagement and soon the fists would be flying. There was no resorting to weapons and no kicking while a combatant was on the ground.

'Night boys!' Mark called as he drew on the rein and rode alongside the brothers. Curled up on his haybag, on the floor of the cart, lay the sleeping form of the father of the family, old Haybags Mullanney. It was a truly profound sleep of the variety that can only be induced by whiskey and from which there is no waking until the participant has snorted and snored his way back to sobriety.

'Who's out there?' The question came from Tom Mullanney.

'It's me, Mark Doran,' Mark replied.

The disclosure was greeted with wild whoops of delight.

It was as though they hadn't seen him for years. They relapsed immediately into a high-pitched, unsustainable song. At its conclusion Mark posed a question which he dared not ask in Tubberlick while Haybags was within ear-shot. Drunk as the brothers seemed to be they suddenly displayed an uncharacteristic caution at the mention of prices.

A whispered exchange took place. The last thing they wanted to do was to adopt a churlish attitude towards a neighbour and proven friend. Mark waited, uneasily. He had qualms about asking in the first place.

'He didn't tell us the exact amount mind you,' Tom Mullanney replied after awhile, indicating the sleeping form at his feet, 'but what he did say was that they made more than he expected.'

Mark Doran knew that he should not have asked in the first place. His mother might say that it was none of his business. He saw the whole matter in another light. The cloak of secrecy which his neighbours insisted in drawing over cattle prices would always militate against their chances of securing just prices for their stock. He knew the shame and degradation he himself had experienced when he was forced to sell cattle at less than their value. He fully understood the reluctance shown by the Mullanney brothers when his curiosity got the better of him. They were too proud to admit that they should have received more and ashamed to admit that they might have been duped. This was the common attitude all over the countryside. Nevertheless, he decided to probe further.

'How much did he get the last time, do you remember?'

Any other question, personal or otherwise, would have elicited an immediate answer from the brothers.

Instead of a response, however, there followed an uneasy silence. It remained thus for several minutes as the cavalcade proceeded on its sluggish way homeward.

It was the same with bonhams and pigs, Mark thought. At the market in Tubberlick, buying and selling were conducted in confessional whispers. At the end of the day there was no means by which one could arrive at an average price. Consequently, there was no method of assessing loss or profit.

Imported maize ground into meal was the basic ingredient in the pig fattening process. It was also used, mixed with flour, in the baking of griddle bread. A griddle-sized disc of dough, flattened by rolling pin, was cut diagonally into four quarters or pointers as they were called in the hill country and baked on both sides on an iron griddle over an open fire of peat coals. Sliced down the middle and liberally smeared with home-produced, salted butter, the yellow meal pointer was the most popular and palatable of all the baked produce common to the hill country.

'Oh for a pointer of my mother's griddle bread with the fresh butter melting on its top!' was the plaint of many a far-flung exile when confronted with less salubrious fare in restaurant or boarding house.

Once while Mark Doran was visiting an elderly grand-uncle, Joss the Badger Doran, in the inner hills the whole question of pig profits received an airing.

'I swear to you,' said the old man as he sat hunched over the hearth, 'I never made a copper profit out of pigs.'

'Why fatten them so?' Mark had asked.

'What other way is there of saving a bit of money?' the old man had replied.

'And what about profit?' Mark had enquired.

'I have no doubt there are some who manage to make profit,' the old man had countered, 'but all I ever found was the bare return for my investment when the time for selling came round. You must allow too for the pig you'll lose. Have you thought of that? The nearest vet is twenty-two miles away and you have to pay for his car as well as his services so I never bothered with vets. I know. I know,' the old man had continued, 'skimp on the vet and you lose more in the long run.'

As well as the yellow meal, fistfuls of pollard and bran were also added to the pig food. The cost of such ingredients was easily totted.

'But then,' asked Mark's grand-uncle, 'how do you put a price on home-produced feed like potatoes and cabbage and the occasional turnip? Riddle me that my boy and I'll pass you for a scholar.'

There was a good deal of truth in what the old man had said. His wife was equally vocal but would seem to be the better economist.

'What ye forget,' said she, 'is that all bar the cows are fed out of the pigs' mess. Turkey, hen, duck and goose, all gets their share and that's where the profit is.'

'I'm taking all that into the reckoning and maybe there's something to what you say,' the old man was always conciliatory when refuting his spouse.

'You'd be setting the potatoes anyway,' she continued as she drew upon the butt of a Woodbine, 'and what great cost is a few bags extra of seed potatoes?'

'Are you forgetting cabbage?' the old man asked.

'Indeed I'm not,' she was quick to reply, 'for cabbage does not come into it.'

'Doesn't come into it,' he scoffed, 'and pray where does all the cabbage our pigs does be eatin' come from?'

'You're talking about the outside leaves now,' she reminded him, 'and not about the body or the heart. You're talking about rough leaves that humans won't stomach, big coarse leaves that's of no use to anyone saving the pig or the cow. Aren't my poor paws blistered from chopping them same leaves. The cabbage and the spud is more than three-quarters of the pig's diet and where are you leaving the waste from the kitchen table? The pig will do for that. The pig isn't choosy. The pig will do for anything.'

Mark was forced to concede that it was a system suited to the small producer. Production on a larger scale was a gamble, often dangerous. If what the old woman said was true, and Mark would not deny that most of it was, then the pig was subsidising the hen and the turkey, two vital sources of income for the hill farmers, the fattened turkeys for the Christmas tables of town and city dwellers and the weekly lay of eggs to barter for flour, tea, sugar, tobacco and all the other household requirements with the occasional luxury such as a pot of jam or a barm brack.

The turkey money, which came once a year a few weeks before Christmas, was traditionally spent on the purchase of clothes and goodies for the Christmas proper, clothes in this instance to mean bibs and underclothes for the females of the household and socks or caps for the menfolk. Heavy clothes were another undertaking financed by the last cattle sales of the year at the Tubberlick quarterly fair near the end of October. Mark Doran was obliged to agree that pigs were profit-making provided that there was no ill-luck and provided that a fair price was assured. The likelihood of the latter happening was the exception rather than the rule unless the producer was presented with access to bigger markets. He never denied that a frugal living might be wrought from the average hill farm but only by dint of hard work, average luck and an able woman in the background. Without the last the struggle for survival would be unbearable.

Mark was roused from his reverie by the argument. Once again he drew rein. The Mullanney brothers had alighted from the rail and were squaring off preparatory to a bout of fisticuffs on the roadway. The horse, a powerful bay gelding of six years stood idly by, well used to the tantrums of his volatile passengers while the father of the combatants slept blissfully on. Had he been astir and able to move he might well have challenged the winner. Even in his supine state it was clear to see that he was an out-sized man. Haybags was never known to use his fists. Rather would he seize an opponent by the lapels or shirt front and shake the victim till the teeth rattled in his head. Another tactic of his was to run at his foes, hobnailed boots clattering, much like a war horse. Resignedly Mark Doran turned the mare and rode to where the brothers stood facing each other, their faces taut, their fists clenched, their eyes wild and bloodshot. Mark dismounted and looked from one to the other and then into the horse-rail. It would be difficult, he told this to himself, to imagine a more bizarre scene. The brothers ignored his arrival and were now involved in some orthodox feinting, feeling each other out, not that there was any need. Neither was been able to remember the number of occasions in which they had been similarly involved since they were children.

'Now boys!' Mark moved between them, hands elevated, palms extended, 'there's no call for this, no call at all!' His words had little effect.

'Keep out of it,' he was warned by each in turn. Then predictably for some reason best known to themselves they decided to opt for a wrestling contest rather than a fistfight. One moment they were sparring like gentlemen and the next they were rolling over on the roadway ending up under the gelding's legs. The creature stood impassively as ever while the brothers extricated themselves, one at either side of the cart. Tom, the more eager to resume where they had left off, vaulted over the back shafts and leaped on his brother's back before he could rise from the roadway.

Bucking like a bronco Jay threw his older brother out over his head and landed him, without apparent hurt, on the grassy margin.

'Quiet!' Mark called loudly and raised a hand. Sitting on his behind on the grass Tom Mullanney, temporarily winded, made no attempt to rise. His brother Jay turned to look in the direction from which the sounds were coming.

'Stragglers from the fair,' Mark extended a hand to Tom and brought him to his feet.

'Into the car now before we're the talk of the countryside.'

'We're that as it is,' Jay Mullanney threw back as he climbed the rail.

Mark remounted hurriedly and soon the party was on its way once more.

'What was that all about?' Mark asked.

'You and your bloody prices!' came the terse reply from Jay Mullanney. 'I was for telling and this fellow wasn't.'

'I was just curious,' Mark tried to sound disinterested. 'I had thought to bring some of my own calves today but I decided I'd check the prices first.'

'Ours didn't do very well,' Jay Mullanney admitted, 'back ten shillings a head on this time last year.'

'Amen't I the lucky man then I didn't take them to Tubberlick,' Mark said, trying hard to conceal his delight and more importantly the fact that his presentiments concerning the Tubberlick prices had proved accurate. His only business at the fair had been as an onlooker. A watching brief was what I had he told himself happily. He was sorry for the Mullanneys but then they didn't have to sell. Theirs was a substantial farm, soggy maybe in some of its more level fields but with the carrying power of twenty-two milch cows, two horses and forty or more assorted dry stock consisting of store bullocks, fat heifers, heifers and weanlings. On top of that Mark never recalled a time when there hadn't been a score of pigs fattening and a sow farrowing. So why sell he asked himself? An outing, of course, a day on the liquor to rouse the brain and shake off the cramps of winter, an escape from the house and outhouses until the blooms of spring brightened the meadows. Partly this was one of the reasons he himself had gone to Tubberlick. All of his neighbours admitted as much to themselves. They offered different excuses to their women-folk, those of them who considered it expedient. Others, like Mark, retained their sucky calves and offered them at the October fairs in Tubberlick and other villages as weanlings. Somehow there was always a market for weanlings. Mark put it down to the high incidence of losses in calves in the early spring and summer.

Mark would attend several fairs between now and the final October fair at Tubberlick. Mostly he would interest himself in prices but if he saw what he believed to be a bargain he would not hesitate about purchasing. The farm was never short of grass between the months of April and October. Despite the death of his father, a shrewd and perceptive farmer, Mark began to see his own function in a clearer light. He regarded himself as an innovator and a speculator and despite the fact that he hadn't a great deal to show for his enterprise he was learning every day and soon, very soon, his investments would begin to realise themselves. The great idea which visited him after he had drenched the grasses through the iron gate was not conceived purely by chance. It was the culmination of much profound thought and observation as well as seemingly fruitless travel through the numerous villages of the hill country that inspired the vision. That was the word that had escaped him since the revelation at the iron gate. He would, however, keep the vision to himself for awhile yet. He would need to add more body to it first and maybe discuss it discreetly with somebody who wasn't given to loose talk, a man with the requisite knowledge and experience to weigh its merits.

'Luckily for me,' said Mark out of hearing of the Mullanneys, 'I know such a man.'

Who else but his grand-uncle Joss the Badger! No better man to sift the chaff and point out the pitfalls and yet never a man to ignore the advantages. Mark resolved there and then that he would visit the old man before Easter. There was a small thatched pub a mile or so from the Badger's dwelling. They had drunk there together many a time when Mark's father was alive but then there seemed to be time for visiting, time for so many things. He would take the mare, put the old man in the saddle and sit behind him on the mare's haunches maintaining a grip on the old man's coat-tails in such a way that neither of them would come to grief, not even when they were returning from the pub in the early hours of the morning.

He would spend the night with the old couple. His mother would handle the cows without difficulty even though the yield would have improved substantially by then. She could have one of the Mullanney girls down to help. She never grew tired of expressing her admiration for their willingness to work.

'And there's many a smart buck,' she would say pointedly to nobody in particular, 'who might travel farther and fare worse.'

As usual she had been telling the truth. Fight they might amongst themselves but shirk never! In the meadow, the bog or the gardens, the boys were capable of putting the best to shame. Jay Mullanney was talking now.

'Come up with us for an hour,' came the expected invitation, 'we'll have a game of cards after we eat. We'll cheat the girls and you can help us unload our cargo.'

Mark considered the invitation before declining. It was a warm and generous household if explosive at times. The girls were buxom, robust, and playful although not Annie. Annie was the youngest and even if she took her mother's side in every argument she was the most reasonable and effective when it became necessary to call a truce at the height of a disturbance. At sixteen she was dark-eyed and sallow but pretty, very pretty in a childish way. Although Mark never failed to notice the more obvious advantages of the other sisters, the sonsy charms, the well-defined buttocks and bosoms which often kept him awake nights and conversely helped him to sleep at the height of his fantasies it was to Annie he would always turn when he visited.

If she were studying he would sit beside her and pretend to be interested in what she was doing or if she was near the fire he would always find a place by her side. Nobody minded, least of all Annie. The other sisters realised that he was simply seeking refuge with the least dangerous member of the household's females. The relationship was filled with banter and everybody saw it as harmless, more like a brother and sister situation than anything else, Mark the protective, overseeing element of the liaison and Annie the girl-child in need of fraternal protection. If he sat near one of the older girls it would be a far more serious matter out of which anything might be read and out of which might emerge the most dangerous complications.

'Come on,' Jay was appealing now, 'for the bare hour only.'

'No but thanks,' Mark explained how it had hardly been fair to leave his mother on her own since early morning with stock to feed and cows to milk.

'Before the end of the week,' he promised. He dismounted from the mare and bade the brothers to take care with their father. It had taken the pair and two other grown men in their prime to lift Haybags from McCarthy's public house in Tubberlick to the horse-rail, the back laths of which had been removed so that he could be laid to rest without too much difficulty on the flat of the cart.

Haybags Mullanney weighed twenty-two stone, or as his son Tom might put it, 'two and three-quarter hundred weights of dead weight, deader than the deadest carcass when he has whiskey inside in him.'

'We'll have no bother with him,' Tom announced

cheerfully. 'We'll take off the back laths first. Then we'll untackle the horse and heel him out like any other load.'

'We could leave him in the rail till morning,' said Jay as soon as he recovered from the convulsions of laughter occasioned by Tom's suggestion.

'And suppose,' said Tom, 'that he woke up in the middle of the night and found himself on his own, under the stars!'

The trio parted company on this sobering note, Mark turning left into the haggard at the side of the dwelling-house. The brothers with another half-mile to go alighted from the rail, Tom leading the gelding by the head up the steep incline towards the Mullanney homestead, Jay following behind with his hands firmly pressed against the back laths lest Haybags be heeled out before his time.

Nonie Doran stood framed in the doorway as Mark entered the haggard. She watched as he led the mare to the stable. Behind her back her hands clutched an oats' satchel.

'Welcome home,' she called as she approached with the oats.

'It's good to be home Ma,' Mark replied, bending to kiss her gently on the forehead.

'Every horse earns its oats,' she laughed as she hung the satchel over the mare's head. 'Your own is on the table. I'll be in shortly.'

Later as he sat replete by the open fire she questioned him about his activities throughout the day. Prices were her paramount interest and then with womanly curiosity she asked about the public houses of Tubberlick and the sayings and doings of the denizens therein. He answered freely. He did not tell her of the idea. She would be the first to know when he started to put it into action. That was her unquestioned entitlement. Theirs was a household which generated a good deal of understandable envy among the hill people. The farm was medium-sized, relatively dry and thriving. His father had left no debts. From a purely commercial point of view his demise turned out to be an outstanding asset. Nonie Doran, in order to avail of the widow's pension, signed the farm, lock, stock and barrel over to her only son, thereby providing them both with a new-found independence which could only succeed in enhancing their relationship. Add to this Nonie's known expertise with all kinds of fowl-rearing, egg-producing, butter-making and calf-rearing, among numerous other attributes and you were left with a model undertaking. The grief which they both felt for the man who had passed on would never really wane but time had brought surcease of the more acute grief.

That night in bed Mark allowed his thoughts to wander to a girl with red hair he had seen in the grocery section of McCarthy's pub in Tubberlick upon his arrival at the village that very morning. He had nodded warmly but courteously in her direction and she had rewarded him with a smile. From the red head his thoughts wandered to the older of the Mullanney girls Ellie and Bridgie. He made no attempt to dispel their buxom figures from his passionate flights of fancy but it was with the dark eyes of young Annie that his night's sleep had to contend. Suddenly he blushed and sat upright recalling an incident from the previous year's corn-threshing in the Mullanney haggard. Without knowing how or why he found himself entangled with her on a deep pile of the loose straw which lay everywhere. His head had been turned somewhat by the two large glasses of whiskey Tom and Jay had handed to him in turn not long before the outrage and that was what he self-righteously called it in the dark of his room.

Suddenly the horseplay stopped and he found himself on his back with Annie kneeling on his chest, her thin hands on his broad shoulders, the sloe-like, wide eyes, infinitely deep, quizzically searching for something he knew not what in his. She had only been fifteen at the time without a breast or a buttock to her as his grand-uncle's wife might say.

'Jesus!' he cried out panic-stricken, 'get up girl, don't your father hang me.'

Frightened and not fully comprehending she stood biting the nails of her right hand her back pressed against an out-house wall. Rising he brushed the straw from his hair and clothes and then noticing her confusion he called out: 'Come on. I'll race you to the house.'

Good God, he thought before he succumbed to sleep, she was only fifteen and me a grown man on top of twenty-six. There had been numerous girls all marriageable but as his grand-uncle had sagely observed: 'You'll be in no hurry. You've a mother who'll look out for you.'

Other mothers with marriageable daughters knew instinctively that Mark was a waste of time, for the present anyway. His mother was a youthful fifty-five and would not be likely to be too favourably disposed towards marriage for her only son. For all their shrewdness and generally unerring instincts they were wrong. Nonie had seen the first grey hair on Mark's curly black head. She had been twenty-eight herself when she walked up the aisle with Mark's father and he had been forty. Mark had been a difficult birth, touch and go throughout the delivery and she had been cautioned about further pregnancy. Life was lonely without her husband and the hills were lonely enough especially in winter. A few grand-children now would change all that.

2

Vester McCarthy, proprietor of McCarthy's bar and grocery in the village of Tubberlick, stood over six feet two inches in his stockings. He was, if one could place any credence in the claims of his female neighbours in the village's only street, as fine a figure of a man as ever took leave of a woman's womb. He carried himself like a field-marshal or so he believed and he sported a fine, flowing moustache which lent authority and dignity to an otherwise unengaging face.

In the dance-hall in his younger days it was said of him that he had a beautiful carriage. In truth he had been a past master of the old time waltz in his heyday and it was taken for granted that he would always be the man to lead the floor when the eximious strains of a Strauss waltz or the wilder music of an Irish reel set the feet tapping and the pulses racing. No one ever dared to usurp his position as floor leader in the Tubberlick Parochial Hall or indeed any of the numerous ballrooms, independent and parochial, within a ten mile radius of Tubberlick.

Among other eminent and prestigious distinctions he was chairman of the local football club, secretary of the Tubberlick trout anglers' association, a leading member of the local confraternity, president of the Parochial Hall Committee and, according to Parson Archibald Reginald Percival Scuttard, Rector of the local Protestant Church, 'as big a bollix as you'd meet in a three week walk'.

There was only one business in which Vester McCarthy did not involve himself and that was politics. These he eschewed with unflagging diligence although he would always subscribe and be seen to subscribe to church gate collections regardless of the party involved.

'My conscience will tell me how to vote when the time comes', he would say whenever he was asked to nominate his choice of candidate.

'I will always do the right thing on the day', was another of his favourite retorts and yet there were very few who would consider him evasive. Pillar of the church he might be and moral fibre of the village but he was no paragon. He had two weaknesses if weaknesses they could be called. He indulged in occasional skites and whenever the opportunity presented itself he liked to allow his hand to linger on a well-designed female posterior. His neighbours would say that there was no great harm in a few drinks now and again.

'And sure,' they attested with tongue in cheek, 'the other thing is no more than a sign of health.'

The women of Tubberlick, especially the older women, tended to be more tolerant than the men in this latter respect and were reluctant to condemn those males of the area who might stand accused of excessive interest in the female form and over-indulgence, true or false, in impure activities of a sexual nature. To give Vester McCarthy no more than his due he knew which buttocks to pat and he knew where and when to pat them. As in all such perilous exercises, however, it is possible to grievously err on the patability or unpatability of certain buttocks with the direst consequences. Vester McCarthy was no exception. His face had been slapped on occasion. He had been threatened with assault from outraged husbands but because of his size and appearance he was never physically attacked.

'Such are the hazards of bottom-patting my boy,' Archie Scuttard was heard to say after it had come to his ears through a crony that Vester McCarthy's shins had been kicked with more vehemence than was strictly necessary by a new and rather prim, young female teacher who had accepted an appointment in the National School of Tubberlick.

Always after a quarterly fair Vester McCarthy divested himself of his shop clothes and donned one of his better suits preparatory to pub-crawling the village but always ending up, still on his feet, at his own licensed premises.

Sometimes he bought a drink for one of the down-and-outs who regularly propped up the four other bars in the village. It depended on Vester's mood. If the fair of the day before had brought exceptional business to his bar and grocery he could be depended upon to buy at least one drink for the regular spongers at each of the four pubs.

Occasionally he joined company with the stronger farmers of the hinterland who might have business in the village and stopped off for a drink or two before returning home; other times it might be a fellow publican on an identical peregrination or, to be fair to Vester, anybody or group with a capacity to buy a round of drinks.

After this particular fair, the first quarterly of the year, Vester McCarthy was not in the most jovial of moods. Business had been anything but booming on the previous day and to crown his worries his over-all sales had been down since the beginning of the year.

Further compounding his woes was the fact that a number of the smaller, poverty-stricken farmers in the hill country were unable to meet their quarterly obligations and he had been obliged to curtail further credit.

As he entered the Widow Hegarty's, the last premises before his return to base, who should he happen to see seated unsteadily on a high stool but his arch-enemy Parson Archibald Reginald Percival Scuttard.

'Scuttard by name and scuttered by nature.' He made certain that the phrase was addressed to himself.

'Nevertheless,' said he still talking to himself, 'it wouldn't do if I didn't offer the ruffian a drink. I could be accused of religious bias although his likes screwed us into the ground for many a year.'

'Care for a drink Archie,' he made the offer as if there never had existed the slightest difference of opinion between them.

'Sorry old boy,' Archie Scuttard replied drunkenly, 'but as you can see I am already in company.'

'Well if your friend has no objection,' Vester McCarthy persisted, 'he's welcome to one too.'

Archie leaned across the counter and muttered something about gift horses to the Widow Hegarty who took the hint and carefully measured two half glasses of Jameson seven-year-old into a pewter measure before transferring them to the already partially filled glasses of Archie Scuttard and his friend.

'You have the advantage over me sir,' Vester addressed the Parson's companion knowing that Archie, out of sheer mischief, would never involve himself in such a mundane rite as formal introduction.

'Oh excuse my ignorance,' Archie turned around on his stool and with an expansive gesture introduced his friend. 'Allow me to present my colleague Monsignor ...' Archie's voice trailed away. He turned to his companion with a quizzical look on his craggy features.

'Monsignor what was it again old boy?' he asked.

'Binge,' came the reply in a soft American accent. 'Monsignor Dan Binge.'

Vester McCarthy did well to contain a deep chuckle. Binge and Scuttard he grinned. What a combination and to think that both were clergymen! The thought gave him a feeling of superiority over the Protestant Rector. It was a rare feeling especially since he had always felt inferior in the scoundrel's company up until then.

'And how is Mary?' the Widow Hegarty asked formally.

'She was often better thank you,' Vester McCarthy did not refer to his wife's current ailment. Always in the spring Mary McCarthy was visited by a blight of ugly boils. These occurred for the most part on the posterior where they were safely concealed from the curious eyes of the villages but this springtime her neck had been invaded by a large and ugly swelling which showed no signs of maturing unlike its undercover kindred which disappeared, unfailingly after a fortnight, allowing Vester to re-establish his rightful sovereignty over that part of the anatomy which he held so dear.

'And Sally?' the Widow Hegarty asked.

'Never better,' Vester lied. The truth was that his only daughter now in her twenty-ninth year was, to put it quite bluntly, starting to feel a real ache for a man. There had been suitors almost from the day she bade farewell to her teens but as in so many similar cases she did not quite fancy what she could have and could not have what she fancied.

Vester and Mary McCarthy had subtly discouraged the less desirable of the suitors and blatantly encouraged others and here we are, thought Vester, at the end of the day back in square one with devil the man to show for all our enterprise. It wasn't that Sally was too choosy. It was rather that she was unfortunate in that the young men which she fancied were either spoken for beforehand or disinclined to have anything to do with marriage. Only the day before she had suffered another disappointment although she had not felt as disheartened afterwards as she might have. The object of her affection, young Mark Doran, had spent the better part of the afternoon in the bar. She had seen him countless times before on the premises and in the street. Occasionally too he would attend the Sunday night dance at the parochial hall but this time he presented a different image. In the hall he had been in the habit of standing at the rear near the door with the assorted recalcitrants of the parish spotting form as they so vulgarly called it but now he seemed to have assumed a new stature. It was as

if he had put that period of wayward youthfulness behind him and come into his own as a man and wouldn't
he be nice too with his own place and a cute, curly head
on his fine square shoulders. He wouldn't be after my
money either. It would be Sally's guess that there was no
scarcity in that respect.

'And I get on well with his mother,' Sally told herself and this was true for Sunday after ten o'clock Mass
Nonie Doran purchased her week's groceries at Mc-
Carthy's while Mark sampled the wares at the Widow
Hegarty's with his friends from the hill country. Sally
had skilfully drawn him into conversation and her
mother, fully alerted to the daughter's strategy, made
sure that they were given ample opportunity to converse. Whenever Sally was called upon to dispense an
order for drink in Sylvester McCarthy's Mary McCarthy
nimbly stepped in and filled the order herself. Haybags
Mullanney in whose company Mark Doran happened to
be at the time, had become engaged in conversation with
one of the local cattle jobbers. Mark Doran, at least as far
as Mary McCarthy could see, seemed interested enough
but that night when mother and daughter sat in the
kitchen counting the day's takings it was revealed that
Mark seemed only mildly interested. Sally had asked
him after an hour's exclusive conversation if he would
be attending the dance on the following Sunday night.
He pretended not to hear at first but when she repeated
the question he mentioned something about having to
visit a grand-uncle. Only too aware that her chances
were running out with every passing year Sally had
persevered.

'I won't see you there so,' she said. Again there followed the calculated hesitation.

'You never know,' he said which, on reflection, in
hill-folk terminology, was as positive an answer as one
was likely to get from the young men in that part of the
world.

'Well,' Sally proposed as she filled a glass of stout for which he had not asked, 'you'll surely be there the following Sunday night.'

He shifted on his stool and shook his head in a thoughtful rather than a negative fashion.

'You'd never know,' he said.

'To tell you the truth,' Sally McCarthy confided, 'I wouldn't be bothered going down there now unless I had a date; too many roughs there for my liking. It's safer to have an escort.'

Mark had nodded agreement and expressed his gratitude when she declined payment for the glass of stout.

'I'll tell you what,' she said, 'why don't you call before the dance for a few drinks and we'll see then.'

'Well I'd be calling for a few drinks anyway,' he answered. It had ended at that.

'Sally McCarthy is a fine and noble cut of a girl,' Archie Scuttard raised his glass respectfully to his benefactor. 'As outgoing and sweet a girl as you'd meet in a three week walk.'

The compliment was grudgingly accepted by Vester. For some reason that he could never fathom his daughter was never happier than when in the company of the emaciated Rector who at fifty-five looked every day of three score and ten.

'He's certainly not God's gift to the ladies,' Vester coldly conveyed his opinion as he preened himself before the large mirror in the haberdashery department which was attached to the grocery which in turn was attached to the pub.

'No,' his daughter had answered, 'but he's respectful and a gentleman after his fashion.'

'You call that bawdy, foul-mouthed wretch a gentleman!' Vester produced a pocket comb and, combing his silvery locks, indented several waves across the dome of his head. Much as she admired and loved him Sally McCarthy was only too painfully aware of her father's vanity and his sanctimonious reaction to all the things which seemed harmless to his daughter. In her view the Parson was a man with little time for cant or hypocrisy and if his language was coarse at times it was so laced with humour that only the most squeamish could possibly take exception except, when deep in his cups, he availed of his comprehensive repertoire of dirty limericks to scandalise any self-righteous patrons he might encounter in public houses after hours.

'You're not a native of these parts Monsignor Binge?' Vester McCarthy posed the question respectfully more for the purpose of making conversation than out of any idle curiosity.

'No Vester. Indeed no. I am a Kilkenny man even if my American twang might suggest that I am a native American.' The Monsignor spoke with a strong Californian accent. He lifted his whiskey glass and like Archie Scuttard conveyed his thanks to the purchaser.

'Are you on holiday then?' Vester McCarthy was curious now but no less respectful.

'I propose to spend a few days in your beautiful countryside Vester, that's if nobody objects.'

'Let me be the first to extend a welcome,' Vester McCarthy drew himself up to his full height as though he was the official spokesman for the entire parish of Tubberlick. He shook the Monsignor's hand with all the fervour that might be expected from such a dignitary.

'You have friends here or relations maybe,' Vester asked.

'My sister lives here,' the Monsignor replied, 'Mrs Tom Heavey at the end of the street.'

'Ah so you're Madge Heavey's brother! I assure you sir that you are now doubly welcome. Madge is a personal friend of mine.'

Vester would have to admit to himself that Madge's

was one of the few posteriors he had not patted or tried to pat. He always got the distinct impression that hers was a posterior not for patting. Several whiskies later Vester was tempted to ask if the clergymen had met by chance of if they had know each other previously.

'We have never met,' Archie Scuttard replied, 'until now and I must confess that I would know very little about him but for your insatiable curiosity McCarthy.'

'Why thank you Parson,' came the amicable reply. It transpired as the night wore on and the witching hour put safely behind them that the Rector and the Monsignor had much in common. Both had been chaplains in France towards the end of the Great War. Both had been wounded, the Rector in the Battle of the Somme as a result of which he had been decorated for gallantry.

The fact that he was the owner of the much-coveted Victoria Cross might never have emerged had not an item appeared in a gazette which a Tubberlick matron had picked up by chance while awaiting her turn in a ladies' hairdressing salon in Killarney. Like any self-respecting product of her native place, worried abut that place's reputation abroad, she transferred the magazine to her handbag when nobody was looking. Her duty done by her village and by her religion which was, of course, Catholic she decided to forego the luxury of the set and wash which she had planned and repaired instead to the lounge of the Great Southern Hotel where she might digest in peace the latest transgression by the Tubberlick Rector. Imagine her disappointment when she discovered that the piece had to do with the number of Trinity College graduates who had been decorated during the 1914–1918 war. Archibald Reginald Percival Scuttard figured in the list as did the hitherto undisclosed fact that he had graduated with honours in classics from Trinity and also had the letters Oxon after his name. The Oxon meant little to the farmers of the

Tubberlick hill country but the Victoria Cross did. Bravery was bravery no matter which side a man took in any conflict. The disclosure endeared him even further to hill people although he didn't have a single parishioner among them.

The twenty Protestant families in the united parishes of Tubberlick, Tubberlee, Ballybo, Kilshunnig and Boherlahan, occupied the valleys and lower slopes of the so-called parishes in question.

'How is it you'll never see a Protestant with bad land?' Mark Doran had once put the question to his father.

'Because they made sure they picked the best of it when the Catholics weren't allowed title,' his father tried to explain.

The Protestant families still survived after hundreds of years. Their numbers had been in serious decline since the War of Independence and many had sold out through fear but there was no intimidation as long as they stayed in the middle of the road throughout the Troubles.

The Tubberlick Protestant community was the last surviving one between the hill village and the town of Trallock thirty miles away while not a single Protestant remained in the vast and mostly fertile countryside between Tubberlick and Killarney. Their decline was to be mourned, all fair-minded Catholics in the five depopulated parishes would agree. They were a thrifty and industrious people, good neighbours and dependable in any emergency. A minority intermarried with local Catholics but nearly always there was trouble when it came to deciding the religion of the children. Tubberlick had experienced its own boycott of a Protestant farmer when he failed to honour a dubious pre-marital promise that the children of the union would be baptised into the Catholic faith. The boycott was vicious and relentless. Many thought it inhuman. The persecuted family sold out and settled in the midlands where many of their own kind still farmed. At the time the hill people disapproved but made no protest such was the influence of the local Catholic clergy backed by their bishop and the more zealous of the villagers. Then there were the young men and women of the district who were easily influenced at the time. Roads were painted with anti-Protestant slogans and, generally speaking, the victim of the boycott was treated like a Pariah. For all his household wants he was obliged to make the long journey to Killarney or Trallock.

The village's sole hackney car was not available to him at any price. Most of those involved would now like to forget the roles they had played, especially the younger people who later saw themselves as dupes. Throughout the entire episode the Rector of Tubberlick had denounced the boycott declaring to anybody who would listen that he didn't care whether the child was brought up Catholic, Protestant or Mohammedan as long as the victimisation ended.

By tacit agreement there was never mention of what happened in the public and business houses of the village thereafter. It would remain a distant cloud however.

Towards the end of the drinking session at two-thirty in the morning an argument broke out between the Rector and Vester McCarthy. Commenting on the decline in the cattle numbers at the quarterly fair the Rector suggested it could well have occurred because of collusion between cattle jobbers. It was rumoured, discreetly as one would expect, that Vester McCarthy was secretly financing at least one of the five jobbers who usually attended the Tubberlick quarterlies. The gentleman in question was a member of a local family of drovers who had a monopoly on all the droving activities of the several villages within the hill country. The Rector didn't have hard proof but the members of the family in question confined all of their drinking to the McCarthy premises and it was well known that they couldn't muster the price of a single Roscrea between the lot of them. Where then did the money come from! The jobber was the father figure of the family which included married sons, daughters and several ne'er do well sons-in-law who seemed not to have the capacity for any form of honest toil other than occasional droving unless one took into account their efficacy in keeping their wives pregnant year in, year out.

'It has come to my attention,' Vester McCarthy's voice rose angrily as he turned on the Rector, 'that you have been advising your flock to withhold their cattle from the Tubberlick fairs. I find this very surprising for a man who lives and works in Tubberlick and who should know better than any that charity begins at home.'

'Charity for whom,' the Rector asked, 'for the jobbers and their puppet master is it?'

Incensed by the reference to his suspected connections with the cattle jobbers Vester drew back his hand to strike at his tormentor but Monsignor Binge succeeded in holding him at bay.

'There's witnesses here,' Vester McCarthy shouted, 'and if you make any more accusations against me you'll answer in a court of law.'

'All I'm trying to say,' the Rector was calm now, 'is that the local cattle jobbers have frightened away many of the farmers.'

'The bloody Protestant farmers only,' Vester shouted back, 'and all primed by you. Your sole aim seems to be the destruction of the business life of the village.'

'Nonsense,' the Rector returned. 'It is the jobbers who are doing that and this should be known to you better than anybody.'

'Is it not true,' Vester was at his most accusatory now, 'that Daisy Popple withdrew her ten store bullocks on your advice even when she had been offered more than she might get at any other fair in the district?'

'Not more and considerably less than she might get in Trallock or Killarney,' the Rector corrected.

'And how the hell,' Vester roared, 'is she going to get them to Trallock or Killarney, on her bloody back is it!'

'Looks like the only way all right with not a drover willing to drive them and I wonder who instructed them? It wasn't off their own bats Mr McCarthy so it had to be someone else. I'll mention no names but that somebody else is an overbearing oul' bollix with waves in his hair and a moustache under his nose.'

Enraged, Vester McCarthy sought to strangle the Rector. The Monsignor, aided by the Widow Hegarty and two other drunken revellers, succeeded in restraining the apoplectic publican, now taunted beyond endurance.

'If there's another word,' the Widow cautioned, 'I'll clear the house.'

'Maybe,' Monsignor Binge suggested, 'it might be a good idea to clear it anyway. My sister will be wondering.'

'Your sister knows you're in good hands Monsignor,' the Widow assured him. There were to be no further exchanges between the Rector and Vester McCarthy on that occasion but word of the ruction would spread far and wide in a matter of weeks, with the hill people coming down firmly on the side of the Rector and the majority of the village backing Vester McCarthy.

As they left the pub not long after the Monsignor's prompting, a cold wind blew up the village street. On his way out Vester had allowed his hand to linger on the ample buttocks of the Widow as she looked up and down the street to make sure no tale-carrier was in the vicinity. If she felt anything; revulsion, shock, joy or elation, it did not register on her face or movements. It would be true to say that it was a backside that had been handled and fondled tenderly, indifferently and savagely down the years and, therefore, it would be fair to assume that she took such liberties in her stride. It would be also true to say that no man had ever been admitted to her private quarters after hours. This *sanctum sanctorum*, which was isolated from the public premises by a locked door at all times, contained a small kitchen, a bedroom and a sitting-room where she would sit and drink tea after the last of the customers had departed. Not only did she never entertain male visitors but she never entertained even a thought of male visitors. She had been a widow for twenty years and she would remain a widow until the end of her days and in case doubt ever arose about her position in this respect she would make an announcement from time to time, especially in the presence of her more amorous regulars, that any sort of intimate relationship with a man was the last thought in her head.

'Can I drop you off?' the invitation came from the Rector as he mounted a large, ungainly-looking motor bike which had been parked, for most of the night and early morning, outside the Widow's door. Monsignor Binge was at first tempted to decline the offer but he reassured himself with the belief that little harm could befall him during a journey which was no more than two hundred yards. He was about to mount the pillion when a mellifluous male voice advised him against it. The proprietor of the pleasant tones was a large, chubby member of the civic guards who had materialised, magically as if from nowhere.

'You go on home now,' the voice was saying, 'and don't worry about the bike Archie. I'll look after it.'

Blearily Archie Scuttard identified the newcomer to the deserted street.

'Ah 'tis you Mick,' he said agreeably, 'allow me to introduce my friend.'

DURANGO

'We've already met,' Mick Malone informed the Rector as he helped him from the bike to the roadway.

What the genial policeman said was true. It was he, in fact, who had directed the Monsignor to the Widow Hegarty's in the first place. The distinguished looking cleric happened to be standing in the doorway talking to his sister and her husband Tom preparatory to indulging in a nightcap or two before retiring. It was his second day in the village. He had come from Cobh in the County Cork where he had disembarked from a transatlantic liner before undertaking the last leg of his long journey from northern California to Tubberlick.

Mick Malone chanced to be passing by when Madge Heavey hailed him and introduced him to the Monsignor. The three had stood talking for awhile. Earlier Tom Heavey had politely refused when his brother-in-law invited him for a drink. Madge was quick to explain that Mick had not consumed intoxicating liquor in years and far from condemning drink had never been averse to a few pints of stout until he developed an ulcer which, regrettably, sidelined him as far as public houses were concerned.

'There's a man won't put you astray if 'tis a decent pub you want. Isn't that right Mick?' The compliment came from Tom Heavey.

'Well now,' said Mick Malone thoughtfully, 'if I were a young chap stepping it out for the first time in this here village I'd be lucky if I was directed to the Widow Hegarty's.'

'Keeps a good drop does she?' asked the Monsignor, entering into the spirit of the thing.

'As good as you'll get anywhere Your Reverence,' Mick Malone retorted as he deferentially touched the peak of his cap, 'and it so happens that I'm going down that way myself on a call of duty so if you have no objection I'll escort you to the very door of the Widow's.'

36

After making his farewells to the Rector the Monsignor sat for awhile in the kitchen of his sister's modest home.

'Is everything all right Danny?' It was Madge's voice from the head of the stairs.

'Fine thank you Madge,' he called back.

'Did you take the key from the door Danny?' she asked gently.

'Yes,' he called back, 'it's on the table.'

'Good, good,' she whispered, 'goodnight Danny.'

'Goodnight Madge.'

She was his only sister. There had been two other brothers and a sister but they had succumbed to tuberculosis back in their native Kilkenny in their early twenties.

'They're in the grave now,' Madge had wept at the time on her sole surviving brother's shoulder, 'that never knew the arm of a sweetheart.'

For awhile it seemed as if she might be smitten too by that most ravaging of all scourges but she survived and when she met Tom Heavey who had been a teacher in the national school in her native parish in Kilkenny she had sold the tiny family farm and moved with him when he was appointed to a school in his native Tubberlick. Their five children were long scattered but they were never visited by ill-health. The eldest girls were nuns in Rhodesia and another was married in London. Their two sons were civil servants in Dublin. Both sons were married with young families. Mercifully the blight of tuberculosis did not cast its vile shadow on any one of them. For this Madge Heavey was truly grateful. Immediately after his arrival by taxi from Cork the Monsignor had placed his cards on the table. He had suffered a nervous breakdown through pressure of work and had been advised by his doctors to take a long break from his pastoral and secretarial duties. For several years he had carried an excessively heavy workload. Due to a scarcity of priests in the diocese he was obliged to act as pastor of the sprawling parish of San Lupino as well as his obligations as full-time secretary to the Bishop of the diocese. One afternoon after a Confirmation ceremony in a remote mountain village he had collapsed, without warning, from sheer fatigue. After a month of convalescing the doctors had advised him against a return to work for a very long time. Reluctantly he had acquiesced and his Bishop had no hesitation in granting him an open-ended leave of absence.

'Danny,' the elderly prelate had confided, 'my days are numbered and if they last longer than I think they will it will be incumbent on me to retire. Either way there will be a new Bishop in a year's time. I am of the opinion that you are the best man for the job and the Archbishop agrees with me as do many of the senior priests of the diocese. Take your break and when you return I will prepare you as best I know how for the onerous task ahead of you. I have absolutely no doubt you will one day be my successor.'

Both clerics had received their secondary schooling in Saint Kieran's College in Kilkenny and had been ordained in the same seminary in California. They held each other in high esteem. The Bishop's last act was to present the Monsignor with a large cheque. They would never meet again. The Bishop died suddenly during an ordination ceremony two days after the Monsignor's departure.

At a hastily convened meeting of the episcopacy and Monsignori of the archdiocese Monsignor Daniel Morgan Binge was unanimously chosen as Bishop Elect of the vacant diocese. It was decided to communicate with him by letter rather than by telegram because of the secret nature of the appointment and because he would need the interlude between the election and ordination to regain his health. It would be some weeks before news of his election reached him. Unaware of his new episcopal status he knelt on the floor beside the table and made the sign of the cross preparatory to beginning the Rosary which he unfailingly recited before retiring since he was a schoolboy. The following day Monsignor Daniel Morgan Binge, MA, Licentiate in Canon Law would wake up a Bishop Elect unawares.

3

On the Friday night following the quarterly cattle fair Mark Doran decided it was high time he paid a visit to the Mullanneys. Aided by his mother he milked the fourteen cows and fed the calves earlier than usual. The question most often asked in the hill country was: 'Have you the cows out?' which was the same as asking if the cows had been released from their indoor winter quarters to partake of the new grass, clover and vetches freshly arrived to the pasturelands in late March and early April.

Mark Doran had released his entire herd the day before which was April Fools' Day. The previous year, because of heavy rains lasting a full week, the stock had been confined until the middle of the second week in April. On the morning of Fools' Day his mother had informed him that two men wearing black clothes and tall hats were awaiting him in the sitting-room. She could not determine for him the nature of their business except to say that they sported long beards and were not communicative. Mark had been puzzled. This would not be the garb of income tax inspectors or agricultural advisers.

'And you have no idea who they might be?' he asked in bafflement.

'Well they aren't poultry instructresses and that's for sure,' his mother had replied.

When he went to the room after first combing his hair, washing his hands, donning a clean shirt, short coat and tie there was nobody there. He returned to the kitchen but there was no sign of his mother. From the haggard he heard her calling, 'Fool, fool the first of April'.

He could not remember a year when she hadn't surprised him with some outlandish story. Also that morning there had been a letter with a Tubberlick postmark from an admirer purporting to be red-haired and blue-eyed and anxious to meet him at the crossroads near his house that very night. He suspected it might be an April Fools' Day letter but he went to the cross that night, nevertheless, at the appointed time only to find, as he expected, that there was nobody there. He had no doubt but that the letter had been the handiwork of Annie Mullanney.

Every day of the week, Sunday excepted, the Mullanney girls together with fifteen year old Florry the youngest brother cycled to the convent secondary school in Tubberlick. Of course the sisters might have been co-authors of Mark's letter but it had, he felt, the singular stamp of Annie. In June when the school would close for the summer holiday the two older girls would depart for England or more particularly for Portsmouth General Hospital where they had been accepted as trainee nurses subject to their examination results which would be a formality for both girls since they were first class students with excellent records.

As Mark climbed the narrow, winding road to the farmhouse he observed with satisfaction the grazing animals on his well-tended, green fields below. As far as the eye could see the cows were out everywhere, heads bent assiduously as they relished each mouthful of the spring grasses. Mark was grateful for the fine weather. His supply of hay was seriously depleted for the good reason that he had not sold a single head of stock since the July quarterly fair of the previous year so that the inroads into his fodder had been more penetrating than ever before. None but the occasional understocked farm would be possessed of sufficient feed to tide them beyond the second week of April. Sometimes, tragically, the fine weather of the first April weeks might change dramatically with hail and snow storms whitening the hills but more often than not there was drenching rain which turned the trampled pastures into morasses. Then the cows were put in again and the demand for hay and turnips exceeded the supply. Mark Doran had vivid memories of gaunt cattle starving and dying on farms where the general husbandry was poor to begin with but made infinitely worse with the famine fodder. These were times for neighbourliness, the hallmark of the true hill man and a trait of which he was inordinately proud when the exaggerated parsimony of lowlanders was cited.

Hay was transported without cost to where it was needed most. Often it was a case of a little having to go a long way but it was a little that made the difference between life and death as far as the cattle were concerned. This annual nightmare which occurred every few years never affected city or towns-people and was of no real concern to them. They had no means of seeing firsthand the appalling sight of emaciated cattle nor was their hearing subjected to the continuous bawling of hungry stock.

Without the neighbourliness of which the hill people were so proud the stench of rotting carcasses would be blown countrywide with every wind. It characterised the lifestyle of the hill people more than anything else. Despite his years Mark realised that it was the dominant factor in the social and religious life of every rural parish. The older he grew the more aware he became of the interdependence of the hill people. The more isolated the region the more powerful the bond that bound the people together.

'Townies don't understand it, don't want to understand it.' How many times had he listened as his granduncle Joss the Badger repeated the accusation which was not altogether true. Townspeople had their own concept of neighbourliness but the awareness was not the same as in the countryside and how could it be with so much hidden from the eye. The hill people are one big family,

Mark Doran thought. Everybody knew what everybody else had. The stalks on the potato drills advertised the density of the crop underneath. Cows, calves and cocks of hay were easily counted from a distance. Hens and chickens as well as turkeys and geese were there for all to see. The evidence confronted even the disinterested day in, day out. It was easy to guess how much milk was being delivered to the creamery, how many eggs were being laid, how many pigs were being killed or being transported to market.

'Want,' Mark spoke the words out loud, 'is every bit as visible as plenty and rural tradition ordains that the strong come to the aid of the weak and the well-off to the aid of the poorly-off.'

He might be echoing Joss the Badger's philosophy but it was a philosophy of which he heartily approved and which he was honoured to espouse. Yet there was another facet to the personality of the hill man which did not quite meet with the approval of the authorities. While the hillfolk might have won fame and renown for their friendliness and hospitality, ranks were quickly closed in the face of overly curious strangers or investigating authority such as the taxman or the warble fly inspector or the civic guards. Even Mick Malone, Tubberlick's sole and revered representative of law and order, confirmed that investigating crime, generally petty in the first place, was a waste of time.

'They will receive you with open arms,' Mick explained to his superintendent as they sat drinking pints of stout in the Widow Hegarty's, 'and you'll be surfeited with food and drink but there is a contrasting stinginess when it comes to imparting information. There is a deeply held belief that God will deal in His own way and in His own good time with the transgressor and they see this as a punishment more terrifying than anything a court of law might hand down.'

As Mark Doran approached Mullanneys he was not

surprised to hear the sound of loud voices coming from the house and a neat house it was as were the hedge-rows and shrubs all around. The cleanliness too was remarkable.

'Almost like a Protestant's,' somebody had once observed.

The Protestant farmers were renowned for their tidy farmyards, always clean and bright and for the spotless-ness of their homes, inside and out and for their farm produce which was always of a better quality than their Catholic counterparts. Neither did the Protestants ever involve themselves in fist-fights amongst themselves or with others. They shunned violence as though it were a plague. The same could not be said for the Mullanneys. Mark decided to wait in the shadows, under a giant sycamore near the house. If he entered in the middle of a row it would be an embarrassment to both sides. He would wait until the din subsided and then he would enter as though he had heard nothing. From the sounds he was able to deduce that it was not a major outbreak. He would wait nevertheless. He had witnessed some rare eruptions in his time.

Elections, local and general, seemed to bring out the worst elements in the warring factions. The outbursts of internal violence seemed to scale unprecedented heights during the run up to polling day.

Outside the confines of the house, all over the coun-tryside, opposing forces often resorted to gable and road daubings, poster peeling and the occasional burning of hay and turf ricks which would be the property of more outspoken party members. The Mullanneys never re-sorted to such tactics. The house was divided into three distinct support groups, Fianna Fáil, Blueshirt and IRA. It was difficult to find more extreme elements anywhere in the constituency.

Haybags and his sons Jay and Tom were IRA sym-pathisers. The elder Mullanney boasted that he was prepared to take up arms at a moment's notice should the need arise. Against whom or what he was not prepared to say but he had the guns and he was ready. Haybags had never fired a shot in either the War of Independence or the Civil War but to hear him vociferate one wondered how a single Black and Tan survived while he was on the warpath. He often spoke half to himself, half to his more youthful listeners, about covert and deadly actions where his life had been at risk and he mourned the loss of unnamed, fallen comrades who had died by his side in action. He had, nevertheless, been a member of the Volunteers in the Troubles and he had the documentation to prove it.

His wife Sheila was an unrepentant Blueshirt and although the organisation had been banned for years by the De Valera government she could be heard above all others shouting: 'Up the Blueshirts!' at the height of the confusion in the home.

When he adjudged it to be proper Mark Doran knocked gently on the back door of the Mullanney dwelling-house before lifting the latch and entering.

'God bless all here,' he said. The blessing was returned with interest from all within. The youngest brother Florry devoted all his energies to the repair of an upturned bicycle. It seemed to Mark that he had never visited the house at a time when there wasn't a puncture being fixed or a bicycle being repaired. He rarely used his own bicycle except on Sunday and holiday nights when he cycled to Tubberlick with Tom and Jay Mullanney and their sisters Ellie and Bridgie and, very often, a large party of boys and girls from the inner hills who might join them on the tar which was the name given to the main road to the village. Of late Mark Doran could not help feeling that he was getting beyond it. Most of the boys and girls of his own age had either emigrated or married. He would give it another year and then reconsider his position. The boys and the girls were no more than children in Mark's eyes and secretly he admitted that he was too old and that this was the real reason he became aware of their youthfulness.

Tom and Sheila Mullanney were seated at the fire. There was no sign of the older boys but it was Mark's guess that they were drilling with the IRA in one of the many empty barns in some secret recess in the hills. Their father knew where and so did anybody with the slightest interest in the rather futile activities of the local company.

Once when his wife asked if he had any idea of the boys whereabouts he had answered solemnly that it was a military secret.

'I know where they are,' Annie chimed in, 'they're above in Maxwell's barn drilling with coarse brushes.'

If Annie had not been his favourite and the light of his life he might well have smacked her bottom. Instead he settled a withering look on her.

The two oldest girls greeted Mark warmly but it was on a chair near Annie's that he sat himself. They smiled at each other but no word passed between them.

'Well Mark and what's new round the world?' Sheila Mullanney asked.

'I heard on the wireless,' Mark informed her, 'that cattle prices are slightly up in the Dublin cattle market.'

'And up they'll go because there will be a war as sure as hell!' Haybags Mullanney was emphatic.

'Anything else?' Sheila Mullanney asked in an endeavour to turn the conversation away from cattle.

'The Pope has made an appeal for peace,' Mark told her, 'and he has asked everyone, everywhere, to pray for peace.'

'Well God blast him, the oul' meddler,' Haybags exploded, 'why don't he keep his oul' bald head out of it and let them at it so's we might get decent prices for our cattle.'

'That's no way to talk about the Pope,' Sheila Mullanney reprimanded.

'I'll talk how I like about him,' Haybags shouted. 'What is he anyway but a pampered oul' dotard with his roast and boiled every day and half the world starving.'

'Oh dear God,' his wife cried out as she made the sign of the cross, 'that's a terrible way to talk about the Holy Father. You'll go straight to hell!'

'Let him stick to his prayers. If there's a war the price of cattle will double before it's over just like it did the last time.'

'Shame on you,' his wife made the sign of the cross a second time.

'And,' Haybags was shouting now, 'the Germans will beat the stuffing out of the British and we'll have a united Ireland, free from head to heel and masters of our own destiny.'

'Give me the British before the Huns any day.' Sheila rose to her feet, her hands on her hips, her eyes flashing, 'and who'll buy the beef off you, you ignorant hoor! Is it the Germans or the British?'

'Sit down woman and don't provoke me.'

'The Germans never bought as much as a dropped calf from us you foolish oul' man.'

Haybags was on his feet now. Mark and Annie were caught between but not for long. Annie surprised him with the ferocity of her contribution.

'Hitler is a madman,' she cried, 'everybody says so.'

'Well by Jasus he's a bloody gentleman compared to Cromwell or the Black and Tans. Hitler will give us the Thirty-two counties and Ireland will be free from the centre to the sea.' Haybags sang the last part hysterically while, in the background, the two oldest girls were making fiery contributions in support of their mother. If Mark could have vanished up the chimney he would cheerfully have done so. He had thought of making for the door but he felt he would have been an unworthy neighbour had he done so. He had two options, the first to sit it out in the hope that it would be of brief duration or, secondly, to intervene in case it grew out of hand. He decided to intervene but before he had a chance to do so Haybags Mullanney stormed out the door threatening his wife with a fractured posterior if she continued to misbehave. Mark decided to follow him. He found him urinating under the shade of the big sycamore with his great head thrown back as he hurled the foulest imprecations at the branches overhead.

'See what I have to put with!' he complained, 'a man who fought for his country when most of his neighbours were under the bed.'

For a moment the moonlight flittered through the branches and lit up his anguished face. Mark was torn between laughter and sympathy. They walked from the tree to the roadway. Overhead, the ragged clouds obscured the crescent moon from time to time but for the most part the night was bright and one could see the lights of Tubberlick village twinkling in the distance.

'See over there,' Haybags pointed towards the south-west where a faint roseate glow hung over a distant township.

'You're looking at Castleisland,' Haybags announced proudly. 'A decent town.' Turning fully on his heel he thrust a mighty hand in a north-westerly direction, 'and that's Trallock town where I gave many a good day and night when I was unfettered by females and I had coins to jingle in my pocket. How's your mother?'

'Never better,' Mark answered.

'Now there's a great woman. You'll never see a poor day while your mother is with you Mark. God be with my own poor mother.' Haybags made the sign of the cross and wiped a tear from his eye. 'That woman is sitting tonight on a silver chair in the halls of heaven. I had a great mother.' Haybags shook his head ruefully and pointed eastwards.

'The city of Limerick lies in that direction. I caught a

glimpse of it one September's morning when there was no haze and no cloud. The air was clear and pure and it was there to be seen. I never saw it since. There's a lot of things I'll never see again Mark.' He shook his great frame and clapped his hands together as though to dismiss the gloom which hung over him since his retreat from the fractiousness where he felt he had been unfairly out-gunned.

There followed a silence. Mark listened as the wind rustled in the sycamore and kept his peace as they watched the shadows of the clouds fleeing across the fields beneath them. Haybags heaved a great sigh as the peace of the out-doors quelled the turbulence within him. For all their squabbling the Mullanneys were a happy-go-lucky family, full of love and concern for each other most of the time. Mark felt the time might be ripe for mention of his idea. He would need the connivance of Haybags and a few others if it was to see fruition. Haybags, breathing easily now and becalmed as a hulk in a backwater, might not be in such a receptive mood for some time.

'Did anybody in this part of the world ever drive cattle to Trallock fair?' Mark asked.

Surprised by the suddenness of the question Haybags found himself in a state of nonplus but not for long.

'Not as I recall,' he replied after a moment or two, 'but it could have happened before my time. You have to remember it's forty miles by road and it's over 35 as the crow flies and you won't do much better than you'll do around here, unless maybe you had the right sort of animals for the October fair.'

'The October fair is what I have in mind,' Mark confessed.

'Wait a minute,' Haybags tweaked his nose as he remembered.

'There was a farmer's boy one time, working beyond in Ballybo for slave wages and starvation diet. This would be all of twenty years ago just after the end of the war. The Scuttler Dawly they called him. You see 'twas the year the German fleet was scuttled at Scapa Flow so they christened him the Scuttler over he rightly scuttling oul' Thade Haragan, the man he was working for. Haragan had a young wife and no children. The Scuttler would sire a parish if he got the run of the females there. Haragan took to beating the wife if the tea was too cold or the spuds overboiled and in the end for no reason at all so the inevitable happened. The wife turned and one morning when Haragan was standing bullocks at the fair of Tubberlick Scuttler Dawly found himself with a woman in his arms. Time passed and the summer flew. Came the October fair in Trallock and the Tubberlick quarterly the very same day. Haragan headed south with in-calf heifers but left the best two behind as herd replacements. No sooner had the old man set foot on the road for Tubberlick at two o'clock in the morning than the lovers hit for Trallock, driving the two in-calf heifers before them. They went over the hills and after eight hours on the road they arrived in the square of Trallock town, just as the Angelus was striking the hour of twelve. It was an almighty journey but they had the practise put in. The in-calf heifers were half dead when they landed. They fetched a good price, enough for tickets from the Cove of Cork to New York and that was the last that was seen of the Scuttler or Haragan's wife.'

'How would a small herd fare on the journey across the hills and through the boglands?'

'There's no doubt it could be done. What kind of herd?' Haybags sounded interested.

'A mixed herd,' Mark replied.

'What kind of mix?' Haybags was genuinely interested.

'In-calf heifers,' Mark answered, 'Roscreas, weanlings and bullocks, milch cows, the devil knows what! The makings of a small fair in themselves.'

'Impractical,' Haybags dismissed the idea.

'But why?' Mark asked.

'It would mean you'd have to send your Roscreas ahead three, four or even five days before to make sure they'd get there in time. You'd want drovers with experience of driving cattle. Weanlings and heifers are wild enough in their own fields but what would they be like if they broke into other fields as ye went through the hills. They could go missing for days. You'd want dogs and we don't have the right dogs around here. There's trained dogs in Tubberlick but they belong to the Drover Mooleys and the Drover Mooleys wouldn't give you the itch and there's another thing you're forgetting. You think that Vester McCarthy and the publicans of Tubberlick and for that matter the publicans and business people of the other hill villages are going to stand back and let you turn their little empires into ghost towns?'

'What can they do?' Mark asked.

'They can canvas against you, point out the gamble involved, promise better prices. Then where are you leaving the jobbers? They'll tell you 'tis their livelihood, that their families will starve. There's other things, hidden dangers that you don't see. There's a lot at stake here. Anything can happen in thirty-five miles of wild country. It's too much of a risk. It's been thought of before too. Of that you may be sure and it's been well reconnoitred by smarter bucks than you or me. If 'twas feasible,' Haybags concluded with doleful finality as far as Mark was concerned, 'it would have been done before this.'

'But,' Mark argued half-heartedly, 'the Scuttler did it and Haragan's wife did it and the heifers did it and they had no dogs.'

'A desperate man don't need dogs and neither does a desperate woman. If the Scuttler was caught he'd find himself looking down the barrels of a shotgun and for sure Haragan would pull the trigger because that's the sort of vile-tempered man he was and who would blame him, certainly no farmer who knew the value of herd replacements and the value of a young woman in her prime and 'tis the farmer that counts in the end for 'tis the farmer that carries the world on his shoulders and 'tis the farmer that feeds the world and 'tis the farmer will go straight to heaven when he dies for he'll have his share suffered surely before he quits this damned vale of tears.'

'I had been hoping,' Mark was surprised by his own persistence, 'that you might contribute to the herd.'

'My in-calf heifers you mean?'

Mark decided to remain silent, to give Haybags his head, to let him waste all his objections.

'You don't see do you? Of course you don't. Young men never do.'

'See what?' Mark asked.

'See how I'm fixed right now,' came the tormented response. 'Ellie and Bridgie, against all my wishes and against my grain as an Irishman, are going to take up nursing in Portsmouth in England in the coming June and I'll want money for them. They'll want new clothes, not one outfit mind you but three if you please and then there's shoes and hats and frillies and there's the cost of their nurses' uniforms and their fare and the mother is talking of going with them to see them settled in and they'll want a few pounds for pocket money till they get paid and who do you think now Mister Doran is going to pay for all of that?'

'The heifers,' Mark replied dutifully.

'The heifers is right and I'm not finished for it has come to my notice that them two Republicans drilling beyond in Maxwell's barn have it in their heads to hit for America before Christmas. I know! I know! I'm not supposed to know but it has trickled to me between women whispering and my own understanding of young men's restlessness. Don't tell them I know for God's sake. It will be hard enough on me when the time comes. That'll be four of my flock gone in the space of six months.'

'You have Florry and you have Annie.'

'Aye,' Haybags echoed sadly, 'I have Annie. I'll never leave Annie go. She's my heartbeat, my weenach. By Jasus if anyone ever tries to carry Annie from me the blood will flow. Dare any man come near her and I'll pull off his head like you'd pull a cork off an ink bottle. No. No. No. I'm too lenient. I'll skin the hoor alive and strangle him with his own pelt.'

Mark found himself trembling. Annie Mullanney was never far from his thoughts. Better, in view of the threats from Haybags, to keep her in his thoughts for the present.

'You'll be letting the heifers go then?' Mark asked despondently.

Aware of his disappointment Haybags placed a hand on the younger man's shoulder.

'I'll be letting go three at the May quarterly of Boher-lahan to cover the girls expenses and the other four at the October quarterly in Tubberlick for the boys.'

'You won't change?' Mark pleaded.

Haybags didn't answer at once. He had a great regard for Mark Doran.

'Why are you so anxious for this drive anyways?' he asked.

Mark informed him of his suspicions about there being a jobbers' ring in Tubberlick and the other villages and how he figured that Vester McCarthy was behind it. He cited prices at home and away in defence of his argument and mentioned numerous cases of collusion where poorly-off farmers had been seriously wronged. Haybags listened without once interrupting. At the end of Mark's denunciations he relented.

'Here's what I'll do,' he promised. 'I have no choice but to sell the three at Boherlahan if you definitely come to a positive decision about the drive to Trallock I won't let you down. The four heifers will travel and so will Tom and Jay because you'll need stout men with you, drilled men that won't let you down.'

They shook hands on the deal and moved towards the house. As they did Annie appeared in the doorway, waiflike in her frock, against the chill of the night. Mark Doran's heart went out to her but he maintained a stern countenance.

'My mother wants to know if ye're coming in for tea?' she called out.

As they passed her in the doorway she seized Mark by the coat sleeve, unseen by her father, who had preceded him.

'Fool, fool the first of April,' she whispered before running before him into the kitchen.

4

On Sunday morning, immediately after ten o'clock Mass in Saint John's Church in Tubberlick, the celebrant, Monsignor Daniel Morgan Binge, former pastor of the parish of San Lupino and Bishop Elect of the diocese of the same name, found himself in the sitting-room of the spacious presbytery which dwarfed every other house in the village. Built in 1919 by the then Parish Priest Canon Freddie Gorman, it was described by various engineers and architects who chanced to pass through the village of Tubberlick over the years, as a barracks, an eye-sore, a mausoleum and, least complimentary of all, a monumental shithouse!

Certainly it was an unprepossessing edifice surrounded by a six foot high wall and fronted by large wrought iron gates which were badly hung and could be heard noisily grating against the concrete forecourt during opening and closing.

Some felt it would have been more practical to have built two smaller houses, one for the Parish Priest and one for the Curate but the Bishop ordained otherwise much to the chagrin of the latter.

Curates who had come and gone since the building was erected felt themselves accountable to the Parish Priest if for no other reason than that they lived under his roof. There were many Parish Priests who imposed curfews on their Curates but these were not always observed.

'I'm sorry Monsignor Binge to trouble you,' the Parish Priest, Father Dugan tendered the apology matter-of-factly, 'but it is rather important and I am most anxious to get it over with. Will you be seated please.'

The Monsignor thought that he detected a veiled tone of peremptory superiority when the Parish Priest suggested, as they sat, that the Monsignor might smoke if he so wished.

'I gave them up years ago,' he explained politely, 'but indulge yourself if you feel like it.'

The Parish Priest looked at his visitor as if the remark had been a gratuitous one.

'I'll come to the point,' he said, resting his eyes upon the gleaming sitting-room table and entwining his fingers together before clearing his throat. After some initial hesitation he began by saying: 'This isn't easy for me but it has to be said, in the line of duty you understand, and there is also the fact that my Bishop has given me certain instructions.'

Monsignor Binge felt glad all of a sudden that he wasn't a member of Father Dugan's congregation at the beginning of one of the long sermons for which he was noted and which accounted for his poorly attended Masses as against the Curate's jam-packed congregations.

'There is word abroad,' Father Dugan untwined his long, puce-nailed fingers and re-entwined them at the back of his head, 'that you were involved in an altercation in a public house in the village long after the legal closing time.'

Father Dugan did not concern himself with the Monsignor's reaction. He simply waited for his words to sink in.

'Naturally I hesitate to bring the matter up. You will feel, no doubt, that it is none of my business but the fact of the matter is that we run things a little differently here. My Bishop was on to me by telephone this morning. Word of this sorry business reached him only yesterday and he is most concerned that a clergyman of your stature should involve himself in such unseemly behaviour.'

Again Father Dugan waited, not for a reply but so that he might compose himself the better for the continuation of his admonishment.

'The Bishop has asked me to convey to you his displeasure and he sincerely hopes that nothing like this will happen again during your stay here.'

'Now,' Father Dugan's posture seemed to say, 'I have kept my own feelings out of it. I have conveyed the wishes of my Bishop to this mischievous Monsignor. All of us, Bishops, Monsignori, Parish Priests and Curates need a little chastening now and then. It might not be very appetising at the time but like all medicine it is the curative properties that matter, not the taste.'

Father Dugan waited for the Monsignor's reaction and after a lapse of several minutes, when no answer or question had been forthcoming, he himself posed a question.

'Have you anything to say?' he asked. He tried not to sound magisterial but he had resolved from the outset not to be influenced by the Monsignor's rank. With many other of his Irish fellow clergymen he felt that most American priests did not deserve such a title.

'If you ask me,' he had once informed a colleague, 'they don't care who they give these titles to.' Certainly older Irish priests would be justifiably peeved that they themselves had not even been elevated to the rank of Canon while younger, brasher American clergymen, without university qualifications or more importantly of sufficiently advanced years, seemed to have no difficulty in attaining to the elevated and pompous-sounding rank of Monsignor. When Monsignor Binge made no attempt to reply Father Dugan eased himself out of his chair. Monsignor Binge did likewise. Both men stood silently confronting each other for a few moments. The interview had not entirely been to the Parish Priest's liking. As they walked from the room the Monsignor suddenly stopped.

'You asked me if I had anything to say Father and you are entitled to an answer. The simple truth is that I have nothing to say. I have never been taken to task before as a priest. Long ago in my seminary days I was the subject of some mild rebukes but never anything like this. I will, of course, mend my ways and try not to be an embarrassment to any of you during the remainder of my stay here.' He extended a hand to the Parish Priest. Father Dugan accepted it eagerly, sensing for the first time that he was in the presence of a devout and submissive man.

'Look,' he explained, 'I am asked to do this sort of thing all the time but the way the Bishop sees it is that you are in one of his parishes, however temporarily. You are celebrating Mass in one of his churches and you are, like the rest of us, expected to give good example. When I was a Curate I was once taken to task by one of my own Parish Priests for playing too much golf in Ballybunion. I hope you understand my position.'

The Monsignor shook his head and smiled.

'That's just it Father. While I fully understand the Bishop's position I don't understand yours. I would respectfully ask you how you personally stand in the matter,' and then after a pause, 'in view of the fact that I will be here for some weeks, maybe months, and will need to say my daily Mass.'

'A fair question,' Father Dugan was obliged to agree.

'Before we had our conversation I was of the same mind as the Bishop but now I'm not so sure. I feel I have no right to criticise your lifestyle personally but I must also say that we have certain standards to maintain. When I feel like a drink I do so in my sitting-room. Another thing that might have irritated His Lordship is the fact that Archie Scuttard was your drinking companion on the occasion to which His Lordship refers.'

'Point taken,' Daniel Binge acknowledged, 'but the trouble with me is that I find drinking in private houses anathema. Hence my preference for the Widow Hegarty's but I shall take all you've said into account and be assured that I will not embarrass you or the Bishop for the remainder of my stay.'

In the afternoon the Monsignor, his sister Madge and her husband Tom, motored to Killarney in Tom Heavey's 1935 Baby Ford. They dined at the Great Southern after partaking of some refreshments in a centrally-situated public house. The Monsignor and Madge spent the time journeying to and fro talking about their childhood. Daniel Binge made no reference, whatsoever, to his interview with Father Dugan. In less than a week his appointment to the diocese of San Lupino would be approved by Rome and he did not want anything made public until then.

Later that night Mick Malone heard from a colleague that a man from the district of Ballybo, a man who had drilled as a boy in Maxwell's barn less than a mile from the uppermost boundary of the Mullanney acres, was sentenced to penal servitude in London for a period of twelve years. He had been charged with several others, all Irishmen, with being in possession of explosive substances and with conspiracy. At the outset he had refused to plead or to ask for legal aid. He told the court that the campaign of the Irish Republican Army would continue until their demands were granted.

'Scum and bastard', were some of the names levelled at him by his captors and by onlookers in the public gallery. The IRA bombing campaign would continue throughout the war with the loss of many innocent lives and numerous maimings of innocent people. The IRA were exploiting the centuries old motto that England's difficulty was Ireland's opportunity and if one were to ask Haybags Mullanney or one of his two sons Tom and Jay, about the character of the man who had been sentenced, they would describe him as a patriot and a grand fellow entirely. In all probability they would not say the same about the several airmen, seamen and soldiers from the same countryside who would die fighting not for Britain, their parents would say, but against Hitler. Then came the sensational statement from Lord Stanhope, First Lord of the Admiralty, that the anti-aircraft of the British Fleet had been suddenly manned so as to be ready for anything and in the Gaelic football grounds of Tubberlick the Ballybo junior football team had its first win of the season. The winning point was notched by centre forward Mark Doran in the failing light. Others to figure prominently in the encounter against champions Kilshunnig were the brothers Tom and Jay Mullanney who, after an unseemly episode between themselves, outshone the opposing backs for the remainder of the hour. Will and Henry Sullivan turned in courageous displays at midfield.

After the game Mark Doran found himself in the company of the aforementioned Sullivans at the Widow Hegarty's licensed premises. Mark had arranged that they would meet after the game. He had approached the older brother Will in the lean-to dressing quarters as they togged out and informed him that he wished to speak to him on a private matter later on.

'I don't know all about that,' Will had answered, alarm registering on his young face.

'What's it all about Mark?' the younger brother Henry asked.

'Don't worry lads,' Mark laughed, 'I'm not recruiting for the IRA if that's what's bothering you.'

The Widow's was crowded after the game. In a corner seated on an upturned firkin of stout was the Protestant Rector. Seated nearby on an empty butter-box was Mick Malone. From time to time Mick placed his hand under the box and extracted his glass, a pint measure, partially filled with stout. Turning his head towards the wall behind him he swallowed copiously and handed the empty glass to the Rector. No one had ever caught Mick Malone in the act of drinking. He accepted a fresh pint from the Rector and turned to the wall so that he might carry out his subterfuge, his broad back hiding his movements from all and sundry. As the after match crowd began to pour in Mick, deftly and unseen, polished off his pint. Rising, he addressed the Widow in a stentorian voice, 'have them all out of here before eleven o'clock,' he cautioned. 'I'll be back to make sure.' Tipping his cap to the Rector he made his way through the crowded bar, the patrons making room for him as he nodded to friends on his way out.

'Good point Mark,' the Rector called, 'very well taken considering the breeze.'

'Will you have a drink Parson?' Mark asked respectfully.

'No thank you,' the Rector replied as he rose to his feet and placed his empty glass on the counter. 'It's a bit too crowded for an old fogy like me.'

Then in a more confidential tone he addressed Mark in a whisper. 'What's this I hear about a cattle drive? Is it in Texas or Tubberlick you think you are?'

Mark kept his voice down as he replied. 'It's just an idea yet,' he explained, 'and anyway it wouldn't be till October.'

'To Trallock I take it?'

'That's the plan,' Mark answered.

'Well Mark,' the Rector shook the younger man's hand, 'if you need a good scout you know where to find me.' As he limped towards the doorway he turned. 'Remember that few have as trusty a steed as I.'

As he sipped his pint Mark recalled their first meeting. He had been sixteen at the time. His father had bought in extra in-calf heifers only to find himself desperately short of hay at the end of March. The extra stock had exhausted all their fodder. They were faced with starvation. The fields were soggy and over-run with water. No grass showed because of a colder than usual spring.

Neighbours had helped but the situation had grown desperate as April entered the scene and bought no improvement in the weather. Then when all seemed lost, word reached Ned Doran that one or more of the Protestant families might have hay to spare. They tackled the horse to the common cart and located binding twine. They borrowed a second horse and cart from Haybags Mullanney and set out on a bitter April morning at seven o'clock in the morning in a do or die effort to purchase hay.

Everywhere they went it was the same story. No hay for love or money. Then by chance they encountered Parson Scuttard dressed in an apron with a broom in his hand outside the Protestant church in Tubberlick.

'In God's name,' his father had begged, 'could you direct us to a few sops of hay Parson?'

The Parson looked long and hard at Mark's father.

'Wait there,' he said. 'I won't be a jiff.' True to his word he was back almost at once with a letter which he handed to Ned Doran.

'You know Daisy Popple's don't you?'

'I do indeed Parson,' Ned Doran had answered.

'Hand her this letter,' the Parson had said.

The hay had been forthcoming and when he went in search of Daisy Popple to settle his account she told him it had been taken care of by the Rector. Mark would never forget. Money was scarce at the time, almost non-existent as far as the hill people were concerned. There was enough to keep body and soul together but no more.

Mark and the Sullivan brothers took over the seats vacated by the Rector and Mick Malone. Mark came to the point at once. In whispers he disclosed his plans for the proposed October cattle drive. The brothers were cautious. Not only had their mother warned them about joining the IRA but she had also made them promise that they would never commit themselves to anything without prior consultation with her. The father was a withdrawn man who rarely appeared in public except to attend Mass. His wife had the handling of the farm income and it was she who made all the decisions about the selling and purchase of stock.

'One thing is sure,' Will Sullivan promised, 'and that is we will go along with you on the day with or without cattle.'

'Oh no thank you,' Mark rejected the offer out of hand. 'I can get half the countryside to come along with me for the fun of the thing. It's cattle I want, not wasters.'

The brothers, with full pints of stout in their hands, promised Mark that they would recommend the drive to their mother. He had to settle for that although Henry Sullivan revealed that they might be obliged to sell some weanlings at the next fair. At the start of the week they had received devastating news. An advertisement had appeared in the local paper announcing the fact that the County Co-Operative Wholesale Society would not accept supplies of porkers until further notice.

'Our pigs are ready for butchering,' Henry Sullivan had complained, 'and now we'll have to hold them and half starve them in case they put on too much fat. It's a cruel decision.'

Mark was unaware of the announcement. He had given up pig production at the beginning of the year.

'I'm lucky,' Mark told the Sullivans of his fortuitous decision.

'There's no doubt,' said Will Sullivan, 'but you're the cutest man in Ballybo.'

'This had to happen,' Mark said. 'There are too many pig producers and not enough consumers.'

Mark went on to advise the brothers to continue with pig production.

'There's a war coming for sure,' he told them, 'and

that means pig prices will soar.'

After several pints Mark decided to move but only after he had extracted a promise from the brothers that they would inveigle their mother into retaining her stock for the drive.

Mark Doran might never have ventured into Vester McCarthy's but for the fact that he had been primed by a rapid succession of pints during his attempted conversion of the Sullivans. The premises was half full when he entered. He declined numerous offers to join the many parties of country folk who had come to the village for the football game. He received all round acclamation for the last minute point he had scored.

In the bar Sally McCarthy indicated to Mark, rather possessively he thought nervously, that the snug near the front of the shop was available. As things turned out it had one occupant, Archie Scuttard.

'What'll you have Mark?' the Rector asked.

'I'll have a pint of stout Rector thank you,' Mark replied.

It was this chance meeting with the Rector of the united parishes that strengthened Mark's resolve to go all out for the drive. The Rector, Mark was surprised to learn, was exceptionally well informed on cattle prices.

'And why wouldn't I be?' he told Mark, 'and every last one of my flock dependent on them.'

The Rector informed him that there had been 545 calves at the Abbeyfeale calf and general market which fell on the same day as the most recent Tubberlick quarterly fair. Calves fetched from 25/– to 65/– under three weeks with some prime four week old Pollies fetching as much as £4 apiece.'

Mark did some hasty mental arithmetic. 'That,' said Mark, 'is 10% to 20% above the prices at Tubberlick.'

'And the villages all around,' the Rector added.

'They're robbing us left, right and centre,' Mark

struck the partition between snug and bar with clenched fist in a show of anger.

'White and inferior calves,' the Rector went on choosing to ignore Mark's outburst, 'fetched from 7/6 to 20/– whereas they made only half that amount in Tubberlick.'

'A good cattle drive to Trallock and they might change their tune in Tubberlick and the villages.' Mark was furious after the Rector's revelations.

'Precisely,' Archie Scuttard concurred. 'You see Mark my boy, while our isolation is spiritually edifying and uncontaminated it also works against us because we are too far out of the buyers' way, saving our own blessed jobbers. A good fright is what they want and by that I mean the threat of competition. Go ahead with your drive, by all means, and let us keep driving until they come to their senses but let us keep our voices down and our plans to ourselves,' the Rector concluded as Vester McCarthy looked in on them from the inside of the counter.

'Faraway cows have long horns,' he said with a smile although he had not heard a solitary word of the conversation.

After a while Sally McCarthy joined them in the snug. Deliberately she chose not to sit near Mark. Instead she sat near the Rector and thrust an arm into his.

'When are you going to convert me Archie?' she asked mischievously.

'I'll immerse you without a stitch this minute,' the Rector replied, 'if you'll come to the river with me.'

'I'll have to tell Daddy about you,' she chided him mockingly. She was gone again after a few moments.

''Tis you she's after,' the Rector informed Mark, 'but I suppose you already know that. I have to go now but we must meet again.'

'Why don't you call some day when you're passing!' Mark suggested.

'I certainly will,' the Rector promised, 'and sooner than you think at that. Do you know that Millstreet in County Cork is only forty miles away?'

'Why Millstreet?' Mark asked.

'Because,' said Archie Scuttard as he rose and gingerly fingered that part of his thigh which had been smashed to pieces by shrapnel, 'there were fifty buyers there the last fair and because it has a railway station and because first-class yearlings made £9 apiece there last time round, the top two year olds made ten guineas and good quality three year old, in-calf heifers broke all records at £15 apiece.'

'Trallock is nearer and easier and it will come up trumps too you'll see,' Mark assured him.

Later on he sat in the snug with Sally McCarthy. She prepared a plate of ham sandwiches and a preciously-filled pint of stout.

'Is that a good pint or isn't it?' she asked. Later they first held hands and then there were some fleeting pecks, followed by longer, more intense kisses which had Mark Doran gasping for breath. Then, unexpectedly, he found himself releasing her left breast from its confines. He expected her to resist but she sat perfectly still. He would never admit it to his more boastful friends but this was as far as he had ever advanced with a woman. Free of its unnatural restrictions the fulsome breast rejoiced in its exposure. Quivering and tantalisingly-nippled, it trembled under his touch. It seemed to Mark to have been designed for no other purpose than the gentle fondling with which he now favoured it.

'God bless you girleen,' he whispered, 'but you're well equipped.'

'Thank you,' she returned gently and then, after a pause, 'I wouldn't like you to go any further Mark if you please.'

'Of course, of course,' came his whispered re-assurance, 'this is plenty for me.'

5

On Easter Saturday Mark Doran, after much agonising, entered the Curate's confessional in Tubberlick. Four months had passed since his last unburdening of conscience. Mark was an annual rather than a regular penitent with no major imperfections to his credit. A cold chill which left a sickening clamminess in its wake assailed him as he neared the confessional. What had been a simple formality until that moment now assumed the awesome guise of an inquisitorial interrogation which might well result in his being refused absolution.

It also occurred to him that he might have been discreetly informed in the past about the morbid and even prurient curiosity of the man to whom he was about to divulge the innermost secrets of his immortal soul. He regretted his decision but he would have to perform his Easter duty. As he wiped the cold sweat from his brow he knew there could be no turning back. It would be the talk of the countryside in the morning if he was seen to balk at the very threshold of the confessional and for evermore, he thought, they'd be wondering what unmentionable perversion came between me and my salvation. Desperately he began to pray. The whispered Hail Marys, an all too familiar exercise at this juncture in the shriving process, poured forth, one after the other as he re-salivated his dried-up mouth and waited for the resident penitent, still mumbling ingloriously, to emerge from the box. He had no doubt in his mind that he would be warned to stay away indefinitely from his most recent occasion of sin, the snug of Vester McCarthy's licensed premises where he had wantonly fondled the bosom of the daughter of the house under her own very roof whilst her father and mother, totally unaware of their visitor's transgressions down below, slept contentedly up above.

After what seemed like hours the shriven but shrunken figure of a Ballybo farmer emerged with his cap clutched firmly between his gnarled hands. Mark and he exchanged a fleeting look but short as it was the older man managed to convey to the younger an inkling of the excruciating examination which awaited him. For a moment Mark wondered if perhaps it was strictly necessary to provide details of his session with Sally McCarthy. After all there had been no intercourse. They had drawn the line.

As he listened to the whispered confession at the other side of the box he decided that it would be perjurious and sacrilegious to withhold the truth. The absolution which he would undoubtedly receive without revealing the outstanding feature of his confession would definitely be questionable. In fact it would constitute an even greater sin than the first. The confession at the far side was a tedious one made longer by the promptings of Father Tapley the Curate who pursued any and all disclosures of a sexual nature with the utmost ruthlessness. Once when upbraided by an outspoken matron of the parish, who had confessed to a solitary impure thought about a film actor, he had pointed out that it was his bounden duty to ferret out every detail and to act as a sort of devil's advocate so that he need have no qualms about giving absolution at the end of the proceedings. The woman had never come back. Most of the female parishioners gave the Curate's confessional a wide berth and confided their sins to the Parish Priest who, after receiving a promise that the penitents would mend their ways, discharged them from his box fully shriven with penances which rarely exceeded a decade of the Rosary.

Mark expelled a deep breath and braced himself as the shutter was drawn across and the outline of Father Tapley's pointed profile revealed itself. Mark opened the proceedings with the usual preliminaries after which he revealed that he had been slightly drunk on 4 different occasions since his last confession. Father Tapley drew on the earlobe visible to Mark and sighed to himself as this latest ploughboy unloaded his commonplace cargo. Father Tapley's greatest difficulty during these mundane recitals was keeping his eyes open. Once or twice he had been known to doze off when the fare was not to his liking. When Mark paused at the end of the introductory items Father Tapley sensed that this unlikely source might be the carrier of some interesting items after all.

'Yes. Yes,' he egged Mark on when the pause turned into a silence.

Mark cleared his throat but nothing came forth.

'Come on man. Was it a girl or what?'

'It was a girl,' Mark blurted out. 'I caught her by the bosom.'

'Inside or outside her clothes?' Father Tapley asked.

'Inside,' from Mark.

'Ah!' said Father Tapley, 'and you come here expecting absolution.'

'Yes,' Mark shot back eagerly in the foolish belief that for once the Curate was about to terminate this uncomfortable line of questioning prematurely.

'Did you remove any of this unfortunate creature's outer garments?' Father Tapley was on the warpath quickly.

'None,' Mark answered truthfully.

'Any inner garments?'

'None,' Mark was now perspiring profusely from every pore.

'You say,' said Father Tapley somewhat baffled for once, 'that you caught this woman by the bosom. This was the expression you used and yet you say you removed no inner garments.'

'That is true Father.'

'But,' Father Tapley was growing annoyed, 'if you removed no inner garments how did you find those forbidden objects in your hands?'

'What objects?' Mark asked innocently.

'The creature's breasts you fool!' Father Tapley exploded and then, realising that his voice might well carry beyond the confines of the confessional, he lowered his tone.

The light of understanding was at last dawning on Mark.

'She wasn't wearing any inner garments,' he explained. 'All she wore was a blouse.'

'And you unbuttoned this blouse,' Father Tapley went on feverishly, 'and you held both of this girls breasts in your sinful hands.'

'One at a time,' Mark was quick to point out.

'All right, all right!' The exasperated voice came back, 'and what did you do then?'

'I held on to just one of·'em,' Mark was relieved that his answer was unambiguous. He hoped the Curate would be satisfied.

'Apart from holding on to it what else did you do with it?'

'I kissed it Father,' Mark whispered the answer, hoping in vain that it would be the last one he would be obliged to give.

'Just kissed it eh?' the Curate was at his most penetrating now. 'Which part exactly did you kiss?'

'The nipple,' Mark answered almost inaudibly.

'You took it in your mouth?' The Curate was unexpectedly conspiratorial all of a sudden.

'I took it in my mouth,' Mark replied, shame and anger in his tones.

'And you drew on it didn't you like one of those ravenous little sucky calves.'

'Yes,' Mark shouted at the top of his voice, the tears surging up in his eyes. 'I drew on it.'

'Now, now,' Father Tapley was alarmed. He hadn't anticipated such a retaliatory outburst.

'It's not the end of the world my son.' He muttered words of absolution while Mark rebelliously embarked upon the *Confiteor*. The Curate had overlooked penance in his anxiety to be rid of this unpredictable penitent. He was struck by the thought, after Mark had stumbled from the confessional, that he should pursue the young man and somehow reassure him but he quickly saw the folly of such a move and turned his attention to the latest arrival.

Mark stood for a few moments in the south porch of the church savouring the night air, crisp and pure, in contrast to the darkness and stuffiness of the confessional. He felt that he had brought some of its foulness with him. He felt none of the elation he had felt on previous post-penitential occasions. Legally, however, he would be entitled to go in the morning to the altar of God, there to receive the sacred host provided, of course, he managed to keep himself in a state of grace in the meanwhile. This at least was something.

Apart from the religious and spiritual values of his visit, it had also helped to emphasise his options in relation to future confessions. He felt that two main choices faced him. One was to avoid Father Frank Tapley's confessional in the future or, failing that, to avoid Vester McCarthy's licensed premises after hours.

It was still bright as he made his way to the Widow Hegarty's. He tried to put all thoughts of Sally McCarthy from his mind.

On the first Monday after Easter the Rector of Tubberlick and the Bishop Elect of San Lupino embarked on a reconnaissance mission to the town of Trallock. Despite the availability of his brother-in-law's Baby Ford and because it was a mild morning with little breeze, Danny Binge was more than sympathetic when the Rector proposed that they undertake the 40 mile journey on his powerful BSA.

In Trallock the clerical pairing of Binge and Scuttard, after an eventful journey from Tubberlick, found themselves in the gents' toilets of the Trallock Arms Hotel. There, after a comprehensive washing, brushing and combing they both thanked God for their safe arrival. They had been particularly fortunate to survive one uncontrollable skid during which they struck a gate. Luckily the structure was an ancient and rickety one, very nearly in a state of collapse. The powerful BSA took the entire contraption in its stride and landed its shocked passengers in the middle of the field into which the gate opened.

After the machine had deposited them without ceremony on the grass they had both rolled downhill for thirty yards and found themselves safely askew in a clover-padded dip. The bike lay on its side, none the worse for its deviations while the clergymen removed their helmets and jackets in a fruitless search for bruises, cuts and fractures. Finding nothing they joined together in a short prayerful session consisting of one Our Father and one Glory. Neither wore clerical collars. Inside the leather jackets, both of which belonged to the Rector, they sported dark grey pullovers, collared shirts and ties of sober hue. The Bishop Elect wore a grey flannel slacks, loaned to him by his brother-in-law, while the Rector wore one of the clerical grey trousers which were part of his everyday garb. An astute observer would have taken them for gentlemen of the cloth at a glance although he might have some doubts about the Rector whose many friends would cheerfully say that the last thing he looked like was a clergyman.

In the lounge bar they took seats by the window which afforded an excellent view of the town square, deserted now because of the bank holiday although there were several other patrons present.

After the second whiskey they examined the menus which had been delivered at the Rector's request.

'The lamb is always excellent here,' he announced, 'although I am more a beef man myself.'

Over lunch Archie Scuttard provided his guest with a short history of the town which had sprung up from the remains of a Norman Castle, destroyed in the Elizabethan wars. In the year 1600 the castle had been surrounded by Elizabethan forces and taken with considerable loss of life. Nothing but an ivied keep remained and this was clearly visible as the Rector pointed out from the dining-room window of the Trallock Arms.

'The square you see before you,' the Rector continued, 'is where the four great quarterly fairs are held. They spill over into the other lanes and streets of the town, even the by-ways and backways during the quarterlies but during the fortnightly fairs the square itself is sufficient in size to contain the smaller numbers of cattle. It has,' the Rector continued, 'the reputation of being the best of all the southern cattle fairs. There is always demand in Trallock or so it is said. There is a thriving railway station with adequate pens. Jobbers and buyers come from as far away as the midlands but more importantly they all come to the quarterlies in large numbers, many of them reputable figures in the cattle business. The question of a ring or cartel never arises and that is why, my friend, you and I are here today. We must look upon ourselves as outriders and scouts or even undercover agents whose function it is to survey the setting in preparation for the the great October cattle drive. Obviously we are unlikely to find any useful information here in this hotel but the town has many excellent public houses where two experienced deputies might find it profitable to keep their ears cocked.'

Over a bottle of wine the Bishop Elect asked a number of pertinent questions relating to the economics of the proposed drive.

'What of the appearance of the cattle after such a drive?' he asked.

'Good question,' the Rector looked into his wine glass and had no difficulty finding the answer.

'It is to be hoped,' he said patiently, 'that the cattle will not be stampeded at any stage or even hurried. A leisurely pace over a two, three or even four day period with good grazing at the end of the day may be the answer to our problems. It is true that cattle look hacked and drawn after long journeys and might not attract the best price as a result but the expedition, if it is planned down to the last detail, can be a success.'

'Do you think,' the Bishop Elect asked, 'that it will be worth the bother? For instance the cattle are sure to lose weight no matter how slowly the drive is paced.'

The Rector was pleased with the question. He raised his glass and thoughtfully sipped the wine therein.

'There can be no doubt,' he replied, 'that we will not gain financially from this particular cattle drive but then it has to be remembered that we are not worried on that score. Our aim is to show that there is an alternative to the fairs of the five villages, particularly to the fairs of Tubberlick. When we have shown that we are capable of conducting a successful cattle drive to Trallock we will bring the villages to their knees. Eventually we might even conduct drives on a monthly or even a fortnightly basis not for the express purpose of doing damage to the economy of the villages but solely to remind them that there is an alternative to the dishonest system which they have supported for years at the expense of the hill farmers. If we were to deliberately set out to destroy the economy of the villages we would eventually destroy ourselves. They are, after all, our villages. All we need is one successful drive and we will have the hill farmers falling over themselves to entrust their cattle to us. The publicans and shopkeepers of Tubberlick will be the first to capitulate with the prospect of empty streets on successive fair days. Empty streets mean empty shops and empty pubs. The business people will eventually see that it is in their own interest as well as the farmers to ensure that the ring of jobbers is smashed and replaced by a larger number of independent buyers, especially invited buyers if needs be. There are buyers nowadays prepared to transport many of the light cattle in trucks. Farming is changing. Farmers are looking further afield. There's a farmer's son in Boherlahan, the smallest of the five villages, who has just purchased a second-hand, two-ton, Dodge truck. He paid £40 for it in Killarney just two weeks ago. It's four years old but it has a twenty-six horsepower engine. Already he's taken three loads of pigs to Limerick and two loads of calves to Killarney. He's prepared to take a load of three bullocks to Trallock but the price is too high just yet. Wait until he gets a bigger truck. Wait until the countryside becomes mechanised.'

'There's a war coming,' Danny Binge warned.

'Agreed,' said the Rector, 'and the longer it lasts the longer we'll have to wait for mechanisation that will liberate us.'

'Will the war mean higher prices for cattle?'

The Rector summoned a nearby waitress and called for a second bottle of wine.

'All this talking has left my mouth as dry as the inside of a crypt,' he explained, 'but to answer your question. Wars in the past have not made all that difference to the price of cattle at least as far as the English are concerned and that's where most of our best cattle go to but this war will be different. The German Navy, and particularly the U-Boat fleet, will pose a major threat to British supremacy on the high seas and this means that imports into Britain will be endangered. The crossing from Ireland is little more than a token crossing and there is the concentration of British warships to defend the food and cattle. Yes, the war will drive up the price of cattle. That's why it's imperative to make this drive, to be ready to exploit the new opportunities for the Irish farmers. The tragedy is,' and here the Rector lowered his voice, 'the farmers will not be the only ones to benefit from exploitation.'

Both men embarked upon a conspiratorial silence as the waitress filled their empty glasses. After she had withdrawn the Rector continued.

'It is a marvellous opportunity for the IRA.'

'I thought,' said the Bishop Elect, 'that they were mainly gone underground, a shadow of what they were.'

'The IRA shadow is different from other shadows,' the Rector explained. 'It's a shadow that can smell opportunity. It can smell war as well, particularly any war that affects the British. This coming war with Germany is heaven-sent as far as the IRA is concerned. Their campaign has already begun and if I were to be asked in the morning why I was so sure that war was inevitable I would point to the IRA bécause they have already started. Instinctively they know that war is brewing, almost upon us in fact.'

'But their support is gone,' the Bishop Elect was surprisingly well informed on the subject.

'They don't make these fellows Monsignori for just being good drinkers,' the Rector thought.

'Their support in the main is gone but they are arming and training in deserted barns, beaches, shells of burned out barracks and great houses. They cannot campaign the way they did in the Civil War. They no longer mount offensives against government forces so they fell back on isolated acts of terrorism at home and abroad and as we speak they are killing innocent civilians in Britain. They maintain that their campaign is targeted against munitions' factories and power installations among other things. They are hated beyond belief in England but they raise the point that they want to drive home the injustice of Irish partition to the English people at large.'

'And the British?' the Bishop Elect asked in a tone which clearly conveyed his Irish-American lack of love for the empire.

'The mass of the English people don't care about us. They don't know about us and they don't really want to know. The British press rail against the atrocities but ignore Loyalist attempts to wreck Catholic churches and memorials in Belfast. Police patrols, present at the time, make no arrests.'

'And the British government?'

'They see us,' said the Rector sadly, 'as a satellite, a satellite that doesn't always conform to the rules but I am hopeful that they will see the light some day.'

After lunch they paid a visit to the keep of the once proud castle, its buttresses embedded deep in the womb of the ancient pool, wide and deep, which partly surrounded it.

'Built by our chaps,' the Rector explained.

'But I thought it was Norman,' Danny Binge protested.

'And so it was,' the Rector assured him, 'and so was I. There was a time my dear Monsignor when my people were called De Scuttards but usage reduced us to Scuttard and we're not De Scuttards anymore.'

Hands behind backs they left the castle grounds and took a turn around the great square, the Rector briefly outlining the history of the Catholic and Protestant Churches with their twin spires and towering Gothic frontages.

'This will be the nub of the great October cattle fair,' he explained as he indicated with his right hand the entire area of the square.

'Not easy to find room for one's herd here with so many traditional claims already established. It will be particularly difficult for us because we have never stood our cattle here before. We would be expected to take our places in the outskirts or at best in one of the minor streets but this is the place to be on the day of the fair.'

'Always stand your nag in the middle of the fair.' The words escaped the Bishop Elect as his eyes took in the Edwardian architecture of the square.

'Where did you hear that?' the Rector asked.

'My mother,' Danny Binge replied.

'Your mother was right,' the Rector concurred. They stopped for a moment to admire the plaster work on one of the most inviting licensed premises ever to confront the eye of the Bishop Elect.

'Should we not indulge,' he suggested to his friend.

'I had rather be a doorkeeper in the house of my God,' the Rector quoted as he wagged a warning finger under the nose of his companion, 'than to dwell in the tents of wickedness.'

'It looks all right to me,' Danny Binge took stock of the frontage a second time.

'Who so diggeth a pit shall fall therein,' cautioned the Rector.

As they continued on their leisurely peregrinations the Rector explained his antipathy to the house which he had rejected.

'The proprietress,' said he, 'of the premises which so captured your fancy is a pillar of the Church and I think you will agree that her persuasion is not the question. What is important, Binge old son, is that the moment we raise a glass to our lips in her presence word of our imbibitions will spread like wildfire through the sainted homes of Tubberlick. We don't want to scandalise the innocent do we?'

'Indeed we do not,' Danny Binge replied.

As they approached the junction of the square and the town's main thoroughfare, a long canyon of three storeyed houses, mainly devoted to business and the licensing trade, the Bishop Elect revealed the details of his exchanges with the Parish Priest of Tubberlick.

'I tell you this,' Danny Binge confided, 'so that you might appreciate my position.'

'I wouldn't worry about Father Dugan,' the Rector threw back, 'nor about the Curate Father Tapley. They have their problems like all of us but they are basically decent enough chaps. It's the boy with the crozier you have to worry about. He should be on a hurley team the way he wields it when the humour is on him. He reported me to my own Bishop one night after I turned into the presbytery by mistake. There used to be a life-size statue of Teresa of Lisieux on a plinth at the right hand side of the presbytery door. Suffice it to say that it isn't there any more. For some reason, best known to herself, she smashed into me, no doubt fearing that I would come to worse harm without her saintly intervention. It was nothing short of a miracle.'

'Were you injured?' Danny Binge asked.

'Not a scratch old boy, not even a bump.'

'There is something I must tell you shortly,' Danny Binge spoke in solemn tones, 'but I hardly think this is the place. Perhaps a decent pub would be better.'

'And where do you think I have been navigating you since we left the hotel,' Archie Scuttard asked indignantly. 'Cast your eyes up this fine street my friend and you will see a sign extending from a noble frontage, less than fifty yards from where we stand. Look well and tell me what is written on the sign.'

Danny Binge peered into the distance and slowly spelled out the letters inscribed on a giant sign in glaring red capitals.

'DURANGO,' he read.

'That is our destination,' the Rector informed his friend. 'I'm well known here. These people are my friends and before this night is over they shall be your friends too.'

6

At four o'clock on a Sunday afternoon Mark Doran
saddled the grey mare and set off at a slow trot for the
abode of his seventy-five year old grand-uncle the Badger Doran. A slight, seasonal drizzle obscured the distant hilltop where the old man had waged an uneven
battle against the inhospitable summit with its in-
sufficient topsoil for two and fifty years of his married
life. There were fertile hollows, all too few, and a flat
well-shaded garden at the lee of the thatched house. The
garden, chiefly devoted to potatoes, turnip, cabbage and
oats, could vie with any in the hill country and despite
the dearth of topsoil was the envy of many with loamier
fields and richly productive cutaway further down in
the valleys.

The great advantage arising from the nature and
dryness of the Badger's carefully nurtured ridges was
the fact that early frost wrought far less havoc on his
potato stalks than those of the watery cutaway fields far
below. The moist soil of the latter would always prove to
be less resistant to the premature frost which was the
bane of all potato growers in the hill country.

As the mare ascended the steep incline along the
boundary of the Mullanney farm Mark caught a fleeting
glimpse of the three Mullanney sisters through the
greening whitethorn bushes that flanked the roadway.

The girls were hastily gathering the dried washing
from the clothes-lines at the rear of the house. As they
called excitedly to each other Mark drew rein for a moment and smiled at their frantic comings and goings. Their
laughter, as they ran with arms full of clothes to the shel-
ter of the house, awoke in him a yearning for a woman's
arms, not any woman but a dark-haired sometimes un-
definable beauty, a girl who always seemed to be about

to materialise in his dreams but then always seemed to recede. As he sat he wiped the water from his face and peered again through the thickening and now cloying mist. He saw her reaching for a white sheet, her slender, angular body almost pathetically frail leaping to open the clothes pegs which held the sheet in place. His heart lifted at once. The movement, lissome and totally free, seemed to him to be a celebration of the childhood which she was about to abandon. He was surprised by the objectivity of his own thoughts. He realised too, for the first time, that he felt a sense of responsibility towards her. He would not compare her with Sally McCarthy, the buxom daughter of Vester the proud and yet he found himself making the comparison and then, as if his conscience had spoken, the mare moved startled by the distant bellowing of Haybags Mullanney, angered no doubt by the bustle and skittishness of his womenfolk. As the bellowing subsided Mark guessed that he would have sought refuge in one of his fields until the frenzied female activities ended. The heavy mist, which triggered off the clothes-clearing operation in the first place, would not trouble him.

As the mare moved slowly uphill towards the summit Mark found himself playing host to a hitherto-unexperienced turbulence which he found disturbing. Mark's mother would always say that his complaisance was his strong point. In fact there had been times during football matches in the heat of the exchanges when he silently congratulated himself on his calm and detachment.

At the root of this newly-arrived inner turmoil were the women in his life, their relationship with him and their likely relationship with each other. At the summit he drew rein for a moment and looked behind him. There she stood, under the green of a whitethorn, her hand lifted in salute, her frailty emphasised by the height of the roadside greenery and the distance between them. He raised his hand and returned her salute. He chided himself for not having stopped by for a moment. Perhaps on the way back in the morning! Yes, without fail, he would look in on the Mullanney household in the morning or sometime later, depending on how the night before him developed and ended.

As he neared Beenablaw which was the name given to the townland where the Badger and his wife Monnie husbanded out their later days he laughed quietly at the prospect of spending the night with the ageing pair.

Beenablaw, Gaelic for summit of the flowers, consisted largely of barren mountain. The exception was the well-tended acreage of the Badger Doran. The couple were without child but there existed between them a degree of respect and affection which had outlasted their many confrontations down the years. The Badger was renowned far and wide for his blasphemous outpourings on any and all topics under the sun. He had also won limited fame for the high quality of his seed potatoes.

Mark's latest recruit to his own farm's workforce of himself and his mother came recommended by the Badger for whom he had occasionally worked. This was during busy periods such as the weeding of turnips and mangolds, the potato planting, the cutting and harvesting of the hay crop and the droving of cattle to the quarterly fairs of the villages.

Mark was immediately impressed with the new arrival Danny Dooley, a pint-sized, moustached man in his late forties who favoured the single state on the grounds that despite years of searching he could not find a woman tall enough to suit him.

A happy-go-lucky bachelor, Danny Dooley had volunteered only a few minutes after his arrival to complete the ploughing of the potato garden which Mark had been forced to postpone because of the unsuitability of the late March weather. Danny Dooley had gone to work with a will. His handling of the two plough horses, the family mare and Mullanney's gelding, was skilled in the extreme. At first Mark had discreetly assessed his ploughing skills from a distance and when he failed to locate a human figure behind the lumbering plough horses he emerged from behind the thicket from where he had been secretly conducting his examination, thinking that some mishap must surely have befallen the ploughman. As he approached the imperturbable team, still moving of their own accord, Mark shouted: 'Whoa, whoa,' from a distance so that he might discover the whereabouts of the missing ploughman. The horses ignored his commands, however, and continued, calmly, leaving behind them a loamy wake, gleaming and straight. Mark stopped in his tracks, mystified by the behaviour of the team. Then inexplicably they stopped and the tiny figure of Danny Dooley appeared, as if from nowhere, at the coulter of the plough.

'What's wrong?' he called with mock surprise.

It became clear to Mark that Danny was well used to the routine. While the orthodox ploughman would raise the plough handles so that the share might penetrate to the appropriate depth as the horses laboured Danny Dooley had no difficulty in raising the handles over his bent head in much the same fashion as a weight lifter. The effect was the same except that Mark had rarely if ever seen furrows as straight. Mark indicated that there was nothing wrong. Danny flicked the reins and soon the gleaming furrow lengthened under his expert guidance.

The following day the potato pit was opened at its more sheltered end and the seed potatoes selected for the summer crop. That night mother, son and labourer expertly cut the seed. The following days were spent planting and drilling.

Danny Dooley brought with him an expertise in

handling potatoes that could only have come from a man whose antecedents had survived the great famine of Black Forty-seven. 'There are tricks in every trade,' he explained to Mark as he later selected certain of the more seeded and wrinkled of the pit potatoes. The tubers remaining in the pit he rearranged and covered with rushes lest they sprout and turn soggy. He removed the seeds from the potatoes chosen earlier and instructed Mark's mother to boil them at once after washing. Although surprised by his request Mark's mother had agreed. Somewhere in the back of her memory was a story she had heard about a similar system of preserving seeding potatoes. When the potatoes were boiled, three stone in all, Danny Dooley transferred them to an ancient skillet, thoroughly cleaned out. The cover was then placed atop the skillet and sealed. The potatoes within would last for weeks and quantities might be removed at mealtimes as required. If they had been allowed to languish in the pit the latent mould of March would have rendered them unfit for human or animal consumption.

There was no day that Mark did not learn something new from Danny Dooley. Let it be turnip, cabbage or mangolds, the new workman more than made up for his lack of height with skill and wisdom. He contracted to stay with Mark until the end of October. He had not come cheaply. Mark had never struck a harder bargain but after the first weeks he came to realise that he had made a good bargain.

At the entrance to Beenablaw House, as the Badger termed his ancient, thatched, one-storeyed farmhouse, Mark dismounted and led the mare to the front door which was opened by Monnie Doran before he had time to knock. She dragged him by both hands into the warm kitchen and sent the Badger, still drowsy after his Sunday snooze to look after the mare. In the kitchen Monnie removed the oilskins. None of the mist had penetrated to his inner garments.

'Sit, sit,' Monnie Doran pushed him downwards onto the sugán chair vacated by his grand-uncle while she hung the wet clothes on a rickety coat-stand near the back door. Her next move was to sit on his lap after which she placed her withered hands at either side of his face before kissing him gently on the crown of the head.

'You grow more like your father with the days,' she said sadly, as she examined his face, 'but you'll have a long life. I've seen it in the leaves often enough.' She then raised his palm until it was within a few inches of her tired eyes. She studied the hard, thorn-pierced surface for several moments.

'You'll be torn between two women, one fair and one dark, the fair one fleshy and the dark one dainty. Fearful ramifications will rear their heads and there will be carnage to boot.'

She traced his life-line while the Badger stood listening at the door. He always took her prognostications seriously. She had often been wrong but there were times when she had been uncannily right.

'Which will it be?' Mark asked as he tried to hide his anxiety.

'Ah!' sighed Monnie Doran, 'so I'm right!'

'Which?' Mark asked, surprised at his persistence.

'That remains to be seen,' the old woman replied, 'but,' she raised the forefinger of her right hand and spoke solemnly, 'me thinks you'll end up with the right one for you have your grand-uncle's luck, especially with women.'

She removed herself from his lap and disappeared into the adjoining room.

'How's Danny Dooley working out?' the Badger asked, knowing full well that there would be an abundance of encomiums for his choice of workman.

'Not bad at all,' his grand-nephew responded with a

sly smile.

'If that man was to stand on his merits,' the Badger boasted, 'he'd be the tallest man in the five parishes.'

'He's good all right,' Mark agreed.

'A good, small man,' said the Badger who was only five feet and two inches himself, 'is better any day than a good big man. You can easily knock a big man but a small man will always stay on his feet.'

Monnie Doran reappeared with a bottle in her hand. The Badger rubbed his hands together as she located three enamelled egg stands in the recesses of the brightly-painted dresser.

'This is as good a drop as ever you'll taste,' the Badger boasted, 'and like all good drops one is enough. Always remember that about poitín. A glass measure or an egg stand full and no more. It's just a primer for porter and we'll have plenty of that soon.'

Poitín as a primer and no more! Mark agreed although he needed no such direction from his granduncle. He had survived a poitín party on his twenty-first birthday, had been ill for several days and learned a lesson he would never forget.

Throughout the Great War in the hill country men had been blinded and one had died from overdoses of the deadly distillation. Yet it was widely imbibed for its alleged curative properties. The Badger Doran would argue that it was the only successful cure for the common cold. Doctors would differ. Some would say that all poitín was poison.

'It's equivalent in the *British Pharmacopoeia* is on the dangerous drugs' list,' they argued.

The Badger was fond of refuting this argument in no uncertain terms. Remembering that it was a Trallock doctor who conducted the inquest on the man who had died the Badger directed his criticism towards the medical fraternity of the market town.

'The doctors in Trallock,' said he, 'wouldn't know

their balls from their tonsils.'

'They say,' said a listener whose only aim was to bring out the best in the Badger, 'that the doctor in charge of the inquest has degrees from all over the world.'

'And I say,' retorted the Badger, 'that for all his letters he can't cure a cold while I that has nothing after my name can cure tonsillitis, laryngitis, bronchitis and bolluxitis.'

The Badger's cronies warned his critics that one of his verbal broadsides left a mental scar far more devastating than any wound inflicted during a physical assault but despite his undoubted predilection for incisive counter-attacks he was nevertheless a popular figure wherever he chose to present himself. Monnie was no less a character. Once a week in the family pony cart she made the journey to Ballybo to dispose of her eggs and to lay in a stock of Woodbines for herself and her man and enough provisions to see them through till her next visit.

Every few months, most likely during the quarterly fairs, she visited Tubberlick from where she originally hailed although none of her kin remained. There she visited old friends, the few remaining from her girlhood. There was a time before they disposed of their milch cows when the pony cart was loaded with sacks of meal, bran and pollard all purchased from the arse-patter extraordinaire as Archie Scuttard, once dubbed the master fondler of Tubberlick.

'And how is Vester McCarthy?' Monnie Doran asked as soon as Mark had finished his poitín.

'Fine as could be,' Mark assured her.

'And Mary his wife and the daughter Sally?'

'All fine,' Mark replied.

Monnie went on to enquire after the Widow Hegarty and the easy-going custodian of the peace, Mick Malone, among others.

'That's a fair cut of a girl, that daughter of Vester's,' she told Mark.

He knew from he way she said it that she must have some inkling of their relationship.

'And is Vester as vigorous as ever?' she asked with a laugh as she drew the cork from the jowl of a porter bottle with an iron corkscrew.

'Oh he's the healthy boy,' Mark accepted the bottle and the tin panny into which the old woman had already poured most of the contents.

'He's nothing but a spoiled arse-catcher,' the Badger declared as he accepted his bottle and panny.

'And pray what's wrong with that?' Monnie Doran asked. 'Don't everyone say that 'tis no more than a sign of health. Sure if a man didn't give a woman the odd smack on the bottom wouldn't they be going around saying that there was something wrong with him. Am I right Mark or amen't I?'

'Oh you're right, of course,' Mark agreed.

The Badger wasn't finished, however.

'God's sake hasn't he the behinds torn off innocent women that says their prayers at night and receives the host every Sunday. That's no way to behave towards God-fearing women.' He gulped back the contents of his panny in disgust.

'A pat on the bottom won't keep 'em from praying or from going to the rails of a Sunday,' Monnie continued, 'and although he never laid a paw on my bony oul' rump I don't see what damage it could do. An arse won't wear from it.'

'He's a randy oul grabber,' the Badger wouldn't let go.

'I'll tell you now so's the pair of you will know,' Monnie's final contribution was to be the conclusive one. 'He's not a grabber,' said she authoritatively, 'and he's not a patter nor a pincher from what I've seen of him in action. He's that way inclined all right and he won't let a well-made bottom pass him by if there's a chance of laying a hand on it and that's all he does is lay the hand on and that way 'tis the bottom itself will give him his answer. Most bottoms will remove, respectable bottoms that is, but there's a share of lonesome bottoms and starved bottoms that will stand their ground because that's the way of the world and that's the way it will be while you have men and women in it.'

The Badger nodded the grey mane from which he derived his nickname. His woman had summed it up well and he would not dispute it.

'Time for us to be going,' he informed his grand-nephew, 'if we're to get to the pub with the light.'

A half-hour later they dismounted from the mare outside Holligan's public house, the only licensed pre-mises in the village of Ballybo, a hamlet consisting of twenty houses but serving a hinterland of a hundred or more small farms which ended half-way up the last of the hills in the five parishes. At the base of the hill at the other side, the Atlantic ebbed and flowed, its thunder sometimes audible, its refreshing tang always in the air. The Badger would boast in distant places that the Protestants had five parishes and hardly any parishion-ers whereas the Catholics had only one parish but twenty times the number of parishioners. He would neg-lect to inform his listeners that the same five Protestant parishes were all contained in the same Catholic parish.

In Holligans they were warmly greeted by the pat-rons already in residence. Some of these were seated at card tables where the game invariably played was a hundred and ten. Mattie and Maud Holligan extended wet hands to the newcomers and enquired after their health and general welfare as well as their womenfolk. The formalities over Mark Doran ordered two pints of stout while the Badger sought out a crony with whom he had already formed a loose agreement in respect of the proposed cattle drive.

'Go back on that Philly,' he instructed the crony in question who chanced to have a near empty pint glass in front of him at the end of the long bar counter. The Badger indicated to Mark that a third pint of stout would be required. Locating a high stool the Badger took his place beside his friend. The agreement between them was revealed to Mark as soon as he took his place beside him. The crony's name was Philly Hinds, a small farmer from the boggy lowlands beyond the hill country. Like the Badger he had disposed of his milch cows because of his age and like the Badger he had kept one and let his fields to a bullock farmer.

'One of those fields he has retained. It is the haggard next to his house,' the Badger explained, 'and this field he will preserve for us from the middle of August to the first week of October while his cow will content herself with the long acre until he puts her in for the winter. The haggard is only an acre and a half and I reckon our herd will strip it to the clay in one evening. For this,' said the Badger, 'he requires two bottles of Paddy Flaherty Whiskey for himself and a bottle of Lourdes' water for his wife for she is a woman of great devotion to the Blessed Virgin. No bottle to be handed over till our cattle enter this man's haggard. Now let us all shake on it as one man to another.'

The three shook hands and quaffed deeply from their pints. Philly Hinds called for a second round and later the Badger called for a third after which Philly went to the spacious open air toilet of over a thousand hilly acres at the rear of the pub.

'Where are we going to get Lourdes' water?' Mark asked.

'All water is the same,' the Badger said solemnly, 'it's the thought that matters and if needs be I'll get my own Monnie to put a blessing on it for she's a devout creature that never wronged anyone. We needn't tell her that she will be transforming ordinary water into

Lourdes' water. One of us is enough to carry the guilt and I now hereby absolve you because the plan was mine.'

As the night wore on the Badger entertained the after-hours drinkers with some ribald songs while Philly Hinds danced a hornpipe to the accomplished puss music of Maud Holligan. Later the Holligans doused the bar lights. Mark, the Badger, Philly Hinds and two other old men sat together in a corner where their conversation would not carry. They spoke in whispers in the first place because it was the norm for the time and place. They were breaking the law by simply being present in a public house after the proscribed hours and should a member of the civic guards arrive at Holligan's front door there would be nothing to suggest that there was any form of illicit activity inside.

The likelihood of a raid was always there, especially if there was excessive IRA activity during the previous week or if some much-abused mother of a large family had complained of a drunken husband who might have badly beaten her. Everyone suffered as a result of the wife beater's cowardly actions. When his identity was revealed, as it always was, he was barred from Holligan's until he mended his ways. It was a punishment more chastening than anything a court of law might hand out. His physical well-being was also at risk. Ballybo was not the only village of the five without a resident civic guard. Tubberlick might be the largest by far of the five but it was not the centre of law and order despite its having a resident civic guard. This honour fell to the smaller village of Boherlahan with its 200 inhabitants, 300 less than Tubberlick but since it sprawled along the main road between Trallock and Killarney it was the most central and boasted not only a civic guard but also a sergeant with responsibility to none save his divisional superintendent.

Kilshunnig was also possessed of one custodian but

as far as the people of Ballybo and Tubberlick were concerned Mick Malone was the supreme authority. Tubberlick was the undisputed ecclesiastical centre with its distinguished, if smaller, Protestant church which catered for the Protestant souls of the same area.

The muted assembly in the corner of Holligan's spoke first of grass and then of sowing. They conferred with great earnestness and concern about the lateness of the potato planting due to the extensive rains. They detailed experiences of similar occurrences and proffered remedies to counter the problem. Mark noted that all of the Badger's utterances concerning potatoes were taken seriously by his listeners. They spoke soberly of the many strains of this indispensable tuber which had sustained them for generations. Philly Hinds argued that for human consumption the Kerr's Pink was without equal and for animal consumption the Aran Banner was a good cut above the rest.

'And where,' the Badger asked politely, 'are you leaving your Aran Victor? The Kerr's Pink I admire and 'tis a nice clean-cut potato with a rosy face but it hasn't the body of the Blueboy.' Blue in colour, the Aran Victor was frequently called the Blueboy. All were agreed that the Banner was the spud for cattle, fowl and porkers but they would never agree on the respective merits of Kerr's Pink and Aran Victor.

'A lot depends on the land,' one old man summed the entire business up before they moved on to cabbage. Round after round of drink was called. The Badger reverted to whiskey on the grounds that he needed it to keep down the several pints of stout consumed since his arrival.

When they finished with their examination of cabbage and kale they moved briefly to turnips and mangolds before, eventually, arriving at the business which had originally moved them to flirt with the laws of the land and remain in Holligan's after hours. The oldest of the party one Moses Madigan was greatly impressed with Mark Doran. While Mark was absent on a visit to the toilet the old chap was heard to say that he would entrust him with his life.

'He's a respectful boy,' he declared. 'He knows how to listen and he don't give guff in spite of being full with drink.'

Later the nonagenarian, for such he was, recounted how he had driven cattle from Ballybo to Trallock, a distance of thirty-three miles always keeping well clear of the main road which, in those days, abounded with cattle thieves, particularly weanling thieves since weanlings could be ran off and made to travel vast distances before they were even missed by their true owners.

'I drove for the Butlers. They're all gone now,' Moses recalled. 'With my brother Cuddeen, God be good to him, we drove thirty in-calf heifers to the October fair in Trallock in 1870 I think. It was a terrible year for potatoes with many good folk dying. It would melt the hardest heart. They used to come out from the bogs asking us for pake or mixed bread, no word of butter, just pake made from maize and as for jam, jam my boys was for wakes alone or maybe Christmas. People complain now but there was real starvation then. Christ boys we have the old-age pension now, 10/– a week and no matter how much bread and butter you eat the pension will pay for it and no matter how much tea you knock back the pension will pay for it. That time there was nothing for the poor only scraps. If a man or his wife wasn't fit for work the family starved. I seen people during that drive that looked more like skeletons than people. I gave what bread I had to a little girl so's she'd carry it home. It was all the potatoes' fault you see. They were after leaving us down again.'

The Badger cut across the old man's reminiscences and asked him if he could help draw a rough map of the terrain they crossed in 1870. The party retired to the kitchen behind the pub and there a sheet of paper was provided by Maud Holligan.

'Cross the bog direct,' the old man advised. 'Follow the donkey and goat paths for safety and your animals won't go bogging. On top of that there's always plenty grass on them same paths. They're well manured from the ponies and asses drawing out the turf.' He stood over Mark Doran as the young man faithfully set down the old man's directions on the paper.

'After you leave home,' the old man seemed sure of his ground, 'you come here by Ballybo and on to Philly Hinds' place where you'll rest up after the herd has stripped his haggard and strip it they will.'

'I don't mind,' Philly Hinds said. 'I'm getting well paid.'

'That's good because I amen't,' the old man laughed, delighted to be part of a plot that might one day be celebrated.

'You leave Philly's at first light and proceed northwards across the bogs until you come to Bessie Lie-Downs. I don't recall her surname because her father vanished when she was young and no one knew who he was, not even Bessie's mother. Bessie isn't called Lie-Down for nothing because, fair dues to her gentle nature, she'd lie down for any man and I hear she's still game although bordering the four score. Take a break at Bessie's. She'll give ye the hot water for the tea and an after-course for anyone that wants that kind of thing. Take care when ye leave Bessie's for knackers that would make off with a weanling no bother and if a crowd of ye goes after him his henchmen will steal another. 'Tis a time for open eyes. Always follow the green paths, never the brown no matter how ye're tempted. The green path will feed the cattle and support the cattle. Keep north until ye come to Crabapple Hill. Give the herd a rest. They'll enjoy the crabapples. The ground is always covered with them at that time of year.

After Crabapple Hill you're in wild country, nothing but snipegrass and briars and black alders. You won't see as much clover as would put a patch on the arse of a lorgadawan's trousers.'

'We'll cure that ailment,' the Badger interposed respectfully, 'by having two wynds of hay transported there a few days beforehand.'

'Good thinking,' said the elder, 'but leave a man with it or you won't find a sop when you arrive.'

There were murmurs of approval and appreciation for the old man's sagacity.

'Now,' the old fellow paused and looked into his glass wherein he saw nothing and by his face it would seem that he would like to see something. The glass was quickly filled. 'Now,' he said again as he blew his nose into the inside of his cap, 'comes the test.' He was a good narrator. He looked from one face to the other, looked into the distance, looked up and looked down and rested his eyes finally upon Mark.

'You are now climbing the Cunnackawneen, which is a haunted hill, and there's many would avoid it but if you want to arrive in Trallock early in the morning with the surety of a good stand for the herd you'll climb the haunted hill and you'll bed down for the night. I don't know how the Cunnackawneen came to be there but it's there and it's green and if it's green it's grass. Arrive there early and let your herd feed. Rest well. The main road to Trallock is only two miles below ye at the other side. Some say that the Cunnackawneen was built by the Danes as a look-out with secret chambers underneath. Others say it was caused by an upheaval when the world was being made. More say 'twas a hanging hill used by English landlords to execute sheep-stealers and rabbit-snarers or any poor man that might steal to feed his wife and young but 'tis most likely inhabited by the old native Irish, tiny, blocky men with ferocious strength, well made and well hung and naked as newborn babies. They have been seen by sane men on May Eve and all through the month of the Holy Souls. There's many a braggart climbed the Cunnackawneen with black hair and came down with white. What I say to you is well known by all that live near that part of the world.'

As they rode homewards the stars gradually faded before the oncoming dawn. The mist had disappeared and a fresh, biting breeze rustled in the roadside bushes. The mare, pleased with herself, at the prospect of lush grass in the home pastures, broke into a strong trot. Mark felt the Badger's grip tightening on the belt of his oilskins as he drew hard on the rein.

'Those chaps at the top of the Cunnackawneen!' the Badger said.

'What chaps?' Mark asked between yawns.

'You know,' the Badger told him, 'those native Irish. How's that he put it again?'

Mark smiled as he remembered the old man's description.

'Tiny, blocky men,' he recalled slowly, 'with ferocious strength, well made and well hung and naked as newborn babies.'

'They're not gone from the world yet,' the Badger straightened himself on the mare's loins and gingerly smacked her haunch. 'There's a few of us left all the time,' he shouted in Mark's ear.

7

Mick Malone was not surprised when he beheld Vester McCarthy's freshly polished Ford saloon parked outside the Drover Mooley's. He decided to bide his time until Vester McCarthy finished with whatever business it was that brought him. Meanwhile he would look around among the furze and thorn scairts in search of the six week old Aberdeen Angus heifer calf which had disappeared three days before from a small farm contiguous to Tubberlee, the third largest of the five villages.

The abode of the chief of the Drover Mooleys, no matter how one approached it, was never visible to the naked eye. Even those familiar with its location were surprised when it suddenly confronted them in the small clearing surrounded totally by an inner ring of overgrown furze bushes and a natural outer fortification of whitethorn thickets or scairts.

On a clear day one might see smoke ascending from somewhere within the almost labyrinthian complex, not always from the spot where the Mooley habitation was centred but from one of several outdoor fireplaces pressed into service whenever the weather was suitable.

The Drover Mooley was himself a lanky, cadaverous fellow, in his early sixties. He never appeared in public without his bowler hat and white silk scarf, worn bandana-like around his neck in all weathers. Both had been lifted by the Drover from a coat rack in the foyer of a hotel in Killarney after a well-attended funeral when the mourners were congregated in the lounge bar drowning their sorrows.

Not only was the Drover Mooley a drover of cattle but also he would assist in the driving of bargains at all fairs in the hill country. His input into successful sales was rewarded with sums ranging from six-penny pieces to half-crowns. He also dealt in calves and weanlings but it was believed that he was secretly acting for Vester McCarthy who financed all his ventures. When sufficient cattle had been accumulated the Drover, with the aid of his two sons-in-law, would dispose of his purchases in Killarney at more than a fair profit.

The people of Tubberlick, especially those who should know, maintained that the Drover worked for Vester on a percentage basis and that the sons-in-law were paid by the mile. Sooner or later their earnings found their way back to Vester through the medium of his bar and grocery.

'Vester McCarthy's is the headquarters of the Drover Mooley's', Mick Malone once informed his superintendent, 'and all their plans are hatched there.'

The sons-in-law, by virtue of their association with their father-in-law, were also known as the Drover Mooleys although their names were O'Dea and O'Connor. For several years they had lived altogether under the Drover's roof of thatch, remaking makeshift beds every night in the kitchen of the one-storeyed abode so expertly hidden from the public eye.

The senior son-in-law answered to the sobriquet of the Ram Mooley because of his sheepish face and the junior to Tiger Mooley because of his propensity towards teeth grinding and snarling whenever he found himself with a chunk of meat in his hands. It was his way too of savouring the prospect of a fight and a sometimes successful method of intimidating likely assailants.

Parents in Tubberlick and the other villages threatened unruly children with a visit from the Tiger Mooley. The ruse always worked and younger children on their way home from school who chanced to encounter him on the way crossed to the other side of the street or made off in the opposite direction.

If one were to ask Mick Malone if the three had anything else in common, apart from cattle-droving,

Mick would answer in the affirmative. 'They are all equally shifty,' he would say. 'They are also lying, cheating, thieving bullies but they know how to drive cattle. They will beat donkeys with cudgels, humans with their hands and feet but cattle they will direct gently with flicks from their long sally rods which goes to show,' Mick would conclude in his homely way, 'that there is some good in every man even the Drover Mooleys.'

After a fruitless search Mick Malone, hickory baton drawn, entered the small clearing surrounding the Mooley headquarters. The drawing of the baton was merely a precaution. Mick always found it a great deterrent whenever he found himself in the presence of cross dogs, as he did now. The seven mongrel sheep dogs sat perfectly still, almost like statues, except that their eyes followed Mick's every movement as he approached the house. In spite of himself he found his scalp tingling and an unfamiliar numbness in the hand that swung the baton. The seven dogs, obviously under the strictest discipline and bound to sit still until the Drover rescinded his commands, constituted a chilling spectacle. Mick knew that they were capable of carrying out any command. He shuddered to think of their murderous potentiality. He had seen them, frequently in the past, snapping at the heels of cattle and he heard that they sometimes ripped marauding canines from outside their domain to shreds. There was no mercy here, none of the frivolity or tail-wagging one might expect from a family dog in the farmyards of the hill country. His lower jaw trembled when he caught the eyes of the pack-leader Dango. Dango was a pure-bred collie, the only one of the seven with pure breeding but he was a renegade and narrowly escaped shooting by his previous master in the mountains south of Killarney. It was rumoured he had deliberately guided seven ewes and their lambs to the edge of a precipice in the darkness of an April night and sent them hurtling to their deaths hundreds of feet below.

Mick Malone stopped within a few feet of the ring-
leader. He dangled the baton in front of the crouching
killer. He might as well have kept it in his sheath. He
swung it as near the creature's jaws as he dared, not
wanting to make contact. The renegade, under strict
orders, never moved.

'Jasus!' Mick whispered, 'I'd hate to meet you and
your comrades in the dark.'

The seven pairs of watchful eyes followed him as he
neared the front door of the hovel. Mick turned slowly
and looked from one to the other, each with a face more
impassive than the next. He knew they would stay put
for a certain period or until commanded to do otherwise.
He was, nevertheless, glad of the baton.

'A good stick makes for a good dog,' Sergeant Mur-
naghan of Boherlahan once told him. 'That is why,' the
Sergeant went on, 'dogs attack postmen but never civic
guards. We have batons; postmen don't.'

'A baton wouldn't be enough here,' Mick Malone
ruefully reminded himself.

The atmosphere was tense, reeking with evil. Mick
felt as if he was in the middle of an arena. He would
have preferred the savage predictability of a lion, however, to the lean, meanfaced crew of curs with bloodshot
eyes, unwavering between narrow slits. Then there came
a yawn from the seemingly disinterested Dango. Mick
guessed it was ploy to catch him off his guard. He had
sensed too that the effects of the last command from
their master were wearing off. Normally this would not
have worried him. He had often seen packs of curs turn
fawning and hangdog with the appearance of his baton
but these were different. There was a casual confidence
here, born of the knowledge that they had worked in
concert many times and always successfully. They were
highly experienced in attack, giving the victim no
chance. Mick knew them individually and had, in fact,
supervised their licensing. None was to be trusted but

Dango was surely in league with the devil. Other dogs, in their moods, might be servile, insolent, blustering or aggressive but Dango was none of these. He made no concession to playfulness and he never threatened. This was his most potent weapon, Mick thought, the ability to look totally innocuous just before an act of treachery. Ordinary dogs would exude menace by snarling and growling but never Dango. As the other dogs began to yawn Dango shook himself as if he were endeavouring to dislodge an irritant such as a tick or a flea. Mick decided it was time to knock upon the door.

Vester McCarthy was, as yet, not unduly worried by the prospect of the drive to Trallock. The friendship between young Mark Doran, the architect of the drive, and his daughter Sally, rather than eventually floundering as he had predicted, was now on a fairly firm footing. This was obvious from the fact that Mark had already called twice to the pub since their first meeting in the snug. Upstairs Vester and Mary McCarthy had gone about their business silently and had not once ventured downstairs while Mark was on the premises. There always seemed to Mark to be an excessive hush, difficult to define, when he found himself alone in the snug with Sally McCarthy. He sensed that the silence was enforced by his presence and it made him uncomfortable.

Mark would not have been pleased had he been privy to the conversation which took place in the smoky kitchen of the Drover Mooley's. Vester had opened the proceedings after the Drover had come from the kitchen innards and escorted him indoors.

'The last cheque,' said he, 'from the proceeds of the Killarney sales was for thirty-nine calves and six weanlings. Is that correct?'

'That's correct,' the Drover shifted his gaze to the floor while his wife squirmed uncomfortably in her sugán chair.

'Yet I am reliably informed that you offered forty-two calves for sale so where did the extra three come from?'

'They were my own,' the Drover replied, his eyes still focused on the mud floor. He could have had a council cottage like his sons-in-law had he so wished but, as the council health officer explained, 'It wouldn't be dirty enough for him.'

'How could the calves be your own,' Vester was persisting, 'when you don't have any land and when all the calves you bought were for me?'

'Strayaways,' the Drover explained.

'You mean they strayed all the way down from the hills to your front door?'

'Not exactly to the front door,' the Drover pointed a filthy, black nailed finger towards the outdoors, 'but they strayed on to my property and I have a rule that anything straying on to my property becomes mine. Possession is nine points of the law Vester. You should know that, an educated man like you.'

The annoyance faded, temporarily, from Vester's face. He had never been called an educated man before. He was immensely flattered. He had come for a specific purpose, however, and that was to caution the Drover about his thieving ways.

'You have a duty,' he wagged a finger under the Drover's nose, now averted as were his eyes. He would have turned them anywhere rather than in Vester's direction. 'A duty to report the presence of strayaways to the civic guards. You'll go to jail again if you're caught.'

'I won't be caught. Malone wouldn't track an elephant through six feet of snow.'

'You were caught before. You'll be caught again and I have my good name to think of.' Vester McCarthy was blessed with an honest face. The Drover decided to indulge him.

'You're an honest man all right Vester. There's no one would deny that.'

'Let this be an end to it now,' Vester sounded somewhat mollified, 'or it will be the end of our dealings.'

'I promise I'll never keep a strayaway again Vester. I promise that on my dead mother!'

Extravagantly and with an extraordinary show of piety he consummated the sign of the Cross and managed to induce a semblance of moisture in his hooded eyes. Vester McCarthy, in all his days, had never witnessed such a travesty of contrition. He found himself laughing in spite of himself. The tears that appeared in his eyes were as authentic as the Drover Mooley's were sham.

'You should be on the stage,' Vester said as he wiped his eyes with a spotless white handkerchief. The seven canines began to grow fidgety outside as the unfamiliar laughter echoed around the enclosure.

'Those dogs give me the creeps,' Vester shuddered, 'particularly that creature you call Dango.'

'Oh they've all got names,' the Drover boasted as he pointed his finger first at the leader.

'There's Dango. Now that's a dotey dog would read your mind. Here's Bubbles. He's mean and cowardly but he does what I tells him and that's Quick wagging his tail. Quick because he's the fastest and that's Doormat because he's fawning and sly but behind it all he's savage and would take the heels from you if the humour caught him. Now we come to the ladies. There's Babs, called after my missus. Babs is a beauty. She's mother to Quick, Doormat and Bubbles but they'd kill her if I gave the order. Next is Queenie. She's a sonsy bitch. I drowned her last litter. They were all deformed but she'll mate soon with Dango and that should be an interesting family when it grows up. Last but not least is Dolly. She's too serious but Dolly's not right in the head so we can't be too hard on her. Still she does what she's told and that's all that matters in a dog. If a dog isn't obedient it should be hanged or drowned. I prefer hanging. It's a lesson to the others.'

Suddenly the Drover went out and clapped his hands. The resultant sound in the confines of the grove was explosive. All the dogs alerted themselves. Rapidly the Drover reeled off their names in a shrill but firm voice.

'Dango, Bubbles, Quick, Doormat, Babs, Queenie, Dolly be upstanding.'

All the canines stood on their hind legs with the exception of Dango. The Drover entered the kitchen and emerged almost immediately with a hazel stick, a shorter and stouter version of the guide sticks he kept to drive cattle. At once Dango came to his feet. The dogs maintained their positions with considerable difficulty for thirty seconds.

'All sit,' the Drover commanded in the same high-pitched tone. The canines sat at once, including Dango.

'They're the best cattle dogs in the county, maybe in the country,' the Drover bragged, 'but don't ever come calling after dark Vester or you'll be sorry.'

'That's one piece of advice I propose to take,' Vester McCarthy assured him.

Before Mick Malone's knuckle connected with the wood the door opened and Vester McCarthy stepped out into the light from the gloom of the kitchen.

'Ah Guard Malone,' said he, surprised to find Mick barring his way.

Mick stood dutifully aside and saluted respectfully. Vester McCarthy would find it unthinkable to call a civic guard by his Christian name.

'Never be familiar with a guard, a soldier or a priest,' his late mother had often cautioned him. 'Post-men isn't too bad,' she said, 'but avoid uniforms and you'll have no regrets.'

Vester always treated civic guards with the height of respect but never with comradeship. Mick Malone was well aware of this attitude. He encountered it every day but he would never grow used to it. A happily married man with a young family and a warm-hearted, good-humoured spouse who cherished his longings and indulged his every whim, he could not understand how people could be so withdrawn in the face of genuine friendship. He put it down to ignorance. He felt it could not be anything else.

'Not a bad day Guard Malone,' Vester spoke breezily and emptily before turning to the Drover.

'I'll see you then my good man,' he said.

'Goodbye Babs,' he called into the kitchen where the Drover's wife sat by a smoking turf fire with a quenched cigarette butt in her mouth. Vester eased himself into the 1935 saloon. In a single instant the engine was turning over smooth as clock-work and in another cruising fluently between the furze bushes.

'What brings you Mick?' the Drover Mooley asked agreeably.

'Nothing but an Aberdeen Angus bull calf,' Mick Malone replied, 'but, of course, you wouldn't know anything about that.'

'Why didn't you ask Vester McCarthy if he had seen this calf? His eyesight is every bit as good as mine.'

'If you're patient I'll tell you why Drover,' Mick Malone withdrew a yard and folded his arms.

'I didn't ask McCarthy because he was never convicted of stealing calves whereas you were, seven times in all, since I came to this neck of the woods. I didn't ask McCarthy because he does not have to steal calves while he has you to do it for him.'

'Down boy! Down!' The Drover issued the command to Dango, the renegade Collie, who had started to move closer to the civic guard. The Drover made no attempt to conceal his delight at Mick's discomfiture.

'You're not afraid surely of a few harmless curs, a big strapping policeman like you!'

'It doesn't matter whether I'm afraid or not,' Mick Malone edged a step nearer the Drover. 'What matters is this! If one of those mangy mongrels touches me I'll have the lot put down and I'll have you in jail for six months. You've been there you thief already and you didn't like it. Now about that calf. I know you and your sons-in-law stole the animal.'

At this juncture in the proceedings Babs Mooley spat the cigarette butt into the fire and hurried to the door with an iron fire tongs in her hand. Brushing past Mick Malone she flung the tongs on the ground and unloosed her apron strings. Instead of falling in a crumpled heap on the ground the apron stood erect like a fender, its coarse material so impregnated by maize and slops from the continuous feeding of fowl that it was now possess-ed of a cement-like consistency. Mick Malone found himself laughing in spite of himself as the Drover re-strained his wife from retrieving the tongs. Mick decided that it was an opportune time to make a dignified re-treat. Whistling as though there wasn't a dog of any kind in the vicinity he returned slowly to the spot where he had left his Raleigh and heaved a sigh of relief when he found his feet on the familiar pedals.

As Vester McCarthy drove through Tubberlick he listen-ed intently to the engine of his gleaming saloon. Gleam-ing she might be but all was not well underneath. He congratulated himself on having successfully traded in the Ford in part exchange for a Vauxhall de Luxe. He would take delivery of the span new ten horse-power vehicle at the weekend. He smiled as he conjured up a picture of his daughter Sally, dressed in her best, driving through the village.

After several weeks, during which he exhausted all the obscenities acquired over a lifetime, he had finally taught her how to drive. Wisely he had decided to break her in before investing in the new wonder car priced at £245 and equipped with hydraulic brakes and tension bar suspension.

The sight of her motoring through the countryside, Vester thought, should shake up every eligible bachelor within a radius of twenty miles, particularly young Doran. It might make him think twice about his proposed cattle drive. The young man wasn't a fool. He must surely know that the Vauxhall and heaven knows what else were there for the taking although he would not be Vester's first choice. There were bigger, better, wealthier farmers who might begin to view things in a new light with the advent of the Vauxhall. Pity Sally couldn't lose weight, not that she was fat. Well-conditioned might be a more apt description. This would appeal to some but not to all. If Vester only knew how thoroughly and hardheadedly his daughter's suitability as a farmer's wife had been evaluated, by the eligible farmers who knew her, he would have been greatly surprised. The inescapable truth was that she had been weighed in the balance and found wanting, weighed not once but a hundred times.

The farmers of the hill country were not given to making hasty decisions. Sally McCarthy was a good mark all right and the fact that she carried a little extra weight made not the slightest difference to the majority of those who had seriously considered her as a lifetime partner. Secretly they would be afraid that she would be a hindrance rather than a help around a farm. She didn't have a farming background and, most importantly, she didn't look in the least like a girl who would sit under a cow or feed calves and pigs and walk through muck and dung swinging full buckets. It wouldn't be right to take her from behind the counter where she was liked and respected and where she was at her best. Far better to marry in to McCarthy's than to take her to where she could only be a round plug in a square hole. To marry in would be the most sensible approach. There was, undoubtedly, a large quantity of cash. The premises was in excellent repair and the business was good. There was also some land so that a farmer's son need not altogether give up his first love. He could dabble in fat stock if he so wished, have a good time to boot and let the McCarthy's worry about the business. Unfortunately, for such aspirants there was little or no hope. They were just the sort of interlopers about whom Vester was forever warning his only child.

While Mark Doran might not have all the qualities desired by Vester McCarthy the older man would not deny that he had many. He was a good footballer, feared and looked up to. He had many friends and admirers and he was honest. Any fool could see that. He would have other long-term projects if Vester knew his man. Vester also guessed that he might not be able to manipulate him. On the credit side he wasn't a headstrong young man and he could carry his drink. Vester would not stand in his way just yet and maybe never if their interests could be made to run parallel.

Vester had not yet discussed the business of the drive with the Drover Mooley for a number of reasons. Chiefly he would have misgivings about teaming up with a trio such as the Mooleys who were capable of extreme violence given the opportunity and Vester could not contemplate any other role for them if the drive was to be successfully obstructed. The dogs would play a big part in such an operation and here again there might be real danger to life and limb.

If the drive were to take place Vester could not be seen to be opposed to it. He could play no visible part. He could not be seen next or near the herd before, during or after the drive and this was where his problem arose. He was determined to sabotage the drive. He felt he was entitled to do this in view of the fact that his livelihood was at stake but in his absence the Drover Mooleys or their dogs would not be subject to any real restraints. If something serious happened to Mark or any of his friends and if it was found out that he, Vester, was implicated the countryside would never forgive him. He would consider every other means before enlisting the aid of the Mooleys.

That night Mick Malone's wife wiped the cold sweat from his brow after he awoke from a nightmare filled with snapping, snarling curs, a hideous experience where he found himself with bound hands and unable to move his legs as he was attacked from all sides by fanged mongrels, hideous to behold.

'It's all right love,' his wife repeated the expression over and over as the children gathered anxiously about the bed of the man they saw as invincible.

Some time afterwards, hands trembling, Mick recounted his experience for Archie Scuttard in a corner of the Widow Hegarty's. He told him of the nightmare and how the fear had spread to his children who thought of him as a God rather than a man. Mick buried his head in his hands at the conclusion. A few moments later a glass of whiskey was thrust into his hand.

'Drink that,' said the Rector, 'and to hell with the Drover and his dogs.'

As Mick began to relax he posed a question for his friend.

'Could you tell me the nature of Vester's business with the Drover Archie? I would dearly love to know.'

'I have my suspicions,' the Rector replied.

'Tell me,' Mick Malone begged him.

'It has to do with our proposed drive to Trallock. Word has somehow reached Vester and he is now in the process of hatching some vile plan to sabotage it. I could be wrong but something tells me that the drive is at the back of it all.'

The Rector, as it turned out, was only partly right.

On the Saturday night after his visit to the Badger, Mark Doran went to the Widow Hegarty's where he found Haybags Mullanney in the company of his two sons, Tom and Jay. Haybags was drunk. He spent the morning mourning the departure of his two daughters, Ellie and Bridgie. Both had been prematurely accepted into Portsmouth General Hospital without having to wait for the results of their Leaving Certificate examinations. The board of the hospital, desperately in need of staff with war looming, had accepted the girls on the strength of their Intermediate examinations.

Mark had made his goodbyes the night before. There had been none of the banter of other visits nor had Annie sat by his side as was her wont. Her attitude toward him had undergone a change. There was a reserve where there had been a girlish playfulness. A wariness had replaced the camaraderie which had existed between them since her childhood. This, he told himself, was to be expected, sooner or later. He felt deflated but it was nothing to what he had felt a few days before when he saw her holding hands with a lanky youth of her own age group. The pair had been walking along a path in the village's deserted commonage as Mark had cycled by. The moment she saw him she moved away at once from her escort. An hour passed before he realised that what he had felt upon surprising her had been painful. Later still, although the hurt remained, he dismissed it as an incidental relationship between schoolmates.

'What will it be?' Haybags asked as Mark took his place at the counter.

'A pint of stout,' came the answer.

It had not escaped Mark's notice that the Widow had not been as effusive in her welcome as she normally might be. Mark attributed this to the proposed October drive. The village would never give such an undertaking its blessing and he fully accepted this. Meanwhile, Haybags Mullanney was bemoaning the departure of his offspring. The girls, with their mother, had left home in the horse and trap, guided by Florry. The womenfolk would catch the early bus for Killarney and travel thence by train to Dublin before embarking on the ship that would take them to their destination.

'I'm going back to a lonely house this night,' Haybags announced sadly between drunken sighs.

'Herself will be back in a week,' Tom Mullanney tried to be consoling.

'And isn't Annie at home,' his brother Jay went further.

'Annie, Annie, Annie!' Haybags shook his swollen head. 'Dare any man take her from me,' he called out the challenge aloud and struck the Widow's counter with powerful, hammerlike blows. Mark glanced anxiously at Tom and Jay. The brothers seemed not in the least uneasy about Haybags' behaviour. They indicated to Mark that he should join them in a corner some distance from where their father was now at the height of his fulminations.

'With a shovel I'll do it,' Haybags was roaring. 'I'll take the head clear and clane from his shoulders with a shovel.'

Mark was now certain that Haybags threats were directed not at him or any known individual but at persons unknown who would defile or carry off his favourite child.

'I'll rip the bastard's heart out,' he told the Widow Hegarty. 'I'll rip out his rotten heart and throw it to the cat!'

In the corner Tom confided to Mark that none of the in-calf heifers had been sold to cover the travelling and other expenses incurred by his sisters and mother. Because of the suddenness of the summons from Portsmouth General there had not been time. His mother had drawn the money from the sub-office of the National Bank in Tubberlick where it had accumulated, known only to her and because of her thriftiness over the years, for the express purpose of dealing with such a contingency.

'Which means,' Jay Mullanney informed Mark, 'that you will now have all of the in-calf heifers for the October drive.'

'The man that touches a hair of her head,' Haybags was now laying it on the line for the Sullivan brothers Will and Henry, 'will wish he was never born. Better for him he came into the world a rat.'

The Sullivans stood meekly just inside the doorway not knowing that Haybags was referring to his sole remaining daughter and those who would molest her. They had come to see Mark and the Mullanney brothers. They had just left a meeting of the district football league and brought news of Ballybo's next encounter against Kilshunnig in the second round of the district league. Successfully sidestepping Haybags they bore even more important tidings to Mark. After a lengthy meeting with their mother, Eleanora, it had been agreed that the Sullivans would hold on to all their saleable stock until the October fair in Trallock, a town to which Will and Henry had never previously ventured. The stock, as far as they could tell, would consist of six in-calf heifers, nine weanlings and three Roscreas, the last in excellent fettle considering their age.

'This is the best news yet,' Mark declared as he rose to purchase a drink for the newcomers.

'You know what this means,' he turned around suddenly from the counter where the Widow Hegarty awaited his order, 'it means that we now have fifty head of cattle between the Sullivans, the Dorans and the Mullanneys and that's only three families.'

The brothers Mullanney and Sullivan were quickly on their feet congratulating each other. As the Widow

Hegarty bent to turn the tap on the half tierce of stout she spoke for the first time since Mark had entered. Her remarks were addressed to nobody in particular but they came across pointed and clear to all concerned.

"Tis a black night,' said she, 'for the shopkeepers of Tubberlick and their families. May Jesus comfort them this night and every other poor cratur with a yard of counter for a livelihood.'

The young men resumed their seats chastened and uncomfortable but their resolve had not suffered in the least. They spoke in whispers after the Widow's deflating retaliation.

'There's a pub there,' Tom Mullanney's whisper drew all heads closer, 'with two blondes and the likes of their tits were never before seen. A man told me they'd feed a parish!'

'What do they call this pub?' Will Sullivan asked.

'It's called Durango,' Tom Mullanney moistened his lips before proceeding. 'Durango!' He allowed the magic of the name to sink in. He lifted his glass.

'Durango!' he toasted.

'Durango,' came back the whispered responses.

'A man told me,' Tom Mullanney was warming to his task, 'that you can have anything you want in Durango.'

'Who saw these tits?' Will Sullivan, who was something of a doubting Thomas, posed the question.

'Never mind who saw them,' Tom Mullanney told him, 'what matters is that they're there. A man told me that these two blondes are mad for it, that they can't get enough of it and they prefer country boys to townies.'

The last piece of information elicited a loud cheer from his listeners. He cautioned them to silence.

'Say nothing about these blondes to our mothers or they'll think that's all that's carrying us.'

The listeners shook their heads solemnly. The mention of the outsize breasts put Mark in mind of a promise he had given to Sally McCarthy at their last meeting. Tubberlick had boasted a small cinema for several years. Some of the more fastidious cinema-goers called it a shed and a flea-trap. What mattered was that films were shown there three nights weekly, Wednesday, Friday and Sunday. Mark had promised to take Sally McCarthy to the double bill which would be showing on the following Sunday night, Gene Autrey in *Springtime in the Rockies* and *Tovarich* starring Claudette Colbert and Charles Boyer. Mark excused himself on the grounds that he would be receiving holy communion in the morning. The Widow Hegarty did not return his goodnight. She did, however, repeat her statement made earlier in the night. This time she addressed it to Vester McCarthy with an addendum which removed any doubt about the course of action he should make after the drive had commenced.

'If I were a man,' the Widow added in plaintive tone, 'I'd block that drive for sure.'

Other interested parties would also let it be known to Vester that it was a shameful business entirely and that something should be done to disrupt it.

On Sunday night Mark Doran and Sally McCarthy sat on the second-hand, plush-covered seats at the rear of Tubberlick's Astoria Cinema. All around them, while Autrey and his sidekick outwitted the bandits on the silver screen, there was frenzied activity of another kind.

'No pawing back there.' The call came from a local idler who sat on one of the wooden forms at the very front of the cinema. His directive was greeted with jeers and catcalls. Thinking that perhaps it might be expected of him Mark placed a hand on the silk-clad knee of Sally McCarthy. It was instantly removed with such alacrity and firmness that he sat upright and rigid as she did until the films ended. As they left the Astoria she linked his arm with hers. Later in the privacy of the snug she compensated for her primness in the cinema with a warmth which almost transported them to the point of no return. She confided to him that she had never gone so far before. In bed that morning she was to ask herself how far she was prepared to go. It was a question she had not asked herself up until now. She resolved to play things by ear but, she told herself sadly, she might eventually be obliged to play her trump card.

8

The Tubberlick reconnaissance unit was well into its third whiskey before the buxom proprietresses of the Durango Bar replaced the temporary barmaid and proffered themselves for the titillation of their customers. The conversations being conducted stopped dead of one accord as they tripped bouncing and glowing into the limelight. Their white, perfectly fitted frocks left little to the imagination. Arriving at the centre of the premises they first curtsied before pirouetting stylishly as though they were modelling the tight-fitting clothes they wore. Both were blonde, blue-eyed and rosy of cheek, with lips rich and ripe as autumn cherries although the more conservative and less charitable matrons of Trallock would say that, without the make-up, the natural features of the Carabim sisters were of a far whiter, even ghastlier hue. Before concluding the prelude to the night's normal activities which would see them behind the bar counter, they shook hands with and extended hearty welcomes to the clientele.

'Archie darling!' Dell, the older sister cried out upon beholding the Rector of Tubberlick. She sat herself on his lap to the astonishment of his companion. She threw her arms round his neck and implanted a juicy kiss on his lips.

'Meet my friend,' Archie Scuttard introduced the Monsignor. 'This is Danny Binge. Danny this is Dell Carabim, the joint owner of the premises.'

The Monsignor was about to rise and formally present himself but before he had time to leave his seat his lap was to play host to the younger sister, Lily Carabim.

'Oh Archie,' Lily screamed delightedly, 'you brought one for me.' Passionately she embraced the Monsignor and then with a toss of her blonde curls im-

planted an even juicier and certainly noisier kiss than
that of her sister. The Monsignor spluttered and squirmed but remained in his seat. He had not received such a
fervent buss since he last embraced a girl at the age of
eighteen, two nights before he entered the seminary. The
occasion had been a purely experimental one. He had
deliberately waylaid one of the more liberally-minded
girls of the locality after a dance and taken her by the
hand to the blind side of an oak tree which grew beside
the dance-hall. Here he flung his arms wildly around her
and squeezed for all he was worth. The girl, it was alleged, was notorious for her venery. Whether there was any
substance to the claim or not he was never to find out for
immediately after he had embraced her she kissed him
with a ferocity that frightened him out of his wits. He
broke free with a startled cry and ran the whole way
home which was no mean jaunt since the family farmhouse was two miles from the dance-hall.

At home, in the silence of his bedroom, he felt elated
that his vocation had withstood such a searching test. He
had to find out before entering the seminary if he was
possessed of the requisite chastity before committing
himself to a lifetime without a woman. Lily Carabim
was intrigued by the Monsignor's bashfulness.

'Don't worry old boy,' Archie Scuttard was saying,
'your celibacy is in no danger. The tastes of these fine
ladies run to the cockerel rather than the rooster.'

Instantly Lily Carabim was on her feet, her face
contrite, profuse apologies pouring from her tinted lips.

'I'm sorry Father, so sorry! I had no idea.'

To add to her embarrassment Archie Scuttard chided her for not addressing him by his correct title of Monsignor.

'Oh Monsignor, how can you ever forgive me?' Lily
knelt at his feet, genuinely affected, and took his hands
in hers.

'Come on. Get up,' the Monsignor urged. 'There's

nothing to be sorry about.'

'You'll have a drink on the house then and that will be my penance,' Lily Carabim insisted.

Meanwhile the Rector had placed Dell Carabim firmly on her feet. Still muttering apologies the sisters hastened to the counter in order to dispense the drinks.

'Younger chaps than us you say. What a pity!' The Monsignor shook his head in mock sorrow. Both clergymen burst out laughing.

'Oh but it's true. It is said that the sisters Carabim will take on any given youth or number of youths at any given time, discreetly of course.'

'And I take it,' the Monsignor said resignedly, 'that they are of the same persuasion as myself?'

'But of course old boy,' Archie Scuttard assured him, 'devout Catholics the pair of them and charitable to a fault.'

'And roughly what ages would they be?' the Monsignor asked.

'Have a guess,' the Rector suggested.

'Middle to late forties,' came the answer.

'You'll have to do better than that,' the Rector chided.

'Early fifties then,' the Monsignor's second conjecture was greeted with scorn.

'Dell Carabim is seventy-one,' the Rector sounded boastful, 'and her little sister is three score and ten.'

'You're joking,' the Monsignor's eyes took in the bosomy pair as they fussed behind the counter.

'It must be the make-up,' he said after a while.

'And the bosoms!' the Rector asked.

'Obviously genuine,' the Monsignor conceded.

'I have it,' Archie informed him, 'on the word of a youth from north of the town – that they are authentic.'

'And is it true about the young men?'

'Yes it is but I should have qualified what I said. They will have nothing to do with the young men of the town or indeed of any town. Able-bodied country boys are the game they're after.'

'I don't see any young people here,' the Monsignor looked about him in case he might have overlooked a likely country lad.

'In the back room you'll find the occasional candidate for the girls' favours. There's no entry from the bar. One has to go behind the counter to gain access unless, of course, you want to use the back entrance. I have been upstairs on these premises many times after hours but since I do not even remotely qualify for admission to the back room I have never been there. There is a back entrance, however, and I am reliably informed that it is used by young men from the countryside, approved youths, preferably in their teens. I have been told that there have been sporadic visits from undesirables but these have been given short shrift. The girls know how to handle themselves and working in tandem are capable of dealing with any trouble maker.'

'There is just one other question,' the Monsignor sounded reluctant.

'Fire away old boy,' Archie placed his entwined hands across his ample paunch and readied himself.

'Regarding the favours which the sisters dispense,' the Monsignor hesitated before proceeding, 'do these young guys hand over money?'

'On the contrary old boy,' the Rector returned, 'the young guys as you call them are wined and dined free of charge provided that their credentials are in order. The girls would never consider disposing of their wares for material reward. These are generous, impulsive, warm-hearted creatures. See what I mean! Here they come now bearing gifts. Their hospitality is boundless. Our chief difficulty will be getting out of here before daybreak.'

Later the Monsignor revealed the news of his forthcoming ordination as Bishop of San Lupino.

'I often had a drink with a Catholic clergyman,' the

Rector confided, 'but never with a Catholic Bishop.'

'The reason I tell you,' the Monsignor continued, 'is that I would not want you to hear it from anybody else. I haven't told my sister or her husband yet nor do I intend to until the morning of my departure.'

'And when will that be My Lord?' the Rector asked.

'I shall be leaving on Thursday morning next but I shall be back. You may or may not have guessed that I do not normally drink as we have been doing. In fact I rarely drink during my administration. I work hard and no doubt I will be expected to work harder after I am ordained Bishop. But,' and here the Bishop Elect was emphatic, 'I shall be returning God willing, to Tubberlick for the October cattle drive so, Archie my friend, I am hereby directing you to reserve a seat for me on the pillion of your BSA.'

'A Bishop on a BSA. Better still, a Bishop on a pillion. What a story for *The News of the World!*'

'Does it come here?'

'Alas yes My Lord,' Archie informed him. 'It's not on sale here but it is dispatched every week by post from Britain, courtesy of our exiles. Carefully concealed within the seamy sheets are thousands of French letters, the last resort of a drained and dilapidated Irish motherhood who might otherwise have doubled their output in recent years and mothered a revolution to boot!'

'French letters are not on sale here then?'

'Not only are they not on sale,' the Rector informed him, 'but as they are proscribed by the state as well as the church those found in possession are subject to prosecution and hell fire!'

As the evening wore on, prompted by his friend, Archie Scuttard disclosed some personal facts. He had been married before joining up to fight the Germans and as had happened to so many others during the the four year long struggle, he found upon his return that his wife had departed to South Africa with a mutual friend who had been wounded during the British offensive of the Somme in 1916. Both had since died but Archie had not remarried although often pressed to do so by his Bishop and friends, notably one Daisy Popple, a strong dairy farmer who was forever advertising, without the least subtlety, her own availability. Archie made no mention of his war wounds nor was there any word of his Victoria Cross. He was at pains to explain about his drinking.

'I am a skite drinker,' he told the Bishop Elect. 'That is to say I am likely to spend three weeks on the booze and as many more off. There have been occasions when my skites have dragged on for months but then I always make it a point to go on the dry for a corresponding period. There is no way my liver could withstand a sustained dousing from alcohol say over a twelve month period. I like drink, particularly whiskey. Not only do I like the taste of it but I also like the look of it and I like the gurgle of it when it's poured from a bottle. I never like going off it but I have to for the sake of my liver and, of course, my purse. When I'm off it I dream every hour of going back on it again. The longer I stay off it the longer and more concentrated the subsequent skite. I fantasise about whiskey the way other men fantasise about women. I am not a drunkard. I was born into this world with a true appreciation of whiskey. When I was a student my father used to say of me that I never went off the booze for the sake of going off the booze.

'Archie,' he would observe to my mother, 'is off the booze so that he can go on it again.'

'Nobody understood my drinking better than my father. What he implied was that I drank until my health had so deteriorated that I was left with no option but to go off it. Off it I would go until I could build up my health once more.'

The Bishop Elect confessed to an equally powerful longing for whiskey but admitted that he confined his drinking to holiday periods and weekends.

'Not a word Archie about this Bishop business.'

'Of course old boy,' the Rector assured him, 'now let us have another whiskey while we may.'

Not long before darkness fell they were introduced to a local apothecary by Dell Carabim. He also turned out to be possessed of a seemingly insatiable appetite for whiskey. Cleverly, or so they believed, the reconnaissance unit created an airing for the subject of cattle fairs.

'The thing that strikes me most about your town,' Archie informed the apothecary, whose name chanced to be Fizz Moran, 'is it's cleanliness. I can't help thinking if it's always like that?'

'You should see it my friend,' Fizz Moran spoke with a trace of boastfulness in his voice 'after the October cattle fair. You'd want the constitution of a duck to put up with the smell and then there's the cowshit! It's everywhere and need I add that the backways are covered with monstrous piles of its human counterpart in every conceivable shape and hue, including the most variegated and bizarre of two-tones.'

Fizz Moran, or Call-Me-Fizz as he was known throughout the town, objected not in the least to the nickname which might offend a man of lesser stature since the implication might very well be that the apothecary's mixtures were fizzy rather than remedial.

Fizz Moran went on to inform them that the October cattle fair was the busiest day of the year for the business houses and licensed premises of the town. 'Debts are paid and old scores are settled. Split heads, broken noses, fractured jaws and the insertion of hundreds of stitches are all part and parcel of the fair.'

From the way the apothecary spoke it became clear that he would not have it otherwise. He was proud of his town, warts and all, and when Archie asked about the most prominent places to stand cattle, the apothecary volunteered to conduct them on a tour of the town.

He took them firstly to the railway station with its many spacious pens, all built as one would expect from discarded wooden sleepers and situated some distance down the track from the passenger platform.

'Here,' said Fizz Moran as if he were conducting a grand tour, 'is where the cattle are loaded on to the wagons for transportation to Mullingar, Cork, Roscrea and God knows where!'

As they left the station grounds they entered a long, quiet street of one-storeyed houses.

'Now this is one place where you don't want to stand your cattle,' Fizz Moran warned.

'Why?' the question came from the Bishop Elect.

'I'll tell you why my dear Monsignor,' Fizz Moran paused and extended snow-white hand in the direction of the railway station they had just vacated, 'because most of the cattle attending the October fair will sooner or later be obliged to pass this way on their journey to the railway station. That means a continuing traffic from morning till evening until the last of the cattle wagons have been filled and where you have continuing traffic you have restless cattle. Now restless Roscreas are no problem. They'll stay put but bullocks and heifers and weanlings are a different matter. They'll try to follow the passing animals and you won't have a minute's peace trying to sort them out all day long. Therefore, you avoid this particular street like a plague.'

The trio journeyed downwards until they came to the town's main street with its centrally situated Durango Bar.

'This is a good street to stand cattle as are the connecting side streets. They are the heart of the town, more or less, and the buyers and the jobbers and the middlemen spend a lot of their time here when they're not in the pubs or the pie-shops.'

The pies to which Fizz Moran referred were a local delicacy made from finely chopped lap of mutton encased in saucer-sized discs of dough and baked to a light brown. The pies would be made in their thousands for several days before the fair and preserved in air-tight tins and boxes until required. Many of the pubs as well as the pie shops and restaurants served the popular and savoury offerings from morning till night. Once removed from their air-tight surrounds the pies were allowed to cook for several minutes in pots of mutton broth and were then served in dishes or soup plates brimming with the steaming hot broth in which they had been simmering. Most countrymen would eat several throughout the duration of the fair. Apart from their celebrated palatability they were also renowned for keeping drunkenness as well as hunger at bay. At a total cost of 1/– the customer was provided with pie and soup and for good measure one half of a baker's tile, known in the countryside as shop bread. Of all the town's eating houses only the Trallock Arms rejected the mutton pie. Its manager would proudly boast that it had never been on the menu: 'And if I have my way,' he was fond of saying, 'it never will.'

The hotel prided itself on the quality of its beef and mutton. It also enjoyed a wide reputation for fillet and sirloin steaks but its manager believed that the pies attracted the wrong type of clientele.

As the apothecary entered the town square, followed by his newly acquired friends, he directed their attention to the four-storeyed hotel standing aloof in a quiet corner.

'That corner,' said Fizz Moran, 'is the best possible place to stand cattle during your October fair.'

The three stood still, taking in the exclusive area which fronted the ivy-covered hostelry. Fizz Moran, a small, dapper, bespectacled man in his late sixties, led the way towards the prime location.

'We may as well have a drink as we're here,' he said. Inside, after he had seen to their wants, he explained that the hotel would play host to a large number of refugees from the town and its more exclusive suburbs on the night before the cattle fair and throughout the following days and nights.

'The reason for this,' Fizz explained, 'is that these brittle suburbanites and local nobs might feel themselves threatened by the presence of farmers and agricultural labourers in the pubs they normally visit. You'll find few rustics in the hotel during fair days. They prefer the pubs.'

'It's the same where I come from,' the Bishop Elect informed them. 'During the festivals when the peons and their families come into town they confine themselves to the cantinas and taverns where there is something thought of them and give the hotels a wide berth.'

'Interesting,' Fizz Moran was elaborating further, 'but what is more interesting my friends is that the wives of these so-called nobs are daughters of the soil themselves not too long married into the professional and the business houses in Trallock. They become quite hysterical at the sight of a man with cowshit on his boots.'

'This is the best cattle stand then?' the Rector looked out of the window on to the square.

'Undoubtedly my friend,' Fizz Moran concurred. 'Despite its antipathy towards our rustic brothers the hotel is the hub of the fair. The square is where the best cattle are gathered. Every prospective buyer at the fair will know about your cattle but, of course, it is impossible to come by a stand here because traditionally most of the landed families nearest the town would have been standing their cattle here since the square was built 140 years ago.'

'And they might not take it too kindly if some ignorant yahoo from Ballybo or Tubberlick were to encroach upon their ground?' the observation came from the Rector.

'They wouldn't like it one bit,' Fizz Moran became suddenly serious, 'in fact I would go so far as to say that there would be bloodshed. The ordinary townsfolk would not mind so much. In fact they might enjoy it but the business section would be on the side of the status quo. Annual accounts are settled on the day after the big fair with thousands involved. Small farmers don't have accounts. They're too big a risk. It's cash on the line for the little fellow. It's the big boys who get the credit. They pay annually so you can imagine how the business interests would feel if their valued clients were mistreated and their accounts put in jeopardy. In the end it all boils down to LSD.'

'And pray what pedigreed dynasty imagine themselves to be lords and masters of this choice piece of public property?'

Fizz Moran savoured the Rector's question even more than the whiskey he had just sipped. Here was a man after his own heart, a man with a fine disregard for conventions that exalted one man and denied another. He had recognised Archie Scuttard before Dell Carabim introduced him. He knew him by sight for some time and had once dispensed a prescription for him many years before when he had been afflicted with a minor rash. By reputation the Rector was a hard drinker, a hard worker, sometimes profane and with the most outrageous collection of filthy limericks in the county. These were not the traits, however, that endeared him to Fizz Moran.

'Here,' thought Fizz, 'is a truly independent man, well, in so far as any man can be independent. Here is a man who has told the world to kiss his royal Irish Protestant arse and gotten away with it. Here is a man who doesn't give a duck-shit about what people think of him.'

'The answer to your question,' Fizz Moran looked the Rector firmly in the eye, 'is the Nob Gobberleys of

Gortnagreena.'

'I've heard of them,' the Rector nodded, 'not a lot but what I did hear was not good.'

'In a nutshell, my dear Rector,' Fizz Moran was in his element now, 'not even their bullocks, and there are many, are capable of producing as much bullshit as the Nob Gobberleys. They have been standing cattle, mostly bullocks, in this very spot for generations and, since they can muster a goodly company of able men between themselves and their workmen, it seems unlikely that anyone will ever take their ground from them.'

'But it could be done,' the Rector had known for some time that he was in the company of a kindred spirit.

'With organisation, with flair, and with the right men it could be done.'

'Say no more for now,' the Rector advised. 'We shall discuss this matter later.'

The three removed themselves from the lounge and entered the darkening square.

'How many cattle do you propose to drive here?' The question caught the clergymen by surprise. They exchanged anxious looks because neither had said a single word about a drive.

'Don't be alarmed,' Fizz Moran put them at ease. 'I'm on your side but I cannot be fully on your side until I know more about your plans.'

'We would hope,' the Rector kept his voice down, 'that between Roscreas, weanlings, bullocks and in-calf heifers to have 150 cattle.'

'A sizeable herd!' The apothecary whistled his surprise.

'It may well be more,' the Rector continued, 'but the drive depends on a lot of factors.'

'Such as?' the apothecary asked.

'Your silence for one thing,' the Rector had grown suddenly conspiratorial.

'That goes without saying,' Fizz Moran assured him. 'Look upon me as an ally. No! Look upon me as a friend in court.'

He extended a pale hand to each of the clergymen. All three shook hands in turn.

'Your project,' Fizz Moran announced passionately, 'is now my project. I shall have my ear to the ground, day and night, and I shall be in touch by letter from time to time. As the hour for the drive draws nearer I shall notify you about the likelihood of high or low prices.'

'That would be great,' the Bishop Elect laid an episcopal palm on the apothecary's frail shoulder as they stopped outside a particular house next but one to the corner of the square which allowed access to the main street and the Durango Bar.

'This is my humble abode,' Fizz Moran announced as he produced a key from his trousers' pocket. 'Here are potions that will improve your sexual drive and restore your hair and all at a moderate cost and, of course, should either of you need mercurial ointment, blue butter to the layman, I shall dispense a three-penny tin for each of you, free of charge.'

The clergymen held their sides to facilitate the peals of laughter which followed Fizz Moran's generous offer.

'Is it as popular as ever?' Archie Scuttard asked.

'On Monday mornings, my dear Rector, it outstrips the sales of all other ointments combined.'

At the rear of the shop was a spacious sitting-room and it was here that the three companions now found themselves.

'Be seated like good fellows.' The invitation from the apothecary was readily accepted. From the dark recesses beyond the sitting-room a frail woman appeared, frailer even than Fizz Moran.

'Gertie, my love, allow me to introduce Archie Scuttard of Tubberlick and Monsignor Danny Binge of California. Gentlemen allow me to present my long-suffering wife.'

Soon the foursome were seated comfortably, glasses in hand.

'Of course, we are all alone now,' Gertie Moran was explaining. 'We have two boys and four girls and to think that they are all fledged and flown.'

'And are there grand-children?' the Monsignor enquired.

'Only seventeen,' Gertie Moran tried hard to sound modest.

At the Monsignor's insistence Gertie produced a bulky album of family photographs. The Rector refused to involve himself in the perusal which followed, on the grounds, that his eyesight might not be up to it. Patiently and with obvious interest the Monsignor listened as Gertie Moran recited the academic attainments of her offspring and the uniquely funny sayings of her grand-children.

'The man is a saint surely,' Fizz Moran whispered.

'He must be one of the most amiable and gentle souls I ever met,' the Rector whispered back.

Leaving the album in Danny Binge's care Gertie withdrew to that place from whence at first she appeared. Despite their protestations she insisted on preparing sandwiches. Later, when they had eaten their fill, Gertie explained that she was a country girl at heart. Influenced by three rapid whiskies she declared her deep mistrust of townspeople.

'I am here in this house for thirty-five years,' she went on vehemently, 'and I have yet to be accepted by them. I am the daughter of a small farmer. My brother Matt still farms along the southern shore of the estuary. He works hard but he hasn't a penny and never will. What do townspeople care if cattle prices fall. Townspeople don't despair when calves die. It makes no difference to them. If prices drop it's the difference between full bellies and empty for the small farmer. The difference between shod feet and bare feet. Farmers have always suffered more than their share. People here with salaries don't care whether it's wet or dry. They'll get their salaries. They'll have silver to rattle in their pockets but my poor father died a pauper after slaving all his life. And my mother! What had she beyond a brown shawl and a black apron and muddy boots and never a day off! May God deliver the small farmer from his misery. May God unite them!'

Gertie Moran was crying now.

'Whiskey gets her down,' Fizz Moran explained. 'It brings back the wrong kind of memories.'

'Women here talk about holidays as if they were a God-given right,' Gertie was off again. 'When I was a girl there were no holidays, not in the country anyway.' Suddenly she sat upright and smiled through her tears.

'What will you think of me at all?' she asked, 'a nice hostess I am! Forgive me Monsignor, Parson Scuttard forgive me.'

'I'll take her upstairs now,' Fizz Moran spoke in an aside to his friends, 'she'll sleep like a top until morning. She'll be all right then.'

'It's the guilt,' he explained later. 'She feels she's not entitled to her lifestyle because of the poverty she knew as a child. She's conscious-stricken about her mother and father as well. They had enough to eat all right but there was never any style or any money. She used to tell me that the family were ashamed of their clothes when they came into town. Their teeth were never seen to either. She'll be all right in the morning.'

There followed a marathon drinking-session at the Durango Bar which lasted until five o'clock in the morning. When the pub closed officially they were invited upstairs with some of the more cherished customers to the living quarters by the sisters Carabim. There, while the others chatted and reminisced, Lily Carabim told Danny Binge the story of her life. In America her father had been an Italian racketeer at the very lowest scale of the ladder. Her mother had been Irish. Both parents were Catholic. When the girls finished school they secured positions as waitresses in downtown Manhattan. When Antonio Carabim passed on, at a young age, the girls spent a long holiday with their mother in the family home in County Leitrim. Neither Lily nor Dell Carabim had ever contemplated marriage.

'I guess,' Lily told the Monsignor, 'we seen enough of it to give us a surfeit.'

Then one fateful New Year's Eve at a party in the restaurant where they worked a friend called Dell Carabim aside. He was an elderly man, a generous and regular customer.

'You and your sister got savings?' he asked.

Dell nodded eagerly, thinking that some priceless inside knowledge was about to come her way. The sisters had benefited from such tips in the past. Dell knew that the man who called her aside was somebody important in one of the many financial institutions in nearby Wall Street.

'You convert all your savings into cash right away,' he advised the older sister, 'and never mind what anybody else tells you.'

'But,' Dell was about to tell him their investments were making money.

'Never mind the buts,' he told her, 'you convert your securities into cash. Look at it like this honey. You got nothing to lose.'

Dell expressed her doubts. His advice was contrary to the norm. Everybody was investing.

'Look sweetheart I don't have time to go into details,' the financier explained. 'I'm with a party and we're moving on. Just take it from me that the market is unsustainable right now. A collapse is inevitable. You and your sister have always looked after me well. Just withdraw your money now, right away, and when

things are settled there's nothing to stop you re-invest-
ing. Now isn't that reasonable. I gotta go honey.'

The Carabim sisters, because they trusted their informant, converted their savings into cash before the
great crash. In the summer of 1932, for the sum of £800,
they purchased the most run down and derelict of all the
saleable buildings in the town of Trallock. Renovations
followed. No expense was spared. The premises opened
with a bang just in time for the great October cattle fair
of 1932. The transition, although she welcomed it in the
beginning, was to prove too much for old Mrs Carabim.
She died peacefully in her sleep and was buried in Trallock where the sisters erected the ancient graveyard's
largest Celtic Cross to the old woman's memory. The
upstairs living quarters of the sisters Carabim was luxurious by Trallock standards. To be invited to spend a
night upstairs in Carabim's was akin to a royal invitation
in the eyes of the humbler townspeople. Those young
men who spent a night downstairs would be equally
enthusiastic about the hospitality to be found there. To
be fair to the Carabims, they rarely entertained downstairs. When they did they would have assured themselves, beforehand, that the young gentleman or gentlemen invited were discreet and of good character. In
recent months the sisters had shied away from all proposals regardless of the suitability of the candidates. In
the first place they liked to make their own choices and
nothing they had seen since Christmas had prompted
them to extend an invitation to the backroom. Maybe the
need had subsided. They would wait and see. After the
first time, in early December of 1932, an elderly customer had respectfully suggested the need for discretion.
The sisters promised to be circumspect but they were to
discover that youth and discretion, rarely if ever, go
hand in hand, that youth was boastful and insensitive,
rash, mulish and heedless, unwary, excitable and impat-
ient and this was the beauty of it, the Carabim sisters

often thought triumphantly. Youth was undoubtedly all these things but, in the execution of its downstairs obligations, youth never failed. Youth was a never-ending wonder in this respect. It might blunder momentarily, come a temporary cropper, misdirect itself, fall foul of its own impetuosity but fail, never. Youth was free, untainted, unmarried, unlimited and impeccably orthodox in the ultimate relationship.

'And that,' as Lily Carabim had once stated in her own inimitable way, 'is the name of the game.'

At five to five in the morning Fizz Moran excused himself on the grounds that his wife might be alarmed if she woke to find him absent.

'It might be a good time for everybody else to go as well,' he suggested. He found none to disagree. Fizz made his good-byes to Danny Binge and the Rector, promising the latter that he would be in touch.

'As for you Monsignor,' he drew Danny Binge aside, 'my wife is a most astute judge of character and she maintains that you are a saint. Bless me before you go.'

Fizz Moran knelt and with joined hands gratefully received the priestly blessing. As the clergymen were about to depart they were restrained by the sisters Carabim who insisted that they stay the night.

'Archie my dear,' Dell Carabim exclaimed, 'you and the Monsignor are staying with us and I am not taking no for an answer.'

In the comfortable beds provided by the sisters the clergymen slept the sleep of the just. At quarter to nine the Bishop Elect made straight for the local convent chapel where he celebrated Mass. Afterwards he breakfasted with the Rector and the sisters Carabim in the upstairs dining-room of the Durango Bar. Before the pair set out on the return journey to Tubberlick Archie promised he would call on a more regular basis while for his part Danny Binge promised that he would write shortly after his return to California. There was a tearful farewell. The sisters were quite distressed that Our Monsignor, as they had christened him, could not spend a few more days with them.

'I'll see you come the end of the Fall with God's help,' he promised.

'There will always be a bed for you too Archie but you know that,' Dell Carabim's eyes filled once more with tears.

'Where would we be without our friends!' The Rector embraced the sisters as did the Bishop Elect. Then they were gone. They stopped, briefly, at Trallock Parish Church. The Rector waited outside while his friend paid his respects. The Rector dismounted and undertook a brief inspection of the grounds. As he stood, hat in hand, admiring the very fine Pugin spire for which the church was famous he was approached by a grim-faced, middle-aged woman, dressed all in black. A sadder sight the Rector had never before beheld. He thrust a hand into his trousers' pocket wherein reposed the sum of three shillings and six pence, his total financial resources at that moment with not the slightest prospect of any more to come. The coins consisted of a florin, one shilling and six-pence. He would give her the shilling and the six-pence. She raised a black-gloved, forestalling hand and produced from her hand-bag a bulky leather purse. From this sombre, one time reliquary, she withdrew a formidable roll of single pounds. Reverently she peeled off one and thrust it into the Rector's hand, pressing as she did, her hand over his when he endeavoured to return the offering.

'You'll say Masses,' she whispered, 'for my late husband.'

The protestations died on his lips as she proceeded. 'He'll be dead a year this coming Saturday. He wants 'em father if ever a man wanted 'em for his soul was as black as the ace of spades.'

Still firmly she pressed his hand as she cleared the

throat which had hoarsened with the harshness of her communication. Repeatedly she shook her head and moaned bitterly at the perfidy of the knave who had preceded her to the seat of judgment. The Rector stood stock still while this most vindictive of widows endeavoured to recompose herself for what he believed would be another damnatory indictment. He was relieved to find that her tone had softened. She wrung the hands which held his.

'His name was Paddy O'Connor Father. Big Paddy they called him. May God forgive him because 'tis not in my power to do so.'

The Rector decided it was time to identify himself – that it was not in his power to say Mass. Despite his financial predicament the last thing he wanted to do was take money under false pretences. The widow, however, held on grimly to his hand.

'Don't forget father,' she was saying, 'Paddy O'Connor, Paddy that's surely in hell but the Masses has to be said all the same.'

Suddenly she released his hand and scurried into the gloom of the church. The Rector opened his hand and looked longingly at the crumpled £1 note.

'This is surely an authentic moral dilemma,' he told himself.

As they later sped over the road to Tubberlick the Rector's conscience pricked him repeatedly. He found himself unable to concentrate on his driving. He swung off the road into a gravelled margin.

'I wonder if you would do me a favour My Lord?'

Surprised by his friend's abject tone Danny Binge replied that he would gladly grant any favour within his power.

'In your spare time, old boy, would you be kind enough to say some Masses for the soul of one Paddy O'Connor.'

'I would consider it an honour my dear Archie. Was

he a friend of yours?' the Bishop Elect asked as he withdrew a small notebook with a tiny pencil attached from his inside coat pocket.

'A friend!' Archie Scuttard repeated the word, thoughtfully, before replying. 'Yes,' he said, 'he was a friend in need you might say.'

'And a friend in need,' the Bishop Elect saw the aphorism to its conclusion, 'is a friend indeed. What's the name again Archie?'

'O'Connor My Lord, Paddy O'Connor, fondly known to his inconsolable wife and family as Big Paddy.'

Danny Binge entered the name and closed his Mass book.

'Not only will I offer my own Mass for him,' he assured a relieved Archie Scuttard, 'but I will see to it that he is remembered in the Masses of every parish in my diocese.'

A short pause followed during which time the Rector considered how he would pose his next, most delicate, question.

'Is there something going to you for all this?' he asked tentatively.

'Something going to me!' Danny Binge took to musing for a moment.

'Yes,' he replied, 'a large whiskey at our next port of call.'

'With a heart and a half,' the Rector agreed.

The twinges of his conscience now diminishing rapidly, the Rector asked the Bishop Elect if he had heard of Mattie and Maud Holligan's pub in Ballybo. The Prelate-to-be shook his head.

'You have never visited Beenablaw House!'

'Never,' came the reply.

'And I take it,' Archie continued, 'that you have never met Joss the Badger or Philly Hinds or Moses Madigan?'

Again the shake of the head.

'Nor have you had your fortune told by the Badger's wife Monnie?'

'Afraid not,' came the reply.

'Your education has been sadly neglected, old boy, but fear not. Deliverance is at hand.'

'Are these people members of your flock?' Danny Binge asked.

'Only Philly Hinds,' the Rector replied. 'However his wife is an implacable Catholic with an insatiable penchant for Lourdes' water. She takes it for her rheumatism with equal parts of poitín. She is aware of the fact that poitín is the devil's brew so she mixes it with the holy water to knock the harm out of it. When there's no poitín she'll take Paddy Flaherty the same as you and me.'

Suddenly the engine roared into life. Before driving off the Rector took the precaution of thrusting his hand into his trousers' pocket in order to remove the widow's pound note. He transferred it to the safety of his buttoned fob pocket.

'I propose,' the Bishop Elect shouted, 'to go on the wagon from tomorrow.'

'Me too,' Archie Scuttard shouted back. 'You won't catch me drinking again until the last week of September.'

'We'll resume where we left off,' Danny Binge shouted as the BSA lunged forward with a powerful roar.

'A pound!' thought the Rector. 'It will buy 22.8 whiskies in Ballybo or, if you're a stout drinker, 22.66 circulating pints of stout.'

9

The September that followed the departure of Bishop Daniel Binge was no different from previous Septembers save for two significant developments at home and one abroad. All three would have far-reaching effects as far as the local farming community was concerned.

At a specially convened meeting in Tubberlick Parochial Hall, the farmers of the five parishes gathered for the first time in living memory to establish a branch of the Kerry Farmers' Association. Surprisingly there were several females in attendance. These included Miss Daisy Popple, the largest landowner in the district and one of the more successful farmers. After votes of sympathy were passed for recently deceased members of the farming community the business proper of the meeting proceeded with the automatic election of the Parish Priest of Tubberlick Father Dugan as president. Although he was not present the proposing and seconding of Father Dugan was a formality. The president of several other bodies in the area the Parish Priest never attended the meetings, general or otherwise, of these organisations. The chairman of most of the other bodies was the genial and ever-approachable Vester McCarthy of Tubberlick. Vester never missed a meeting and it was said of him that he mostly conducted the business of these meetings fairly and impartially.

After the elevation of the Parish Priest to the highest office in the branch the next item on the agenda was the election of officers. These would consist of chairman, secretary, treasurer and committee. Father Frank Tapley, the Curate of Tubberlick very kindly consented to preside as acting chairman until the permanent officers had been appointed. The first proposal came from a Boherlahan milch cow farmer. He proposed Vester McCarthy

138

for the office of chairman. The proposal was immediately seconded by a score of voices. There followed a lengthy silence during which Father Tapley waited for further nominations. None seemed to be forthcoming.

'I take it then,' Father Tapley addressed the meeting in a voice loud and clear, 'that there are to be no further nominations for the post of chairman.'

'I propose Parson Scuttard.' The voice was that of one Haybags Mullanney. He did not rise to his feet. Rather did he keep his head down but such was the power of his voice that Father Tapley had no difficulty in recognising its owner.

'Very well,' the Curate spoke in tones formal and solemn. 'We have the Rector of Tubberlick and the United Parishes proposed by Tom Mullanney of Ballybo. Do I have a seconder?'

'I second that,' Daisy Popple was on her feet on behalf of her friend and the minority religion.

'Do I have any further proposals?' the Curate asked as he tried to suppress a smile. He withdrew a while linen handkerchief and loudly blew into it. He spent several seconds wiping away an imaginary nasal discharge whereas he was secretly celebrating the nomination of his friend Archie Scuttard but was determined to conceal it. The Curate had two pet hates. One of these was the person who could not or would not speak up in the confessional and the other was Vester McCarthy. Not once in his seven years as Curate at Tubberlick had he received a Mass offering from the McCarthy household All donations in this respect went straight to the Parish Priest. Father Tapley received an abundance of pietistic claptrap from Vester whenever the pair happened to meet but, of the coin of the realm, he had never received as much as a single penny.

'A vote!' the call came from Tom Mullanney.

'A vote!' his demand was echoed from one end of the hall to the other. Father Tapley waited a decent interval to accommodate any last minute nomination.

'Very well then,' he announced, 'a vote it shall be.'

So it was that Archie Scuttard was elected the first chairman of the Tubberlick branch of the Kerry Farmers' Association. Vester McCarthy was visibly shocked at the outcome. The farmers of the five parishes knew before a vote was cast what the outcome would be. Archie Scuttard, whatever else, had the interests of the farmers at heart. He might go on monumental skites and he might be a Protestant but he was fair and above board and it would be foreign to the man's nature to do any person a mean turn. He had also been proposed by Haybags Mullanney. Yes, the farmers would agree, he is a blusterer and a blowhole but he's one of us and when it comes to farming he has the shrewdest head of any man in the district. Father Frank Tapley was mightily pleased with himself. One might have thought, for a man whose mental gratification ran somewhat parallel with the aspirations of the last of the great Gaelic arse-patters as he had been dubbed, that the Curate would have a certain amount of sympathy for Vester. He had none whatsoever. He was delighted at the Rector's appointment. It had been close, only three votes between the pair in the end out of two hundred cast. The office of secretary went unanimously to Mark Doran and the offices of joint treasurer to the brothers Will and Henry Sullivan. The Ballybo boys had been proposed by their mother Eleanor and seconded by Jay Mullanney. Some passionate speeches were made on the occasion, the first and longest by Haybags Mullanney who stressed the need for unity among farmers and ended up with a fuming condemnation of all things British. By far the most appreciated comments of the evening were contributed by the Rector who spoke for several minutes on the need for local branches in each of the five parishes. The Rector spoke of the farmers' organisations as political forces and predicted that it was inevitable that a farmers' candidate would contest the next general election and, more-over, that a farmers' candidate would win the seat if the farmers voted to a man. His speech was greeted with loud cheers and as the night wore on it became apparent that the farming communities of the parishes were intent on unity.

'Only by unity,' Mark Doran pointed out, 'can we achieve anything. Let us back any farmer's candidate 100%. Let us work towards that goal from this day for-ward and let us have prominent speakers down here on a regular basis from now on. We want to know what's happening. We want to have a stake in our own futures and I think that every man and woman here tonight will agree on that. We have no voice and without a voice we are nothing.'

Mark's contribution was cheered by the enthusiastic attendance. There was no one there on the occasion who did not feel that there was a new awareness, a new pride and, most important, a new sense of power.

'We hold our destiny in our own hands.' Will Sulli-van spread his arms wide, 'and the sooner we invest in our own cattle co-op the sooner we'll get just prices.' Will Sullivan, who had been well coached by his mother, spoke of the four impoverished farming families in the remote townland of Shannyvalley. Will spoke passion-ately. His contribution was greeted with rapt silence. None of the farmers in question had more than twenty acres of land and none had more than six milch cows.

'What I say to you is this,' Will Sullivan spoke now with his hands behind his back, 'these poor people of Shannyvalley are without shoes and without decent clothes. The fathers of these families can't even afford to smoke. Their combined incomes amount to £7 a week which is the same as one national teacher. Now I have nothing against national teachers. They taught me well. I wouldn't be here tonight talking to you but for my teachers and not forgetting my mother either. But listen

DURANGO

to this. The teachers say they haven't enough and I believe them. But if teachers haven't enough what chance
has a farmer with one quarter of a teacher's salary! I'll
tell you what he has. He has no chance at all.'

Will's analogy was much appreciated even if it
weighed somewhat in the farmer's favour. The farmer
did not have to buy potatoes or vegetables and since
bacon and cabbage or bacon and turnip was the staple
diet it could be fairly argued that he did not have to buy
meat. It could be argued too that he did not have to buy
fruit since most of the houses had small orchards which
intruded in no way into the farm resources since the
grass in such orchards provided prime fodder for most
of the year. Fish for the most part he would have to buy.
The local streams provided trout of stunted growth and
few salmon since only spawning fish came so far up-
stream from the main rivers. The only other fish available would be mackerel and herring on a seasonal basis.
By the time they finally reached the villages by rail, lorry
and horse or pony cart, they weren't always as fresh as
they might be. Fresh or no they were eaten with relish.
When fish wasn't available on Fridays and fast days
there was onion dip, a sauce made from milk and flour
and flavoured with onions. With good potatoes it provided a satisfying and tasty dish. Cash was the paramount problem. Only the big farmers had a bare sufficiency. None had cash to spare for luxuries. The small
farmer never had sufficient cash. The lucky ones might
earn enough from their holdings to clothe and feed their
families but the majority wore hand-me-downs and the
children went barefoot the year round. Clothes were
bought at the second-hand hustings in the villages during the quarterly fairs. Mark Doran, the Mullanneys and
the Sullivans together with other young men saw the
whole business as a monstrous conspiracy by city, town
and even village dwellers against the farmers. Certainly
there was no sympathy for the farmer outside of his own

142

community. Still there wasn't a farmer who wasn't greatly heartened by the inaugural meeting of the Tubberlick branch of the Kerry Farmers' Association.

Before the meeting closed Henry Sullivan, the second joint treasurer, made a short speech in which he thanked the Parish Priest and the parochial committee for the use of the hall. Then, innocently, he requested the audience to pay special attention to the important announcement he was about to make.

'People of Tubberlick, Ballybo, Tubberlee, Kilshunnig and Boherlahan and any other interested parties,' Henry Sullivan opened, 'I have been delegated to inform you that a drive of cattle will take place to Trallock town commencing at twelve noon on Friday, 29 September for old cows; on Saturday morning at seven for weanlings and on Saturday afternoon at three for incalf heifers, bullocks and other prime stock, all cattle to meet on the hill known as the Cunnackawneen on or before Sunday night, 1 October. All cattle will depart the Cunnackawneen for Trallock town at first light on the morning of 2 October where they will be stood for the great October fair.'

Vester McCarthy was instantly on his feet.

'I object,' Vester shouted, 'this is an advertisement for a private consortium whose aim is to destroy Tubberlick and the other villages. Damn well you know Henry Sullivan that the Tubberlick quarterly fair takes place on the same day as the great fair in Trallock.'

Vester shook his fist at Henry Sullivan.

'It's a bad night for you and yours Sullivan to renege on Tubberlick for 'tis well you know that we carried you and a lot of the other deserters here in the hard times.' What Vester said was true enough. What he failed to say was that the village shopkeepers were nearly always paid and the prices charged for provisions, while not exorbitant, were above the norm.

'I would like to remind you Mr McCarthy,' Henry

Sullivan had thrust his hands under his galluses as he had seen Raymond Massey do in a recent film, 'that we live in a free country and that we can sell our cattle wherever we damn well like!'

Consternation now broke loose in the hall and there was a melee near the door between the younger farmers and the representatives of the business interests in the five villages, many of whom would have fields or small farms themselves to supplement their often inadequate incomes from trading. The drive to Trallock, if it succeeded, would be the cause of a falling off in these incomes and it would be particularly damaging to the businesses of Tubberlick. But for the timely intervention of Mick Malone matters might have got seriously out of hand. Arms raised Mick went among the trouble-makers with a smile on his face, joking, cajoling and addressing the more bellicose of the participants by their first names.

'What pleases me most,' the newly elected chairman, Archie Scuttard, informed his crony Mick Malone later in the pub, 'was the large number of ladies and young people present. After this night I think I can safely say that we are not as helpless as we were.'

The Rector swallowed from the glass of lemonade which Mick Malone had bought him. Mick hinted that Vester McCarthy might not take his rebuff lying down.

'It's not so much himself,' Mick warned, 'but his henchmen. Mark Doran would want to be on his guard.'

Suddenly Mick Malone changed tack and enquired about the Bishop of San Lupino.

'It's been some time,' the Rector replied, 'since I heard but if I know the man he will be here on the day.'

'And,' Mick proceeded, 'regarding your long abstention from the liquor. Dare we hope that the end of your suffering is at hand?'

'Take this foul liquid from my hand,' the Rector entreated his longtime friend, 'and replace it with a drop of Paddy Flaherty.'

'You're sure?' Mick Malone asked.

'As you so often say yourself Mick,' the Rector tried to sound grave, 'the end of my suffering is at hand.'

In the nearby presbytery the Parish Priest, Father Aloysius Dugan sat in his sitting-room, listening to his Curate's account of the meeting. The pair had a good relationship but the Parish Priest felt there were a few inconsistencies in the make-up of the younger man. There had been complaints from female parishioners about his attitude in the confessional. One woman had gone over his head and written to the Bishop and for this the Parish Priest was truly grateful for it meant that the matter was out of his hands, temporarily at least. He had been obliged to reveal the number and nature of the previous complaints to the Bishop. If he had deliberately concealed them, even with the best intentions in the world, he would have placed himself in breach of normal ecclesiastical procedure. Frank Tapley had survived the Bishop's admonitions and explained that the questioning was absolutely imperative because of the tradition of belittling or even the withholding of vital parts of the transgressions in question so that mortal sins became venial sins in the process. Hence the necessity for extraction as Father Tapley termed it.

'Some of them would not confess their sins at all,' he told the Bishop, 'without the special type of interrogation to which I must subject them. All they have to do is tell the truth in the first place. It's the hesitancy, the mumbling and the incoherence. Half of them would leave the confessional worse than when they entered if I wasn't there to coax the sins out of them.'

The Bishop decided to let the Curate off with a caution.

Both Father Dugan and his Curate were heavy smokers. Lacking in ventilation of any form, like most presbytery sitting-rooms of the period, a blue haze enveloped the entire room as they exchanged views about the meeting.

'Still,' Father Dugan shook his head gravely, 'it's a shame that Vester wasn't elected. Vester is a good man. If he has a flaw or two, and which of us hasn't Father, he makes up for them with the good work he performs voluntarily in so many organisations and he's a decent man, a good friend to the Church and ever mindful of our needs. We must never forget who our friends are Father.'

'Of course, of course but it will show how broad-minded we are in this neck of the woods. I mean electing a Protestant against all the odds and a minister at that.'

'Who was his nominator?' Father Dugan asked.

'Tom Mullanney,' came the muffled reply.

'Who?' the Parish Priest shouted.

'Tom Mullanney,' the Curate raised his voice.

The Parish Priest crushed his barely smoked cigarette in the ashtray and rose to his feet.

'Haybags Mullanney!' Father Dugan exploded, 'the so-called Republican, the Pope-hater and heaven knows what else. That fellow never had a good word for the Catholic Church. Why doesn't he join the other crowd altogether!'

'The positive aspect of the meeting,' Father Tapley decided to risk going on as if he hadn't heard, 'is that there was no word of Nationalism except for Haybags who is not taken seriously. This meeting was the first of its kind that I have attended where all the issues raised had to do with farming and the future of farming.'

'And this drive?' Father Dugan asked.

'The drive is all set to go ahead. There was an announcement tonight. It seems that the first of the cattle will leave on Friday week.'

'That's only nine days away,' the Parish Priest lit another cigarette. 'Can nothing be done to stop it?'

'Oh nothing whatsoever. These young men are

determined.'

'Don't they know what they're doing? Don't they know what this will do to Tubberlick.'

'They're not all that worried about Tubberlick. The only thing that concerns them right now is the welfare of the farmer.'

'That's a very selfish attitude in a time of war.'

'Most of them will ask you whose war it is. They say it doesn't concern them.'

'Oh but it does. We could be invaded at any moment. If not this year then certainly next year.'

'That doesn't occur to them,' Father Tapley replied. 'It may occur to those who don't own land. They're getting out to join the British army or the Irish army but the farmers are not unduly concerned. The war is an opportunity and they see it as their duty to exploit that opportunity. It seems to me that by the end of the war, whenever that is, there won't be anybody left in this part of the world but farmers. There's very little here for anybody else. You see Father,' Frank Tapley patiently expanded his hands to clarify his viewpoint, 'every young Irishman, whether he's town or country, has too many options, all ready-made. There isn't a young Irishman who hasn't an aunt or an uncle or a relative in America, Australia, England or Canada. The language is the same and the relatives receive them with open arms. They have a headstart over other European emigrants. The youth of Ireland is born into ready-made, inescapable options.'

The second significant local development which would have long-term effects was a large scale search of the haunts and houses of IRA suspects. There were many arrests nation-wide under the Offences against the State Act and in mid-September a large number of IRA members and suspects were interned at the Curragh where many would remain for the duration of the war. The dwelling houses and outhouses of Haybags Mullanney were searched for arms and explosives but nothing was found nor was there the slightest trace of any illegal activities when a party of local civic guards, led by Mick Malone, conducted a thorough search of Maxwell's Barn. In Ballybo a small farmer, arrested and charged with possession of guns and ammunition, was transported to the Curragh in County Kildare where he was interned despite pleas from Father Dugan and the Rector. The murder of the innocent civilians in Coventry earlier in the year proved to be one of the sticks with which the IRA would beat themselves throughout the entire war. Also in mid-September a blackout was imposed on Trallock town, on a trial basis, and thereafter whenever the sound of a plane was heard at night, curtains were drawn and lights were quickly doused. But not for long because the novelty of the war wore off as time went on. The sympathy of 90% of the Irish people was with the British.

The truly significant happening abroad was the declaration of war by Britain and France on Germany on 3 September. At the same time De Valera embarked on a course of neutrality and was attacked in turn by Churchill and Roosevelt. The Irish government was accused of cowardice, abandonment, treachery and it was ridiculed most of all for its declaration of the Emergency. De Valera succeeded in keeping Ireland out of the war and he was repeatedly reviled for his stance. His enemies claimed that the numbers of young men from the Irish Free State who died fighting on the English side, 50,000 in all, might have been substantially less if Ireland had joined with the Allies and had a say in how its young men might be deployed and, most important of all, that the majority of young men would have been chosen from all walks of life rather than the less prosperous. Poverty, lack of opportunity and frustration, were the new recruiting sergeants who worked relentlessly on behalf of the British army in Ireland.

Mark Doran paid no great attention to the war. His mind was too taken up with other matters, chief of which was the cattle drive and in this respect the day of reckoning was almost at hand. He secretly prayed that England would not be invaded. It figured hugely in his plans, plans he would not translate into action until the drive had been completed.

Immediately after the war's outbreak thousands of young Irishmen joined the RAF and the British army. Others, not so many, joined the IRA exhorted by that organisation's recruitment officers, still emphasising the grim philosophy that England's difficulty was Ireland's opportunity. All through the war lone young Irishmen on furlough and wearing British uniforms would be waylaid and severely beaten up often in their own streets and on their own doorsteps by IRA sympathisers. Nothing, however, could impede the outward flow of British sympathisers. The native Irish army doubled in strength in a short time until its numbers stopped short of 40,000 fighting men of high morale ready to fight and die in defence of their country. They were never called upon to do so but this can never take away from their exceptional commitment to the defence of the Twenty-six counties, and should England be overwhelmed by the Axis, to the sundered six in Ulster as well. Nobody doubted but that they would go down in such an eventuality. Neither did anybody doubt that they would do so gamely and to the last man. Still there were powerful voices demanding active and immediate participation in the fight against Hitler. Only the IRA and their sympathisers expressed any support for Germany.

The writing was on the wall for Germany's mainland victims when on the 14 September the German High Command announced that their advancing troops were less than a hundred miles east of Warsaw and that the nearby city of Lodz to the south-east was on the point of capitulation. When Russia invaded Poland on

16 September Polish resistance was effectively finished.

In Tubberlick Vester McCarthy's chief concern was not the forthcoming cattle drive, for which his plans were well advanced, but the dazzling ten horse-power Vauxhall de Luxe which had done so much to enhance the image of his only daughter across the summer and early autumn. The liquor business in the McCarthy licensed premises had picked up considerably since the disastrous quarterly cattle and pig fair of July. Old suitors surfaced from every side and Sally found herself being pursued by several young and not so young bachelors of unquestionable eligibility. Many were rejects from former, short-lived liaisons. Then there were those whose attentions had never been more than lukewarm and a chosen few for whom Vester's only daughter had cast her amorous nets in vain. All had returned and in various ways, direct and indirect, had intimated their availability. Sally most definitely cut a dramatic and dashing figure as she sped with driving window open through the leafy highways and byways of the countryside. Her rich fair hair swept loosely behind, her clear skinned pleasant face was always advantageously highlighted by a selection of fresh white blouses. Often she applied the brakes in order to pass the time of day with one of her many suitors. She never dallied long. This, she discovered, was the secret. Let them savour her fragrance, catch glimpses of her infectious smile, laugh at their commonplace and often crude jests but never totally reject. Her time was running out. Most of all she took to calling on a regular basis at Mark Doran's. Oddly enough he was rarely in. He was always out in the meadows or the pastures or the garden, a fact that did not escape the notice of his mother. Sally McCarthy was a welcome visitor. She always brought news. The real reason behind her visits did not dawn on Nonie Doran at once. This happened when the older woman noted the younger's movements to and from the kitchen windows

and door. Then the smiling young face would turn serious as her perplexed eyes sought the whereabouts of
the object of her visit.

Whether by accident or design his mother noted that
Mark never put in an appearance during one of her
visits which was in sharp contrast to his attitude towards the childlike Annie Mullanney. But then Nonie
Doran could never be sure whether Mark's intentions
towards the dark-eyed teenager, on the threshold of her
seventeenth year, were serious or playful. She was forced to conclude, in the absence of evidence to the contrary, that the friendship between the pair, although
somewhat less boisterous than of yore, was not something that should cause her undue concern, at least not
yet. Annie Mullanney had grown slightly self-conscious
across the summer. Nonie Doran understood this fully.
The girl was no more than a grown-up child but slowly
and surely she was shaping into a presentable slip of a
girl. Sally McCarthy now was different proposition. She
had never made any secret of the fact her cap was set for
Mark Doran. Things had not gone altogether as Sally
had planned but she would change all that before Mark
set out on his crazy drive. While her father had denounced the idea several times in the presence of Sally and her
mother they both felt that Mark would be all the better
for having put the drive behind him. Mrs McCarthy was
convinced that the drive was a sort of last fling after
which Mark would be clearer about his intentions. Sally
had found him tough and non-committal on matters
nearest and dearest to her heart. It wasn't that his interest had waned. Rather was it static. Mark reminded her
of a tide which could not make up its mind whether to
ebb or flow. Still, of all the renewed interest by those she
had once fancied or rejected, he was the one young man
she would choose above them all. They had met several
times since that first time and on occasion they had gone
driving together but it had always been dark. The ex-

cuses he gave for his nocturnal preference varied. There was the training for the five villages football championship. There were the meadows. The summer and autumn days had provided mixed weather. Then there was his obsession with the drive to Trallock which seemed to take up all of his waking hours. Their courting sessions had been less intense than that night when the ports were nearly surrendered. There was great pressure at the time on the Irish government to surrender the Irish ports for the duration of the war to English shipping but De Valera steadfastly refused to hand them over on the grounds that it would compromise Irish neutrality. Consequently, there was much banter on the subject. When a young man met his friends after he had seen a girl of advanced years home from a dance he would be asked if she had surrendered the ports. Sally McCarthy promised herself on the day that England and France declared war on Germany that, one way or the other, she would be a married woman before the same date the following year. With this in view she sought out Mark Doran.

On this occasion she by-passed the dwelling house and went directly to the cowshed where, to her great surprise, she beheld Nonie Doran seated on a three-legged milking stool with a bucket between her legs. She wore a heavy sack apron and crooned a love song vaguely familiar to Sally McCarthy as she drew on the paps of the cow she was milking. Nearby sat Mark Doran, similarly engaged whilst at the farthest end sat Danny Dooley, gently humming. Such was the degree of concentration by all three that Sally's presence at the doorway went unnoticed. The only other sounds were the occasional swishes of the cows' tails and the sibilances, rich and deep, as the jets of milk lathered the contents of the buckets. She had never been privy to a milking session of such a kind in her life. Her father had cows but the cowshed was the province of the workman who looked after the cattle. Milking time at Doran's despite the soft singing was a businesslike operation which, by its very nature, would not brook interference unless in the case of emergency. Sally McCarthy was well aware of this. She withdrew into a cobbled yard. She decided to wait until one of the trio emerged with a contribution for the creamery tank which stood outside the back door of the house. As she stood with folded arms, her eyes fixed on the hills to the west, she remembered her father's last words as she entered the car.

'Drive while you can Sal,' he had enjoined her, 'there won't be a private car on the road come Christmas.' Vester had been disgusted when on 3 September the British again proved their perfidy by making a mockery of his forecast that there would be no war.

'It's a phony war,' he had told his many friends on countless occasions before the declaration, 'there will be no war.' Now he was stuck with an expensive car which would probably lie idle on his hands for years for the good reason that there would be no petrol.

When Danny Dooley appeared with a bucket of milk for the creamery tank he stopped in his tracks on beholding the unfamiliar visitor. Danny knew Sally McCarthy well enough but confronting her on his own was a different matter. He nodded politely and was surprised by the effusiveness of her response. She called him by his Christian name and enquired after his welfare as though she really meant it.

'I'll get him for you,' Danny Dooley said after he had poured his milk into the tank. Politely Sally refused his offer and cautioned him to make no mention of her presence. Eventually when Mark emerged from the cowshed, milk bucket in hand, he was surprised but not overjoyed when he saw her standing at the gable end of the house with her eyes fixed on the distant hills. Silently he lifted the cover of the milk tank and tilted the bucket so that the creamy contents spilled silently through the muslin mesh which had been tied around the mouth of the tank to prevent impurities from joining the milk already inside.

'This is a surprise,' Mark called out pleasantly. She came towards him at once and without a word threw her arms around his neck in spite of his protestations that he was covered with dirt and heaven knows what.

'I don't mind,' she said as she held him firmly, 'unless you do.'

'Of course not,' he broke from her suddenly as his mother appeared in the door of the cowshed.

'Sunday night,' she whispered as Nonie Doran stayed put, then turned and exchanged words with Danny Dooley. Mark was about to explain that he would be tied up with arrangements for the Trallock drive which would begin on the following Friday.

'Don't let me down,' she pleaded, 'come after the pub is shut.'

Sally looked to see if Nonie Doran's back was still turned towards them. She was gratified to note that she had re-entered the cowshed. Sally was convinced that the guilt which was uppermost in her mind would surely show in her face if she were to exchange looks with Nonie Doran at that moment. The older woman would instinctively know that the younger's latest plans for the permanent ensnarement of her son had been hatched out of sheer desperation and that she would stop at nothing to achieve her goal. Sally saw her prospective mother-in-law as an astute and practical woman who would see through her, would instantly recognise the change of tack for what it was, the seduction of her only son by a desperate woman. Sally McCarthy was not altogether correct. Nonie Doran was, as she had deduced, astute and practical but most of all she was experienced and being experienced would be alive to the wiles of girls in Sally's position, particularly in relation to Mark's future. The last thing Nonie Doran needed was a look at Sally McCarthy's face. She had known for some time that Sally would play every card in her hand before she gambled with her final throw. Nonie Doran knew that the time for that throw had come. The fleeting glance which she had been afforded as she was about to leave the cowshed with her milking pail only served to confirm what she already knew. It was to conceal her own embarrassment rather than highlight Sally McCarthy's that she had retraced her steps. In the shed she entrusted the bucket to Danny Dooley as he was about to depart with his own. She would wait until Sally McCarthy had left the cobbled yard before showing herself. The girl wouldn't stay long, no longer than was necessary, to extract a promise which Mark would give but which, Nonie Doran was certain, he would never keep. She knew, in her heart, that Mark had other plans, long term maybe, but positive nevertheless and she knew, or believed she knew, where Mark would turn when the time was ripe.

10

The thirty Roscreas assembled in Mark Doran's haggard, some old and a few venerable had arrived singly, in pairs and otherwise all through the evening prior to the morning of departure for Philly Hinds' haggard. Their owners, for the most part farmers and cottiers, had deposited the beasts in Mark's care and wished him luck before returning to their homesteads. There had been no difficulty in procuring this particular contingent of the herd. Mark let it be known that he was prepared to pay thirty-two shillings and six pence per head, cash on delivery at the Doran haggard. The likelihood was that the ancient cows would fetch up to £2 per head at the fair of Trallock but even the most tight-fisted owners would concede that there was no guarantee. Add to this that there was always the likelihood that the overland journey might prove too much for a milch cow nearing the end of her days. There was also the fact that old cows, by their nature, were a decidedly risky investment so that the only fair conclusion to be drawn was that Mark Doran's offer was a reasonable one.

The Badger Doran and Philly Hinds supervised the arrivals. In the process they rejected several of the more emaciated. From a feedbag slung across his shoulder the Badger distributed the going rate of a pound, a ten shilling note and a half-crown. In return he received luck money to the tune of a shilling per head. This he divided with his friend Philly Hinds. When added to the sixpences and shillings they had saved across the summer they would find themselves with £3 a man, sufficient surely they believed to pay for two nights' lodgings in the town of Trallock with enough left over for drink, food and any unforeseen contingency which might arise. Lodgings had been arranged for some time by the Trallock apothecary Fizz Moran. Neither Philly nor the Badger had ever laid eyes on Moran but by all accounts he was a decent sort and, according to Parson Scuttard, his wife was a countrywoman, the daughter of a small farmer and proud of her agricultural background.

Early in the morning Danny Dooley led the grey mare in from the moist pasture at the rear of the haggard where the old cows, unaware of the demanding trek that lay before them, browsed leisurely on the plenteous grass, especially reserved over several weeks. In the farmyard Danny Dooley went about the tricky business of tackling the mare to the railed cart. In the rail would go the provisions for the journey as well as fresh clothes and shoes in readiness for the night life of Trallock. There would be shovels and ropes in case an animal went a-bogging or slipped into a drain. There would be a ration of oats for the mare and the luggage of the entire party. As well as shoes and clothing this would include razors and in some cases hair oil, fresh socks, shirts, soap, towels, sacks of bedding straw and a quantity of dry turf and bogdeal to facilitate the starting of fires.

Gently stroking the sensitive ears Danny Dooley inserted the bit in the mare's mouth. He then placed the winkers, with reins already attached, over the head. Then came the heavy collar which he slung with both hands over the neck, then came the inelegant hames fitting perfectly into the collar, then the straddle over the broad back and bound under the abdomen with buckled strap, then the britching on the rump and the band of the britching between thigh and point of buttock and attached to the straddle again with strap and buckle, then the reins through the rings of the hames. Up then with the shaft, then wheel the horse around until the rump is between the shafts and facing the body of the car. Then on with the backband on the bridge of the straddle, then the traces into the hooks of the hames and the tying of the chains to the two crooks of the greased slides, then the simple bellyband to stop the cart from heeling if the load should shift.

'Tackling a horse is not a fool's job. Never forget that,' Danny Dooley had spoken curtly to Mark one fair morning when the younger man tended to take the exercise for granted.

'Tackling a horse properly will save your horse's life and maybe your own. What if the two traces are not tied to the same length! How about the damage such carelessness will cause to your horse's breast! How about if the slides are not greased and the straddle shifts! You'll scorch your horse's breast for sure. What if you forget your bellyband and your horse bolts! I knew chaps that tackled horses and they didn't know a common bit from a running bit. Wronging a horse is as bad as wronging a woman. A good woman or a good horse will never let you down. Remember that always and you won't go far wrong.'

Mark had responded at the time with a respectful nodding of the head. Watching Danny Dooley from the gable of the out-house Mark noted the unhurried and methodical movements of his workman. He had timed him on one occasion and was astonished to discover that Danny could tackle the mare in half the time he himself had taken.

At the conclusion of breakfast in Doran's kitchen on the morning of the twenty-ninth it was agreed that Danny Dooley would guide the mare. The terrain ahead would never be less than challenging and very often dangerous. Accompanying Danny would be Philly Hinds, the Badger Doran and Jay Mullanney.

'Now my friends,' Mark Doran addressed his drovers prior to their departure, 'keep your eyes open at all times and remember that at no time is the horse and rail to be left unattended. You'll proceed to Philly's with two stops on the way to give the cows a breathing space. Don't hurry them. You can make tea and partake of the cold bacon and cabbage when you arrive. Don't forget to leave ours. Release your cows into the haggard and make four watches, each man to take a watch of two hours. At cockcrow you'll breakfast well and proceed with your herd as far as Bessie Lie-Down's. Remember that this woman is mental for men, young or old and is best left to herself but she'll have a fire going and she'll wet tea for you and there's good green grass in the cut-aways all around. Don't let your cows wander on to soft bog. On Sunday you'll be obliged to miss Mass but you're doing God's work because you're helping the poor. You will proceed all day, wet or dry, to Crabapple Hill and God willing we'll all meet at the Cunnackaw-neen on the evening before the fair. God speed now and good luck.'

Before anyone could move Nonie Doran ran from the kitchen doorway where she had been waiting for Mark to conclude his address. She sprinkled each in turn with holy water and cast a drop or two in the general direction of the Roscreas whose sole interest, alas, was centred on the half-eaten haggard which they had been forced to vacate. As the cavalcade, led by the mare, emptied onto the roadway it was halted by a mighty roar from Haybags Mullanney.

'Don't go without this poor chap,' he called to Danny Dooley.

The lumbering eight year old Shorthorn bull, roan in colour, which trailed Haybags at the end of a thick rope, surveyed the lack-lustre sorority, some of them old acquaintances, with baleful eyes, comparing them no doubt unfavourably with the wanton young libertines he had so zealously serviced throughout the hazy days of summer.

Danny Dooley drew rein while Haybags released the Shorthorn. 'Hasn't been doing his duty lately,' the big man explained, 'and gone a bit choosy to boot. Spends more time chewing than screwing!'

'You can't have that,' Danny Dooley concurred.

'He was a good one,' the Badger guided the bull towards the Roscreas, his slender ashplant brooking no nonsense.

'He's still a good one,' Haybags shook his head mournfully, 'if only he'd put his mind to it.'

'You have to admit,' Philly Hinds reminded Haybags, 'that he's had his share of it. You have a suitable replacement I take it.'

'Indeed I have,' Haybags boasted, 'only eighteen months and he'd mount a gate pier. He'll throw good calves too. You can always tell.'

'What kind of money?' Mark Doran asked as he advanced to take a closer look at the discarded Shorthorn.

'Take what you get,' Haybags replied, 'he's only a liability to me. I'll say this about him though. He was the most attractive animal I ever owned. He's just lost interest so I decided only an hour ago that he had to go.'

'The interest could come back,' Philly Hinds observed.

'His own story he's telling,' the Badger pointed his ashcrop in the direction of his friend.

'A bull has a great life,' Philly returned, 'all he has to do is mount heifers and cows day in day out. He'll have a sad end I know poor chap but there's no one can deny he had his fair share of fun.'

'Let's go boys!' the command came from Danny Dooley as he flicked the reins. The mare moved forward slowly followed by the listless Shorthorn and the assorted oldsters of the five parishes. At the rear came the Badger and Philly Hinds. On the right flank which afforded access to countless acres of undrained cutaway Jay Mullanney, agile and exuberant, ran back and forth exhorting the less energetic of his charges with shouts and whoops.

'It's a historic day,' Mark raised a hand aloft in farewell. With luck he would join them with the remainder of the herd at the Cunnackawneen on the Sunday evening before the fair. They stood silently, Haybags and Mark, side by side. Nonie Doran looked on from the doorway, her Rosary beads clutched in her hands as she prayed fervently and silently for the safe passage of the adventurers but chiefly for Danny Dooley whose welfare she secretly cherished. Had he not been like a father to her son Mark from the moment of his arrival and had he not always behaved like a perfect gentleman towards herself and yet, for all his gentle ways and his diminutive stature, she sensed that he would be a rare man in the face of setback. She prayed to the Blessed Virgin that she might intercede with her son Jesus for the safe return of Danny Dooley and for all the others who would embark upon the long journey to Trallock. The trio stood watching until the slow-moving livestock reached the crossroads where the turning to the left would take them to the village of Ballybo and beyond it to the holding of Philly Hinds where they would settle for the night. Although it was no more than an eleven mile journey all told it would test every last cow to the utmost. The drovers also would have to take into account the second and third stages of the journey, each as long as the first before the final descent from the Cunnackawneen to the main road and thence to the town of Trallock. Any loss would put a severe dent on Mark Doran's investment and might well militate against further drives of a similar nature. Not until the entire party had disappeared at the crossroads did Mark remind himself of his next commitment. He dared not think of all the things that might go wrong. He had, in so far as it was in his power, covered every eventuality but one. This was the threat from the villages, Tubberlick in particular, and the form it might take. He had already mentioned his worries in this respect to Haybags. The bluff Republican dismissed the idea.

'Look at your numbers,' he told Mark. 'Look at the quality of the men you have with you. Your only concern should be to ensure that the older bucks don't drink themselves to death.'

'You won't change your mind and come along with us!' Mark urged.

'Too old Mark,' Haybags answered, 'but I'll be with ye in spirit.' They stood silently for a while. Mark anxiously recalled how Haybags had surprised him on the road one evening as he held Annie's hands in his.

'That evening on the road!' Mark flinched, wondering what was to come.

It was as though Haybags had read his thoughts. 'You had a great chat with Annie!' The tone was accusatory as though Mark was guilty of some form of complicity. 'Anything I should know about!' Haybags asked throatily.

Mark found that his knees tended to knock.

'Nothing. Nothing at all,' he replied.

'I'm glad to hear it,' Haybags heaved a sigh of relief and patted Mark on the back.

'Annie is special,' he confided, 'and she's little more than a child. She's very dear to me.'

Mark Doran vowed there and then that he would never again mention Annie Mullanney's name in the presence of her father. He had spoken at length with her on the occasion in question and he knew from the way she squeezed his hand that she cared for him. They had made certain tentative arrangements to meet again at the crossroads. When Haybags turned to enter a roadside field he managed to kiss her flush on the lips. Her response removed all doubt.

After consultation with the Rector of Tubberlick Daisy Popple had volunteered ten prime bullocks towards the drive. The main body of the herd would consist of bullocks, heifers with and without calf, some young milch cows and other prime stock, all due to leave the Doran haggard at four in the afternoon the following day. These would be preceded in the morning by seventy weanlings, the combined stock of over fifteen farmers, including Mullanney's, Will and Henry Sullivan's, Mark Doran's and most of the successful hill farmers within a radius of eight miles. The weanlings would leave at daybreak and would follow the route taken by the Roscreas and Haybags' retired Shorthorn. They would be accompanied by Mark Doran, Will Sullivan, Tom Mullanney and Mattie Holligan, the Ballybo publican, who professed after he had heard about the drive that he had never in his life felt so much in the need of a break. He had also accumulated several weanlings over the spring and summer months in lieu of cash to meet outstanding dues which had been put on the long finger from Christmas orders. These, he explained to his wife Maud, would contribute handsomely to the drive and since Ballybo was the only one of the five villages not hostilely disposed to the venture, his decision met with the approval of the farmers thereabouts.

At Daisy Popple's the bullocks were waiting in the farmyard, always spick and span despite numerous intrusions by the farm population. Mark sat sipping the second glass of elderberry wine while Daisy held forth from the other end of the table about the conniving clique of local jobbers and most notably the Drover Mooleys whose curs, according to Daisy, were not above killing other dogs when the bloodlust was upon them.

'Have another glass,' Daisy suggested eagerly after Mark had finished praising the wine. Up until this time he had always associated elderberry wine with genteel old ladies.

On his way home in charge of the Popple bullocks he found that his bicycle was possessed of a freshly acquired imbalance whenever he endeavoured to keep the well-conditioned cattle on the straight and narrow.

Daisy Popple sat amused in her Baby Ford at the rear of the group. Mark Doran was not the first newly-inducted imbiber to be deceived by her elderberry wine. She had refused to put a reserve on the bullocks.

'I'm in this thing win, lose or draw.' She had quivered indignantly all over like the grandiose blancmange to which she had frequently been compared. The ripples of obesity appeared whenever she wished to emphasise or underline a particular point. Mark had averted his eyes with considerable embarrassment when the two double chins shuddered and shivered, barely restraining a third which threatened to join the dominant pair whenever she lowered her head. He had come across many overweight females in town and village but none had the liveliness or heartiness of Daisy Popple and none had the glowing peachlike colouring There was a freshness and a rosiness to her. She seemed to glow all of the time. Her presence had the effect of energising the withdrawn and the lackadaisical. She had the power to alert people to her presence and, most importantly, the innate unawareness of her own corpulence compelled people, who might otherwise stand and stare, to take her for granted. She was possessed of a breeziness and a bluffness which made her welcome everywhere. There were two loves in her life, her bullocks and her pastor, Archibald Reginald Percival Scuttard.

On one occasion, shortly after his wife died, despite the combined efforts of his Bishop and physician to have him committed to a sanatorium for the alcoholically ill, she had insisted in nursing him back to health herself. Aided by other concerned members of the Rector's ever-declining flock she had converted the modest parlour next to the kitchen into a sick bay. She had engaged a tradesman to seal the latticed windows lest her patient escape and undo all her good work with a visit to one of the all too accommodating taverns in the vicinity. To counter-act such a possibility she contacted the Rector's friend Mick Malone who took it upon himself to call upon each of the publicans in the five villages letting it be known that the Rector was not to be supplied with intoxicating drink under pain of personal annihilation and, worse still, the threat of an objection to the granting of a liquor license at the appropriate court hearing. Despite this and despite the vigilance of Daisy and her helpers the Rector remained drunk and delirious in his room for the first few days of his confinement.

The only conclusion that Daisy Popple could draw was that the Rector had smuggled the liquor past her on the very first day of his confinement. If this was so and it seemed the most likely answer she asked herself where he had concealed it. A thorough search directed by Mick Malone was instituted. Although the Rector, reeking with the fumes of whiskey freshly-consumed, was patently drunk, nobody had seen him with a bottle to his lips and none had discovered the presence of a bottle in the sick room although several empty bottles were found.

The only time the room was vacated was when the Rector was obliged to relieve himself in the commode provided for such a purpose. Mick Malone retired as did Daisy when the patient expressed a desire for privacy so that he could engage the commode. As he was leaving the room Mick Malone allowed the door to remain partly ajar. At the same time he silently intimated to Daisy that she should douse the kitchen lamp, making it impossible for the Rector to discern anything beyond the bedroom door. Mick, safely concealed in the shadows, awaited the next move from the figure in the bed. With an agonising groan the occupant sat painfully upright and eased himself from the bed. Instead of availing himself of the commode as he had indicated he knelt by the side of the bed and, thrusting his trembling hand beneath it, withdrew a supplementary chamber pot more decorative than truly functional. Holding the vessel in both hands he lifted it to his mouth and swilled therefrom like a starving bonham, spluttering and wheezing as he did.

He placed it on the bedroom floor temporarily as he sat on his haunches gasping for breath.

'That will do my poor man,' the voice was that of Mick Malone who advanced upon the drunken Rector and kneeling beside him lifted the surprised tippler into his bed. Archie Scuttard soon recovered from his bewilderment.

'Fair cop,' he gurgled. It was now obvious that Archie's first act upon arrival at the Popple parlour had been to locate a suitable hiding place for the illicit noggins and half pints concealed all over his person. The pot under the bed had been an inspired choice after he had failed to find a worthy cache for the assortment of whiskey and gin with which he had stocked up after promising Daisy that he would present himself at her abode rather than a hospital or sanatorium. He improved rapidly after the discovery. In less than a fortnight he was tending to his parochial duties. He had not embarked on a rampage of similar intensity afterwards. He had always drawn the line when he found his indulgence encroaching upon his duties. As he said himself to Mick Malone when he refused to join him one winter's night at the Widow's: 'Thank you Mick but I know exactly how far I can go and I've just arrived.'

At such times he would go on the dry for months until he found that he had recovered sufficiently to begin all over again.

As they turned the bullocks into the haggard Daisy Popple recalled what the Rector had said about the man to whom she was entrusting her cattle.

'A leader,' Archie Scuttard had confided when he had first approached her about the possibility of lending her stock to the drive, 'and not just that but an innovator as well. He is exactly what this countryside needs. He also has visions of a central mart for the five parishes and the countryside around. There will be changes after this bloody war. If you ask me we're lucky to have such a young man.'

Daisy had agreed at once but voiced her unease about a cattle mart.

'The villages will be against it,' she said.

'Of course they'll be up against it and so would I if I had a vested interest but farmers and villagers alike will benefit in the long run. They can't see that now but they must be made to see it.'

The Rector paced the farmhouse kitchen, his pudgy hands extended, his voice high-pitched. It was towards the end of his latest abstemious period. His perception was at its sharpest. At such times he would outline the country's ills with clarity and accuracy and prescribe the cures required for its betterment.

'Mark Doran knows where he's going. He has a following and it wouldn't surprise me if he had politics at the back of his head in the long run. We must give him every support in this drive of his.' The Rector of Tubberlick knew that he was preaching to the converted to begin with but he knew that Daisy had influence far and wide.

When the bullocks were safely deposited in the Doran haggard they repaired to the kitchen where Nonie had spread a spotless white tablecloth over the workaday table. After tea Mark made out a makeshift receipt which Daisy Popple declined.

'They'll lose a bit on the journey,' Mark told her, 'but I promise you they'll make as good a price as any.'

Daisy Popple rose to her feet and shook hands with Mark.

'I hope you have a trouble-free journey. You carry all our hopes with you. I know you won't fail us.'

It was the first time that Mark became fully aware of the heavy responsibility he shouldered. Daisy's words had placed the undertaking in its proper perspective. He thought of the thousand things which could go wrong, of the huge sum of money involved, of the families dependent on his enterprise and who was really to say whether it was a foolhardy enterprise or not. He would depart at seven o'clock in the morning with the seventy weanlings. The main body of the herd, consisting of a hundred mixed stock, would leave at noon.

That night before sleep came, long after its time, he had prayed and fantasised futilely to induce slumber. He squirmed when he thought of his final meeting with Sally McCarthy. He forced himself to go through the nightmarish encounter once more. He had arrived at her request to the pub shortly after closing time. They had embraced at once, passionately, and without the expected preliminaries.

Vester, she explained, and her mother were in Killarney and would not be home until the morning hours. She had taken his hand and led him to the upstairs sitting-room.

'Wait there,' she had said in a husky voice. She slipped silently out of the room. A bright fire burned in the grate. An ornate clock ticked loudly on the mantelpiece. Otherwise there was silence. The minutes passed and Mark began to grow anxious. He rose and paced the room. He was overcome by an inexplicable uneasiness and there was a sense too of not belonging. What in the name of God and His holy mother was she up to! He resumed his seat. Just then she appeared in the doorway sporting exactly the same apparel as she did when she first entered the world save for a pair of white bedroom slippers with pink pompons.

Never before in the history of his life had Mark Doran been confronted by a naked woman. Here was no scraggy slip of a girl, no puny, bony, underdeveloped adolescent. Here was, as his grand-uncle the Badger Doran might put it, a fine ball of a woman. Sally McCarthy stood before him, a strange smile on her freshly made-up face, her dun-coloured nipples highlighting the delightful symmetry of her twin protuberances, shapely and round and delectable, complimented by a soft white belly with highlighting navel at its centre, complimented in turn by a magical cluster of hairs, naturally and indifferently deployed but incomparable in ensemble. Underneath were sturdy, inviting thighs atop well-shaped legs. The whole presentation left Mark stunned and confused. It had now become a deadly serious business. What should he do! How should he react! Should he seize her there and then! Should he wait! A wild excitement took hold of him. He rose unsteadily and went towards her. Then with a fierce cry of anguish he rushed past her, down the stairs, into the street, forgetting in his haste to close the door behind him.

Later when Vester and Mary McCarthy returned home they found their only daughter fully dressed but somewhat distraught in the sitting-room. The fire had gone out. There was a chill in the room. Listlessly their daughter answered the many questions posed by her concerned parents. Where was Mark Doran? Why had she allowed the fire to go out and subject herself needlessly to the cold of the night? Who had left the street door open?

'All I'm saying,' Sally McCarthy spoke from between clenched teeth, 'is that there's something wrong with that fellow.'

'What fellow? What fellow?' both her parents asked eagerly.

'That Doran fellow,' came the icy response, 'that weird son of a bitch out the Ballybo road. What other fellow would there be?'

The tears came immediately after she had identified the cause of her woe. At once her mother threw both arms around her weeping daughter.

'What did he do to you?' Vester McCarthy fumed. 'I'll have the bastard castrated so I will.'

'He did nothing,' his daughter put in quickly, 'he's just a hick, a hayseed. I don't know what I ever saw in him. There's something the matter with him. He's peculiar.'

'I'll fix him,' Vester McCarthy vowed. 'I'll fix him good I promise you.'

So saying he went downstairs and filled himself a glass of whiskey. He would visit the Drover Mooley's first thing in the morning. He was convinced that Doran had degraded his daughter in some way. Why else would she weep? Why else would she be distressed? It was just the sort of deceitful behaviour one would expect from such a man, from a disrupter of calf markets and cattle fairs. At first he had been somewhat disinclined to interfere with the drive to Trallock. His daughter's tear-stained face changed his mind.

In his bed, after his flight from the sitting-room, Mark Doran drew the clothes over his head in a vain attempt to shut out the naked form, the plump and shivering form, the pink and enticing form of buxom Sally McCarthy.

'I am a man of iron,' he thought, 'to flee such a golden opportunity. Not only did I see Sally McCarthy's naked body,' he told himself with ruthless honesty, 'but I also saw my future and I didn't like what I saw. One false move in that sitting-room and I would be a martyr for the rest of my days. There is also the fact,' he whispered to the dark walls and ceiling, 'that I don't love her. I love Annie Mullanney and nothing can change that.'

In the morning, after a fitful night, he was awakened by the arrival of the weanlings. Their bawls of protest, Mark thought, would surely wake the dead! He pulled on his trousers and looked out of the bedroom window onto the haggard. There they were, intermingling with

Daisy Popple's bullocks, their combined breaths forming a white vapourish cloud in the frosty morning air. Mark drew on his socks and boots. What a blessing for the weather to be fine! The prospect of the adventure before him instilled in him a rare headiness which made him giddy when he rose to don his coat.

'Get out of bed you lazy hoor!'

It was the voice of Will Sullivan. The sentiments were echoed by Mattie Holligan, the Ballybo publican, who had cycled the seven miles to keep his appointment. His weanlings were safely in the haggard. The rest arrived from dawn onwards. The owners stood around silently, awaiting Mark's appearance. They would depart as soon as he acknowledged the numbers and identities of their weanlings. His arrival out of doors was greeted by a loud cheer. Mark was excited beyond words. Now the real drive could begin. He hoped he had spaced the times of the three departures right and that the Roscreas were making modest headway.

'Let's all go in for our breakfast,' he called, magnanimously, 'but let there be no delay. The road beckons!'

11

Acting upon instructions from the Badger Doran, Jay Mullanney went ahead to reconnoitre the ground between Philly Hinds' and Bessie Lie-Down's.

During the moments before daybreak Danny Dooley, whose watch it chanced to be, had been alerted by what he believed was the whimpering of dogs in the distance and then came a human command followed by silence.

He rose silently and found the mare standing under a sycamore. The cattle had bedded down for the night in a grove of black alder. All seemed well. Dawn broke and with it came the first twitterings from the sally and alder groves which surrounded the Hinds' homestead on every side. Other birds joined in, linnet and lark, thrush and robin, finch and tit, from every grove, every bower, every conceivable cover.

'Welcoming the new day,' Danny Dooley informed the mare as he led her towards the house. 'They'll be like that now till the morning is well advanced. They don't care that there's a war on or that Poland has fallen.'

In the Hinds' kitchen they breakfasted on tea and fresh pointers. After breakfast they were well and truly sprayed with the spurious Lourdes' water.

As Jay Mullanney neared the crumbling abode of Bessie Lie-Down's he climbed a solitary conifer which towered above the roadway. Two miles to his rear he could barely discern the cattle, now no more than a carelessly-applied, dark blob on the landscape. He peered in every direction in a vain search for the whereabouts of any canines which might be a threat to the herd. He turned his attention to the house but there was no sign of activity. He returned to the soft pathway and, singing at the top of his voice, directed his footsteps towards

Bessie Lie-Down's. As he neared the doorway he was astonished to behold a small, fat man, wearing not a stitch of clothes, emerge from a gable window before disappearing into a sally grove near the house. Jay had hardly recovered from the shock when a large woman of advanced years and covered with several layers of clothes appeared in the doorway.

'Are you the army, so is it?' she called out.

'I'm the Republican army,' Jay Mullanney stiffened and called back proudly.

'Oh them is it?' Bessie Lie-Down sounded relieved.

'Any sign of regulars back along?' the woman whose chin was whiskered and whose face was smeared with grime asked.

'No regulars,' Jay informed her, 'but we'll be wanting hot water for our supper if you'll be so kind.'

'Who else is with you?' Her eyes narrowed. She brushed a lock of dank hair from her face and stood on her toes to look past his shoulder.

'Danny Dooley,' Jay began.

'Never heard of him,' she cut across him dismissively.

'The Badger Doran and Philly Hinds,' he continued.

'Beelzebub's brothers,' she cackled.

'And your own monicker. What would that be?' she enquired with a hideous grin.

'Jay Mullanney,' came the ready answer. 'I'm a son of Haybags.'

'Haybags is it and did he free Ireland yet the ould blatherskite?'

Not waiting for his reply she cupped her hands to her mouth and called: 'Algie, Algie! 'Tis only a garsún from beyond the ways. Come on away in at once lovie or you'll catch pneumonia.'

They both waited in silence for the reappearance of the naked man. Some time passed before he showed himself. Making no attempt to conceal his private parts

173

he ran past them into the house..

'Tell the Badger and Philly they're welcome to all I have. How long will they be?'

'They'll be an hour at least, maybe an hour and a half. Roscreas and an old bull we have.'

'What would you say to a Roscrea and a young bull,' she cackled, this time revealing a mouthful of teeth blacker than any Jay Mullanney had ever seen.

'Who is Algie?' he asked.

'He's a deserter, God bless him,' Bessie Lie-Down explained. 'He thinks everyone is a regular, even the hare on the mountain.'

The small fat man reappeared, this time dressed in a woman's coat. He stood behind his hostess from where he leisurely surveyed the young man with the ashplant.

'Seen any soldiers?' he asked.

'Not one,' Jay assured him.

'Why is he dressed like that?' Jay put the question to Bessie Lie-Down.

'He's dressed like that because I'm dyeing his trousers navy blue.'

'And where's his shoes?' Jay asked suspiciously.

'Boots he has boy. Army boots. When he's leaving I promised him these.' She pointed downwards to her mud-stained wellingtons.

'Do you think he'll pass muster?' she asked.

Jay Mullanney answered with a question.

'Where are you headed?' he asked the small man.

'England,' came the carefree response.

'Why England?' Jay asked.

'To join the army of course.'

'You'd join the British army!' Jay Mullanney exploded and he ran at this likely addition to the ranks of the old enemy. The older man stepped aside and floored the younger with a text-book right cross. Later, when Jay came around he was still groggy.

'No hard feelings,' the small man extended a hand

and helped him to his feet.

'It's twelve months' detention for me if I'm caught,' he explained.

'Does that mean jail?' Jay asked, rubbing his jaw.

'Worse than jail,' came the reply.

'Have you ever heard of the Cork Detention Centre?'

'Not that I recall,' Jay replied.

'I hope you never spend time there,' said the small man. 'Hell is a picnic by comparison.'

Shaking free her scarf-covered locks of grey, Bessie Lie-Down led the way indoors. A black, iron kettle hung from a crane over a turf fire in the hearth. On the hob sat a bastable oven. Bessie lifted the cover and with the handle of the house brush removed the dripping army trousers, once khaki-coloured but now dark blue. She bore it out of doors and tossed it on the ground.

'It won't dry out here,' she informed them, 'not this time of the day. Wring the last drop out of it the pair of ye and I'll throw it over a chair near the fire.'

The small man introduced himself as they wrung the dripping trousers.

'My name is Algie Clawhammer,' he informed Jay.

'That's not your real name is it?' Jay asked.

'It's my name now,' Algie Clawhammer replied.

With bare feet and wearing the woman's green coat Algie accompanied Jay Mullanney to where the slow-moving Roscreas dawdled, not for the first time that day, a little more than a mile from Bessie Lie-Down's.

'Who's your girlfriend?' the Badger called as soon as they came within hailing distance.

'It's a he,' Jay was at pains to point out.

'Has she knickers on under that coat?' The query came from Philly Hinds. Jay explained the necessity for the female garb.

'But why,' Danny Dooley asked, 'should you leave the Irish army for the British?'

'A lot of reasons,' Algie Clawhammer replied. 'First

is I'll get eighteen months in the Cork Detention Centre if I'm caught by my own army. Number two is I want to fight Hitler.'

'And number three?' Danny Dooley asked when he sensed a reluctance on the part of the visitor to continue.

'Number three is money,' Algie Clawhammer explained. 'I'm a fully trained Vickers machine-gunner and that would entitle me to an extra 10/6 a week in the British army.

'Give us a good reason why we shouldn't turn you in? The Irish army is our army and you're a deserter.' Danny Dooley alighted from the horse rail and confronted the newcomer. The interrogation was continued by Philly Hinds.

'How do we know,' he asked with a serious face, 'that you're not a German spy?'

'Don't be ridiculous,' Algie Clawhammer, panicky now, looked from one to the other as he considered flight. Jay Mullanney was amused to note that each of the four in the cat and mouse game were of equal height. It was strange indeed, he thought, to find so many small men in such an out of the way place at the same time.

'Look,' Algie Clawhammer explained, 'there's a Bedford truck in the area with a bastard of a Sergeant and eight military policemen. This Sergeant's name is Rowley and he's the greatest unhung monster walking the earth today. I've already spent a one hundred and fifty-six days in the Cork Detention Centre and if I'm caught it looks like I'll sit out the war there.'

'But what crime did you commit to warrant such a sentence?' The question came from Philly Hinds.

'If stealing army socks and selling them to farmers is a crime then I'm a guilty man. I don't mind the glass-house so much. It's that pervert Rowley. You don't know what it's like in there. Morning till night scrubbing floors, on your knees with your feet in the air behind you. Then there's the arse-lickers who want to keep in with Rowley. Look!'

Algie Clawhammer raised the front of the coat to reveal his discoloured testicles and blackened loins.

'There's this poor fellow there,' Algie Clawhammer continued, tears appearing at the corners of his eyes, 'he was caught with a sheep and he was sent up for a year. Rowley would arrive to his cell at night with an armful of grass.'

'Eat that you bugger,' he'd say. 'It was good enough for your girlfriend. It should be good enough for you. I'm telling you boys,' Algie wiped the tears from his eyes, 'I'll do myself in before I go back there. It's no place for a human being. If Rowley gets me back in there I'm finished anyway.'

A lengthy silence ensued. His interrogators hung their heads. None knew what to say. They left it to the Badger to break the silence.

'Why don't you climb into the rail,' he suggested, 'and come back to Bessie Lie-Down's with us.'

'And Trallock?' Algie Clawhammer asked.

'We'll see. We'll see.' The Badger replied as he stroked the grey stubble on his chin.

Slowly the journey was resumed. Led by the mare and rail they moved towards their destination. Overhead the evening star, brightest of all the heavenly spheres, shone brightly in the evening sky. On every side, milk white vapours covered the broad boglands as far as the eye could see. To the left of the cavalcade a huge flock of lapwing, wheeled and re-wheeled with military precision before settling down for the night. A full moon, still deathly pale, shone serenely on the flat countryside. To the west the mountains and hills submitted themselves to the approaching dusk and in the rail Algie Clawhammer trembled as the penetrating frost intensified its assault on man and beast. Danny Dooley knelt down in the body of the cart and, fumbling through his possessions, located a trousers.

'Here,' he called as he flung it in Algie Claw-hammer's direction, 'pull that on.'

'Oh may God spare you, you're a true Christian,' came the grateful response. After he had donned the trousers Algie sat in a corner of the rail with his legs tucked beneath him.

'How did you come to this pass my poor man?' Danny Dooley asked, the sympathy evident in his voice.

'It wasn't always like this,' the soldier replied, 'for there was a time when I was going great. I had a young wife, a steady job and not a care in the world. Then the wife took sick and when she grew worse they took her away on me to that TB place in North Cork. She rallied for awhile poor thing but then the end came and with it you might say came the end of me.'

'The Lord have mercy on the poor woman,' Danny Dooley made the sign of the cross.

'I knew when she left for that place that I'd never see her again. Just like them poor oul' bitches following behind us,' Algie went on as he pointed to the plodding Roscreas in their wake. 'She was on a one-way ticket. There's no coming back from those places.'

'Don't I know boy,' Danny Dooley lifted his cap and bent his balding head in sorrowful memory. No words passed between them for awhile. They listened to the laboured breathing of the tired beasts behind them without comment.

'What outfit were you in?' Danny Dooley asked after a while.

'First Division of the Southern Command, so-called light infantry. Couldn't keep out of trouble. Joined up after the wife passed away.'

'They'll spot you no bother,' said Danny Dooley, 'with that soldier's haircut.

'That's detention centre regulation,' Algie confirmed. 'At no part of the head may the hair exceed a half inch in length. I'll have to get a cap or a hat.'

'What happened your uniform?' Danny asked.

'Well the trousers is being dyed. I sold my great coat and cap to a farmer. I'll need the money to get to Dublin. There's a woman there. Once your army she'll fix you up with clothes and cash. Next thing you're in London station called Goragh Wood and that's it!'

'I wish you luck,' Danny Dooley said.

'Meeting you people is the first piece of luck I've had since I deserted,' Algie Clawhammer told his benefactor.

'What happened your jacket?' Danny asked.

'It's hid,' Algie confessed, 'under Bessie's mattress. Well there's only one bed!' he raised his voice defensively 'and I was freezing to death when I arrived. It was her body heat that saved me. She might be advanced in the years but by God she's a right roaster in bed!'

'I believe you,' Danny Dooley found himself laughing. He had seen Bessie Lie-Down several times.

'She wouldn't be my kettle of fish,' he said.

'You might not say that if you were numb with the cold.'

'Maybe not, maybe not,' Danny conceded.

'Any port will do in a storm,' Algie concluded for by now they had arrived at Bessie Lie-Down's. The Badger and Philly Hinds were rapturously received. Bessie produced a pint bottle of poitín from the voluminous garments smelling faintly of stale urine. From a dresser, partly filled with cracked delph, she lifted the halves of several eggshells to serve as containers for the bottle's contents. Later when it was drained they sat and stood around the ancient deal table. There were only two chairs and the same number of cups. Wisely the visitors had brought along their own tin pannies. The Badger had drawn a pannyful of fresh milk from a cow not yet gone dry.

'It will colour our tea,' he said.

Danny Dooley who acted as quartermaster, as well

as teamster, opened his sack of provisions and saw to it that no one was hungry. There was butter, fresh from Nonie Doran's churn, pointers from Tess Hinds, scalding tea, sweetened and coloured, an abundance of sliced bacon and cabbage, always more palatable to Ballybo folk when cold and especially so after a drop or two of the hot stuff. They dined well and afterwards they sat around the warm fire swapping yarns while Bessie Lie-Down endeavoured to stitch folds on Algie Clawhammer's dyed trousers.

'The material's too coarse and too thick,' she explained after all her efforts had failed.

'I'll take it,' Danny Dooley declared magnanimously, 'and you keep mine. I'll also have your jacket and here's my shortcoat in return.' Danny would not hear of refusal.

If Bessie Lie-Down's first undertaking was a failure her second was the opposite. She wrung the sweetest music ever heard by any of the company from a tattered concertina which she kept in a hatbox under her bed. Sometimes the visitors sang along and other times they listened while the old woman played and replayed her wide repertoire of reels and jigs.

At eleven o'clock Bessie Lie-Down dangled a long Rosary from her two discoloured hands, its large mahogany beads shining and worn. All knelt while the Rosary was recited. No word was spoken, the only sound coming from the crumbling turf fire which had served them so well.

Between watches they slept soundly. In the morning they breakfasted on boiled eggs and the remainder of the Hinds' pointers, still quite palatable, although staler than they would have liked. The white of the night's frost lingered for most of the morning on the surrounding boglands but before noon it had disappeared altogether. The Roscreas made good headway, considering their ages, and the Shorthorn had a spring in his step.

"'Tis all them females,' Philly Hinds explained. 'They bring out the best in him.'

The roadside was covered with an abundance of the most luxurious grasses, as yet undamaged by the frost. Earlier that month the department of agriculture had notified the Kerry Farmers' Association regarding the advisability of sowing catch crops because of the poor hay harvest, chiefly due to weather factors. While the hay crops had been generally light the weather conditions during the latter half of September had encouraged a heavy growth of good quality grass and more particularly aftergrass. Aftergrass, especially where it contained a mixture of clover, was extremely high in protein content, the ingredient which was generally obtained through the medium of imported foods.

Mark and many of his younger friends in the Tubberlick Branch of the Kerry Farmers' Association had already sown rye and winter vetches which would be available in the spring to supplement the food supply. Others in the cutaways would plant large tracts of cabbage for the same purpose.

As the cattle moved forward the humped outline of Crabapple Hill came clearly into view for the first time. The hill like the Cunnackawneen, nearer Trallock, was an unusual feature of the boglands. In reality it was no more than a mound of boulder clay elevated above the surrounding bog. Some quarrying, which had once taken place there, revealed the unstratified clay loaded with stones, sand and gravel. Such features occurred when the finely-ground boulder clay was dragged along in the lower part of glacier ice and was left behind when the ice melted. Unlike the Cunnackawneen, which was widely renowned as the resort of little people and other denizens of the underworld, the hill was famous for crab-apples.

There was no trace of the two cocks of hay which had been deposited by Philly Hinds two days before the drive had begun, not that the hay was now an absolute requirement. Because of the intense day-time sun over a period of several hours there was still excellent growth so that there was no fear the ancient bovines and the lumbering Shorthorn would go hungry.

Still and for all, Philly thought, the oncoming prime cattle would benefit more from the hay and then there was the novelty after the long months in the pastures. It was decided that Jay Mullanney be dispatched to investigate. They were now at the entrance to a narrow causeway with quaking peat morass of unknown depth at the left hand side. Scarifying tales about bottomless areas in this still developing bogland were legion. It was rumoured that in former times instead of hanging a poacher or a cattle thief his hands were tied together behind his back and he was flung, without mercy, into the quagmire where it might take hours and often days for his body to sink into the depths. The reality was that the morass was no deeper than any of the turf-banks which they had passed earlier in the morning. These rarely exceeded seven or eight feet.

Because the bog was virgin there was none of the normal drainage which turf-cutting incursion made possible. Hence the soft expanses at the left of the upraised causeway which itself was impassable in the aftermath of heavy rains. It was decided to await Jay's findings before venturing on to the quarter mile long passage. The sun was now at its zenith. From time to time the drowsy cattle would lift their heads appreciative of the unexpected warmth. The bogland breezes were pure and crisp and refreshingly cool despite the hot sun.

'I don't like this at all,' the Badger took to fingering his grey stubble. 'No hay where hay should be! You'd think we'd have ruzz some sort of a bird or a hare over the past mile but devil the cratur of any kind in sight!'

'Maybe we should wait for Mark and the wean-

lings!' Philly Hinds put forward the proposal and looked at the others for support.

'We can't do that,' Danny Dooley was emphatic. 'If
we wait, these cows won't arrive in Trallock in time for
the fair and that's why we left a day ahead of the others
in the first place. We have to keep moving.'

'Could we get them to go any faster?' Algie Clawhammer asked.

'Oh sure,' the Badger was sarcastic now, 'no bother
and the faster you make them go the faster they'll drop
and when they drop they'll most likely drop for good!'

'Here he comes.' The observation came from Danny
Dooley, resplendent in his neat army jacket, its buttons
glinting under the bright sun. They watched as Jay Mullanney ran swiftly towards them. He had been gone less
than half an hour. He had covered the two miles back
and forth in a little more than twelve minutes. He ran in
his bare feet. When he arrived, breathless and pale-
faced, he had discouraging tidings to relate.

There had been no sign of the hay, nothing save two
circular areas of scorched earth covered in white ash.

'Burned!' Philly Hinds danced with rage as he considered his wasted journey.

'To the ground,' Jay Mullanney, still heaving after
his run, raised a hand to indicate that there was worse to
follow.

'Dogs!' he announced dramatically between intakes
of breath. 'I'd swear I heard dogs.'

'Did you see dogs?' the Badger asked.

'No,' Jay answered truthfully. 'I didn't see dogs but I
heard dogs, a lot of dogs.'

'How near?' again from the Badger.

'Very near,' from Jay.

'All the more reason why we should wait for Mark,'
Philly Hinds persisted.

'We have our orders and there's nothing about waiting in them,' Danny Dooley climbed down from the rail

with a shovel which he handed to the Badger. He held the mare under close rein.

'I'll take her by the head,' he told the others, 'the causeway's too narrow. When she's safely over I'll come back and we'll move the cows. Nobody's to do anything rash until I get back.'

As they awaited Danny Dooley's return, apprehensive glances were exchanged.

'It has to be those scutterin' miscarriages of Mooley's and their danged mongrels!'

The outburst came from the Badger.

'And we know who's behind them don't we?' Philly Hinds added menacingly. 'I'm making a vow now that when this is over he'll never pat another arse because I'll personally break his two hands!'

'I'll have something to say to the hoor too,' the Badger promised.

'God almighty!' Philly Hinds exclaimed helplessly, 'we're in the middle of nowhere with no recourse to help. Mark and the weanlings must be ten miles back or more and here we are without a gun between us!'

'What do you think they'll do?' Jay Mullanney asked anxiously.

'I can't say for sure,' Philly dolefully informed him, 'but it won't be anything good. There's a thousand acres of snipegrass out there with nothing but sallies, furze and black alder. You could disappear a hundred cattle there and nobody would know whether or which.'

When Danny Dooley arrived his urgency transmitted itself to his companions.

'No time for delay,' he shouted, 'the sooner we get this lot to the hill the better. At least we'll be able to see what's coming.'

In single file the weary Roscreas lumbered across the causeway, the Shorthorn in their midst. Each was anxious to have him as a companion for all his years. It was a tedious crossing. The five human escorts deployed themselves evenly along the file of cattle at the side where the morass beckoned the unwary. There was no danger at the other side, just a soft, minor, depression. As the leading cows neared the end of the causeway the dogs, seven in number, suddenly appeared as if out of the ground. The attack was swift and terrible with deadly consequences. Led by the arch-practitioner of demonry, the blood-thirsty Dango, the vicious pack members, barking frenziedly, swept along the safe side of the causeway, snapping and snarling. They came and went with a fury that was terrifying to behold. Only the Shorthorn was ready for the onslaught. His undercarriage safely concealed at the herd's centre he managed to butt and trample the unsuspecting Bubbles, leaving him still and bloodied on the causeway. The others, Dango, Quick, Doormat, Babs, Queenie and Dolly, ignored the anguished yelping of their dying comrade and disappeared as quickly as they had come. Only then did the herdsmen have time to take stock of their losses. Two cows lay sprawling beyond redemption in the morass, their piteous bawling and terror-filled eyes unheeded as the remainder of the herd pressed forward urgently now with the presentiment that worse was to come.

This time the dogs came from the blind side. They moved like shadows behind their new leader Quick. From behind too came the unheralded sounds of gunshot, one, two, three discharges in quick succession. There came a loud cheer of delight and relief from the hard-pressed herdsmen. The pack slunk into the snipegrass, vanishing without trace, as the Rector of Tubberlick, his service revolver aloft, alighted from the BSA followed by his friend Danny Binge. There was only one casualty from the second affray and that was the unfortunate bitch Queenie whose left rear leg was smashed to pieces by the last of the Rector's bullets. She would have somehow managed to belly her way into the snipegrass but the Badger Doran, shovel in hand, beheaded her summarily with a single, expert stroke. The slowly-sinking cows were beyond help when the Rector, from close range, disposed of them both.

12

Monsignor Daniel Binge on his return to San Lupino after the protracted break, reported at once to his Archbishop to be told that Rome had unconditionally approved his elevation to Bishop. To facilitate a smooth transfer of authority it was decided to postpone the ordination till the Fall. There was much to be done in the interim. After a busy summer during which he prepared himself, to the exclusion of all secular activities, for what lay ahead he embarked on a fortnight-long retreat in a hillside monastery, situated in a remote area of the archdiocese. Here he spent long hours in prayer and meditation. So impressed were the abbot and monks of the impoverished community by his apparent grace and sanctity that they requested his blessing and prayers on the day prior to his departure. His first act upon returning to San Lupino proper was to visit his physician, a third generation Californian of Irish ancestry. There followed what seemed to the Monsignor to be no more than a cursory examination but there was none of the customary banter when the business was over. If anything Doctor Coffey was more serious than was his wont.

'You can tell me,' Danny Binge assured him.

'No I can't,' Doctor Coffey returned, 'because there's nothing to tell, at least not yet. I'm sending you for x-rays just as a precaution.'

'Can you tell me anything?' the Monsignor pleaded.

'Nothing.' Doctor Coffey was emphatic.

The visit had ended without further exchanges. Their next meeting was of longer duration.

'Have a seat.' The doctor had said as soon as the Monsignor had entered the consulting-room. It was the way he said it that prompted the cleric to demand a frank and uncompromising revelation of the true facts.

'Just tell me straight up,' he said.

'I wish,' the doctor spoke wistfully, 'it was as simple as that. I've been in a hundred situations like this and I still don't know how to handle it. You're sure you want this straight up?'

'I wouldn't have it any other way,' the Monsignor assured him.

The doctor, still hesitant, made a poor pretence of clearing his throat.

'From the look of things,' he began, 'it would seem that we are dealing here with cancer. However there is always the outside possibility of a reversal or a remission.'

'It's terminal then?' the Monsignor's voice almost failed him as he requested confirmation of his worst fears.

'Afraid so,' came the subdued reply. The two men looked at each other without speaking for several moments. What more does one say, the doctor thought. This priest is either a very good actor or he has extremely deep reserves of resignation to call upon.

'How long do I have?' the Monsignor asked matter-of-factly.

The doctor did not reply at once. He tweaked his nose and considered the question carefully.

'I don't know exactly,' he replied. 'It's not as cut and dried as that I'm afraid.'

'But judging from all the information at your disposal.' The irritation was apparent in the cleric's voice, 'and your own experience in such matters you must have a rough idea.'

'A rough idea would be the best I could offer and even then I could be off target. I would say that you have eight months, give or take a few weeks, but that's just an opinion,' the doctor added hastily.

'Time for a holiday before they hospitalise me?'

'Yes,' the doctor answered, glad to be able to dispense some modicum of comfort.

'I have some unfinished business in Ireland,' Daniel Binge explained, 'and with your say-so I would consider crossing on the next available liner.'

'Go by all means and when you return we can talk of hospices. There are some good ones and even if it does sound like poor consolation they do make a difference.

'You're a brave man,' Doctor Coffey looked him squarely in the eye as they shook hands. 'I'm sorry I didn't have better news.'

'You can't win 'em all Doc,' the Monsignor was at his most consolatory.

As he walked away from the consulting-room he half expected to be assailed by pain or weariness but he felt nothing. There was no physical change that he could pinpoint. His mental attitude he knew must change. He must learn to adapt. At least there was the holiday. He hoped he would survive it without any great degree of stress. He would have to tell his Archbishop. His sister and her husband would have to be told sooner or later. He would not disclose the nature of the illness nor the fact that it was terminal. She would draw her own conclusion inevitably. He stood for a moment looking down at the bonnet of his car.

'It's tough,' he whispered, 'sweet Christ but it's tough!' Unable to restrain the tears which started to course down his cheeks he placed both hands on the car bonnet and shook his head at the awfulness of what he would have to face. He had seen men die from lung cancer. He had been with them at the end and it had always been a mercy when they had drawn their last breaths. He wiped his eyes with his handkerchief and resolved there and then that there would be no more tears and no more self-pity.

'Next stop Tubberlick,' he spoke the words aloud.

The moment Monsignor Daniel Binge arrived at his sister's house in Tubberlick he made contact with his friend the Rector. The drive had not yet begun although the Roscreas were on the point of departure from Doran's haggard. The Monsignor explained to his sister Madge and her husband Tom about the illness which necessitated his withdrawal from the ordination to Bishop. He had tried to sound casual and had glossed over the nature of the illness but Madge had been persistent.

'The neighbours will be curious,' she told him, 'and what am I to tell Father Dugan? He is the Parish Priest after all.'

'Just tell him I've had a physical setback and I have been obliged to put the interests of the diocese first. He'll understand.'

'But Danny,' Madge would not be easily dismissed, 'you haven't told us exactly what's the matter with you.'

'Now, now,' he said placatingly, 'it's nothing that should cause you concern.' He was glad when he heard Archie Scuttard's voice in the hallway that led to the kitchen. Later as they sped over the uneven road which led to the Badger Doran's residence in Beenablaw the Monsignor decided that he must reveal the true nature of his illness to his friend. Anyway the Rector would know that a minor illness would only mean a deferment of the ordination and would guess that his friend was afflicted with something more grievous.

On their arrival at Beenablaw Monnie the Badger informed them that they had only just missed Philly Hinds and the Badger who had taken the short-cut by the fields to Mark Doran's haggard and their rendezvous with the Roscreas. Monnie produced a bottle from a recess near the fireplace and soon the three were sipping from brimming egg-cups. Since it would have been unthinkable to refuse the tea which Monnie had drawn in a chocolate coloured teapot the moment she heard the sound of the bike, they decided to relax before moving on to Mattie

Holligan's pub in Ballybo.

After the tea had been drunk the Rector submitted his cup for inspection. He had made certain that there would be a sufficiency of tea leaves remaining at the bottom so that Monnie would experience no difficulty in realising her prognosis of his future. He was surprised to see a shadow cross her face. Normally there would be a cheerful forecast but it would seem from Monnie's clouded features that the disposition of the tea leaves boded no good for the Rector. She declined to comment when he pressed her for what surely must be a portentous prospect. He had never before seen her so doleful about the future. As they were leaving he turned and asked her to reveal what she had seen. The Monsignor had wandered absently towards the BSA and was gazing into the green valleys far below.

'Coffins,' Monnie whispered the word.

'That's because there's a war in Europe,' the Rector chided.

'No,' Monnie was adamant, 'there will be coffins, a lot of coffins before this drive is over.'

'Well then,' the Rector tried to cheer her up, 'they will be the coffins of our enemies.'

'Amen to that!' Monnie shrugged off her gloom and wished them luck.

Later as they sat in Mattie Holligan's the Monsignor unfolded his tale of woe. The Rector was silent throughout. He thought of Monnie the Badger's prophesy. As a rule he paid no heed to such divinations but Monnie had a local reputation for being occasionally accurate. The Badger swore that she was uncanny. Always he instantly rinsed out his cup after the tea lest she find some disquieting news about his future prospects as a tenant of the living world.

'What can I say to you my dear friend!' The Rector laid a hand on the Monsignor's shoulder but was unable to look into his eyes. After a long session at Holligan's they had spent the night at Monnie the Badger's. Late in the morning after they had breakfasted on boiled eggs, freshly lain, and pointers hot from the griddle they headed out after the first segment of the herd. But for their intervention at the morass there might well have been catastrophic losses among the Roscreas. Neither the Rector or the Monsignor brought up the matter of the latter's illness again. They plunged themselves into their duties as liaison officers and all-round troubleshooters of the drive.

13

'It was God sent ye.' The Badger wrung the Monsignor's hand while the others crowded round the Rector, the hero of the hour, his still-smoking service revolver poised for any contingency, his face ghastly pale, his eyes bloodshot from the initial shock of the engagement. The cattle, minus the two casualties, were all safely over the causeway and were now grazing contentedly as though nothing had happened.

'It's Mark's loss poor fellow more than anybody's,' the Badger shook his head sadly. 'Down two before the fair starts.'

'I shouldn't worry,' Archie Scuttard proved to be the bearer of good tidings as far as their prospects at the fair of Trallock were concerned. 'Last week at Millstreet,' he informed his listeners with unconcealed joy, 'prices were at their highest for any fair this year and particularly Roscreas which ranged from £2 to £2. 5s.'

Immediately the Badger's gloom lifted. As if to celebrate the prospect of unprecedented prices the Rector produced a half pint flask from inside his leather jacket. It went the rounds until the contents were exhausted.

'Now,' said Archie Scuttard as though he were the commander-in-chief of their combined forces, 'I propose to return forthwith and inform the others of the possibility of further attacks from these accursed curs.'

'Tell them the hay is burned as well,' Jay Mullanney called.

The weanlings had proved a handful from the very moment of their departure. Totally unused to travel they had broken up in several directions after a series of unexplained explosions from the general direction of the deeper heather, profuse and purple the whole way to the main Trallock–Killarney road. There were also outcrops of heavy gorse. The explosions sounded remarkably like discharges from a double-barrelled gun.

Mark was tempted to forget about the weanlings for a moment and make off in hot pursuit but Mattie Holligan was quick to point out that it might well be a carefully planned ruse for that very purpose. Mark's suspicions were directed towards the father of his would-be seducer. Sylvester would have been well used to the terrain. Indeed he would know every bogpool and declivity like the back of his hand. Was he not the secretary of the Tubberlick Anglers' and Gun Club and without doubt the most accomplished fowler in the five parishes. How often had Mark and Will Sullivan seen him striding, purposefully, through the boglands, his gun across his arm, his fowler's bag across his shoulders and, at the side of his head his rakishly perched tweed hat, festooned with trout flies. He liked to think of himself as a sportsman.

Simple, Mark thought, to park his gleaming Vauxhall de Luxe at the roadside and embark on a lightning foray, firing over the heads of the weanlings at relatively close range, and then disappear. The effects might well have been catastrophic but for the area where the surprise attack took place. Also there was the nimble-footedness of the weanlings. If the shots had been discharged a half mile further on there would most certainly have been losses since the region was largely soggy, cutaway, dotted with dangerous bogholes. As it was two of the weanlings sustained injury from stray pellets.

'We'll keep our powder dry,' Mattie Holligan cautioned, 'our turn will come in due course.'

The largest and final contingent of the herd left Doran's haggard on Saturday, 30 September at two o'clock in the afternoon. The aim was to proceed without stop until the hundred and one prime stock were safely deposited in

Philly Hinds' two acre plot where they would graze and rest up for the following day's journey. This second and final stage would see them cover a distance of over twenty miles past Bessie Lie-Down's and Crabapple Hill until they reached the Cunnackawneen for the grand reunion with the Roscreas and the weanlings before proceeding to Trallock on the Monday morning of the fair.

In charge of the motley assembly, consisting chiefly of Aberdeen Angus and Shorthorn, was Will Sullivan's brother Henry, Sandy Hassett who happened to be Daisy Popple's workman, 15 year old Florry Mullanney and, for the final part of the journey, from Bessie Lie-Down's onwards, the intrepid clergymen, Archie Scuttard and Daniel Binge. Throughout the entire proceedings the pair liaised between the three segments of the herd and at night there would be a trip to Trallock where they would meet with Fizz Moran. Fizz would outline for them the procedure which might be best adopted on the day of the fair. He had earlier in the month been in contact with Archie Scuttard and there had also been an exchange of letters between the apothecary and the Monsignor.

In his letter to the Rector, Fizz Moran had pointed out that a dawn invasion of Trallock square would be an absolute necessity if the prime stock were to be exhibited in the most advantageous position.

'By dawn and by this I mean at the very first light,' Fizz had written, 'before the Long Gobberley beef arrives on the scene. Remember it is customary for the Gobberleys to drive their cattle to the town square at six-thirty in the morning which is not too long after the official breaking of the day. But before that,' he continued, 'and this is important, two of the Gobberley retainers and a Gobberley elder, one William Joseph, the patriarch you might say of the whole Gobberley tribe, inappropriately nicknamed Bollicky Bill Gobberley because he has only one, will take up their positions outside the Trallock Arms and prohibit any and all members of the bovine species from usurping their traditional ground. They are usually armed with ash knopsticks and maybe concealed weapons such as batons or iron bars. They will actively discourage farmers, jobbers and drovers from standing a solitary weanling in their hallowed space. I don't know how best you should counteract this unnatural and undemocratic remnant of disgusting feudalism. I will leave it in your own capable hands and those of your friends but remember that I will be available for consultation at any time. Herself sends her fond regards. Her day was made when this morning she received a long letter from your dear friend Monsignor Binge who hopes to be with us on the great occasion.'

In the extended postscript there was reference to the Carabim sisters, Lily and Dell, whose spirits as always were in the ascendancy and who wished to be fondly remembered.

The weanlings arrived without further mishap at Bessie Lie-Down's but alas the three drovers found the grime-covered creature in a most distraught state. Earlier in the day she had collapsed with fright and had been at death's door as a result of an attack on her meagre stock of fowl by several dogs she had never seen before. They had savaged and partially devoured the fowl in front of the house without fear of retribution. When Bessie came around she locked herself into her cabin in fear of her life.

'Did you see any human?' Mark asked.

'Not a single Christian,' Bessie assured him. 'All I heard was whistles for all the world like the pee-weeing of a plover although sometimes it changed and was like a seagull. Then, finally, there was a long whistle like you'd hear from a curlew. The dogs made off. They dragged the carcasses of my lovely birds behind them.'

That night there was no concertina playing but they dined well on the provisions left by Danny Dooley.

'I tell you this now,' Mark Doran promised the still agitated Bessie, 'that you will never more be visited by these dogs and I promise you that their masters will be made to pay and that you will be compensated.'

'Better still,' Mattie promised, 'there will be pullets for sale in the market at Trallock on this coming Monday and you shall have ten of the best or my name isn't Mattie Holligan.'

'And which is more,' Will Sullivan added generously, 'I will arrive with one of my mother's finest Sussex Blue roosters and he's a boy won't leave you long without chicks.'

It had taken considerable time and effort to cheer her up. In the end they succeeded but only after Mark had faithfully promised that she would be visited by Monsignor Daniel Binge who would celebrate the holy sacrament of the Mass in the very kitchen where they sat.

'And I have the holy water,' she said, 'direct from Lourdes and the stumps of sacred candles left over from Christmas.'

Mark Doran was as good as his word for that evening the Rector and the Monsignor arranged a makeshift altar from which the latter said his Mass and beforehand forgave Bessie Lie-Down all her transgressions great and small.

Arriving at Crabapple Hill with the mare and rail some time before the others Danny Dooley had started a fire. They heated the last of the bacon and cabbage in their tin pannies. There was also some cold boiled potatoes in the provisions. These served as an after-course and a special treat they were, beloved of journeymen and drovers since the potato was first introduced in the countryside. By simply raking a heap of smaller coals to one side, placing the unpeeled potatoes thereon and turning them over and over or smothering them with the coals, there emerged a blackened tuber, unappetising to the eye but a delight to the palate. The blacker areas of the skin were picked away by the fingers. A perforation was made to a depth of two inches or two-thirds the depth of a mature potato. Butter and salt were inserted and allowed to melt. Then and only then might the finished product be savoured. The prized delicacies were called re-heater and if you were to ask any of the four if there was better fare to be found on the face of creation they would proudly answer nay.

The Roscreas and the Shorthorn munched late on the ripe crabs, all windfalls, before settling down for the night on the less exposed side of Crabapple Hill.

"Tis a brave man would stand behind those to-morrow,' the Badger cautioned, 'because they'll leave a trail of scutter behind them right up to the top of the Cunnackawneen.'

That night as darkness fell they were visited by the Rector and the Monsignor·who had made a thorough survey of the ground that lay between the Roscreas and the fairy knoll. They brought a dozen of stout and a half pint of whiskey but refused to participate with the four drovers and Algie on the grounds that they had already over-indulged and needed all their senses as they proposed to maintain a ceaseless vigil until dawn broke. They thanked God for the continuing fine weather.

'Look at that for a display,' the Rector pointed upwards to the vast star-beset dome of the heavens, brightened by a waning moon. They had feared that the change in the moon would result in a change in the perfect weather conditions with which the drive had been blessed so far. They were delighted to observe that no change had come about.

Further back Mark and his party and further back still Henry Sullivan and his companions were partaking of the same fare left behind in caches at pre-arranged spots by the quartermaster-general Danny Dooley. The night was one of peace and contentment among the three different groups. The Rector's news regarding the dramatic upswing in the price of Irish beef, bacon and butter was the very tonic the drovers of the five parishes required to boost their morale. The loss of the two Roscreas had been temporarily forgotten, again thanks to the Rector's news from the Millstreet Mart.

As the fire burned the Badger enacted a playlet in which he compelled Jay Mullanney to act as fool. The Badger pretended he was a jobber and that Jay was a witless country lad. The result was that by a series of lies and threats he exchanged a rail of rotten turnips for Jay's prime milch cow. The playlet was loudly applauded by the trio of onlookers.

'I have nothing agin' jobbers,' Philly Hinds was heard to say, 'but there are jobbers and jobbers.'

'Agreed to be sure,' the Badger drained his bottle.

'There's good and bad in every outfit,' Algie Clawhammer put in, 'in the jobber world, in farming, in droving and in the army.' The tears welled up in his eyes as he recalled, for the fireside group, the death of his wife and his unimaginable suffering at the hands of Sergeant Rowley in the Detention Centre.

'If I go to hell,' Algie Clawhammer boasted, 'it will be a picnic because compared to Rowley the devil is a gentleman. Rowley very nearly drove me clear and clane out of my mind.' He looked into the fire, tears streaming down his face. It was apparent that the three bottles of stout and the mouthful of whiskey he had swallowed had made him drunk.

'Can't handle the stuff,' Philly Hinds whispered to Jay Mullanney, 'and maybe that's the root cause of this poor fellow's trouble.'

'You may be facing worse than Rowley where you're going,' the Badger cut across the drunken soldier.

'No! No! There's nothing worse than Rowley,' he

cried out. 'I'll die if I have to and I won't be found wanting but I'll not be humiliated ever again. I'll swing before I go back.'

The Badger decided it was time to change the subject.

'If you ever watch a jobber at a fair,' he rose to his feet and resumed his earlier role, 'you'll notice your real jobber will give the impression that he has not come to the fair to buy cattle at all. He'll take off his hat and scratch his head and pretend he's come sightseeing, that buying cattle is the last thought in his head. If he decides to buy a bashte from you it's because he's sorry for you and wants to take the creature off your hands as a special favour because he's after taking a liking to you.'

Later they slept soundly in their bags of straw. Danny Dooley took the first watch. He had the uneasy feeling that he was being watched.

14

Upon their arrival at the causeway which led to the base
of the Cunnackawneen the Badger Doran and his party
were surprised to see a herd of donkeys arriving at the
summit. The donkeys, fifty in number, upon beholding
the luscious but limited green pasturage at the top of the
tiny hill, kicked their heels high in the air and brayed
uproariously as their handlers, five in number, urged
them upwards where they might graze to satiety without interference.

They had come eastward out of the heather and
most likely, the Badger guessed, had abandoned the
main Trallock–Killarney road because of the inhospitable farmers whose lands bordered this busy highway.
The donkeys were more surprised than the Ballybo drovers who had never seen so many gluttonous members
of the asinine species congregated together in the same
place. The chief of the donkey men called the others
around him as soon as the herd had arrived at the summit. There followed a most elaborate series of gestures
which seemed to suggest to the cattlemen that while it
was all right for donkeys to ascend the summit it was
not all right for humans.

'They're afraid, the ignorant hoors, they're afraid!'
Philly Hinds exclaimed.

'That might be our trump card,' the Badger smiled
grimly as he fingered the lengthening bristle on his jaw,
always a sign that the Beenablaw pensioner had something up his sleeve.

'They're afraid of the little men,' the Badger whipped off his coat and signalled to Philly and Danny
Dooley that they should do likewise.

'Go on over a ways the pair of ye,' he curtly instructed Jay Mullanney and Algie Clawhammer. 'Keep a right

eye on things. We'll be missing for a short while. See to the mare and rail above all.'

So saying the trio disappeared behind some gorse bushes where they disrobed. They covered their faces and their bodies with clay and waited until the donkeys were concentrating to the fullest on their grazing and had abandoned their playfulness.

A frisky stallion, black in colour and of Spanish strain flanked by two young mares, playfully bit each on the crests of their submissive necks before settling down to savour the clover-bedecked grass. Normally these placid creatures would be infinitely more circumspect about how they might best approach such an oasis. Their handlers too, under a different set of circumstances, might have waited until nightfall before releasing the ravenous herd on grazing land wherever that might present itself but this was different. Here was a sacred place, a haunted place and it was their experience from frequent illicit invasions of graveyards and fallow glebe-land that while some interested parties might be outraged there would be no repercussions.

Generally speaking these sacred areas were deserted so that the donkeys recognised a safe haven when they saw one. Moreover, had not their handlers urged them onwards and upwards as soon as the hallowed mound came into sight. The five donkey herders had seen the cattle herd from afar and had made haste to be at the Cunnackawneen first. To their credit it should be said that they exercised no monopoly. They always said in their defence that they were not covetous the way farmers and small-holders were. The Roscreas were welcome to participate as well. They sat at the foot of the hillock and ignored the drovers. Soon the tinkling of coins was heard and they were seen to be playing cards. The chief cast a precautionary glance in the direction of the Roscreas but all he could see was a small man in charge of a mare and rail and a younger man who seemed intent on minding his own business. He was well satisfied to let things rest but he kept a wary eye sideways for any unexpected development. They admitted to each other that they would rather face the fires of hell than stay on the summit of the Cunnackawneen where rumour had it that the over-curious had expired without rhyme or reason and where the unwary could be dragged into the bowels of the earth and never seen in the natural world again.

The five were well pleased with themselves. More than three-quarters of the donkeys had been stolen and the others, largely strays, driven from lanes and byways to where they had escaped from cruel masters. The donkeys should fetch record prices. Word was abroad that there was an unparalleled demand on the north-western shoulder of the continent.

Normally in September and early October there was a heavy demand anyway. Horse meat and donkey meat was much in demand in Belgium, France and Holland where convents and colleges and other educational institutions had re-opened after the long summer holidays. They knew that the herd which had begun to settle into a steady pattern of grazing above them might well be one of the last to be exported because of the worsening situation in Europe. The donkey herders were in no way prepared for what followed. It was the chief of the group who noticed the agitation on the slope. The herd was restless, its collective head now directed downwards to the humans who had brought them safely thus far. Slowly the herd began to move away from the summit, sensitively and silently and then with urgency and then at a trot as the three naked, mud-covered trolls advanced upon them from the other side.

'See what's up boy!' The chief issued the order to the youngest member of the group.

The boy sped upwards obediently, his heart racing wildly, not knowing what monster might confront him.

The terrified donkeys, now galloping, passed him by at either side. He made no attempt to stop them. To obstruct them in any way would have been suicidal. After they passed he beheld the three monsters approaching. At first he thought they must be apes but if they were apes where was the hair and if they were apes why were their private parts dangling in front of them. For a moment he stood dumbfounded and petrified, his legs refusing to respond to his terror. Suddenly he managed to regain his voice.

'Lorgadawans!' he screamed but still his legs refused to come to his aid.

One of the fearful creatures stopped unexpectedly, bent over backwards and cocked his posterior towards the terrified youngster who had never beheld any creature so ugly or so awesome in his entire life. The creature broke wind. The sound was sharper, louder and longer than any the hapless youth had ever heard before but it was to be catalyst that would fuse brain and foot and permit him to take flight.

'Lorgadawans,' he screamed as he ran down the hillock, a plentiful supply of the same commodity as that which had been earlier discharged by the crab-loosened Roscreas, soiling his trousers at ever step. He did not pause upon reaching his astounded comrades who stood paralysed with their mouths wide open. He ran past them still shouting 'Lorgadawans!' at the top of his voice.

Upon beholding the three mud-painted demons from the underworld the donkey herders too took up the cry 'Lorgadawans, Lorgadawans!' and disappeared after the still fleeing donkeys. Later when they felt it was safe to do so they paused for breath. They found the youngster, who had first beheld the fairy folk, in a state of collapse, gasping for his very breath in the middle of a cluster of black alder. They managed to bring him around in time but he insisted that he would never be the same again. He described the grotesque faces and bodies of the macabre trio and averred with a hand over his fiercely thumping heart that the fart he had heard on that day was the equivalent of a clap of thunder.

'I will never forget it as long as I live,' he told his listeners, 'that is if I live.' He went on and on, babbling incoherently, until he was brought temporarily to his senses by his chief who slapped his face forcefully in an attempt to restore his coherency.

'Tell us boy,' he held the youth firmly by the shoulders and looked steadfastly into his wild eyes. 'Tell me true now boy for what your life is worth and tell me only once. How were these men hung?'

Like a flash the youth answered. 'I only saw one from behind and he was hung like a bull.'

His listeners exchanged terrified glances. It was true then what the old people had always maintained, that though small they might be and gnarled and old as the hills where they resided in their secret caverns, the hallmark of the true lorgadawan, the ponderous rear appendage was present. Had they not heard it from their own fathers and had not they heard it from their fathers' fathers and so forth and so on.

'The man I saw,' the youth was rock steady now, his speech reasoned and carefully paced, 'was as old as ever I saw and yet there was a seam at the rear of his balls the very same as a sliotar.'* This final revelation elicited gasps of astonishment from the four listeners.

The Badger and his party made no attempt to replace the donkeys with their own animals after the evacuation of the Cunnackawneen. They decided to rest the cattle at the base of the hillock and to dispatch Jay Mullanney and Algie Clawhammer to the summit where they would watch the surrounding countryside with the field glasses issued to each of the three groups by the Rector of Tubberlick after the losses at the morass. At the

*[Leather hurley ball.]

first sign of trouble half of each of two groups would hasten to the aid of the third should that group be compromised.

The two clerics had held a council of war with Mark Doran, Mattie Holligan and Tom Mullanney. The last-named insisted that they should visit Tubberlick on the Parson's BSA, under cover of darkness, drag Sylvester McCarthy from his bed and submerge his head for long periods in a horse trough at the rear of his premises until he owned up to everything and implicated the Drover Mooleys as well so that all four might be subjected to stiff prison sentences. Nobody took him seriously. It was the sort of unbalanced outburst that one would expect from Tom but they felt that it was important, nevertheless, that he be allowed to make a contribution.

'Let us,' said Mark, 'look at the possibilities. First of all I believe we should eliminate the Roscreas who must surely be very close to the Cunnackawneen if the Rector's reports are accurate and you are generally spot on Parson,' the younger man conceded.

Archibald Reginald Percival Scuttard nodded his finely-wrought grey-topped head in gratitude and was seen to blush for although he was a man who never fished for compliments he was certainly possessed of the grace to accept one when it came his way.

'Without him,' Monsignor Binge interjected, 'we would have sustained incalculable losses.'

'With the Roscreas safely at base,' Mark went on, 'you might say we need only worry about ourselves and the bulk of the herd which is only eleven miles behind.' Mark paused for a moment to allow his words sink in. 'I am firmly of the opinion,' he continued, 'that the enemy will try to pull one daring stroke and I think he will concentrate all his firepower as a result on the third group.'

'Good thinking,' the Rector rose and stood with his hands behind his back surveying the distant mountains.

'I cannot see them trying to come at us at the morass

where they attacked the Roscreas. They know we'll be ready for them. They know we will be better armed than the last time.'

He stroked the shining stock of the double-barrelled shot-gun which was strapped across Mark's shoulders. The Rector, acting on Mark's instructions, had requested it from Nonie Doran with her blessing but with the proviso that it would not be used against a fellow human. The Rector had assured her that it would not be used unless one of their own lives was at stake.

'I have myself been through a war,' he informed her, 'and I never pointed a gun at a human being so I don't propose to start now.'

He had considered briefly reporting the shooting incidents to his friend Mick Malone but he had the feeling that Mark might not approve. Mark had his own way of doing things and the Rector would be the first to admit that it would be the way best suited to the attitudes of the countryside and to the circumstances.

'The question we must ask ourselves,' Mark Doran was at his most earnest now, 'is what we might do in like circumstances. Mattie?'

The Ballybo publican was a shrewd man not given to idle speculation or to exaggeration. He carefully considered the question before answering.

'I am inclined to believe,' he said solemnly, 'that we should prepare ourselves for an attack on the main body of the herd. After all the bullocks and in-calf heifers are by far the most valuable animals we have and from the looks of things they could well attract record prices. A blow here would be the worst thing that could happen to us. Even the loss of a solitary animal would be a severe financial setback. We have an awful responsibility.'

'But,' Mark persisted, 'what do you think they are likely to do?'

'I don't know,' Mattie replied, 'but I feel in my bones that it will be soon.'

'Fair enough,' Mark turned next to Tom Mullanney.

'I think,' Tom said evenly, 'we should reinforce the bulk of the herd ourselves. We would seem to have the worst of our journey behind us and these weanlings are spry. They'll sprint out of trouble and we can always regroup them afterwards. I say reinforce the main herd!'

There were murmurs of assent all round.

'And you Mark. What do you say?' the Rector asked.

'We can have this lot on the Cunnackawneen and safe in less than two and a half hours,' Mark answered, 'if we push them. I've given this a lot of thought,' he became confidential. 'I've asked myself what are the worst things that could happen to us apart from an attack by the Mooley dogs. The dogs won't take on the main herd, not with the Parson's revolver at the ready. They know him now and they'll be anxious to avoid him. Then there's my gun. So what have we to look out for?'

'Stampede,' Tom Mullanney replied instantly.

'Hardly,' Mark replied, 'the cattle are mature and besides there aren't enough of them. Anyway the ground is too soft for a stampede. No with all due respects we can write off a stampede.'

'Fire!' the contribution came from Monsignor Binge.

'Exactly,' Mark returned. This was the answer for which he had been fishing. 'Fire and only fire can stop us now.'

'Would they stoop to that?' There was alarm in the Rector's tone.

'They'd stoop to anything,' Mattie Holligan assured him.

'Fire!' The Monsignor considered the implications. 'We cannot put the possibility to one side.' He plucked a fistful of dry sedge and tossed it in the air. The others did likewise and always the sedge was blown in the same direction, towards the north-east, driven thither by the prevailing wind which for nine-tenths of the year was south-westerly.

'So if it's to come,' the Monsignor pointed ahead to where the entire landscape was rust and yellow-coloured by the withering grasses, coarse and tinder dry, 'it will most certainly come from the southernmost portion of that coloured area we see before us. Fanned by that fresh breeze there is no way it can be stopped or diverted until it burns itself out. Our danger area lies ahead.'

'Then our best course,' Mark was speaking again, 'is to make sure the bullocks and in-calf heifers go around.'

'But that will add five miles on to our journey,' Tom Mullanney pointed out.

'We can't take a chance,' Mark was adamant. 'Let's move these and get them to the Cunnackawneen. It's back then to the bulk of the herd.'

The area in question ran along the left hand side of the up-raised bogland over which they had been travelling up till this. To the right was a deep ravine into which the cattle would certainly run if fire threatened them from the south-west. There would as Mark had anticipated, be no place else to run. Since the ravine was virtually impassable as far as cattle were concerned for over a distance of three miles a fire could be the cause of decimating the herd. Mark was not prepared to gamble that there would be no fire.

Word was dispatched through the Rector that the circuitous but safer route should be taken. The ground was less firm and there was the danger that cattle might go a-bogging but to be on the safe side it was worth the risk. A shiver ran along the back of his neck as he saw in his mind's eye the swiftly-moving sheet of flame on its way from the south-west.

The weanlings and their escorts were now moved at a trot. Mark was anxious to have the danger area well to their rear. The weanlings showed no signs of tiring and Mark was hopeful that he would reach the comparative safety of the Cunnackawneen in far less than the two and a half hours which he had previously estimated.

Meanwhile the powerful BSA headed towards the bulk of the herd with the fresh dispatch for the drovers, Sandy Hassett, Henry Sullivan and Florry Mullanney. They were a reliable enough trio. Florry Mullanney was a resourceful individual of fifteen, just a year younger than Annie. Mark's heart raced as he thought of the girl of his dreams and of his secret plans for their future, not a word of which had been revealed to anyone save Annie herself. He longed with all his heart for her presence by his side with nobody else near, in their own world where words would be unnecessary and where a single glance could set the heart racing and the blood to surge, where the smile on her full lips would dispel the clouds and the shadows and light up his world with such unbelievable brightness and radiance that it became unbearable even to contemplate. She was never far from his thoughts and always her smiling face would obscure the perils and the darknesses that lay ahead. She had become the paramount driving force in his life. He had known with over a year now that nobody could ever fill the void he felt while he was away from her. He had told her so one night as she walked with him under the sycamores. It had all gushed out in a raving torrent of love words and phrases which he considered himself incapable of creating. Such was the spate of his outflow that he never realised he was holding her in his arms, his lips brushing her cheek and pressing upon her neck. When it had all been said he felt confused but her smiling face had reassured him and he knew that the tumbling, tempestuous words had been well received, that she shared his feelings and that of all the people in the world there would always be something special and sacred between them alone.

Jay Mullanney had never ascended the summit of the Cunnackawneen before. Neither was he in the least bit superstitious but Algie Clawhammer and himself were exceptionally curious.

'Look!' Algie pointed downwards, 'you can see every street in the town and look,' he grew wildly excited, 'there's a train, maybe the very same train that will take me out of this accursed country and over to Goragh Station in London.'

'This country is not accursed!' Jay Mullanney fumed and clenched his fists ready to do battle for his native land in spite of his adversary's devastating left hand.

'All right, all right,' Algie Clawhammer was full of apology. 'I didn't mean that. I love this country. It's some of the bastards that's in it I don't like. Here. Try these and see what's to be seen.' He handed the field glasses to Jay. Mollified the young man focused on the streets and the square.

Now it was Jay's turn to get excited. 'I can see people,' he called out, 'and it's like they'd be standing beside me.'

'Any soldiers?' Algie asked anxiously, 'soldiers with red bands on their caps.'

'I don't see any,' Jay threw back. 'Here why don't you have a look for yourself.'

Algie spent ten minutes focusing on street after street, laneway after laneway.

'There's an army lorry,' he told Jay, 'but I don't see any soldiers.'

He returned the glasses to Jay who resumed his examination of the town's inhabitants. Satisfied that the streets had no more to offer he turned his attention to the approach roads. Already there were sizeable numbers of cattle converging on the town. However, he could see none in the immediate vicinity of the town or in the town itself.

'Ah,' Jay was quick to draw the correct conclusion, 'they'll settle 'em down for the night in outlying farms owned by friends or relations and then move them into the town first thing in the morning.'

Most of the cattle would have come from no further afield than fifteen or sixteen miles, unlike the Ballybo herd which would cover twice that distance, in spite of hazards and obstructions. He returned the glasses to Algie and took a walk around the fabled hill. He could discern nothing of note, no secret hollows or caves, nothing save some ancient hawthorns halfway down on the Trallock side. Even in their midst he could detect nothing of interest. Hawthorn raths or circles had the reputation of being likely places for housing fairies. Jay was disappointed. Suddenly he leaped into the air as the hand fell on his shoulder. When he reached the ground again he found himself paralysed and facing a red-faced military policeman. Jay recognised the fellow at once from the description given to him by Algie Clawhammer. Sergeant Rowley had small blue eyes beneath surprisingly long lashes and hardly any eyebrows. He had the sort of face which was devoid of the liberal lineaments necessary for creating a smile.

'Seen any soldiers boy?' he asked in an icy tone.

'No,' Jay replied, 'and if I did I'd be danged if I'd tell you mister.'

'You would, would you!' There was no trace of emotion in Rowley's voice. Two other soldiers appeared as though from out of the ground. Suddenly Rowley seized Jay by the right wrist and held him vice-like in the wake of a simple twist.

'Maybe I can jog your memory boy,' Rowley's tone was laden with menace as he kneed Jay into the small of the back so that the young man cried out in pain.

'Now!' Rowley barked, 'did you see e'er a soldier?'

'Yes. Yes,' Jay screamed in mock agony as he thought of Danny Dooley and his soldier's jacket.

'At the foot of the hill,' Jay cried at the top of his voice as Rowley applied pressure. Jay prayed that Algie would be alerted by his cries. In this respect he was right. Algie had made himself scarce. He had seen the canvas cover of the Bedford hidden between the hedges in a narrow roadway which ran from the town to the northern base of the hill. Algie was now nowhere to be seen.

'Let's ramble down boy and check out your story,' Rowley, still holding Jay's wrist, pushed him downwards to where Danny Dooley and the Badger were discussing the probable nightlife of Trallock town.

'Better let him go,' one of the soldiers suggested as the pair came into view.

'Remember he's a civvy,' the other, a younger man, cautioned.

'Civvies!' Rowley spat out the word contemptuously, 'there won't be many civvies when this war finishes.'

'He's not a soldier,' the young military men laughed as he pointed in the direction of Danny Dooley, 'he's too old.'

'All right, all right,' Sergeant Rowley snapped, 'where did you get the jacket then?'

'Found it,' Danny Dooley replied.

'You didn't find it,' Rowley told him, 'but you can keep it if you tell me where that little gobshite Conway is hiding.'

So that was his name Danny Dooley smiled as he climbed down from the rail.

'Conway. I don't know any Conway,' Danny faced up to the Sergeant.

'Well if you don't you'd better get that jacket off or I'll have the police on you for illegal possession of army property. If we were at war you could be shot.'

'Sure,' said the Badger Doran who had taken an active dislike to the Sergeant, 'and if my aunt had balls she'd be my uncle wouldn't she.'

Sergeant Rowley decided to ignore the crabbed little man who looked eighty if he looked a day.

'We're on the right track,' he told his companions. 'He'll be looking for transport to Dublin. You tell him,'

he addressed himself to the Badger, 'that Sergeant Rowley was here. Tell him I'll have his bed nice and warm at
the centre.'

'You deliver your own messages,' the Badger advised him.

'You'll hear more about this,' Rowley warned, 'con-
cealing a deserter and refusing to disclose his whereabouts is punishable by law. This makes you traitors as
well as thieves.'

'I'm in command here,' the Badger twirled his ashplant and swished it no more than an inch from the Sergeant's nose. The action had no effect whatsoever on
Rowley. He stood his ground.

'Let's get back to the lorry,' he turned smartly and
followed by his companions returned the way he had
come.

'Nasty bugger,' the Badger stuck his knopstick into
the ground.

'You,' he turned on Jay Mullanney. 'How the hell
did you let him surprise you? You were supposed to be
on the lookout.'

'Where do you suppose Algie's gone?' the question
came from Danny Dooley.

'Forget Algie for a while,' the Badger was clearly
annoyed with Jay. 'You go back up the slope young man
and scour the countryside with the glasses.'

Glad to be let off so lightly Jay Mullanney obeyed
cheerfully.

'And keep your eyes open this time,' the Badger called after him. 'Watch for weanlings. Watch for dogs and
make sure you know the difference. You hear?'

'Sure, sure. Take it easy old boy. Take it easy. Bad
for your heart,' Jay called lackadaisically, safely out of
range of the Badger's blistering tongue.

'Just like Haybags,' the Badger turned to Danny
Dooley, 'wouldn't know his flute from his fingers only
for the nails.'

'He's a good lad, just young,' Danny Dooley looked upward to where Jay was sweeping the countryside with the powerful field glasses.

'I don't care how young he is,' the Badger was un-relenting, 'there's too much at stake here.'

'Weanlings, weanlings!' Jay was calling from the summit.

'Where boy where?' the Badger called out as he hurried up the slopes of the Cunnackawneen, followed by Danny Dooley.

'Where?' the Badger asked breathlessly upon reaching Jay Mullanney's side.

'Just around the bend, less than half a mile,' Jay danced a jig as he handed over the field glasses to the Badger.

'Well I'll be danged!' the old man cried out with delight, 'the jigsaw's starting to fall into place. If we had the fat stock now and the in-calves we could tell the world kiss our arses!'

He handed the glasses to Danny Dooley. Gifted with exceptional sight the younger man lifted them to his eyes and was instantly focused on the herd of weanlings. He could clearly see the features of the drovers. Mark half walked, half ran with bent head; Mattie Holligan did likewise whilst Tom Mullanney, although walking, easily matched weanlings and drovers alike with long strides. Danny Dooley could distinctly hear the whistles and other sounds of exhortation as the cattle drew near. Satisfied that all was well he focused the powerful lenses on the more distant expanses of the bleak boglands, all owned as far as the foot of the hills, by some foreign landlord whose name he had forgotten but whose agent charged turbary rights each season to all those requiring turf for their hearths, hobs and iron ranges. Likewise this faraway Lord would exact tolls from the owners of every head of cattle, every horse, cob, pony, mule, ass and jennet, present at the great fair of Trallock.

Satisfied that there was no danger apparent in the countryside about to be vacated by the weanlings Danny Dooley turned his attention to the area between the Cunnackawneen and the outskirts of Trallock. He was confronted by a dramatic change in the landscape. As far as the eye could see there were green pastures, highlighted here and there and everywhere by the bright yellows and burnished russets of stubble fields. He turned his gaze towards the east of the town where the boglands dared to encroach once more on the pasturelands and tillage. He was intrigued by the numerous green pathways which criss-crossed each other all the way into the depths of the boglands. Then he saw the goats moving slowly over the raised brown bog and greener cutaway. Their droppings would account for the green of the paths, Danny thought. His examination swept onward, aided by the glasses. It was then that he saw the human figures for the first time. He searched for dogs and had difficulty in finding any but locate them he eventually did. Like flies on a blanket he thought.

'Dogs!' he shouted, 'dogs and men.' He pointed to the south-west where the figures were fading fast.

The Badger and Jay Mullanney had been investigating the ancient ring of hawthorn where Sergeant Rowley had surprised the negligent Jay. They hurried at once to Danny's side.

'You sure,' the Badger asked.

'Certain,' came Danny Dooley's response, 'five dogs, five men, in one hell of a hurry.'

'Let's have a look!' Jay appropriated the glasses.

'It won't do you any good,' Danny told him. 'They've gone from view.'

'Five men.' The Badger fingered his stubble. 'I would have thought three.' He was clearly puzzled. 'There's the Drover Mooley himself, the Ram and Tiger Mooley. Vester McCarthy would not be seen dead with them but he's behind it, make no mistake. It has to be someone from Tubberlick.'

'Not quite Tubberlick,' Danny Dooley raised a finger the better to air his suspicions. 'You remember when we were buying the Roscreas?'

'I always remember things I pay for,' the Badger said.

'Then you'll remember the Lullagys, cousins they were, one with a half-dead Dexter and the other with a Kerry as old as a bush. You refused to buy on the grounds that Kerrys and Dexters were too small and wouldn't stand up to the journey.'

'I remember. Blasht it we even sent out word in advance that we wouldn't be taking small cattle. Too near the ground. They wouldn't have a sign of a pap or an udder between them by the time they reached Trallock. So you think 'tis them Lullagys, the dirty rotten degenerates?'

'It has to be them. I heard them vow they'd get even with the Badger when they were leaving with their rejects.'

When Mark Doran arrived with the weanlings there were great scenes of rejoicing but the sobering news of the dogs' presence and the five men moving swiftly towards the south-west was final proof, if any was now needed, that fire was indeed the motive behind this last effort to subvert the drive. Mark was glad that he had alerted the trio in charge of the mature cattle, one hundred and one in number and worth a king's ransom all told. Reinforcements in the shape of Monsignor Binge and the Rector were already at the scene. Five good men and true, Mark thought, even if Florry Mullanney was only a boy. He was bred to play a man's part should he be needed.

'The Mullanneys often remind me of mules,' the Badger once said, 'they can be stubborn as hell and thick as ditches but if there's trouble they won't run.'

'Now,' Mark knelt on the ground and signalled to

217

the others that they were to gather round.

'It's my guess,' he began, 'that the Mooleys and their friends the Lullagys will start a fire with a view towards destroying the last part of the herd. Vester McCarthy would have spotted us earlier in the day and reckoned that we'd be exposed at a particular time. Well we won't be exposed because by now the herd will be well on its way to safe ground. They'll be late but they won't be roast beef. What we need now is that horse and rail. How many will she carry Danny?'

'She'll carry the lot of us if she has to,' Danny said proudly.

'Somebody will have to stay behind. You take charge here Mattie. Jay will keep you company ...'

'No!' Jay protested, 'I'm not missing the action.'

'You'll stay here with Mattie and you'll answer to your father if anything goes wrong. Now Danny! How fast can she go with passengers?'

'Faster than the wind,' Danny Dooley shouted back as he climbed into the rail.

15

The Rector and Monsignor Binge now found themselves with the main body of the herd, the Rector some way ahead on his BSA as the soft ground would not sustain the extra weight of the Monsignor who seemed well pleased with himself as he twirled his ash knop-stick at the more recalcitrant of the steers and heifers under his control. Earlier they had abandoned the ancient track which had been traversed by the Roscreas and weanlings, now safely settled at the Cunnackawneen. Florry Mullanney, young and fleet of foot, made frequent incursions into the heather-covered mounds and alder groves along the way, the better to view the surrounding countryside. Sandy Hassett and Henry Sullivan acted as flankers while the Monsignor brought up the rear. Occasionally the Rector back-tracked and with the mud flying from beneath his spinning wheels, made circles of the entire group until he was certain no danger threatened. He was worried, however, and would not feel safe until Mark and his party arrived to reinforce them.

'If I were starting a fire,' the Rector stopped for a moment to speak to the Monsignor, 'I would start igniting somewhere around here, that is if I wanted the fire to engulf a herd of cattle which should be over there.' He pointed to the north-east where the herd should, at that precise time, have been moving towards Crabapple Hill. A fresh, cool south-westerly wind, gentle and fragrant blew down from the hills on their left. It was the sort of even paced, fanning wind that would impel a grass fire more devastatingly than a gale force or a blustery wind.

'There's salt in it,' the Monsignor made the observation as he inhaled. He heard something crackle in his chest. It was sound he had never heard before. A deep racking cough assailed him. The Rector, sensing his embarrassment, drove off to resume his role as pathfinder at the front of the herd.

'Fire!' the call came from Florry Mullanney perched fifteen feet above the ground on the uppermost branch of a sturdy alder. He pointed a finger to where three distinct, pencil-thin stems of smoke had just risen from the nearby sea of snipegrass. The stems, caught by the breeze, dipped and faltered for a moment or two before righting themselves and ascending the ether once more, this time stronger and with red bases which indicated that the flames were catching hold and that a mighty blaze was in the offing. With an unholy chuckle, frightening to the listener, the flames took hold and ran in long sheets northwards and westwards. If, thought the Monsignor, the wind was blowing our way the cattle would be half-blinded by smoke and would be running for their lives by now. As it was they stood placidly, sensing as only cattle could, that the searing tongues would in no way endanger them. The flames had taken off at terrifying speed and in less than a minute there was a smouldering area of ever-increasing, pitch black cutaway, to its rear. Not a rib of snipegrass was to be seen in this burnt-out tract. The fire sped onwards inexorably. Occasionally breakaway ribbons and wider sorties of flame made inroads into flammable coverts and thickets but generally it continued on its course to the north-west without major diversion. As the herd arrived at a particularly rough stretch of terrain, covered with thickets of briar and furze, Florry Mullanney raised a hand for silence.

'I hear someone laughing,' he called back from where he had been flanking the left hand side of the herd. The others paused to listen as the cattle moved soundlessly northwards in the general direction of the Cunnackawneen. They had now safely passed the danger spot and the fire which had run riot up till then had now burned itself out at the other side of the boglands where the herd might well have been but for the foresight of Mark and the Monsignor. Several lesser fires still raged, uncertain of which direction they should take, dependent on the fickleness of stray gusts for guidance. The herders listened.

'It's laughter all right,' the Rector agreed. As they penetrated the thickets and came out on the other side they came across the source of the laughter. There were the five arsonists, followed by the dogs. To say that they were astounded by the unexpected appearance of the herd and herders would be to put it mildly. They stood, aghast, unable to believe their eyes. By all reckoning the cattle should be at the other side of the boglands and should be well scorched by now and yet here they were without as much as a blister. Two shots suddenly rang out, splitting the silence.

Two dogs dropped dead, victims of the Parson's revolver, whereat the other three canines turned tail and took to their heels only to run into the first discharge from the barrels of Mark Doran's shotgun. Mark had just arrived on the scene. A second discharge followed swiftly on the first. A third member of the murderous pack was killed instantly while a fourth, piteously whining, lay writing on the ground.

The casualties included the fleetest of the pack, the mercurial Quick, the bitches, Babs and Dolly and the wounded Doormat, pellet-riddled and bloody. The Rector quickly disposed of the pathetic creature. Death was instantaneous after he had pressed the service revolver to its ear and pulled the trigger. Including the two at the morass, Bubbles and Queenie, six of the Mooley canines had now been accounted for. Dango the deadliest was still at large. He ran between the mare's legs when he saw the danger from the occupants of the rail. The animal had lunged violently and would have overturned the rail but for the skill of Danny Dooley.

When the commotion had died down there was no

sign of the pack leader. The Lullagy cousins lay on the ground, their heads covered by their hands, afraid to move. They lay there from the beginning, afraid to stir because of the vicious cross-fire.

The Drover Mooleys were nowhere to be seen. Their familiarity with the terrain had come to their aid. It would take at least a hundred men to locate them in such a wilderness.

As soon as the Badger alighted from the rail he grabbed Mark's double barrel and poked the Lullagys in their respective midriffs before ordering them to their feet.

'What are you going to do?' Philly Hinds asked in mock apprehension.

'Dang it man,' the Badger returned, 'I'm not a bloody pagan. I'm going to let them say their prayers.'

The Lullagy cousins exchanged woeful glances and then the tears began to fall, large round and beautifully shaped. They coursed down the sides of the cousins' faces in streams, accompanied by convulsive sobs. One soiled himself. The other, more continent, began to retch violently. The retcher recovered quickly when the Badger slipped the cartridges into the breach. Wailing aloud the retcher recited the first part of the Hail Mary. His cousin responded by falling to his knees and offering the response to the heavens overhead where, as far as he knew, dwelt the God who would presently seek out a detailed account of his earthly transgressions. All the while the onlookers remained silent, afraid to utter a word lest the performance be recognised by the Lullagys for the charade it was. As they continued to pray their lamentations grew louder. Tearful mention was made of the mother of one and the wife and family of the other.

'Ye should have thought of them,' the Badger reminded them, 'when ye were trying to burn us to death.'

His charge was refuted by the most pathetic pillalooing during which they endeavoured to explain their positions. They had been forced to go along. They had no idea that the Mooleys would resort to fire. They swore on their solemn oaths that as sure as their grandmothers and grandfathers were in their graves they were innocent victims of an evil conspiracy.

'Enough!' the Badger cried. 'Do ye want handkerchiefs?' Not fully comprehending the Lullagys wiped their eyes with the backs of their hands but the tears till coursed down as beautifully formed as they had been at the beginning.

'Do ye want blindfolds?' the Badger asked.

It was obvious now to the Lullagys that his patience was growing thin, that the time for execution was at hand. The Badger ordered them to stand to attention and raised his gun. Then and only then did Philly Hinds intervene.

'You're a sportsman, are you not,' he reproved the Badger.

'I am a sportsman sir,' the Badger replied proudly.

'Then you'll give these men a sporting chance.'

'I don't follow,' the Badger feigned ignorance, annoying his questioner.

'If you're a true sportsman,' Philly Hinds pressed his case, 'you'll give these poor fellows a sporting chance.'

'Explain yourself,' the Badger aimed his gun over the heads of the cringing Lullagys.

'Give them a run for their money! Give them a space of fifty yards before you start shooting.'

At this unexpected development the tears on the faces of the Lullagys ceased to flow. Sniffling yes and woebegone and shaking with fear but now at least there was a faint glimmer of hope. Swallowing hard they keenly watched the Badger's face for a relenting sign. It was slow to appear but appear it did as he good-naturedly agreed to the proposal from Philly Hinds.

'Fifty paces it will be,' he said.

'Count yourselves lucky to have met a true Christian,' Archie Scuttard spoke with feeling, 'to have met a man not indifferent to distress and with a fine sense of sportsmanship. However, since there are two of you in it it would be fairer if there were two of us.'

So saying he drew his service revolver from the pocket of his leather jacket and twirled it expertly in his right hand.

'Could not be fairer,' Mark Doran stepped forward.

'Let's do it then!' the Rector's stentorian tones sounded like a death-knell as far as the Lullagy cousins were concerned. Joe, the older and the taller, was a natural coward and bully whereas Duckface, which was the second cousin's unwished-for sobriquet, was a weaker character who went along with anything prompted by the older cousin so long as it was well outside the circle of the law. Both had a tendency never to acknowledge the rights or the property of others.

'I take it sir,' the Rector addressed himself to Mark Doran, 'that you will act as arbiter!'

'Delighted!' from Mark.

'Any last words?' the Badger asked as Mark faced the doomed pair in the opposite direction to that taken by the sprawling herd. Since no answer was forthcoming Mark raised his right hand and made his announcement.

'At the count of three,' he spoke at the top of his voice, 'you will get ready and get set and remember that after fifty paces you're fair game. Now the count begins. One, two, three!'

A loud cheer was raised by the eager onlookers at the sounding of the final numeral. The cousins started well and matched each other, step for step, as Mark called out the paces so that all could hear. One would have imagined that the longer Lullagy must surely edge his way to the front but long as his legs were they were not possessed of the piston-like power of the shorter cousin. After twenty yards it was still neck and neck and as the fatal count began to draw to a close the shorter cousin began, slowly but surely to inch his way ahead. This in itself was lawful and sporting. What was neither, however, in the eyes of the longer Lullagy, was the way the shorter cousin ran directly in front of him so that he was obliged to shield him from the fusillade which must surely sound from behind them at any moment. At the count of fifty the Rector fired twice into the air. Although the bullets went nowhere near him a scream of mortal anguish escaped the trembling lips of the longer Lullagy. Then, realising that he had not been hit, he stretched a hand, proportionately long as the legs which should have aided him, and seized the coat tails of the man in front of him. The victim of this most foul interpretation of the rules swung his hands backwards defensively but they were too short. In an instant he was trailing his longer cousin who now employed the same subterfuge which had placed his life at risk during the early paces. The Badger fired secondly, barely over the heads of the runners so that the murderous pellets whined about their ears.

In a despairing but mighty effort the shorter Lullagy threw himself forward and seized the coat tails of the longer. Again he found himself in the van but it was short-lived for his adversary now employed the same tactic. They ran thus for over a mile until the shorter man collapsed in a panting heap. The longer Lullagy did not draw his breath until he reached that blessed area of sanctuary under the double bed in his mother's room.

Meanwhile, the enactors of the deadly parody hugged themselves, danced, leaped and rolled over in exquisite paroxysms of mirth. Then they guided the herd towards the north country but every so often one or another would sit on the ground and hold himself until the most recent bout of laughter was exhausted. To add further to the enjoyment Philly Hinds recalled their encounter with the donkey herders and the terror which they had instilled in man and beast alike.

16

As night fell the cattle lowed loud and long, not with hunger, as they had neatly denuded the hillock of clovers, vetches and grasses as the most carefully tended suburban lawn, or with fatigue but to reassure themselves in the face of darkness and the unknown. One by one they laid themselves down on the high, dry ground until all were resting. They mingled easily without rancour, the old with the young, the heifers with the bullocks and the Shorthorn safely surrounded by many of those he had serviced throughout the languorous days of summer. Now it seemed that the tender act of procreation was the very last thought in his mind. If one listened, the cud chewing of powerful jaws could be plainly heard above the other noises of the night. It was a soothing, comforting sound, an assurance that all was well with the herd now swollen to two hundred after the arrival of the in-calf heifers and bullocks.

To the north of the well-shorn elevation the lights of Trallock town twinkled merrily, less than two miles distant. After the rout of the Drover Mooleys it had been a far less eventful evening. The cattle had been counted and recounted but no further losses had been sustained. All were agreed that the unfortunate Roscreas which had floundered had met a tragic end but the story might well have been worse.

It now seemed certain that prices would be well above average with an unprecedented demand for Roscreas. The last of the bullocks had hardly ascended the hillock when two men alighted from a hired Ford onto the grass covered roadway which ended at the base of Cunnackawneen. Mark Doran knew at once that they were jobbers or cattle-buyers representing one of the meat factories. It was not uncommon for buyers to explore the surrounding countryside the evening before the fair and proffer bids for the cattle they required. They would have a certain quota to fill and this was true, more often than not, in respect of Roscreas. If supply fell behind demand it meant work stoppages at the canneries. It transpired that the better-dressed of the visitors was a representative from the Roscrea factory. After a walk amongst the cattle he asked if he might speak to whoever was in charge. All eyes were suddenly focused on Mark Doran.

'I counted twenty-eight Roscreas.' The buyer whose name was Flannery looked Mark up and down, 'would that be right?'

'Right!' Mark replied.

'I won't quibble with you,' Flannery looked Mark in the eye and paused so that his assistant might confirm that the statement was accurate.

'He don't quibble and that's the gospel truth,' the assistant, a dark-visaged, unshaven fellow with a gruff voice by the name of Gubbins faced up to Mark and then turned on the other onlookers. 'This here is Mister Flannery the buyer,' he explained, 'a man what don't quibble like he says. He offers a price and you takes it or leaves it.'

'What's the price?' the Badger asked.

'The price is two pounds and two shillings a head for the Roscreas and it's a price that might not be there against the time morning comes around.'

Flannery's statement was greeted by silence. Mark Doran was pleasantly surprised. He had hoped for thirty-five shillings to two pounds per head maximum and here was this unexpected bonus without having to stand the weary animals at the fair. They could be driven direct from the Cunnackawneen to the railway station first thing in the morning. Mark considered the amount of his initial investment, thirty head at thirty-two shillings and six pence a head which came to forty-eight pounds and fifteen shillings. Taking the losses into account there would still be a decent margin of profit. Twenty-eight times forty-two shillings amounted to fifty-eight pounds and fifteen shillings, a profit of ten pounds and one shilling. It was, without doubt, a fair profit.

'You'll have to do better than that,' Mark dismissed the offer as he turned away to consult with his friends. They were of one accord. Take the offer while it was still there. Remember the old saying, 'always take the first offer'. Mark turned back to parley further with Flannery who was now being forcibly restrained from flight by his friend Gubbins. Flannery, enraged by this rebuff to his magnanimity, succeeded in breaking away and even managed to reach the car. Before he could enter the vehicle, however, he was dragged back by Gubbins.

'All right, all right.' Flannery reluctantly acceded to his assistant's whispered advice. 'My final offer is forty-three shillings a head.'

'Forty-five,' Mark returned.

Again Flannery escaped the clutches of the man who would restrain him. This time he ran to the car and managed to seat himself in the front. Mark had serious misgivings as the engine started and the car began to move slowly away from the base of the hillock. At risk to his life, or so it would seem to an onlooker unaccustomed to the ways of jobbers, Gubbins stood in front of the moving vehicle as though defying the driver to run over him. With both hands pressing on the bonnet he brought the car to a halt. He then proceeded to drag the still reluctant Flannery from its front seat.

The Badger and Danny entered into the spirit of the exchanges and dragged Mark forward until he and the buyer faced each other once more.

'Make him a last offer,' Gubbins urged his master whose hand he now lifted and brought it down forcibly on Mark's which had been extended, palm upward, by

Danny and the Badger. The others crowded around sensing that a bargain would be struck at any moment.

'My final offer,' Flannery broke free and raised a warning finger in front of Mark's face, 'is forty-three shillings and six pence a head.'

'Forty-four shillings and six pence,' Mark raised a finger to match the bidder. Flannery sought to escape the clutches of his handler but there was now no place to turn. Mark and he were surrounded.

'Give him forty-four shillings and let that be the end of it!' Gubbins seized the buyer's right hand and endeavoured to bring it down on Mark's in an effort to seal the bargain.

'By Christ no!' Flannery roared as he bucked and reared in defiance of his handler's behest. 'I'd cut the hoor's throat,' he shouted, 'from ear to ear before I'd raise him another copper.'

'Give him,' his handler shouted, well equal to the occasion, 'forty-four shillings a head and he'll give you a decent luck penny. Tell him you will sir,' Gubbins entreated Mark.

'I will,' Mark nodded solemnly and allowed his hand to be thrust into Flannery's.

'It's a deal then,' Gubbins raised his hands aloft as Mark and Flannery shook hands of their own accord.

'Raddle 'em,' the buyer called out to Gubbins as he located a large red raddle stick which he handed to his assistant.

'You'll deliver to the station first thing in the morning,' Flannery insisted.

'First thing,' Mark promised.

'I'll be paying out at the Durango Bar all day,' Flannery informed him. 'The women there know me. Just ask for Jacko Flannery. Here's a fiver in earnest. I'll put the rest in your hand tomorrow when you present me with a loader's receipt.'

They shook hands a second time after which Mark

introduced himself and his friends. Flannery informed them that in his humble opinion the bullocks would fetch record prices and the others, weanlings and in-calf heifers, would not be far behind.

Jacko Flannery intended to purchase as many Roscreas as possible before the fair was over as a large number were urgently required by the cannery to meet growing demands for its produce. With volunteers flocking to the Irish army from every corner of the land the retired milch cow assumed a more important role in the nation's economy. An English war correspondent stated that the Irish army was the worst equipped but the best fed of all the armies in Europe. He did not acknowledge the role of the Roscrea in the latter part of his assessment.

Later that night the camp fire at the base of the Cunnackawneen was visited by Fizz Moran and the Rector of Tubberlick. Both men were in an excited frame of mind. Fizz Moran's connections in the bailiwick of the enemy had secretly informed him that the Long Gobberleys would be standing more bullocks than was their normal wont at the October fair. The reason for this, Fizz pointed out, was that the Gobberleys had been buying up bullocks and fat heifers since the British entry into the war on 3 September. Not only would they require their normal standing grounds in the square but in order to accommodate their extra purchases they would need as much more at least. That was the reason why there would be three retainers instead of two in the company of Bollicky Bill Gobberley when he took up his position as guardian of the traditional Gobberley rights in front of the Trallock Arms.

The Rector was in the company of Fizz Moran when the apothecary's source had confided his information. Their informant had once worked for the Long Gobberleys and had always found them parsimonious in the extreme. Terms such as holiday pay and overtime did not exist in their vocabularies. If a man was prepared to work from dawn till dark, wet and dry and survive on leftovers, his job with the Gobberleys was assured.

'Bollicky Bill and the boys will arrive in town about four in the morning on the day of the fair,' the source informed them. He extracted a promise from them given on their solemn oaths that they would never divulge his identity.

'I live near them,' he explained, 'and a rich neighbour is better than a poor neighbour any day because you have nothing to get off a poor neighbour except sympathy whereas there's always something to be had from a neighbour with means, even if you have to go on your knees for it.'

The source's only concern seemed to be the feeding and clothing of his ample family and, whenever possible through any and all means, a few pints of stout to banish his cares for awhile. He was provided with a sufficiency of drink in return for his disclosures.

'The men with Bollicky Bill,' he told the Rector, 'are no chickens. They are wary oul' codgers, long in the tooth and will not be frightened easily. They can box a bit too. There's a set of gloves in the Gobberley stables and there's nothing they enjoy better than to watch the hired help hammering the daylights out of each other. It don't cost nothing and that suits the Gobberleys fine. They'll have knopsticks as well and maybe a pocketful of nice, roundy stones, the size of bantam eggs, handy lads these for pelting at cattle or them that drives cattle. For sure and certain Bollicky Bill will have a blackjack up the sleeve of his coat and no man knows better how to use it. There's many a farmer's boy with a fractured skull that would testify to that. I got a rub of it myself once across the back and all I was doing was trying to come around a new milkmaid for a kiss or two.'

The former Gobberley workman went on to inform

them that the Gobberleys would have in excess of two hundred bullocks and would brook no infringement of their standing grounds.

'Remember too,' he sounded another warning, 'that they will have call on four more men within an hour and there's Bollicky's brother Thade Joe, long as a telephone pole and lean as a lath but shifty and wouldn't be long giving you a nice box of a fist from behind or a tasty tap with the shoe into the poll when you'd be down. Oh a sneaky boyo! Then there's their relations and most of them will be at the fair and although the Gobberley blood is thin 'tis still thicker than water and then there's their own kind, the strong farmers that goes by the same rules and that is keep the poor man down and the servant boy down and everything down that might look for a halfpenny more or a mouthful more or a place in the light. They'll all be on the one side when the trouble breaks out and while they mightn't be much in themselves they have strong willing bucks working for them who would think nothing of kicking the daylights out of one of their own kind.'

The would-be usurpers around the campfire listened in silence as the Rector and the apothecary in turn recounted all they had been told by the one-time Gobberley employee.

'Seems we have our work cut out,' the Badger looked from one face to the other in the light of the blazing fire.

'Not you my friend,' Mark laid a hand on his shoulder, 'and while I have no doubt you'd be as good if not better than any of us I am depending on you to take the Roscreas to the station. They're valuable now remember and I stand to make a profit so you're in charge of that department and when you have the twenty-eight loaded you're free to come back to us because by that time I hope to have our herd standing outside the Trallock Arms come hell or high water!'

A rousing cheer went up at this. Mark continued with his plans for the Roscreas.

'You will take Jay and Danny with you. Danny you will find stabling for the mare and see that she gets her oats.'

'There's a stable at the rear of my premises in the square,' Fizz Moran volunteered, 'you can use that. There's oats at the ready and there's hay and the wife is expecting you. There are also beds for those who require them.'

Those who had not seen him before looked the apothecary over as best they could in the flamelight. He did not look like a man who would espouse the cause of small farmers or law-breakers nor did he look quite like a townie either. He was a nimble fellow for his years and he exhibited a rare sprightliness when he went around the fire and shook hands with every man present assuring them of his backing and friendship at all times.

'This is all very fine,' the Rector raised himself to his knees and asked the question which none had dared to put until that time.

'How,' he asked grimly, 'are we going to dispose of our problem?'

There was no answer forthcoming. All present were aware of the fact that the Rector never posed a question without having an answer at the ready.

'Force will be needed,' he began, 'and I don't mean brute force. What I mean really is a display of force, enough to scatter Gobberley and his henchmen far and wide enough until our herd is settled. Mark!' He turned to the man from whom everybody would expect the final solution.

'I've been thinking about it,' Mark did not move from his place near the fire, 'and may I say Parson that it might be better if you were to return to the Monsignor and take Fizz with you because we don't want you involved in this particular action.'

The Rector was about to protest but already Fizz Moran had seated himself on the pillion of the BSA.

'You're in command here Mark,' the Rector saluted smartly, 'if you require me you will find me at the Durango Bar.'

'Leave the bike outside the Durango,' Tom Mullanney made his first contribution to the conversation and it became clear at once to the Rector of Tubberlick that plans for the inevitable engagement with the Long Gobberleys were well advanced.

'You will find the bike in Fizz Moran's stable tomorrow,' Mark informed the Rector. 'That's all you need to know. If I were to tell you more you would be part of a so-called criminal conspiracy.'

What Mark did not tell the Rector was they had already requisitioned the service revolver and ammunition which had been handed over to Danny Dooley for safe-keeping. It would not be used to endanger life. On the way back to Trallock it began to dawn on the Rector that his pillion passenger was surely the brains behind Mark Doran's plan of campaign. Why else would he have mounted the bike so speedily after Mark had suggested that they return to Trallock and to the Monsignor who had retired early so that he might be fully revived to celebrate morning Mass and thereafter the festivities of the fair. Fizz's stable would seem to be the base of operations and why not! After all he was the only member of the party with true local knowledge and more importantly was not his wife a willing accomplice in all that had transpired and all that would transpire.

'I chose my wife as she did her wedding gown,' the Rector called out aloud, 'not for a fine glossy surface but for such qualities as would wear well.'

'How true! How true!' Fizz Moran shouted into the driver's ear.

'*Vicar of Wakefield* as I recall,' the Rector of Tubberlick threw back.

Upon entering Trallock, before repairing for night-
caps to the Durango Bar, the pair cleared the rear entrance, which led to Fizz Moran's unused stables, of all
obstructions. Even the public laneway where the uncivil
and the unco-ordinated were fond of dumping unwant-
ed articles from holed chamber-pots to sacks of hedge
clippings, was cleared of every obstacle so as to facilitate
the breakneck incursion of a powerful motor bike. The
laneway also offered access to the open countryside and
a network of narrow dirt tracks.

Shortly after the departure of the Roscreas Mark
Doran and the remaining Ballyboites conducted a count
of the herd, now reduced to one hundred and seventy-
two without the Roscreas who would soon be travelling
by rail on a one-way ticket to the midland town from
which they received their name. The remainder of the
herd was intact. This greatly pleased Mark. Weanlings
had a habit of disappearing on occasion, especially in the
vicinity of towns and villages. They rarely reappeared of
their own accord.

'Prime cattle to the fore,' Mark called out, 'weanlings
behind.'

The drovers, more united now and filled with resolve after their experiences together on the drive, gathered round their leader, determined to do his bidding
no matter what. All were eager to see the drive to its
conclusion. They were prepared for anything. They
would follow Mark to any lengths. Their plan of campaign had been agreed. All that now remained was to
launch it into action. Each man knew what he must do.
There could be no turning back, no shelving of plans.
Something needed to be proved on this October morning. There was more than money at stake. The rights of
farmers and freedom to stand cattle at will were as important as the financial aspects.

'Roll on Trallock,' Mattie Holligan shouted as the
first of the bullocks moved down the hillock. The main

road to Trallock, which they joined as soon as they left the grass-covered path which led from the boglands, was crowded with cattle, transports and people.

'The world and his wife are here,' Henry Sullivan had never witnessed such a long and varied cavalcade. Only Sandy Hassett remembered such a scene from a time when, as a young man, he drove fat stock from the Popple pastures with Daisy's late father.

'That was the year after the Great War,' Sandy informed Florry Mullanney, 'and it was the May fair which is not as big as the October one. It was six months after the Armistice. We didn't all come back. I left a brother behind at Passchendale.'

Florry Mullanney had never spoken to Sandy Hassett before. He had seen him often enough standing outside the Protestant Church at Tubberlick on Sundays. Everybody said he was a quiet man and honest too who minded his own business. He was a big man with a frank, round face and the bluest eyes Florry Mullanney had ever seen.

'Was your brother older or younger than you?' Florry asked.

'Younger,' Sandy Hassett replied, 'he was only sixteen but he was big like me and he passed for a man.'

'And what age were you?' Florry asked.

'I joined up at eighteen and I was home in time to spend my twenty-first birthday in Vester McCarthy's. Spent all my discharge money too but I was glad to be home. You won't catch me volunteering this time!'

As they neared the town they passed numerous hay-carts loaded with wynds of hay, assloads of thatching scollops in neatly tied bundles of one hundred and countless butt carts filled with potatoes. There were horse-rails of mangolds and turnips and hundreds of weary Roscreas, all ambling wearily towards town, singly and in small groups. There were novelty items also, thrushes and finches in home-made cages of sally bough, decorated walking sticks of holly, hazel and blackthorn, clowns hats of plaited straw, wicker-work baskets and panniers and strings of golden onions several yards long. There were clamped rails of turf, black, brown and mixed drawn by horses, ponies, mules and donkeys. There were open carts laden with boxes of apples, pears and plums.

'Take it all in Florry,' Sandy Hassett extended a hand all around, 'it will never be the same again. It never is lad.'

'At Passchendale,' Florry Mullanney asked, 'how did your brother die?'

'His head was blown off.'

'Sorry,' Florry whispered.

'War!' said the older man, 'bloody war.' They walked silently for awhile after that, Florry vainly trying to match steps with is new-found friend.

'I'll have to leave you now for awhile,' Sandy Hassett declared.

He withdrew the service revolver from inside his trousers and spun the full chamber before returning it to its resting place. Tom Mullanney joined him with Mark Doran's double-barrelled shotgun neatly bound in hessian. The pair took their leave in turn of the others, of Mark Doran, the brothers Will and Henry Sullivan, of Mattie Holligan and finally, of Florry Mullanney. They ran, one behind the other through the suburbs. They attracted no attention. The covered shotgun was taken for a cudgel and the running pair for no more than small farmers endeavouring to forestall break-away heifers.

As they passed through the town they noted that the bigger streets were already filled to overflowing with cattle. They had already passed many stationary groups in the suburbs where they would spend the morning and forenoon until disposed of by their owners. Indeed on more disastrous occasions they would be obliged to wait until nightfall before the cattle were bought at deflated prices. It had been clear from over-night and early morning bidding that this would not be one of those occasions. Demand was brisk.

Outside the Trallock Arms Bollicky Bill Gobberley stood with a knopstick in his hand and a wad of Bendigo tobacco in his mouth. Occasionally he spat. All around on the dry flag-walk were the circular stains of rheumy, discoloured discharges. It was clear that Bill Gobberley was as determined to hold onto his own personal space as he was to that of the Gobberley bullocks which would shortly appear. This time, as if forewarned by some sixth sense, the Gobberleys had taken the precaution of erecting flimsy, wooden barriers, three in number, but so well assigned that the three retainers had little difficulty in keeping all bovine trespassers at bay. All around, outside the enclosed space, hundreds of cattle in groups of varying sizes submitted themselves for constant inspection. None would escape the discerning scrutinisation of jobbers, buyers and, very often, knackers dispatched by their masters to pinpoint the locations of likely bargains.

Jacko Flannery who stood in the hotel foyer with a glass of whiskey in his hand often marvelled at the cunning of local knackers whose true vocations lay not in locating under-priced cattle but rather in identifying backward and uninformed rustics who could be panicked into selling in a hurry if the knacker was proficient at his job. Only that morning a knacker had complained to Flannery that he would require an extra commission as his immortal soul was in danger of damnation. Intrigued, Jacko Flannery asked for details.

'The last time I was in confession,' the knacker lamented, 'the priest told me he could not give me absolution over I taking down small farmers all the time.'

'Next time you go to confession,' Flannery advised him, 'you tell the priest your sins and keep your business to yourself.'

Marvel as he so frequently did at the wiles of knackers he marvelled even more at the sheer audacity of the Long Gobberleys of Gortnagreena. On his way into the hotel he had asked good-humouredly if there would be any Roscreas among the arrivals which were due to appear within the hour at the sacred precincts in front of the hotel. Bollicky Bill Gobberley had answered with a heavily reinforced spit which missed Jacko Flannery's brown boots by a fraction of an inch. Everyone in the cattle business were aware of the fact that the Gobberleys had been poaching space for years but all would likewise admit that as far as well-finished bullocks were concerned the Gobberleys led the field.

'Bullocks is their business,' the knackers admitted. 'Bullocks is what they're good at. Bullocks is all they're good at!'

Jacko Flannery saw the motor bike before he heard it. He saw the driver and the pillion passenger. He saw the guns but because of the helmets and goggles he could not see the faces of the armed men, the driver now revving relentlessly, scattering cattle as well as men and boys to left and right, the shattering staccato of the powerful engine alerting the entire square to the imminence of what might well be deadly action.

The pair of riders, by their very appearance, were enough in themselves to instil fear into the most stouthearted. The helmets and goggles provided them with the most outlandish appearance. Mark had chosen his assault unit after the most careful consideration, Tom Mullanney because he was fearless and a hothead and Sandy Hassett firstly because he had been a dispatch rider in France during the Great War and secondly because he was ice-cool. He was also a crack shot with a revolver or indeed any other kind of firearm. Sandy Hassett was in command of the operation. Mark had made it quite clear to Tom that the former dispatch rider was to be obeyed unconditionally and immediately. As the speeding bike bore down upon an astonished and almost paralysed Bollicky Bill Gobberley he gulped in terror and accidentally swallowed the juicy tobacco wad as well as a mouthful of enriched spittle which he had been accumulating for some time preparatory to squirting it on to the flagstones at his feet.

The bike screeched to a sudden halt inches from where Bill Gobberley stood. Not for all the tobacco in Virginia could he have moved a foot even if he had wanted to. The helmeted, goggled driver had temporarily hypnotised him with the intensity and ferocity of his gaze. Suddenly Tom leaped from the pillion and raised the gun aloft.

'In the name of the Republic,' he shouted for all to hear, 'I declare this ground the property of the people of Ireland from this day forth and I order all imperialists to quit this ground this instant minute under pain of death!' So saying he discharged the first barrel of the shotgun into the air. At that moment, without dismounting, Sandy Hassett aimed his revolver at the feet of Bollicky Bill Gobberley. He fired not once but six times as the elderly bullock producer danced as he had never danced before. Bollicky Bill Gobberley had been a man renowned for his composure, a sort of deadpan character who could not and would not be ruffled. That image of Bill Gobberley was to change forever after his dancing display on the spit-covered flagstones outside the Trallock Arms Hotel.

In the doorway of the same establishment Jacko Flannery knew not whether to laugh or cry; to laugh at the dancing figure of Bollicky Bill or to cry because one of the bullets might well put a sudden end to his own eventful life!

Onlookers, all it must be said from a safe distance, whispered that it must surely be an IRA unit, specially mobilised for the occasion such was the suddenness and violence of the attack, such was the daring and the co-ordination.

The Gobberley retainers had remained absolutely stockstill from the moment Tom had dismounted. Not a word or a look was exchanged. They might be loyal enough to the Gobberleys as long as they were fed and paid but there was nothing in their agreement which obliged them to put their lives at risk.

When the revolver fire ceased Bollicky Bill Gobberley took advantage of the lull to make good his escape. He ran through the fair, mouthing unintelligible warnings about woeful events to come. Looking behind him fearfully and, by means of eye-rolling and terror-inducing signals, he urged all and sundry to run for their lives as he was doing. At the entrance to Healy Street he was arrested by a relative who shook him soundly and slapped his face several times in an effort to restore him to normality. When this failed he dragged him into a brimming hostelry, known as the Bus Bar, and poured a brandy down his throat. Only then did he muster sufficient coherence to make himself understood.

'Thade Joe won't like this,' the relative said. 'Thade Joe won't like this at all!'

'If you're not gone out of here before the count of three,' Tom aimed the shotgun in the direction of the Gobberley retainers, 'I'll blow the balls off the three of you.'

The retainers were streaking through the fair before he could even commence his count.

From the doorway of the Trallock Arms Jacko Flannery observed the figure of Mark Doran at the head of the mixed herd from which Jacko had purchased the twenty-eight Roscreas the evening before. The lightweight barriers were thrown aside by an old man. Jacko recognised him from the previous evening. It took all of five minutes to fill the space in front of the hotel.

'Well done young man!' Jacko Flannery shook hands with Mark Doran and looked around for the BSA. There was no trace of the powerful bike or its goggled riders.

Shortly afterwards they breakfasted lavishly in Moran's kitchen. Gertie and her husband Fizz had a grandstand view of the action from beginning to end. Later there might be retribution but for the moment there was the sweet taste of victory. An ancient wrong had been righted and the incident would go down in the history of Trallock town as one of the more significant happenings of the early decades of the twentieth century.

When the Gobberley bullocks and fat heifers arrived at the town's outskirts, their drovers were told of all that transpired by Bollicky Bill who had already reported the incident to the barracks of the civic guards. The orderly immediately contacted his superintendent who set an investigation in motion since it was believed that a local unit of the IRA was involved. Meanwhile, for the first time in the history of the Gobberley family, they had to settle for a place in one of the town's unfrequented laneways which, and everybody agreed, was a terrible come down for people who thought they owned the world. 'As well as being long,' Jacko Flannery warned, 'the Gobberleys are also deep!'

'Which means?' Mark asked.

'Which means,' Jacko replied, 'that this affair is not over yet but I suspect you know that already without my telling you!'

Less than half an hour after the Gobberley flight two armed detectives, an uniformed sergeant and the local superintendent arrived at the scene of the shooting. Despite repeated questioning they failed to glean one iota of information from the cattle owners. When asked what make of motor cycle was involved every man and boy, without exception, asked: 'What motor cycle?'

When asked if he had given his motor cycle to any unauthorised person the Rector of Tubberlick answered that he had not. When asked if the cycle might have been stolen he answered that it might well have been.

When asked if he knew of its present whereabouts he answered, truthfully, that he did not.

17

When Algie Clawhammer eventually made his way to Trallock Station he found an empty wagon without difficulty. A friendly loader had provided him with a canvas coverlet, a billycan of tea and a sandwich. Algie Clawhammer, formerly, Patsy Conway, weak and exhausted, fell into a deep sleep. When he awoke several hours later he found himself looking up into the smiling face of Sergeant Greg Rowley.

'If there's three things that annoy me more than anything else in this world,' Sergeant Rowley knelt on Algie Clawhammer's chest as he spoke, 'they are the sight of a soldier without a uniform, a soldier who's dirty and a soldier who has deserted and you Pom Conway are all three rolled up in one. You dirty little gobshite. If we get into this war and I hope we do you'll be shot for sure. All right get up!'

Algie Clawhammer rose to his feet, his eyes dazzled by the pair of torchlights which were fully trained on his features by the two military policemen who accompanied the Sergeant.

'Stand to attention or have you forgotten!' Sergeant Rowley produced a belt from his overcoat pocket.

'Seen this before Pom!' He held the double-buckled leather belt aloft the better for Algie to view.

'Don't call me Pom!' Algie's voice sounded tranquil and composed.

'I'll call you whatever I bloody well like Pom because you are a Pom. Isn't he a Pom soldier?' He turned to the nearest of the two Corporals for affirmation.

'He looks like a Pom all right,' came the response. There was some truth to what the Corporal said. The Pom Conway, as Algie was called by those who wished to provoke him, bore a certain facial resemblance to the

Prussian Pomeranian so beloved of old ladies of the so-called ascendancy. They and many of their imitators retained the crinkly-faced toy dogs and moth-eaten furs to show that they were still special even if the sovereign decrees of the Irish Free State ordained otherwise. Unfortunately, for any tiny man or woman with excessively wizened or wrinkled features, the tag of Pom became inevitable in the course of time.

Algie's full Christian name was Patrick Desmond Conway. Paddy was the name by which his late parents and his friends always addressed him.

'You will call me,' fully aware that he was well within his rights, Algie spoke manfully, 'by my rank which is Private and by my surname which is Conway.'

Sergeant Rowley was, for once, speechless. Instead of attempting to make verbal retort to this inalienable right he spun the luckless Algie around and, seizing his hands, tied them together with the double-buckled belt.

'Let's see you get out of this one you stinking little Pom!' Sergeant Rowley turned him about face and delivered a staccato of spittle-enriched, army swear-words straight into Algie Clawhammer's face.

"Tenshun!' He finally shouted at which Algie immediately sprung to regulation attention, his eyes looking through those of Sergeant Rowley, much to the secret delight of the two Corporals standing dutifully in the background, their torches still beaming on the shackled Private's face.

'I have certain rights,' Algie drew himself unsuccessfully upwards.

'You have no rights soldier,' the Sergeant shot back. 'A private soldier has no rights and no property. The army owns your clothes and the army owns your body and the army owns your balls and the army owns your soul. Therefore, I own your soul. Remember that when you're in front of a firing squad you little pom-faced prick!'

The Corporals laughed dutifully when their Sergeant turned on them reproachfully for the approbation which they had forgotten to contribute.

'You know what you own Private?' Rowley was in his element in a role which he knew by heart and in which he had given star performances a hundred times or more, 'you own the twenty-seven inches of ground between your boots unless you die, of course, and then we'll do better by you but for the present that is exactly what you own soldier, twenty-seven inches between your boots and that's just the line between your boots, not the area, and it is an invisible line which means you effectively own sweet bugger all. Now, by the left, quick march!'

The foursome alighted from the wagon, led by Sergeant Rowley who was in turn followed by the prisoner. The two military policemen, in close order, brought up the rear. On the platform the air was cold and crisp. The dawn, freshly-broken, had shed its earlier greyness and dispelled its mistiness to reveal a bright blue sky overhead. The platform was alive with movement. A passenger train, still empty, awaiting its morning complement stood idle while further down the line engines shunted cattle trucks to their appointed sidings. Most of the activity stopped as the noisy tramp of army boots made itself heard. All unoccupied eyes were trained upon the prisoner. The man who had earlier given Algie the billy-can of tea and the sandwich looked on in dismay. He was a conductor on the passenger train which must shortly vacate the station for Limerick, Dublin and Holyhead. From his experience of people he would judge the prisoner to be a decent man. If he knew anything he knew that the poor fellow had also seen his share of trouble, and most likely, would see more. He also felt, but again he was only guessing, that he was a man who would always be in trouble. He had that sort of face. Looking neither to left or right the three escorts and prisoner marched smartly along the platform past a waiting room where startled passengers leaned forward to have a peek at the cause of all the furore. He must be a terrible fellow indeed, they thought, this insignificant but obviously dangerous creature who required three well made soldiers to guard him. It reinforced the views of the more cautious of the observers that one should never judge by appearances. The fellow was surely a thief, maybe even a murderer.

As he marched, Algie Clawhammer thought about his wife's funeral. He had felt little at the graveside. From all sides his hands had been pumped by friends and relations. His tears although plentiful were nevertheless, he felt, more ritual than anything else. Anyway he had been sustained by a brother and sister, the former dead and buried like his wife, both victims of a scourge as bad as Cromwell, the accursed plague of tuberculosis.

It was when he went home to the little room they had rented after they married that he was physically smitten by the most overpowering grief. The aftermath of her death had been the blackest time of his life. There would be bad times after that but none would ever compare with that first shock when he found himself deserted and alone in the tiny confines where they had loved each other so dearly for so short a time.

The moment they left the platform Sergeant Rowley called a halt. Realising that it might not be wise to march their prisoner through the fair which had now spilled over almost to the very area where they stood it was decided that the local gardaí should be contacted. One of the force could then be dispatched to the outskirts of the town where the Bedford truck with its driver, a Second Lieutenant and twelve armed troops were waiting. There was the danger that the prisoner might be taken for a member of the IRA and since the town would play an innocent host to many sympathisers on such an occasion there was no point in taking chances. Antigovernment and anti-British feeling was high among a number of local families, some of them influential. Some days before, a man from the town had been arrested with his English girlfriend in the vicinity of Salisbury Plain in England. Maps had been found in his possession and a subsequent search of the car revealed that there were explosive substances and a notebook with incriminating names and addresses in the book. In Coventry a young man from the north of Trallock parish had been arrested after a raid on his flat. Several rounds of ammunition, a rifle and a large quantity of explosive substances were found beneath the floorboards. There was no doubt in anybody's mind but that the materials found would have been used against British army personnel and, as a consequence, against innocent civilians. Both suspects faced long prison sentences and the girlfriend of the first, who was a mere dupe, would not be spared either. In its blindness the English legal system unwittingly fostered numerous atrocities because of its pomposity, its ignorance of history and its bias towards Irish suspects. There had been demonstrations outside the gates of the Trallock Catholic Church the previous Sunday and there would undoubtedly be further demonstrations during the fair although many townspeople declared with some emphasis that while the demonstrators consisted of a small hard core of IRA members the majority were ne'er-do-wells and petty criminals attracted to the Republican cause by what seemed to them to be its anti-establishment, anti-law-and-order ethos. Then there were the hotheads who were anti-everything. These too found comfort under the IRA umbrella, an umbrella which folded and unfolded and whose radius lengthened and shortened with the ebb and tide of the war. The international policy of the movement at the time of the great October fair of Trallock was clear-cut and unequivocal. It was anti-British and pro-German.

Sergeant Rowley dispatched one of his Corporals to the station ticket office with instructions to ring the garda barracks. He returned briskly with the news that the clerk in charge of the ticket office had adamantly refused to let him use the phone without written instructions from the Superintendent of the garda síochána or the Corporal's commanding officer. In a rage Sergeant Rowley went to the ticket office and confronted the clerk, a mild-mannered, moustachioed man, with rimless spectacles and a quizzical air.

'Listen you son of a bitch,' Rowley opened, 'I am hereby commandeering this phone under the Emergency Act!'

'And I,' said the clerk, 'am requesting you for your identity papers under the same act.'

'Here is a warrant,' Rowley produced the requisite document, 'for the arrest of three army deserters. You will see that two names have been crossed out. The third is waiting outside for army transport which will take him to the nearest army barracks where the commanding officer will conduct a preliminary hearing since this is a court-martial charge.'

What Rowley said was true enough. The nearest barracks was Ballymullen in Tralee and already the OC in this Kerry outpost had presided over the two preliminary hearings the previous week. Both the accused were returned for court-martial to the Curragh army headquarters in County Kildare. There they would be held in the glasshouse until their trial.

'You may use the phone,' the clerk returned to his paper work after he had admitted Rowley to the ticket office.

Sergeant Rowley made contact with the local police. The barrack orderly advised him that there would be some delay, not on the part of the gardaí but the driver of the Bedford would have his work cut out to negotiate the busy streets, jam-packed with cattle and people not to mention horses, mules and asses. The orderly offered the use of a cell pending the lorry's arrival but Sergeant Rowley declined on the grounds that there were too many unruly elements in the town.

'If there's any confusion,' he told the orderly, 'my prisoner could escape and we can't have that.'

When the orderly suggested that a member of the force could be made available he was assured that the army was in command of the situation. It was the dismissive manner in which his kind offer had been turned down that disgruntled the orderly.

'Just so long as you're sure,' he said bitingly as though Sergeant Rowley might not have the acumen to handle a civilian incident.

'Just send somebody for the bloody lorry will you!' His aggravation was meat and drink to the orderly whose indifferent whistling nettled Rowley.

'Listen officer,' he spoke in low tones, 'if I had those troops behind me I could take over this bloody town in ten minutes!'

'Ah 'tisn't here you should be at all,' said the orderly, 'but over in Poland.' He hung up at once knowing that this lop-sided compliment would further exasperate the unpleasant man at the other end.

The first cattle were moving upwards from the fair towards the loading sidings. Already several groups had by-passed the passenger entrance and were now milling near the entrance to the sidings where the railway loaders awaited them. Without a receipt from the loading porters the downtown cattle buyers would refuse to hand over money for their purchases. After the bargain had been struck the cattle would be streaked with raddle or their rumps clipped of small quantities of hair with scissors or shears to a particular design. Each cattle buyer and each jobber had his own particular brand. As soon as the cattle were boarded at an average of twelve to the wagon the loaders would issue receipts for size, breed, age and numbers of cattle. These receipts were handed over by the drovers to the cattle owners who repaired to the pub favoured by the jobber or buyer who had purchased their cattle. Upon examination of the loaders' dockets the buyers handed over the money but not before they demanded and received luck money on every head of cattle paid for.

The loading of cattle to the wooden wagons was a job which demanded great skill and deep understanding of the moods and precocity of the unpredictable bovines which arrived at this point of dispatch all day and all night in their hundreds until by the following morning a grand total of 2,280 cattle in 240 wagons would leave the Trallock sidings for their various destinations. Drovers from the surrounding villages and towns accounted for another 4,000 on the hoof while small-holders and individual farmers accounted for another 1,500 composed of ones and twos and threes.

Altogether 8,500 head of cattle changed hands at the great October fair of 1939. There were no returns, that is to say cattle which would be taken home again due to poor prices regardless of the journey. Because of an insatiable demand by the native canneries and overseas agencies, exclusively British, everything on offer was purchased by early evening. The Ballybo Roscreas were among the first groups to arrive at the entrance to the railway station. Considering all they had been through they might have looked far worse. There were a few among them almost overcome by fatigue and drowsiness but they were carried along albeit reluctantly, by the general impetus of the herd and the cajoling, the whistling, the whooping and all known forms of verbal inducement. When all these failed sticks were used but at all times with great skill and care. Not once during the entire drive was a single Roscrea struck in anger or with any great force. The only damage inflicted was by canines and always at the instigation of the human.

When the Badger, Danny and Jay arrived at the station entrance with the twenty-eight Roscreas they had been held up by two tollsters with leather satchels slung across their backs and ticket machines in their hands. Also in the vicinity was a supervisor, a craggy-faced individual, whose function was to make immediate contact with the gardaí should owners refuse to pay the toll for the cattle in their care. The first act of deception perpetrated by the Badger was to shoo Jay Mullanney on ahead with several of the Roscreas. When the supervisor blocked their way with a string of oaths and a cudgel he was roundly derided by the Badger.

'Can't you see he's deaf and dumb,' the Badger said.

Suspicious but taken aback nevertheless the supervisor moderated his profanations and resorted to a form of sign language which clearly indicated that the mute would be deprived of his teeth and maybe other objects unless he paid six-pence toll money on each of the seven Roscreas which had broken away from the others.

'Blasht you for a heartless hoor!' the Badger leaped in front of the supervisor and flourished his ash knopstick, 'that poor young fellow hasn't a copper to his name and he's a widow's son to boot!'

The supervisor although well used to all the forms of subterfuge employed by cattle owners to avoid paying toll was seen to be in some perplexity but still determined to extract his dues.

'Here's a shilling out of my own pocket,' the Badger extended a palm with a solitary shilling glistening on its surface. The supervisor looked around and saw that his lackeys were taken up with the remainder of the herd from which the trespassers had broken away. Skilfully he palmed the shilling and placed it in a coat pocket which had already been partially filled with sawdust to stifle any clinking which might occur when the new arrival joined the other outlawed tribute already accumulating there. Reluctantly the Badger paid the toll on the remainder of the Roscreas and, since the supervisor and the tollsters were under each other's gaze, there was no opportunity to defraud further the absent earl and his unwary agents.

The Badger Doran waited patiently while the chief loader meticulously completed the receipt which would account for the surviving twenty-eight Roscreas. All were now safely aboard the wagons which would transport them to their final destination.

'I wonder if they have any idea?' Jay Mullanney put the question to Danny Dooley.

'Naw,' Danny replied, 'cows think grass and maybe hay and the bull once a year.

The Badger carefully folded the receipt and secreted it in a leather purse which he wore round his neck. Calling the chief loader aside he handed him a florin for a drink. The token would be added to the many others which the loaders received all through the day. The money was evenly divided after the last head of cattle had been placed aboard. The Badger would recoup the amount later from Mark as he would the toll money which he had partially paid under pressure before being granted permission to enter the station precincts by the toll collectors, especially hired for the day by the solicitors who were the agents for the absentee landlord, the Earl of Trallock.

The ninth earl resided, according to newspaper reports, in Rhodesia, where he farmed extensively and was a keen polo player. One of the agents had once discreetly disclosed that the earl, in his youth, had played off an international handicap of plus three. The family biographers had been fulsome in their praise of the earl's ancestors who, by all accounts, had never hanged grainstealers or poachers as their peers so frequently did but saw to it that they were instead transported for life to the colonies.

Jay Mullanney it was who first spotted the prisoner.
He alerted the Badger and Danny Dooley. Danny was
now on foot having stabled the horse at the rear of Fizz
Moran's shop. All three, on the Badger's instructions,
moved quickly to the farther side of the Roscreas where
they were concealed from the soldiers. As the last of the
cattle passed by the Badger called out in a high-pitched
voice: 'Algie Clawhammer! Algie Clawhammer! Run
boy run! This way boy!'

The Badger appeared for an instant at the rear of the
herd and beckoned to his friend. Before the MP's could
restrain him Algie made his break and, although imped-
ed by the double-buckled belt which entwined his
wrists, had a head start before his two larger and clums-
ier custodians were aware of what was happening.

'In among the cows and keep down,' Danny Dooley
turned to face the oncoming soldiers now panic-stricken
at the prospect of facing their Sergeant without the prisoner. Jay Mullanney set about unbuckling the leather
belt while the Badger and Danny tussled with the soldiers. The efforts of the latter to fling the maddening little
men to one side turned out to be fruitless. They ran
among the cows with their smaller assailants hanging on
like leeches. The loosening of the double-buckled belt
proved to be no simple task since Jay and Algie had to
keep on the run in order to stay ahead of the soldiers.
Eventually Algie Clawhammer was loosed from his
bonds. One of the soldiers also broke free and with
powerful outstretched hands sought to catch hold of the
diminutive Algie. Algie dropped to his knees and craw-
led under the belly of the nearest cow. Like a minnow he
darted in and out among the others and then through
the cattle which formed the next contingent for the
railway sidings. The entire action had lasted no more
than sixty seconds.

Look where they might the dismayed soldiers could
see no trace of Algie Clawhammer. One took off towards

the entrance which provided access to the sidings and the other ran into the passenger area of the platform. Algie was nowhere to be seen. Both soldiers almost collided when they met at the ticket office.

'Any sign of a small man, the prisoner we had earlier?' the soldiers asked breathlessly.

The clerk shook his head.

'Now you must excuse me,' he explained. 'I have work to do.'

Ignoring the soldiers he addressed himself to a ledger which earlier occupied his attention. Crouched in the corner at his left hand side, visible only to the clerk, a shaking Algie Clawhammer prayed silently with eyes closed.

'What in Christ's name did you do man?' the clerk asked without raising his head from the ledger.

'All I ever did was steal a few pairs of socks to buy drink,' Algie whispered back.

'Look,' the clerk whispered, his head still studiously bent over his ledger 'I have a job to keep down and I have a wife and two young children so you'd better be moving.'

'I had a wife too,' Algie played for time, 'but she died on me and that was the start of my trouble.'

'I'm sorry to hear that but you can be certain that the station master will arrive here any minute now with those Corporals and you can be sure he'll contact the gardaí. He's obliged to co-operate with the civil authorities and, dammit, so am I so move man and do us all a favour.'

'But where will I go?' Algie asked desperately, 'what direction will I take?'

The clerk made no answer. He opened the door of the ticket office and looked up and down the platform. There was no trace of the Corporals.

'Quick!' he called. 'Get down onto the tracks and keep your head below the platform. Keep going until

you come to the turntable. On the left is open countryside. Follow the tracks at night and you'll get wherever
you want of go if you're patient.'

'God spare you,' Algie wrung the clerk's hands, 'and
God spare your wife and children to you always.' Algie
speedily took off in the direction recommended by his
mild-mannered benefactor. At the other end of the station the loaders had little difficulty with the Roscreas.
Here was none of the butting or bawling or scuttering of
younger cattle. Here was blind obedience.

Later when the Second Lieutenant arrived in the
Bedford he deployed his troops along both sides of the
platform. He dispatched a look-out to the top of the iron
foot-bridge which spanned the railway line. It was the
highest point in the platform and afforded a wide view
of the countryside. The Lieutenant was met at the ticket
office by the station master and clerk.

While they stood rigorously at attention at the rear
of the Bedford Sergeant Rowley harangued the Corporals. After threatening them initially with the most
painful form of castration, executed with uneven slivers
of corrugated iron, he went on to tell them that this
would be followed by the removal of every last fragment
of their genitalia using a rusty hacksaw with every
second tooth missing. Then would come the extraction
with a steel pincers of any roots that might remain behind. This initial disciplinary action would be followed
by the dismembering of each and every one of their ten
toes with a blunt-edged chisel. The toes, one after the
other, would then be stuffed up the rear aperture which
would be immediately sealed by stitching the two
cheeks of the posterior together with thorny wire.

'And I also guarantee you,' Rowley went on, 'with
twelve months apiece in the detention centre where you
will be under my personal supervision. I am hereby
charging you with neglect of duty and I am confining
you to this lorry until such time as you come up for a

preliminary hearing and court-martial.'

'Christ give us a chance Sergeant!' the younger of the Corporals pleaded as he whipped off his cap and squeezed it between his hands.

'You're wasting your time,' his companion advised him.

'Into that lorry and stay there,' Rowley barked.

'You'll never get him back without us.' The younger Corporal saw the months ahead with a less resigned eye than the older.

'Nobody else knows him but us,' the younger man pressed his advantage as he saw the innate cunning replace the anger on the Sergeant's face.

'We're the only two from the detention centre. The others wouldn't know their arses from a hole in the ground. We're your last chance.'

'All right.' Rowley's tone dropped dramatically. 'I'm suspending the charge. Follow me. On the double now!' He led the way into the station, stopping short in front of the Lieutenant and saluting smartly.

'Sorr!' he opened, 'the prisoner will stay near the tracks. It's his only chance Sorr.'

'That's right Sorr,' the Corporals eagerly echoed their Sergeant's reasoning.

'What do you propose Sergeant?' the Second Lieutenant with his six months' old commission reflected in his chubby, boyish face swaggered down the platform, his hands clasped behind his back.

'Sonofabitch!' the Sergeant made sure he spoke the words to himself. He was left with no option but to tag along after the officer.

'Needs putting in his place,' Lieutenant Cobb reflected silently. 'Thinks he knows it all, probably does too. One thing is sure and that is he knows more than I do.'

'He's headed for Limerick Sorr and from there to Dublin Sorr!' The Lieutenant increased his gait. Lieutenant Brinsley Cobb was six feet three inches tall. Sergeant

Rowley was five feet eight inches. He was obliged to break into a trot when the Lieutenant decided to stretch his long legs to the full.

'I propose Sorr we take half of us along the track in the Limerick direction and the other half to go in the lorry to the next station.'

'Very well Sergeant. You take the track and I'll take the lorry. Spread your men out into the fields at either side of the track and give me one of your MPs. We don't want to waste time chasing the wrong quarry eh!'

'You can have Corporal Kelly Sorr. He knows Private Conway well.'

Sergeant Rowley saluted and hurried back to the platoon. He dispatched one detachment to the lorry and ordered the younger Corporal to accompany them

'Now you sorry bunch of pimps,' he turned on the remaining troops, 'I'll keep you out till we find him and I promise that none of you will taste a bite of food till he's captured.'

As they left the station grounds the Badger expressed his sorrow that Philly Hinds had not been with them. Philly had been requisitioned by Mark to assist with the weanlings and the rest of the herd. Apart from the minor engagements with the tollsters and the military the Badger and his party felt they handled the transportation of the Roscreas with great skill. There had been several other eruptions of violence in the vicinity and on the approaches to the cattle sidings but none worthy of police intervention.

'You know what I long for now,' the Badger exclaimed as the saliva trickled down both sides of his bristle jaw.

'A double whiskey!' Danny Dooley volunteered.

The Badger shook his head.

'A double whiskey followed by a pint of stout!' Jay Mullanney proposed.

'Later yes,' the Badger's reply suggested that he was never a man to discourage youthful contributions, 'but now, right now what I am going to have is a mutton pie and when I have it eaten ...'

'You'll have a second mutton pie,' Jay Mullanney interjected.

'The very thing my boy. The very thing.' The Badger lay a paternal hand on Jay's shoulder, 'and you my friends will have pies with me at my expense.'

Later when they were sated they repaired to the Durango Bar which was crowded with buyers and farmers, jobbers and knackers, thimble-riggers and three-card-tricksters and others of every conceivable disposition but all now intent on temporarily segregating themselves from the cares of the world which, as they all knew only too well, awaited them as soon as they forsook the happy confines presided over by the sisters Carabim. Preside was the operative word for it was a day when the sisters employed several local girls to act as barmaids whilst they themselves played the parts of hostesses as only they could.

To the casual observer it seemed that the sisters in all their finery, bosoms and buttocks generously and especially taken into account, were radiant and beautiful to such a degree that the serving girls were left altogether in the shade. To the keen observer, however, it was apparent that the serving girls had been in the shade long before they graduated into the bright presence of the sisters Carabim and, in fact, this was only one of the stratagems employed by the sisters in order to accentuate their own charms at the expense of their employees. Always they were careful to choose the very plainest and the least charming of all the available females in the locality.

No sooner had the Ballybo trio stepped inside the door of the premises than they were greeted by the Rector of Tubberlick and his friend Monsignor Binge. It was here they heard for the first time of the skirmish in the town square and it was an indication of serious trouble to come. After his first drink Jay Mullanney found himself being led by the hand to a back room behind the bar. His guide was Lily Carabim.

'You'll sleep here tonight,' she said pressing the fingers of both hands gently to his lips in order to silence his protests.

'I'll show you to your bed,' she said gently. 'It's there for you at any time.' He followed her up the stairs, intoxicated by the flickering of her sensuously projected buttocks. He would have followed such a prospect all around the world and back.

'Here it is,' she said with as demure and as beguiling a smile as ever Jay Mullanney had seen. It was the way she looked into his eyes that made him blush and want to avert his gaze.

'We're shy aren't we?' She undid his flies. She inserted her hand, still smiling, and as she allowed it free range to roam at will she only uttered one phrase and that one under her breath.

'Just as I thought,' she whispered.

Jay found himself unexpectedly without any clothes lying on his back on a large double bed with Lily Carabim astride him, an energetic, acrobatic and beautifully balanced Lily Carabim, truly determined that they should both make the most of their good fortune.

Later as she sat on the side of the bed re-arranging her hair she asked him if he was alone with the older men. She cooed with delight and fairly beamed when he revealed that he was only one of a party of five young men and a boy all, more or less, from the same part of the world.

'You must all stay here with us,' she said. 'I won't hear no for an answer and the boy,' she asked, 'what age is the boy?'

'He's only fifteen,' Jay explained.

'Only fifteen!' she savoured the words several times before insisting that Jay bring him along with the others.

'While you stay with us you'll want for nothing,' she promised. 'My sister and I will be in and out all the while. You come and go as you please and,' she gently took his hand, 'you'll tell nobody but your friends.'

Unable to mouth words that would make sense Jay Mullanney nodded.

'Your word,' she whispered gently as she went astride him for the second time.

'My word, my word,' Jay shot back.

18

Danny Dooley, the Badger Doran and Jay Mullanney sampled many of the delights on offer at the great fair of Trallock before noon when they presented themselves to their leader Mark Doran.

'Reporting for duty sir,' the Badger saluted and stood to attention, his whiskey-flavoured breath belied by his sober stance. Danny Dooley and he had consumed four half glasses of whiskey each and were none the worse for their modest indulgence.

'You cannot drink if you don't eat,' Danny Dooley had warned Jay Mullanney after he had come downstairs in the Durango Bar.

'Drink is the last thought in that man's head,' the Badger winked at his companion and urged him to take note of Jay's drooping eyelids, his heavy breathing and general drowsiness. If they had not constantly nudged him and drawn him into conversation he must surely have drifted into sleep.

'Isn't nature wonderful,' the Badger observed, 'see the balm on that man's dial and will you look at the cut of his mount. I declare there's twenty years after droppin' off her. What will herself and the sister be like when they've serviced the rest of 'em!'

'There's a cure in it for sure,' Danny Dooley was forced to agree, 'they say them that hold on to it is poisoned by it and what's their reward in the end?'

The Badger allowed himself one of his rare angelic smiles.

'Heaven!' he answered.

'To be sure,' Danny Dooley agreed.

'There's one man will benefit and he's not here at all,' the Badger laughed as he spoke.

'And pray who would he be?' Danny Dooley asked.

'Frankie Tapley,' the Badger responded. 'The Curate in Tubberlick.'

"Tis an ill wind ...' Danny Dooley laughed.

'God moves in mysterious ways,' the Badger intoned the words.

They bade their temporary goodbyes after that to the Rector and the Monsignor and to the beaming sisters Lily and Dell Carabim, Lily extracting a whispered promise from Jay Mullanney before releasing him from a fierce embrace.

As they walked through the long bar they could not help but hear of the rout of the Long Gobberleys. It seemed to be the sole topic of conversation in every corner and the victory was savoured while it was hot.

The bullocks and in-calf heifers might have been disposed of upon arrival at the area outside the Trallock Arms for prices well above the reserves which had been placed upon them by their owners but Mark, after consultation with the Sullivan brothers and Tom Mullanney, decided to hold out. It had been a wise decision. Cattle of similar quality had been bought up the moment they went on offer at better than normal prices. Mark had been tempted. One of the offers had come from a member of the Long Gobberley clan, a lean fellow with a haggard face and sallow features. He towered over Mark as he asked if the cattle were for sale. He made a reasonable offer and Mark was tempted, especially when the fellow produced a wad of twenty pound notes, several inches thick and proceeded to flaunt it under Mark's nose.

It had been recognised for generations as one of the better-known and heavily-exploited weaknesses of the small and middle-sized farmer, that he would always capitulate for an inadequate price when confronted with a sizeable wad of notes. It was a powerful ploy but a time was coming when it would be seen for what it was, another ruse as though there were not enough already, to enrich the jobber and the middle-man and drive another nail into the coffin of the small producer.

Mark had been privy shortly after his arrival at the fair to some priceless information and he had nobody to thank for it but Jacko Flannery who had taken a liking to the younger man after his impressive dismissal of the Long Gobberleys. Flannery had no doubt but that Mark was the brain behind the rout.

'Hold your bullocks till out in the day,' he advised, 'and you won't go far wrong.'

The member of the Gobberley clan who had made the offer to Mark was a distant cousin of Thade Joe's and Bollicky Bill's. He had scoured the fair from the break of day making similar offers. He had invested in four score prime bullocks on behalf of his better-off kinsmen. Later they would sell them at a substantial profit. By exploiting the fear and ignorance of the more impoverished members of the farming community they had forced them once again into accepting unrealistic prices.

The in-calf heifers were a different proposition. They were sought for the most part by farmers within a twenty mile radius who required them as herd replacements. The remainder were bought up by jobbers who dispatched them by rail to distant counties where they would be disposed of at a modest profit to widows and to elderly folk with whom the jobbers had been dealing for years and who were not possessed of the expertise to differentiate between a good cow and a doubtful one. The jobbers were rarely wrong and if they were wrong would they not have to live in the vicinity of their mistakes and would they not be expected to make good next time round!

Theirs was a specialist trade. They never bought at random. The owner of the in-calf heifer for sale would be known to them or would come recommended. They were excellent judges and could tell from the gait, the eyes and the smell of the animal whether she would throw good calves or bad and whether she would be a profuse milker or a modest one. Livelihoods depended upon their judgment. The fair was full of such specialists. There were jobbers who could stand back five paces and survey a weanling speculatively from every angle so that in the end they could visualise her as a heifer and later as a cow. Again, livelihoods depended upon their judgment. After fairs such as Trallock men and women would come to their farms and small-holdings in search of suitable weanlings and particular breeds of weanlings, men and women who were known to them and to whom they would be responsible should the weanlings turn out to be misfits. There were bullock specialists such as the Gobberleys and there were Roscrea specialists such as Jacko Flannery who could look in an old cow's eye or listen to her breathing and determine in a thrice whether she would be alive at the end of a rail journey or not. There were bull specialists one of whom was now circling the Shorthorn, his keen eye searching for defects as he measured shoulder and head, rump and undercarriage from a respectable distance.

'He's Drangen,' the Badger whispered to Jay Mullanney. 'Neddy Drangen from a place called Lacca about twenty miles from here. Wouldn't give you the dirt under his toe nails if he thought 'twould do you any good and that's his brother-in-law with the hazel staff and the zipped-up gansey standing beyond, Dinny O'Day, wouldn't give you a black hair off his arse to save you from hells' fire!'

'Who owns?' Neddy Drangen shouted at Mark. Mark indicated the Badger who approached with hands behind back.

'His danglers is low!' Neddy Drangen spoke without looking again at the Badger.

'If they're low itself,' the Badger returned, 'they're no lower than your own!'

'How much do you want for him?' Neddy Drangen

asked, ignoring the reference to his private para-
phernalia.

'Twenty single notes,' the Badger replied.

'You're sure you wouldn't take twenty fivers?'
Neddy Drangen sneered as he called to his brother-in-
law so that he might participate in the negotiations.

'I'll give you fifteen pounds and not a penny more!'
Neddy Drangen sounded adamant.

'Give me nineteen pounds into my hand now and
he's yours,' the Badger was smiling. For all his astute-
ness Neddy Drangen was offering more than the bull
was worth.

'What age is he?' he asked.

'Six years and two months,' the Badger lied.

'Nearer to ten I would say.' Neddy took another
turn around the bull who suddenly ignored the proceedings and made straight for a heifer who had ogled him
several times since his arrival and whose comely after-
parts now further provoked him from an assailable distance. She positioned herself perfectly for the assault
which she had subtly engineered and, without looking
around her, allowed his bright tapering organ thrusting
access to where it was required. It was a thoroughly
comprehensive coverage. It was seen, when the ancient
rite was completed, that the Shorthorn for all his years
was deficient in neither seed nor energy and at the end
of the day there was one replete heifer and one
thoroughly satisfied bull!

'I'll take him,' Neddy Drangen extended a hand to
his brother-in-law for the wherewithal to purchase the
Shorthorn. The deal was quickly closed.

'We'll be back in two hours for to take him to the
station,' Neddy Drangen counted the notes into the
Badger's joined hands. The Badger in turn counted them
into Jay Mullanney's open palm. Mark Doran's safety-
pinned breast pocket was to be the final resting place of
the nineteen pounds.

'I'll have my luck money now if you please!' Dinny O'Day the nasal-voiced brother-in-law spoke for the first time.

'Give him a half-crown,' the Badger advised Mark.

'A crown at least,' Dinny O'Day protested.

'I'll divide it with you,' Mark said.

Mark handed over a half-crown and for good measure a shilling piece and a three penny piece.

Dinny O'Day pocketed the money and departed without a word.

'Mind you keep him away from those heifers!' Drangen cautioned. 'He's had his nuff for one day.'

Rarely were there more than three of the Ballybo Brigade as the Rector had christened them to be found in the vicinity of the Trallock Arms from noon onwards. No sooner had one group returned after depositing cattle at the railway sidings than another was dispatched to the same destination with a freshly sold contingent of mature cattle. Others took turns to visit public houses in the immediate area. Here they partook of Trallock mutton pies sitting on hard benches at long wooden tables savouring every last mouthful of the mouth-watering delicacies.

The rule was that each man would consume only one pie at a sitting. The day was long the older men would vouchsafe and there would be many a drink between morning and night. A pie every two hours or, for outsized countrymen, a pie at more frequent intervals, was a guarantee of relative sobriety for the duration of the fair in particular and thereafter for as long as was necessary. The larger farmers, the wealthy jobbers and buyers were not above eating pies in the town's numerous public houses but their eating tastes ran to red meat as a rule and their drinking tastes largely to whiskey. As soon as the Ballybo drovers had consumed a pie they would repair straightaway to the bar where no more than two mediums of stout were permitted for the dur-

DURANGO

ation of any visit. It was a good rule for no sooner had they wined and dined than they returned to their duties and allowed their colleagues to indulge in similar repasts. There was also no danger of drunkenness whereas those who succumbed to long early sessions without food inevitably wound up drunk and spent the remainder of the day asleep in the corner of a tolerant hostelry or seated on their posteriors on the dung-covered street wherever they might find room. Now and then it was permissible to indulge in the occasional half whiskey but only as a sort of booster when spirits tended to flag or fatigue overcame the travel-weary.

'All a chap has to do,' Philly Hinds warned, 'is follow the rules. That way you won't get drunk at the start of the day and be a nuisance to everybody. You won't get drunk in the middle of the day and have to fall asleep. If you get drunk it will be at the end of the day and your horse or your ass will carry you home and if you have no horse and no ass you can go to the barracks and if there's room in the cells you won't be short of a mattress for the night.'

It was during a sojourn at the Bus Bar, an establishment noted for the quality of the meat in its mutton pies, that Jay Mullanney described his visit to the upstairs bedroom of the Durango Bar. He lingered over the delightful details and pointed out that there was not just one of these most accommodating females but rather were there two. His friends nodded eagerly, already partially informed with regard to the accomplishments of the Carabim sisters and their fortunate preference for youths of the rustic persuasion. As much as their mouths had watered earlier at the prospect of mutton pies they were now drenched altogether in the lascivious saliva of uncontaminated prurience. Will and Henry Sullivan begged for further details of Jay Mullanney's visit but for the second time since morning that worthy's head tended to droop and his tired eyes tended to close.

'I think I'll have to go to bed for an hour or two,' he admitted.

'You know where to go,' his brother Tom shook him by the shoulder, 'so go there now and sleep your fill. We'll call you quick if anything comes up. Tell the sisters that we'll be along shortly, to be expecting us.'

Assisted by Will and Henry Sullivan Tom Mullanney succeeded in getting Jay to his feet.

'He's groggier than if he was in a fight,' Will Sullivan laughed as Jay staggered against the table where they had been sitting. Tom Mullanney helped his weak-kneed brother out of doors. In the bright sunlight he revived a little but he was still a trifle uncertain of his exact whereabouts.

'You'd better go with him,' Will Sullivan addressed himself to Florry Mullanney, the fifteen year old.

'And mind,' his brother Tom seized him firmly by the shoulders, 'you return here straightaway or you'll hear about it from me!'

'Oh I'll be back,' Florry promised earnestly and from the look on his face it was apparent that he meant what he said.

Aided by his younger brother Jay Mullanney staggered across the square, now more than three-quarters empty and emptying further by the moment as its bovine population drifted without let-up to the jammed railway sidings in the northern part of town. Not much notice was taken of the drunken garsún and his escort. The town was filled with his likes and at least he was on his feet. He might not be for long but his brother seemed a sharp enough lad who would eventually get him to his destination.

One of the last animals to leave the square was the hand-some, roan Shorthorn, once the proud possession of Haybags Mullanney. Having gratified himself earlier through contact with the heifer from the neighbouring herd he found that his appetite for such natural activities had been merely whetted.

'Watch the hoor,' the Badger Doran drew Philly Hinds' attention to the Shorthorn as he made further overtures to a heifer who chanced to be part of a small herd which had replaced the Doran contingents already on their way by train to distant places. The owner of the herd, an inoffensive small farmer from County Limerick respectfully enquired from the Badger if he might allow his charges access to the vacated ground. The Badger had agreed and thus began the Shorthorn's second venture into the realms of romance. The Limerick man asked the Badger if he would keep an eye on the heifers while he and his young son indulged themselves with sorely-needed mutton pies. The Badger graciously acquiesced. It was while the owner slaked his thirst and satisfied his appetite that the Shorthorn made his second move of the afternoon.

'It's the change of scenery,' Philly Hinds opined.

'It's the change of heifers,' the Badger contradicted.

'Shouldn't we stop him?' Philly Hinds turned to his companion who stood impassively resting on his knopstick while the Shorthorn readied himself for his second encounter.

'Don't stand in the way of nature,' the Badger said.

After he had performed, the Shorthorn ambled back to the spot where he had been standing before spotting the heifer. For the first time that day he sat down.

'You won't catch him rising again in a hurry,' the Badger observed.

'The taspy is gone from the poor chap all right,' Philly Hinds concurred.

Shortly afterwards when Neddy Drangen and his brother-in-law Dinny O'Day arrived to collect the bull they were surprised to find him fatigued.

'What's the matter with him at all?' Dinny O'Day asked through his nose.

'The same as yourself would be,' the Badger told him, 'if you were called into action twice in the space of a few hours.'

Viciously Neddy Drangen raised his knopstick and held it close to the Badger's smiling face.

'I thought I told you,' he fumed, 'that he was to be kept away from heifers till we gathered him.'

Reluctantly the bull rose to his feet prodded and smacked by the sticks of the new owners.

'Is he the same bull at all?' Dinny Day asked in his plaintive way.

'He's the same bull all right,' his brother-in-law assured him, 'but we'd better take him to the railway because he'll never make home the condition he's in.'

Slowly, painfully the Shorthorn trudged stationwards, ignoring the glances of occasional heifers along the route, as step by step, he made his way through the streets of the town. He would have cheerfully rested but there was to be no stopping. Relentlessly his owners drove him onwards, ignoring the rolling of his eyes and the laboured breathing which sounded like a giant bellows piping harshly beneath his ribs.

'He'll be all right,' Neddy Drangen promised his anxious brother-in-law. Despite his assurance there was little confidence in his tone.

'Shouldn't we rest him awhile?' Dinny O'Day's persistence was beginning to grate upon Neddy Drangen, not the most patient of men at the best of times. Besides he had his fill of nasal nattering from the moment they left the square. He carefully considered his brother-in-law's request nevertheless. His reputation might very well be at stake should the bull fail to negotiate the journey to the railway. Despite his impatience he decided that their charge should be rested for a brief period, long enough to restore sufficient energy for the remainder of the journey. Just then the bull stopped of his own accord. A massive scutter erupted without warning from his rear. Dinny O'Day was sprayed from head to toe. Luckily for Neddy Drangen he happened to be standing at the animal's side. The bull made no attempt to move forward. He extended his tongue but failed lamentably to make any sound. Eyes rolling he slid to the ground where a mighty shudder seized his entire frame. His legs shot out from under him and he rolled over on his side.

'He's dead!' Dinny O'Day wiped the sage-green scutter from his mouth and knelt on the ground where his protestations attracted a large number of passers-by.

'He's dead. He's dead!' he wailed as though the once brawny procreator had belonged to the human species. Mortified, his brother-in-law vainly endeavoured to raise him to his feet but Dinny O'Day, his eyes raised heavenwards at the woeful injustice of it all, was pilla-looing like a rejected foster pup.

A large crowd had now gathered. There was none among the many onlookers who was not astounded by the eerie lamentations of the dung-sprayed figure kneeling on the ground. None who knew him intimately would have been surprised. The year before he had stood tearless at the graveside of the sainted mother who had slaved for his advancement in the world from the day he was born. At his father's burial, although he had inherited every acre of the family farm, he had fretted at the delay of the mumbling priest who presided over the final obsequies and yet when a prize heifer had drowned in a flash flood during the November of the previous year he had wept until not a single tear remained and he had wailed and groaned till he was hoarse. It had been the same when a prime Hereford bull had been accidentally poisoned. He would not be consoled and now here was this latest misfortune to try him further.

'Get up man or we'll be the talk of the fair,' Neddy Drangen dragged him, still olagóning, to his feet. Just then a civic guard put in his appearance.

'Are you aware,' he addressed Neddy Drangen,

'that you are causing an obstruction?'

'Sorry guard.' Neddy sounded as if he meant it. Under his breath he silently cursed this meddlesome interloper who added to their tale of woe by demanding that the obstruction be removed forthwith. Eventually a local butcher arrived, a grease-covered, cadaverous-looking fellow who specialised in selling suspect beef to greyhound-owners. With the help of the onlookers the bull was loaded onto a dray and transported to the rear of the butcher's premises. Before he departed, the butcher took Dinny O'Day's hand and placed a pound note therein.

"Tis the best I can do,' he whispered, 'there's some would give you nothing.'

Dinny O'Day looked at the solitary note and recommenced the baleful caterwauling which had so intrigued his audience. Neddy Drangen led his still sobbing, stinking brother-in-law to the Trallock Arms where he spent a half hour fruitlessly endeavouring to remove the dung which discoloured his face, his boots and his clothes.

At exactly quarter to one Mark Doran disposed of the last of the bullocks. The ten, belonging to Daisy Popple, had fetched sixteen pounds and ten shillings a head. She confided to Mark that she would be happy if they fetched fourteen pounds a piece .

Shed of his backbreaking responsibility Mark had his first drink of the day, a half whiskey paid for by his grand-uncle, the Badger Doran. Mark should have been a happy man. He should have been congratulating himself but he dare not. He carried several hundred pounds in cash on his person. He sat in the Bus Bar with the Badger and Danny Dooley. All three had already eaten several mutton pies. Mark confessed his worries to his two companions.

'I have in my breast pocket,' he confided, 'more money than I ever saw in my life. It's the proceeds from the sales of the in-calf heifers and the most of the weanlings. I have still to collect for the Roscreas and the bullocks so I propose we go shortly to the Durango Bar where I have an appointment with Flannery and the other buyers.'

Over a medium of stout Mark produced the several receipts from the railway loaders. Meticulously they went through the sheaf of papers until every last head of cattle had been accounted for. Mark then outlined his proposals for the safekeeping of the money in his possession and the payments he would collect at the Durango Bar.

'It is my intention,' he told Danny Dooley and the Badger, 'to retain that which is mine, that is to say, the price of the Roscreas and my own stock which were part of the herd. The rest of the money I will deposit in the National Bank which is just across the road. I have an account there. I will sign cheques for each and every person who contributed cattle to the herd less, of course, the luck money and the toll money. These cheques I will entrust to you Danny and in case of accident you will deliver them personally. If you lose them it won't make all that difference because they can only be cashed by their rightful owners.

'But ...' a perplexed Badger intervened.

'Let there be no buts,' Mark struck the wooden table with the base of his empty glass, 'just do as you're told and I'll explain later. Now we'll have another drink before we set out for the Durango and meanwhile you will not depart from my side for any reason whatsoever. If I piddle you'll piddle with me. If I go forward you'll go forward and if I go sideways you'll go sideways until such time as the money is deposited in the National Bank.'

It was Fizz Moran who introduced Mark Doran to the immaculately dressed manager of the National Bank on the morning of the fair. By arrangement Mark had called for the genial apothecary at half-nine in the morning. Mark had deposited a modest sum and was presented with a National Bank cheque book. The manager had extended credit to the tune of £200 with Fizz Moran acting as guarantor. Later, after collecting at the Durango, when Mark deposited the returns from the sale of the herd the bank manager came from his office to shake hands with him and to assure him of prompt and personal attention at all time.

'Should you need further credit for any other enterprises you have in mind,' the manager shook Mark's hand, 'you know where to come my boy!'

The Badger and Danny Dooley stood by. Not a whisper escaped their lips. Here was a come-around in the world. Here was a day to be remembered. His companions regarded him with newfound respect. To their knowledge only priests, teachers, big shopkeepers, doctors and the like had bank accounts. In all their years and they were many they had never heard of, much less encountered, a small farmer who had a bank account.

On their arrival at the Durango Bar Jay and Florry Mullanney were greeted so effusively by the sisters Carabim that the latter was quite overcome.

'You show them up dear,' Lily managed to conceal her longing by embracing Florry Mullanney so warmly and yet so tenderly that he wished it was she and not her sister who was conducting them upstairs. Florry need not have worried. No sooner did they find themselves in the bedroom vacated earlier by Jay and Lily than Dell, with nothing more than a flick of her wrist and a twiddle of her fingers, summoned to the surface every ounce of manhood which had resided in the loins of Florry Mullanney uninduced and unprovoked since his arrival at the age of puberty. Between them Dell and he lifted the sleeping body of Jay and bore it to a neighbouring room where they laid it on a bed. When they were leaving their ears were assailed by deep, satisfying snores of a kind that can only be induced by a mixture of drink, debauch and exhaustion and on the other side of the coin by honest toil, rectitude and righteousness. There are those who would argue that this might be a most odious comparison but for those who believe that comparisons are not odious the end result might seem to justify the means.

Florry Mullanney had two advantages over his older brother; he was a youth of inexhaustible physical reserves as he had demonstrated all too often during the drive. Also he had been forewarned and could hardly contain himself. This delighted Dell Carabim. His urgency amused her.

She stripped slowly, deliberately pausing to divest him of a shoe or a sock or a vest so that they might be reduced together to an original state. Casually, or so it seemed to Florry Mullanney, she positioned herself seductively but strategically. Had he but known it was a stratagem which had taken years to perfect and was derived from both the realms of reality and fantasy and had almost but never quite been comprehensively realised.

In theory the fulfilment of her fantasising was feasible but it had never quite come off in the harsher more physical realms of reality. When they embraced she cried out aloud, grasping his slender body to her bosom, shutting out all thoughts of the world around with its distant lowing, its coin-jingling, its shouting, swearing and its general pandemonium. Bells tinkled in Florry Mullanney's ears.

'What is age,' Dell Carabim thought to herself as her dream neared its realisation, 'but a figment of the imagination. Only this is real and it defies age because when age and youth commingle like this, age is secondary. I will use my age for matters that need age but here is soundly invested the last vestiges of my youth!'

She chortled a deep chortle from the depths of her

feminity as her captive struggled and writhed and moaned. They both arrived at the threshold of delirium together. They both cried out before collapsing exhausted on their backs, totally relaxed and fully relieved of the weighty strains and tensions that chain the human species from the beginning to the end of life.

Suddenly Florry Mullanney vaulted across his first and only conquest with a cry of alarm. Dell Carabim sat instantly upright.

'What's wrong lover?' she asked, her deep voice filled with concern.

It was now Florry's turn to experience concern. He had never in his life been addressed as lover. He looked behind and about him affrighted lest she be addressing somebody else. Assuring himself that there was nobody else in the room he explained to Dell Carabim that he had promised his brothers that he would return immediately.

'They told him,' he directed his thumb to the room where Tom slept, 'to tell you that they would be calling soon.'

'And you lover!' Dell asked fearfully, 'will you not be coming back again?' Her lips pouted like a little girl's and her eyes grew moist as she watched Florry Mullanney draw on his clothes.

'I'll be back with the boys,' he assured her.

'You're sure it isn't your conscience?' she asked as he bent to tie his bootlaces.

'My conscience?' he asked, perplexed beyond words.

'I'll put it another way,' she took one of his hands in hers. 'Are you worried by what we have just done?'

'No,' Florry answered truthfully.

'But it's in your head isn't it?' she asked, curious now, 'to go to confession at the next available opportunity.'

'Confession,' Florry laughed, 'sure you couldn't tell

a thing like that in confession. The priest would throw you out of the box.'

'Oh no he wouldn't,' Dell Carabim assured him.

'Maybe. Maybe not,' Florry showed no relish for the turn the conversation was taking, 'but I'm not taking any chances. I'll just tell him I committed an impure act and that's all he'll get out of me.'

For the first time Dell realised she was in the presence of an amoral Irish country boy. He was the first of his kind to have crossed her path. She was intrigued but as far as he was concerned the conversation was over, at least for the moment.

After he was gone she lay on the bed relishing his lack of complication and inhibition remembering other boys not all that older who, not long after the act was completed, confided their fears about facing the confessional where the wrong kind of priest could turn the sacrament of penance into an instrument of mental torture. It was always the first thought to enter their heads as they drew on their clothes, a sort of thorn-topped hurdle, extremely difficult which had to be cleared before life might resume its normal course.

There was never a word about confessions beforehand, nothing to impede the urgency which possessed the young men and boys who could not wait to have it over and done with. She conceded that some were painstaking and deliberate but, without doubt, Florry Mullanney was the best to date. His liveliness and spontaneity, his sense of timing which was so natural and, most of all, his innocence imbued her with fresh vitality. She resolved there and then that Florry Mullanney would be the note on which she would make her final farewell from such relationships but there was a long day there yet and there was a morning to follow.

'Morning is often best,' she thought as she drew on her silk stockings and re-fastened her suspenders.

She sat on the bed awhile and cast her mind back

over the years to that first time when, crazily without forethought or explanation, her sister and she had embarked upon their relationship with country lads. This would be their last fling. It was time to ease into a little flesh, to eat a little more and to drink a little more and to grow old with grace and gentility. There would be no room for young men in their lives once the final step had been taken. They would dispose of the premises within months and retire to a detached house in the suburbs already under construction but first the grand finale! It had been nearly two years now since the last debauch and there had only been occasional lapses prior to that. They both agreed that they had needed to splurge on occasion but now it was time for respectability, for religion and for good works. It was a time to begin the all-important quest for the grace of God. Dell prayed that God in His mercy and compassion would grant time for such a quest. It would be unthinkable if it was not forthcoming! It would be damnable! Silently she opened the door of the room where Jay Mullanney slept. The snoring had now grown intermittent with long periods of deep, even breathing. His handsome face looked boyish, almost babyish. A faint cry of alarm escaped him and he stirred uneasily. At once she knelt by the bedside and stroked the forehead, free of wrinkles. She smoothed back his hair and kissed him gently on the lips. For a moment her hand lingered on the coverlet and she was tempted. She arose quickly and departed the room, closing the door silently behind her, whispering a prayer for his welfare as she silently tripped down the carpeted stairs.

19

Algie Clawhammer knew after the first mile that he would never shake off his pursuers unless he was granted the time and privacy to restore his flagging energies with a sufficiency of sleep. He would also need at least one decent meal before his debilitation turned him into an easy quarry. The way ahead was fraught with danger. It was his guess that already troops were advancing in his direction from the next station. Then there was the danger from cattle and passenger trains should he risk travelling along the railway line when the sun went down. He was in no condition to go on unless the food and sleep he so desperately required was immediately forthcoming. He eventually came to the conclusion that his only hope was to go back to Trallock. At least he would find friends there but with troops behind him and troops ahead of him his dilemma seemed unresolvable. There was also the nightmare of Sergeant Rowley. He could imagine him haranguing the military policemen and the troops with language so coarse and vile that even the most hardened veterans must recoil when bombarded with it. There was no other solution. He had to turn round.

After traversing a few hundred yards of rough ground he came upon a narrow by-road which ran parallel with the railway line. On either side it was flanked by high hawthorn hedges. His heart skipped a beat when a blackbird, chattering frantically, suddenly broke from the undercover at his feet and winged its way down the sheltered roadway before turning sharply into the whitethorn on its right.

Then unexpectedly a break appeared in the hedgerows on his left. He drew back hurriedly and peered through the whitethorn. All he could see was an old woman in front of a white-washed, thatched cottage. Keeping perfectly still and hardly daring to breathe he watched her every movement. She disappeared for a moment into the house and returned with a bucketful of wet clothes. She proceeded to hang the dripping garments on a makeshift line which hung between two timber posts. As she lay the clothes across the line she crooned softly to herself. From where he crouched the words were indistinguishable to Algie Clawhammer but he recalled the melody easily enough. At the same time he heard the sound of voices in the distance. These would undoubtedly be the troops who had set out a short while before from Trallock station. With them was Sergeant Rowley. At any moment they must appear round the nearby bend on the bóithrín. If they spotted him all would be lost. The old woman, her curiosity aroused by the unfamiliar voices, slowly made her way to the side of the house from where she might view the approaches to her domain.

Seizing his chance Algie ran towards the house, the front door of which was open. In the tiny kitchen a turf fire smouldered in an open hearth. Above it a black kettle, its bottom soot-covered, hung from a hook attached to a grimy crane. He listened without daring to move. At the side of the fireplace was a small hen coop. Its two feathered inmates, unperturbed by his presence, were deeply involved in the process of egg-laying. Outside he heard Sergeant Rowley questioning the old woman. No, she had not seen hide nor light of a small man. No, she didn't mind if they looked in the house but they must not wake the old man. Algie hastily withdrew from the window where he had been standing. He guessed that the open door at the other end of the kitchen must lead to the room where the old man in question lay sleeping.

'Cover the rear,' Rowley's voice was unmistakable.

Algie heard the sound of running feet as the troops

hurried to obey the Sergeant's command. In the bedroom an old man lay on the bed, his head propped by
pillows. He slept soundly. Suddenly his eyes opened
and he beheld the form of Algie Clawhammer standing
beside the bed.

'Is that you Sonny?' he asked.

'It's Sonny,' Algie replied reassuringly. The old man
seemed relieved to learn that it was indeed Sonny. He
rambled on incoherently after that and closed his eyes.

'Who's in that room?' Algie moved quickly to the
farther side of the bed at the sound of Sergeant Rowley's
voice.

'There's nobody there but the old man,' the woman
answered.

'Mind if I look?' Sergeant Rowley asked.

'Look away,' the old woman said, 'but mind you
don't wake him.'

In an instant Algie was in the bed, at the side farthest from the door, his small body shielded by the bulk of
the old man. Startled, the old fellow sat upright and
began to babble unintelligibly.

'See,' the old woman chided, 'he's awake. I told
you!'

'Go to sleep old man.' Rowley issued the command
as though he were addressing an underling. Surprisingly the old man closed his eyes and fell into an instant
sleep much to the relief of the fugitive.

Algie stayed put until the voices of the searchers
faded in the distance. Only then did he ease himself
from the bed. In the kitchen the old woman stood by the
doorway, her eyes fixed on the forms of the disappearing soldiers.

'Don't be frightened,' Algie raised a finger to his
lips.

'Ah,' she said, 'you must be the one they were
searching for. Go on out of here this minute you wretch
or I'll call them back.'

'I'm gone, I'm gone!' Algie shook her hand and ran along the boíthrín until he reached the northern suburbs of the town. He made his way through a laneway choc-a-block with cattle. From the laneway he entered a broader even more crowded thoroughfare. He had never seen so many cattle in all his days. He had been to fairs during the days when he laboured for his hire with farmers but he had never experienced anything like this. A man could hardly move a foot in any direction without bumping into a beast. He knew where he must go. He had heard mention often enough during the drive of the intention to take over the area outside the hotel. That surely was where his friends must be. On his way through the town he dawdled now and then, standing sometimes, as drovers do, alongside groups of cattle to divert attention and other times requesting the price of isolated cows or heifers as though he were in the market for such animals. All the time he drifted towards the square until at last he found himself within fifty yards of his destination. He stopped dead in his tracks when he beheld the uniformed members of the civic guards. They seemed to be questioning Mark and the others. Convinced that they were searching for him he retreated hastily until he found himself in the vicinity of the Durango Bar. He dared not go in for fear of being re-cognised. He froze when he heard himself being ad-dressed by his name of convenience. He hardly knew whether to turn round or make a run for it.

'Monsignor,' he called out gratefully, 'it was God who sent you.'

'How can I help Algie?' There was no mistaking the sincerity of Monsignor Binge's tone.

'I need food, sleep. I need help. The guards are searching for me. Already they're questioning Mark and the others. I've just escaped the army and now I'm in the worst pucker I ever was in!'

'Oh dear!' the Monsignor stood helplessly wonder-

ing what he could do to aid the stricken soul who needed his help so badly.

'First,' the Monsignor took Algie by the hand, 'we
must get some food inside you and then some sleep.'

'If I could rest up until nightfall,' the words poured
out of Algie Clawhammer, knowing he had a sympathetic listener, 'I could try the railway line again. If I could
only get as far as Limerick I know I could make it the
whole way.'

'Follow me,' the Monsignor led the way into the
crowded bar where Algie was quickly introduced to Lily
and Dell Carabim. The pair turned out to be even more
sympathetic than the Monsignor. A half hour later, after
he had devoured an enormous meal of rashers, sausages
and eggs he sank into the downy depths of Lily Carabim's very own bed in a third storey room which overlooked the street. From the landing outside through a
tiny window at the rear of the premises much of the
town and countryside all around could be clearly seen.

Knocking gently on the door Dell and the Monsignor entered. Dell Carabim opened the wardrobe where
she pointed to a chamber pot.

'You don't even have to leave the room,' she told the
figure in the bed.

'You'll be safe here,' the Monsignor assured him.
His words fell upon deaf ears. Algie Clawhammer had
fallen into a deep sleep from which he would not
awaken for several hours.

'Father,' Dell Carabim forestalled the Monsignor on
the landing after she had closed the bedroom door.

'Yes Dell,' he asked gently, sensing that his hostess
had something important to convey.

'If you please Monsignor,' Dell opened hesitantly,
'Lily and I would like to make general confessions, if
that's all right with you.'

'Of course it's all right,' the Monsignor assured her.

'Say tomorrow then.' Dell bent her head modestly.

'Tomorrow,' the Monsignor agreed, 'but let it be before twelve o'clock. The Rector and I will be departing at noon.'

Dell led the way down the stairs, glad that she had committed herself and Lily to general confession and in the process saying goodbye to all liaisons with all young men for once and for all and as another consequence opening the way to a new and better life, a life to be filled with faith and charity until such time as the good Lord saw fit to call them to everlasting life.

Dell Carabim felt as though she were already shriven. Her step was lighter as she led the way downstairs. The Monsignor had already declined the offer of breakfast. His wants, in this respect, had been seen to by the Presentation nuns who looked after the tiny chapel where he had celebrated Mass. He looked at his watch. Nine o'clock.

No matter how hard he tried he could never escape the shadow which hung over every waking hour. There were times when his mind was mercifully taken up with other matters but these periods were short-lived and always after all too short a respite he was confronted by what lay ahead. There was no escape. He was resigned in so far as any human being with an incommutable death sentence could be resigned. He was glad that his illness had not subjected him to bouts of depression, that he still had time for the tribulations of others. Lately, however, he had found the days interminably long. Also he tired easily and there was considerable pain from time to time. He went to his room for an hour or two. Later he would make contact with the Rector and the others. Fine if he could sleep but that incomparable balm for all forms of weariness was not always forthcoming when he found himself alone. When it did eventually come it was fretful and uneasy. It allowed him too much scope to dwell on his misfortune. He had no fear of the hereafter. There was nothing on his conscience. The God he served so faithfully for so long would surely be compassionate but that was all some time away. For the present he must put down the days and the nights until his hour came for the hospice. He would spend the time in between with his sister Madge and her husband Tom but he would need highly specialised care towards the end. Meanwhile he would rest and then he could spread his energies over the remainder of the day, buttressed by the occasional drink and by short periods of rest in between. Suddenly he felt cheered. He would stay away from the death chamber until the very last minute and he would stay on his feet until he collapsed.

In a corner of the Durango Bar the Ballybo herders had appropriated an area especially for themselves. The hour was three o'clock in the afternoon. The bar was filled from its front door to its rear. Now and again voices were raised in song and occasionally an itinerant musician, hat in hand, solicited financial contributions from those present. Half-pence, pence and three-penny pieces were thrown into the hat. Other musicians were followed by shawled females who extended long leather purses, loudly rattling the contents under the noses of recalcitrants. From time to time shawled tinker women would appear bearing timber trays of camphor balls, cardboard representations of the Sacred Heart of Jesus, paper flowers, cards of common pins and safety pins and other odds and ends never exceeding a penny in price.

'There's a market for everything at the October fair,' the Badger Doran declared to Philly Hinds.

Mark Doran sat between the pair. During the first lull in conversation he called for order. He had written the cheques for each and every one of the contributors to the drive. The luck money had changed hands and there had been no complaints. Now had come a time when the men who participated in the drive must be rewarded.

They would be the first to say, Badger Doran and Philly Hinds excepted, that nothing was expected or indeed deserved by way of financial incentive, that they had merely served their own ends, that the reverse might even be the case for had not Mark Doran out-generalled their enemies! Had he not held out for better prices when a weaker man might have panicked and given in! Had he not routed the Long Gobberleys and would he not be giving an extra half-crown to the owners of the Roscreas when he was in no way obliged to do so! This last move was seen to be a truly generous one especially since the owners of the Roscreas had been happy with the prices paid at Doran's haggard on the first morning of the drive. After he had concluded his business at the bank he had called the Badger and Philly Hinds aside and pressed a ten shilling note into the hands of each. Already they considered themselves adequately compensated by the luck money they had received at the haggard but they accepted the crisp notes nevertheless. The Badger spent most of his on Woodbines for the insatiable Monnie. She would look askance at any other sort of gift.

When Mark produced the paper bag of half-crowns and stood it on the table all present leaned forward eagerly. When he poured the contents of the bag onto the wet surface, empty glasses were quickly removed and placed on the bar counter by willing hands.

'There are three half-crowns drinking money for every man here,' Mark made the announcement proudly because it often seemed before and during the drive that there would be nothing but empty pockets at the conclusion. One by one the drovers accepted the coins, some jingling them in their pockets, others admiring their feel and lustre.

'Where is Henry Sullivan?' Mark asked.

'I'll hold his money for him,' his brother Will volunteered.

'But where is he?' Mark asked, perplexed by the nudging and the poorly-concealed giggling which greeted his question.

'No need to worry about him,' a well-rested Jay Mullanney finally answered. 'He's in good hands.'

Still perplexed Mark handed three half-crowns to Sandy Hassett. It was at that exact moment that Jacko Flannery entered the bar. He made straight for the table occupied by Mark and his friends. He gasped for breath and there was a worried look on his face.

'I've come from the Trallock Arms,' he informed the gathering, 'and unless I'm greatly mistaken you will have unpleasant company shortly.'

Suddenly there was silence. The drovers had half expected some form of retribution from the Long Gobberleys and their retainers but as the day wore on the likelihood of a confrontation grew more unlikely. Indeed the Long Gobberleys might have merely swallowed their pride such was their delight at the upturn in prices and there was also the mitigating factor that Bollicky Bill had not suffered physical injury. However, another factor entered the picture. It was an influence which proved to be distinctly advantageous to the Long Gobberleys.

As in all wars, great and small, the opposing factions are fully aware beforehand of each other's strengths and weaknesses. Without such knowledge, most of which is generally common to begin with, few factions would initiate wars deliberately. Better, they believed, to stay at home than tangle with the unknown.

The Long Gobberleys, after the morning's rout, sent members of their intelligence out into the wider world of the fair to find out all they could about the enemy. The member of the clan who approached Mark Doran, ostensibly to buy bullocks was a shrewd and experienced observer. Before approaching Mark he had stood unobtrusively in the wings taking careful note of the

comings and goings of the drovers attached to the tres-
passing herd. He was a man who had little recourse to
the five parishes so that his knowledge of Mark's following was practically nil. He knew the number and he was
able to make a reasonable guess at the ages but he knew
little of the character or the mettle of these hill men who
had so brazenly disregarded the standing rights of his
kinsmen. His brief exchange with Mark left him no wiser
regarding the fighting potential of the leader but he
came away with the distinct impression that the rout of
Bollicky Bill and the retainers was organised by the man
who had refused his offer for the bullocks.

All day long the Gobberleys together with their
relations, retainers and friends made their secret en-
quiries regarding the potential of the Ballybo men. Mark
Doran it emerged was the undisputed leader of the
group, a skilful and fearless footballer, a useful man
with his fists and deadly cool in the face of danger, in
summation, more desirable as a friend than an enemy
and best left alone. His grand-uncle, the Badger Doran,
was better known with an estimated age of seventy-five.
According to some he should have been hanged years
before while others would maintain that he was a man
of his word as well as a man to be feared in combat. It
was revealed that he also fought with distinction in the
Black and Tan war. Philly Hinds, it would seem, was of
the same mould. Little was known of the Mullanneys.
Although hearsay had it that they were trustworthy men
in a fight and did not know how to go backwards.

The Sullivans, it was reported, were also footballers.
Amiable, easy-going lads, not given to bickering or
fighting, they would be certain to follow Mark Doran to
the sacrificial altar. The latter estimation was Archie
Scuttard's. He had been unwittingly quizzed by a Gobberley sympathiser as he and Fizz Moran enjoyed a quiet
drink in a rather musty and unfrequented premises next
door to the Moran pharmacy. Neither Fizz nor the Rect-

or showed the least sign of drink. They had imbibed guardedly since morning. They promised to meet later in the day at the Durango Bar where the Rector had an appointment with his friend the Monsignor.

The Gobberley retainers had little stomach for a full-scale confrontation with the ruthless pair who had shattered the morning's normality. Whether they were members of the IRA or not was immaterial.

When they enquired about the big man who was part of the Ballybo contingent they had no idea that he was the sharp-shooter who had riddled the pavements under Bollicky Bill's feet. They immediately drew their own conclusions when it transpired that Sandy Hassett had been a dispatch rider in the Great War. Their informant had served with Sandy in France. When asked to deliver judgment on Sandy's character their source announced that he would rather face a raging lion than face Sandy Hassett.

Mattie Holligan, it transpired, was well known even in Trallock. According to Long Gobberley sources he had been something of a playboy before he decided to settle down. His had been one of the more familiar faces at wakes, weddings, patterns and football fixtures throughout the land until Maud Cooley, for such was her maiden name, had set her cap for him. He stood no chance at all when she turned her laughing eyes in his direction.

After marriage his hankering for the road quickly subsided except for rare outings which Maud saw fit to encourage. She was a subscriber to the view that a good man needs a good break occasionally. As to his potential in a fight the Long Gobberleys contacts were all of the same accord. Mattie Holligan was a man not to be trifled with. He was, without doubt, a good humoured, generous fellow but if he took a notion to assault a body that body would be well advised to take off without delay in the opposite direction.

When the Long Gobberleys added up the findings of their intelligence units they were agreed that it would be foolhardy to take on such formidable adversaries. In short there were too many Ballybo men and too few Gobberleys. In point of fact the numbers on either side were equal but the Gobberley rules of war saw equality in a different light. Their idea of a fair contest was where the Gobberleys out-numbered the opposition by at least two to one. They decided therefore that it would not be in their best interest to wage war upon the usurpers who took over their territory. It had not yet been driven home to them that their power had been broken but the truth was that everything had changed. The square would never again be looked upon as the sacred domain of the Long Gobberleys. From that day forward it would be regarded as open ground nor would the men who had taken it over that morning by compulsory acquisition have it otherwise. It was not their aim to establish sham rights the way the Long Gobberleys had. All they had ever wanted to do, and they would swear to this in any court of law, was to strike a blow for the small and the middling farmer.

When Jacko Flannery regained his breath and subsequently his equilibrium he related the grim news which he had overheard at the Trallock Arms. Apparently the Long Gobberleys were prepared to swallow their pride and allow matters to rest. Their humour was partially restored and they had dined well. They were now in the process of addressing themselves to some serious drinking in the bar of the Trallock Arms. Their profits from the day were enormous by previous standards and there was a promise of better days to come. The Economic War with Britain was a thing of the past. There would be a demand for beef unlike any experienced by Irish farmers within living memory. Well might the Long Gobberleys congratulate themselves.

Now to add to their already brimming cups there was the prospect of an alliance from a most unlikely quarter as Neddy Drangen and his brother-in-law, Dinny O'Day, told their tale of woe to Thade Joe Gobberley and his kinsmen. It gave the leader of the Long Gobberleys all he could to to suppress a smile. Instead he presented a visage most grave and most sympathetic.

'You'll not take this lying down I hope.' He looked from Dinny O'Day to Neddy Drangen who by this time had been joined by Neddy's two brothers and some near relatives of Dinny O'Day's.

'All we want is our money back,' Neddy Drangen was pleased to see so many commiserating faces.

'You're entitled to your money back,' Bollicky Bill Gobberley forced his way between the disgruntled brothers-in-law and placed a friendly hand around the shoulders of each. Thrusting the partially-chewed wad of tobacco to one side of his mouth he turned his head and with considerable skill first assembled and then lodged a substantial spit under a table behind him.

'Listen boys,' Bollicky Bill outlined the situation as he saw it. 'It would appear to me,' he began, 'as it would to any honest man that you have been badly wronged. Go after your bull money. Demand it and if you don't get it we'll be outside the door of the Durango awaiting your call. If we don't get it fair we'll beat it out of them!'

The allies, for such they were from that moment and would be until they no longer needed each other, muttered approval. They numbered seventeen in all but the ranks swelled to a score of fighting men when Bollicky Bill commissioned three local thugs to align themselves with the Drangen–Gobberley alliance. The trio came from one of the town's back lanes and were possessed of the same sense of fair play as the Gobberleys. One had seen the inside of jail several times while the other two had been lucky to receive suspended sentences when prison seemed likely.

'Go now,' Bollicky Bill urged the brothers-in-law and their following, 'and we will follow.'

By Bollicky Bill's reckoning the combined forces of the adversary amounted of no more than eleven. He took into account also that two of the eleven were elderly and one was only a garsún. It was unlikely that they would attract support from onlookers. Their native haunts were too far distant and the clergymen would hardly take part.

'Easy meat as far as I can make out,' he thought as he went over the numbers a second time and concluded happily that there was no way the Drangen–Gobberley alliance could be beaten.

The moment the brothers-in-law entered the Durango Bar Mark Doran knew that trouble had arrived with them. He turned to Will Sullivan.

'Fetch Henry,' he whispered urgently, 'and fetch him now!'

Sandy Hassett counted the newcomers. They numbered nine.

'They'd never take us on without back-up,' he told Mark.

'The Gobberleys are behind them and that's for sure,' the Badger rose as did his companions when Neddy Drangen approached the table.

The bar, packed as it was from wall to wall, fell silent. Lily Carabim in the absence of Dell who was otherwise engaged, faced up to the newcomers.

'We will not tolerate any trouble here,' she cautioned. 'If there is trouble I'll have the cops on top of you before you can blink.'

'Don't worry,' Neddy Drangen assured her, 'the trouble will be outside not inside and if we get what's due to us there won't be no trouble at all.'

'You're in the wrong shop my poor man,' the Badger informed him, 'because you're owed nothing here.'

'I'm owed for the price of a bull that dropped dead from old age,' came the nasal interjection from Dinny O'Day.

'A bull that died because of your carelessness,' Neddy Drangen added bitterly, 'so we'll have our money back this minute and we'll be on our way.'

'Go,' the Badger commanded, 'while you can.'

'For the last time,' Neddy Drangen's demeanour suddenly grew more menacing, 'hand over the money or 'twill be beaten out of you!'

'I'm the man with the money,' Mark Doran made his first contribution to the argument, 'and there's nobody going to beat it out of me so be on your way before I lose my patience.'

'So be it,' Neddy Drangen opened the door and called upon the Gobberleys. Only Thade Joe entered. A gaunter specimen of manhood had never set foot in the Durango. He stood six feet four inches, long and lean and gnarly and not an ounce of excess flesh on his bones. His cheekbones stood high in his sallow face, his bushy, black eyebrows meeting over his bloodshot eyes, partly hooded by heavy lids. His long jaw when he used it to issue his challenge seemed to be an object foreign altogether to his face. His teeth were large and yellow, almost equine when his thin lips bared them for all to see.

'You Doran,' he addressed himself to Mark, 'you're in charge here are you not?'

'Correct,' Mark answered, his eyes unflinchingly fixed on those of Thade Joe Gobberley.

'Then let you and me settle it one way or the other. Let the price of the bull be the stake. If you win you keep it. If you lose it goes to this man here,' he pointed to the dung-encrusted Dinny O'Day for now the dead bull's discharge had dried on his clothes and hair.

'Fair fight or rough and tumble?' Sandy Hassett posed the question.

'Rough and tumble,' from Thade Joe Gobberley.

'Fair enough,' from Mark Doran.

Every man and boy in the bar trooped out into the square where an impromptu human ring was formed by common consent.

'To the finish,' Thade Joe Gobberley announced to one and all.

'To the finish,' Mark Doran agreed.

Mark's only apparent advantage was his age. He was ten years younger than his opponent. Thade Joe Gobberley feinted before delivering a devastating straight left to Mark's jaw. The younger man staggered but he did not fall. Had he met the ground the longer man would have finished him off there and then with a kick from his size 12 cattle boot. Mark easily avoided the rush of blows which followed. All landed on thin air. Both men paused for a moment to draw breath. On the resumption Thade Joe was on target for the second time with a shattering straight left. Again Mark staggered. Groggily he kept his distance from the murderous left hand. It began to dawn on him that he must surely go down unless he managed to get inside the long man's guard. Again came the left, grazing his temple this time but quickly followed by another which caught him on the ear.

They fought warily for a long spell, Mark absorbing further punishment although nothing as damaging as the first two blows. Suddenly Thade Joe struck again, a straight left, a classic of its kind sent Mark reeling into the crowd. Quickly Thade Joe followed up his advantage but a sympathetic push from behind sent Mark stumbling into the centre of the arena and out of range of the wild but potentially stunning blows of the Gobberley leader.

'Bide your time,' the advice came from the Badger Doran who stood rigidly with clenched fists in the front ranks of the crowd. Mark was bleeding from a number of cuts. Only one, just above the temple, would need stitching. He wiped the blood away from his eyes.

When Thade Joe Gobberley turned there was no trace of his opponent. Mark had stepped back a few paces so that he seemed part of the crowd. Shading his eyes with his right hand Thade Joe peered all around. Suddenly Mark was upon him, raining lethal right hands on his face and body. Thade Joe Gobberley was taken by surprise. He seized Mark around the back and squeezed for all he was worth. Unluckily for him he did not have shoulders proportionate to his height. Mark broke away easily and moved quickly around the ring, tiring his adversary. Goaded into action by his henchmen the long man struck again and again, but never on target. Now he paused and rested, his hands on his hips, his chest heaving. Mark was upon him a second time before he had a chance to raise his guard. This time Mark landed a left cross followed by a telling blow to the midriff. Again Thade Joe Gobberley held on for dear life. Mark broke quickly away, the long man catching him with a powerful left as he tried to dance out of reach. Mark found himself on his knees. Fortunately for him Thade Joe was too groggy to take advantage. He lunged forward but Mark rolled out of his way and struggled to his feet.

The crowd, wild and crazed from the beginning were now berserk, one section calling for Long Gobberley blood and another for the blood of Mark Doran. From where the Badger stood the fight was over. He knew that the leader of the Gobberleys had shot his bolt, that his only hope lay in treachery.

The pair in the ring were now at it hammer and tongs with no holds barred. The crowd closed in as the pair of bloodied, weakening adversaries fought it out to a finish. Thade Joe Gobberley it was who first backed away. Mark followed up ruthlessly, landing a smashing right fist on the long man's nose. It was then that Bol-

licky Bill Gobberley took a hand. Unseen by Mark he
struck the younger man from behind. It was a savage
blow. Mark managed to stay on his feet. Luckily Thade
Joe Gobberley was winded, his long hands hanging use-
lessly by his sides. Not for the price of a prime bullock
could he have raised one even if he thought it would
have finished the fight. Bollicky Bill's unsporting blow
was the signal for which the Gobberley–Drangen alliance had been waiting. The Badger caught the perpet-
rator of the foul blow across the small of the back with
his ash knopstick. Slender and pliant it stung to the
quick. Angrily Bollicky Bill turned but again the Badger,
dexterously twirling his stick, landed a second stunning
blow on the top of Bollicky Bill's head. He fell on his
posterior. The Badger turned away to aid his outnumbered friends. He was seized from behind by one of the
laneway mercenaries and dispossessed of his stick.
While one held him another drew back his hand to
strike. Fizz Moran saw to it that the blow never landed.
Up the sleeve of his coat was an apothecary's pestle.
Smiling sweetly he allowed it to slip into his grasp.
Gently he allowed it to fall upon the head of the unsuspecting thug. He fell at once to the ground. A young
member of the Gobberley–Drangen alliance ran at Fizz
Moran from behind. He never achieved his objective.
Archibald Scuttard, Rector of Tubberlick, extended a
foot at precisely the right moment and the youthful
assailant fell on his face and eyes, not knowing what had
tripped him. The Rector stood with his hands behind his
back, his lips pursed in a silent whistle. Despite the
timely interventions of the apothecary and Archie Scuttard it seemed that the alliance must carry the day.
Sandy Hassett found himself fighting three opponents
but he yielded not so much as a solitary inch. The Sullivan brothers, despite their several engagements with the
sisters Carabim, fought valiantly as did the Mullanneys
although young Florry was knocked unconscious early

in the proceedings after receiving a blow from behind on the cheek-bone from Dinny O'Day. The cowardly act was quickly avenged by his brother Tom who floored the culprit with a savage right hand. When Jay Mullanney was knocked to the ground outside the door of the Durango it seemed that he must be kicked senseless. Dell Carabim appeared in the nick of time with a kettleful of boiling water.

'I'll scald the first bastard to use a boot,' she screamed while her sister dragged the senseless Jay indoors.

Philly Hinds and Danny Dooley fought back to back and gave a good account of themselves. The Badger wearied and bloodstained fought with his back to the wall. Beside him Mattie Holligan refused to yield. Every so often he would rush into the melee and floor an unsuspecting member of the alliance. As the fight drew to a close the Ballyboites surrounded the Badger. All were resolved to fight to the last gasp although outnumbered two to one even after Jay Mullanney, revitalised by the motherly ministrations of the sisters Carabim, rejoined them for a last stand. Florry Mullanney too had come around. Their adversaries, sticks at the ready, fists clenched, readied themselves to move in for the kill.

'Get the civic guards,' a woman's voice called. She sensed maiming or maybe worse in the offing. Truth to tell two civic guards had entered the square a few moments earlier and, standing at the farthest corner, had viewed the disturbance from a distance.

'What will we do?' the younger guard asked.

'Nothing,' replied his senior. 'If we attempt to intervene, the sight of our uniforms will only inflame them and we'll have made a bad situation worse. Let's do a round of the town and come back when it's over.'

They left the scene and would not return until peace and harmony were restored. Any reasonable man would agree that it was a wise decision.

Just as the Alliance closed in, the besieged were joined by an unlikely ally. In his upstairs bedroom, in the Durango, Algie Clawhammer was awakened by the clamour below. From the window he saw the tiny knot of Ballyboites surrounded by twice their number. There were soldiers in the watching crowd. On the edge he spotted Sergeant Rowley. Agonising as to what he should do he watched when the Monsignor, with hands raised, placed himself between the opposing factions. He no longer wore his priestly garb. If he had he might have escaped the blow which Bollicky Bill landed on the back of his head. He crumpled to the ground. The treatment of the man who had befriended him that morning so nauseated Algie Clawhammer that he decided, Rowley or not, to join his friends. His arrival was greeted with a cheer. Even with his presence the Ballyboites stood no chance. Then a remarkable thing happened. The action was initiated by the Rector who wore sunglasses and a black overcoat to hide his identity. He had been watching in despair when Daisy Popple's Baby Ford drew up outside the Durango. There was one other occupant. His size and girth almost filled the car's interior. With difficulty he managed to extricate his mighty frame.

'What's going on here?' he asked the Rector.

'It looks like your sons are about to be slaughtered!'

'Slaughtered!' Haybags roared, 'my sons!'

He advanced upon the Gobberley–Drangen alliance roaring at the top of his voice. Onlookers scattered in fear before him. Others he seized and cast aside and then he broke into a run. In his hurry to accept Daisy Popple's invitation of a lift to Trallock he had forgotten to change the hobnailed boots which he had been wearing when she arrived. He had donned a collar and tie and a bright sports coat to suit the occasion but he had neglected his feet.

As Haybags Mullanney ran he roared and as he roared people fled. The hobnailed boots fell with the force of Mills bombs on the pavement. The Gobberley retainers who were nearest the approaching giant fled as one. The thugs from the laneway followed suit lest he seize and devour them. Haybags rushed at the remnants of the Alliance, hands extended to embrace as many of the enemy as he could. When he fell they fell with him and when he rose they ran. He stood bellowing, entreating them to come back so that he might massacre each and every one of them. He then threw his hat on the ground and offered out any three men in the crowd. Nobody accepted his challenge. He looked a fearsome sight with his massive girth and great height and leonine head and swelling chest and bull-like neck and snarling mouth and ham-like fists.

Finding nobody to take him on he turned to the Rector and invited him for a drink. The sons and neighbours whose lives he had saved followed him meekly. He might be the worst fist fighter and the worst wrestler ever to descend upon the town of Trallock but he had fearlessly carried the day and would be remembered for his courage when others, more skilful, would be long forgotten.

Mark reached an agreement with Jacko Flannery for a bimonthly supply of Roscreas at a price that would move steadily upwards until the end of the war.

'Unfortunately for all concerned,' Flannery noted, 'the nearest rail link with Tubberlick or Ballybo is too far but if you have the right politics you might persuade the railway to construct a temporary siding at the line's nearest point which is only fourteen miles.'

Mark had promised to look into the matter at which the Rector of Tubberlick who had been present declared that there would be no need of political lobbying if only Mark would consider contesting a government seat under the banner of the freshly-founded Farmers Party.

'With the right man,' the Rector pursued the idea over which he had been mulling for some time, 'there's a seat there for the taking.'

'I know nothing about politics,' Mark was quick to counter.

'There's time enough to learn,' Jacko Flannery put in, 'and if there's a seat to be won on the farmers' behalf you're the man to win it.'

Mark had remained silent as Danny Dooley later recalled. Certainly a huge majority of the hill-country votes would be cast in favour of Mark Doran, his own among them although he was an avowed supporter of the Fine Gael party. The Republican vote would also go Mark's way if he played his cards right.

After a long pause Mark excused himself on the grounds that he had to engage in some shopping on his mother's behalf much to the surprise of Danny Dooley who had been entrusted before the drive started with a sizeable list of items which he had already purchased on Nonie Doran's behalf. Sooner or later he would have to face up to Mark and reveal the deep feelings which had developed between the well-preserved widow and himself since his arrival at the farm. He had already spoken to Nonie Doran on the matter and was delighted to hear that his honourable overtures were welcome and provided Mark had no objection she would gladly exchange vows with him as soon as the summer hay of the following year was saved and safely in the shed. So daunting did Danny Dooley find the prospect of facing his prospective stepson that he approached his friend the Badger who promised to bring the matter to Mark's attention at the first opportunity.

'I foresee no difficulties,' the Badger had assured him. 'Mark has marriage in his eye and if he's to bring a new woman in he'll have to make alternative arrangements for the woman already inside.'

20

Sergeant Greg Rowley, terror of the army detention centre and all those who found themselves temporarily under his command, decided to bide his time. He had resisted the urge to effect the arrest of Algie Clawhammer after Corporal Kelly had identified him among the beleaguered Ballybo men. He might have, if he so wished, enlisted the aid of the civic guards but felt it prudent to wait until the deserter happened to be on his own. Attempting to take Algie into custody while he was in the company of his friends would require a company of soldiers and even then there was the likelihood that he might escape in the ensuing confusion.

'Sooner or later,' Rowley told his Corporals Kelly and Mannix, 'he's going to make a break for the railway line and that's where we'll nail him.'

The Corporals exchanged dubious glances. The Bedford and the troops under the command of Lieutenant Brinsley Cobb had returned to Sarsfield Barracks in Limerick city and would not be returning until morning when the search for the last of the fugitives would be resumed. Cobb's commanding officer might well decide that the Lieutenant's platoon should be reinforced. The capture of Algie Clawhammer had become a priority. Word of his exploits and the futile attempts to capture him had spread among the rank and file of the division and there were many who secretly wished him well especially after hearing that Sergeant Rowley was involved in pursuit. It was doubtful if there was a more unpopular non-commissioned officer in the Southern Command. The Sergeant was only too well aware of his superiors' concern regarding the absentee Private. The capture of such an elusive and notorious character should serve as a warning to others who might entertain notions of deserting to the British army, especially Vickers' machine-gunners.

The Corporals Kelly and Mannix, in their private exchanges, often tried to find the reason underlying the Sergeant's obsession with the Pom Conway. He had never before been so dedicated or so determined.

'There has to be something,' Kelly who was the younger of the pair and who heartily detested his Sergeant declared.

'But what?' Mannix asked, 'it couldn't be jealousy. I mean who could possibly be jealous of the Pom!'

Inadvertently Corporal Mannix had struck the nail upon the head but the question he posed was still a perplexing one. The answer surprisingly lay in a rebuff which the Sergeant experienced one pay night on the pavements of a sometimes proscribed area near the entrance to Collins Barracks in the city of Cork.

As was their wont on pay nights a number of girls had discreetly established themselves where they might waylay compliant off-duty men with money in their pockets. These erring sisters of the darkness were much in demand on Wednesday nights when the private soldier, provided there were no withholdings by way of fines, found himself with the weekly wage of thirteen shillings and two pence in his pocket. For a modest percentage of this equally modest subvention the easygoing ladies of the city provided temporary relief and entertainment of a non-horizontal variety in a matter of minutes. Such activities were not condoned by the authorities but neither were there any serious attempts to curb them. So it was that the Sergeant found himself in the vicinity of the barracks on a night when demand exceeded supply. Indeed only a mousy-haired, anaemic-looking woman in a black shawl remained on offer when the Sergeant put in an appearance freshly shaved, hair trimmed and brilliantined, brown shoes gleaming, Sergeant's stripes newly carminated, cap forward. Sergeant Rowley was a text-book soldier. The Pom Conway was the opposite.

Sergeant Rowley had never seen him before but he would remember him with unconcealed bitterness. The one remaining temptress out of the droves of girls allowed her shawl to fall from her shoulders to her waistline. The Private and the Sergeant arrived at either side of her at exactly the same time. After the briefest of glances at both she made her selection instantly. To Sergeant Rowley's disgust she elected for the private soldier. Rowley could hardly contain his fury. His teeth chattered with hurt and indignation. Either the girl did not like Sergeants or she must have found him extraordinarily repulsive. He never conceded that the Pom Conway might be in some way attractive to women or could it be that the bawdy stories concerning the sexual abnormality of small men might have some foundation after all!

'How in Christ,' the Sergeant asked himself, 'did the wretch even pass inspection! Everything about him was wrong. His hair exceeded regulation. There was mud on his uppers and there was a button missing from his tunic.'

Some months later a young Lieutenant and two Private soldiers arrived at the gates of the detention centre in a single-wheeled Bedford for the express purpose of delivering a prisoner. As Sergeant Rowley wrote out the receipt, for the live body and equipment of Private Patrick Desmond Conway, he looked briefly at the prisoner to make sure that he was really in one piece. He immediately recognised the unkept, unsoldierly specimen, almost unidentifiable under the fifty-six pound pack. That evening, before he collapsed after countless rounds in full pack of the detention centre square, he received a short lecture from Sergeant Rowley on the subject of sock stealing.

'Don't you believe,' Rowley, hands behind back, addressed the tiny, panting figure still marking time, 'what

Napoleon said about an army marching on its stomach?'

'It wasn't Napoleon said that. It was an army cook said it. Napoleon said an army marches on its socks.' Breathless and barely able to stand the luckless Private listened as his chest heaved and his legs buckled under the pack.

'Now you listen to me, you sock-stealing Pom, a soldier's socks are part of his weaponry, the same as his gun or his bayonet. A soldier without socks is restricted in his capacity as a fighting man. When you steal the socks of a fellow-soldier you put his life at risk. If I ever again hear of you stealing a sock no matter how sweaty or how full of holes I'll deracinate your cobbles with my bare hands. Now sing after me!'

In double time Rowley led the way round the square chanting raucously: 'I'm a dirty, sock-stealing Pom. That's what I am. That's what I am!'

When the nightmare in the detention centre ended Algie Clawhammer enjoyed a short period of freedom if ever an out-of-favour soldier's sojourn in an army can be described as freedom. In less than two months he found himself in the detention centre for a second six month period. This time he had stolen shirts as well as socks, all to satisfy his craving for drink. On this occasion the urge had seized him when he saw a girl on a bicycle one morning who reminded him of his late wife.

Now happily ensconced among his friends in the Durango he began to formulate a plan which he hoped would see him safely out of the country. With the assistance of Sandy Hassett who would again borrow the Rector's bike, without his permission, he would be deposited at a small railway station about twelve miles from Limerick city. With any luck he should find himself in the city's marshalling yards with plenty of time in hand to catch the earliest of the passenger trains to Dublin and thence to London by boat.

In addition to a smart grey overcoat which the Badger had lifted from a rack in the Trallock Arms on the grounds that its new wearer would need it more than its legitimate owner, Algie found himself with a pocketful of silver amounting to several pounds, all subscribed willingly by the drovers of Ballybo and the assorted clergy of Tubberlick and California.

'Don't you go buying no ticket at the station. If they're still after you that's the first place they'll ask.' The advice was tendered by Mattie Holligan through a badly-swollen upper lip.

'You hang around the goods area till the train is just pulling out of the station,' Mattie continued, 'then you board her. You can pay your fare when the conductor asks you for the ticket.'

There were prolonged goodbyes, some drunken but all genuine. There were tears and fond embraces from the sisters Carabim and blessings from both clerics.

When Sandy Hassett arrived with the bike his passenger was waiting in the Durango doorway with Mattie Holligan and Danny Dooley. Promising to write and acquaint them of his safe arrival, Algie Clawhammer perched himself upon the pillion. Racing the powerful engine, Sandy accelerated. They moved slowly out of the square and into a little-used laneway which would eventually take them onto the main Limerick road. During their sojourn in the Durango after the fight the wind had strengthened considerably, growing more assertive by the moment as they sped over the even surface on the first phase of Algie Clawhammer's long journey.

Algie breathed his first sigh of relief since his fortuitous escape of the morning. He might not have breathed so easily had he known that Sergeant Rowley and the Corporals Kelly and Mannix were not far behind. After the victorious Ballybo men had retired to the Durango Rowley had gone immediately to the barracks of the civic guards where he identified himself to the young orderly who chanced to be on duty. The orderly excused himself while he went in search of the Sergeant-in-residence. He found him seated by the fire in the tiny sitting-room of the married quarters. His wife sat opposite, darning studiously. Their three children sat on the linoleum-covered floor, their school books spread all around.

'What is it now?' the Sergeant asked angrily. It was the third time since his supper that the much-prized and peaceful sojourn with his family had been interrupted.

'It's an army Sergeant sir,' the orderly informed his drowsy superior after he had first excused himself.

Later after the formalities had been dispensed with and they had been many, including calls to the Commandant of the detention centre and the Chief Superintendent of the county, Sergeant Rowley found himself seated in the local patrol car, a cumbersome V-8 badly in need of replacement. The detective-driver, a middle-aged man, taciturn and disinterested, sat with Rowley and the Corporals in the battered vehicle strategically parked under an archway from where the front and side exits of the Durango were observable to the car's occupants.

When Sandy Hassett emerged and made his way to the laneway entrance which would take him to the rear of Fizz Moran's, Sergeant Rowley presumed that the big man was merely attending to the needs of a horse or pony, stabled over-night in one of the laneway's many outhouses. Some moments later when he heard the sound of a motor cycle it dawned on him that they might well be listening to the sounds of a getaway vehicle. The sound also alerted the indifferent sleuth, his elbows resting on the steering wheel. A motor cycle had been involved in the morning's affray outside the Trallock Arms. The investigation into this particular disturbance was still on-going and had turned an unwelcome spotlight on the local Superintendent and, inevitably, generated a good deal of hassle for those under his command.

The four occupants of the police car watched while Algie Clawhammer mounted the pillion of the BSA. They did not attempt to overtake when the driver, helmeted and goggled, unexpectedly turned into the little-used laneway. Detective Colligy followed at a respectful distance knowing full well where the laneway led. Even if he found it necessary to over-take he was only too well aware that the powerful bike would leave them far behind in a matter of minutes. Sooner or later the fugitive and his accomplice would arrive at their destination.

From an early stage Detective Colligy decided to drive without lights. Despite the high wind the skies were clear. A generous moon threw sufficient light on the wide roadway. From time to time they passed groups of cattle with vigilant drovers conspicuous at front and rear. Always Colligy slowed down to avoid collision with errant heifers or weanlings and to enquire if a motor cycle had passed. Always came the reassuring responses that it had just passed or was just up ahead. Always too he would ask if there was a pillion passenger. The answer was always in the affirmative.

Even after they had driven twenty miles the car occupants were still filled with wonder at the steady gait of the cattle and drovers, particularly the latter. Cattle were expected to travel all day and night but these men seemed capable of going on forever. Many, even if they had desperately required a rest, dared not stop lest the cattle wander afar in the darkness, availing of gaps and hidden by-ways. To be certain that their charges never strayed the only solution was to keep moving as briskly as possible.

'Looks like they're headed for the city,' Detective Colligy made the observation to himself.

'I doubt it,' Sergeant Rowley based his disagreement on the certainty that the city terminal would be under

DURANGO

constant surveillance by the police and the army not just
for the fugitive Private but for other wartime interlopers
as well.

'No!' Rowley was adamant, 'he dare not show himself at the ticket office and you won't catch him on the
passenger platform. They'll stop any minute now. You'll
see.' Rowley was to remain silent and thoughtful until
their next sighting which turned out to be a substantial
herd of mixed cattle.

'No,' the drovers had not seen a motor cycle with a
pillion passenger. In fact the only traffic they had encountered in several miles was a drunken farmers' boy
cycling home from the fair. How could they forget him!
Hadn't he fallen from his cycle several times.

'The last village,' there was urgency in Rowley's
voice. 'We passed it just two minutes ago. There's a station there. The city is only ten or twelve miles. He'll walk
it inside three hours no bother. The way I see it he'll hole
up in the marshalling yards till morning and make a
break for the early passenger train.'

On their way back to the village, this time with
lights fully on, they saw the BSA minus its pillion passenger leaving the station grounds on its way back to
Trallock.

Sandy Hassett had no way of knowing that the re-
ceding car's passengers were in pursuit of his friend. For
one thing the vehicle had come from the direction of the
city and therefore its occupants could not know that he
had deposited the fugitive at the station. Sandy decided
to drive the bike to the stable at the rear of Fizz Moran's
and rejoin his companions at the Durango. He might
even go to the Trallock and District Farmers' Ball, an
annual affair in the parochial hall where, according to
reports, there was a new maple floor which greatly fac-
ilitated smooth dancing, particularly the old time waltz.
He might even find a wife. Sandy laughed out loud. He
could converse without difficulty with old women and

309

young girls but he was struck dumb whenever he found himself confronted by a marriageable prospect.

'I've never had a woman,' he informed the night. 'What would the boys think if they knew! They would not believe it of Sandy Hassett, dispatch rider, fist-fighter and farm manager you might say. Never had a woman! Sandy Hassett! You're joking man.'

He decided against the dance.

'I'm a Protestant and there won't be Protestants at the dance and if there were Protestant girls itself how would I know them!' He resumed his conversation with the night, 'and anyway,' he lied 'I'm quite happy the way I am.' His thoughts turned to the carousel at the Durango as the BSA shot from twenty-five to forty miles an hour.

The high winds had turned into a storm as Sergeant Rowley set out along the tracks from the station. On his orders Detective Colligy had transported the Corporals Kelly and Mannix to the next station. At some point in between they would meet up with Algie Clawhammer and there would be a private moment of reckoning before he was formally taken into custody.

'As for you,' he turned to the detective, 'as soon as you drop this pair I want you to patrol the road between both stations. If our man escapes us and manages to make a run for it you follow him and arrest him. I don't care if you run the bastard down or shoot him so long as you don't kill him altogether.'

If Detective Colligy entertained any ideas to the contrary he kept them to himself. It wasn't that he disliked the Sergeant or that he resented taking orders from a man he regarded as his subordinate. Rather did he feel distaste for army procedures. In his own case if he wished to leave the police force all he had to do was retire or if he had not served the requisite pensionable years he could resign. He failed to see why a man could not also resign from the army if he felt like it. Different if there was conscription but keeping a man on year after year against his will was tantamount to coercion and after all it was supposed to be a free state. Where is the freedom in such inhumanity, Colligy asked himself. All right, there were bastards in the civic guards and they could make life hell. There were also bastards in the professions but you could always opt out. Soldiering was the only profession from which there was no escape. Colligy had gathered that the man they were after was wanted for petty crimes, notably sock stealing for which he seemed to have a habitual proclivity. Why all the fuss then over a sock stealer absent without leave! It was beyond the detective's comprehension. He would patrol the roadway as requested and he would keep an eye out for the missing man as requested but he's be damned if he'd open fire or run the unfortunate fellow down.

A strong, north-westerly gale, blustery and gusty, blew into the faces of Algie Clawhammer and his lone pursuer less than three hundred yards behind. For the first time in four days the high overhead pressure showed signs of weakening. Scudding, expanding clouds occasionally obscured the moon, shredding and sometimes totally obliterating its light. It was during these periods of darkness that Sergeant Rowley doubled his pace, taking two wooden sleepers in his stride instead of one. After one such burst he found himself only yards behind the unsuspecting Algie Clawhammer. The smaller man walked with his head bent, intent on locating a sleeper at every extended footfall. He was obliged to stretch his legs to their utmost lest he slip and fall on the crushed rock underneath the cross-ties. It accounted for all his concentration. If the wind had been blowing from behind he would have heard the footsteps in time to take evasive action. Instead he was taken completely by surprise and brought down by the sheer weight of his assailant. The Sergeant might have drawn his side-arm but contemptuously he quickly and skilfully seized the fugitive's left wrist and twisted the hand diagonally across his back. Algie Clawhammer cried out in pain. Sergeant Rowley increased the pressure, enjoying the grimacing and screaming of his captive. Raising his free hand to the side of his mouth the Sergeant called out in the direction from which his Corporals must at any moment approach. His voice failed to carry against the boisterous wind. By now the moon had shaken off the ever-increasing clouds which had shuttered its light. Once again its rays had transformed the parallel steel rails into gleaming silver. Sergeant Rowley released the imprisoned hand and shook the luckless prisoner as a cat might shake a mouse.

'You should have known better Pom,' he taunted, 'didn't you know that I would always find you, you dirty little gobshite. Didn't you know that you can't escape me. I am your nemesis. Do you know what a nemesis is Pom? Course you don't you horrid apology for a soldier. I seen rats Pom and they smelled better than you and I seen pigs Pom that looked cleaner than you. You know what you really are Pom? You are the worlds' dirtiest living soldier.'

As Rowley spoke he shook the unfortunate Algie with one hand and slapped his face with the other. The Sergeant might have used his fists but he was under orders to return the live body of his captive intact as per army regulations. Slapping, administered consistently and with the right amount of force, was more effective than striking with the bare knuckles and besides, the victim suffered more. There was a greater sense of shock and the subject stayed conscious for a much longer period. Rowley's well-tried system was guaranteed to inflict the maximum amount of suffering with the minimum amount of physical damage. He spat in disgust on his captive's face when he felt the undersized body go limp in his hands. When he released his hold Algie Clawhammer fell noiselessly to the ground.

'Don't die on me you whore's melt,' Rowley whispered the words passionately before cupping his hands around his mouth and shouting with all his might into the wind. There was no answering call. Then suddenly the Corporals appeared in the distance, clearly visible as the bright moonlight flooded the landscape. Now that they could distinguish the Sergeant and his prisoner they began to wave their arms wildly. As they drew nearer they began to shout but even though their voices were carried further than was normal by the northwesterly their efforts to communicate with Rowley failed abysmally. Realising that he could not hear they began to gesticulate furiously. He convinced himself that the pair were clowning and, worst of all, clowning at his expense. He would have something to say when they met. He raised a warning fist and as he did he was caught by the most stunning blow of his entire life. So pre-occupied had he been with the antics of the Corporals that he had not noticed when Algie Clawhammer raised himself to his knees nor had he the slightest opportunity to dodge the powerful, left-handed uppercut which caught him on the jaw. Never in his life had Algie Clawhammer struck anybody so hard with the naked fist and yet he failed to bring his tormentor down. Both men were now standing but before Algie could strike a second blow the Sergeant threw his arms around him and held on in a desperate bid to clear his head. Then all of a sudden as though they had been forewarned simultaneously by the same instinct for survival they turned in horror to see the mighty J-class engine bearing down upon them. For the first time the Sergeant understood why the Corporals had been signalling with such abandon. The icy chill of fear paralysed him as he realised that death seemed unavoidable. Then the looming, towering engine was upon him. He screamed and covered his face but miraculously he found himself being pushed into a briar clump at the side of the line. Algie Clawhammer died instantly. When his legs failed to respond he pushed Sergeant Rowley with all his remaining strength. The fugitive's body was found in a field next to the railway line by Sergeant Rowley and his Corporals.

'You owe him your life.' The words were spoken by Corporal Kelly after he had whispered an Act of Contrition into the dead man's ear.

'I owe that git nothing,' the Sergeant was quick to deny the victim's role in his last-minute deliverance.

'Remember it was I who put my life at risk. It was I who was doing my duty. I was in the right.'

'He pushed you Sarge. You can't take away from that,' Corporal Mannix took his colleague's side.

'And I say I jumped.' The Sergeant was emphatic but for all his assurance his bravado seemed to have deserted him. He was badly shaken. His hands trembled as he stood with head averted after they had laid the body on an iron seat in the exposed platform.

'If either of you breathe another word about my being pushed you'll spend the next twelve months in the detention centre.'

Rowley's threat carried little conviction. The Corporals, by unspoken consent, decided to keep their own counsel until a later date. At the subsequent inquest, however, they would speak of the dead man's gallant action.

21

On the day after the fair the winds died. The weather reverted to its previously composed conditions with bright sunshine and the reviving tingle of autumnal frost in the morning air. The odour of stale cowdung dominated every street and laneway, often wafting its way indoors through open doors and windows on gentle currents of air. Gone was the stifling pungency of the day before, extenuated and even made bearable by the wind and rain of the night.

'That's a healthy smell boy,' the shopkeepers of Trallock insisted good-humouredly when strangers, unaccustomed to the still-cloying if diminishing graveolence, wrinkled their noses in disgust, feigned or otherwise.

'That's the smell of money boy so take a good whiff because it isn't everywhere you'll find it.'

In the square a few cattle still squatted. Three were Roscreas, consumption-ridden, emaciated rejects and there was one scour-infected white weanling with the bones barely contained in its sickly hide, abandoned by his owner after fruitless attempts to dispose of the creature the day before. Sooner or later all would be claimed or bought by knackers for little more than pittances. There were also human rejects, many of them sprawled under archways, others curled up from the cold in doorways and corners. One, a shawled tinker woman sat with her back to a house-front, her bare legs askew, her mouth porter-stained, her cracked voice feebly raised in song when she was not cursing passers-by. She too would be claimed before the morning gave way to noon.

Florry Mullanney was the first of the Ballybo men to open his eyes. A mantelpiece clock informed him of the time. Twenty to nine. He had no recollection of going to bed. He had vague memories of a dance and of being

315

transported on his brother Tom's back. Beside him Dell Carabim lay becalmed in smiling sleep. At her other side Will Sullivan snored as though his craving for sleep would never be satisfied. On the floor between bed and doorway lay Tom Mullanney, a blanket drawn over his head, his bare bottom exposed for all to behold, his breathing deep and powerful. Dell Carabim stirred and breathed a gentle sigh as Florry Mullanney addressed himself at once to his duties.

'To woo is to waste,' his paramour whispered encouragingly. If Florry heard or understood he gave no sign. Rather did he commit himself silently and industriously to the task in hand. His was the sort of urgency that brooked neither foreplay nor blandishment. If brief in itself, his performance was so high-powered and assertive that Dell Carabim was quite overwhelmed. After, he lay silently on his back hardly breathing. Dell was surprised that there was none of the panting and breathlessness peculiar to the male of the species after such encounters. She turned to see if he was all right only to be silently restored to her original position in readiness for a second assault of a slightly longer duration but no less vigorous and no less red-blooded so that, at the conclusion of the final engagement, Dell Carabim lay gloriously realised.

There was more to come for as Florry Mullanney struggled with his trousers there were stirrings from the other occupants of the room and he was not surprised to see that the place he vacated was filled by the powerful body, freckled and bare, of his brother Tom.

As Florry Mullanney left the room he was assailed by a most unholy hunger for food. He turned to see Dell Carabim extend plump white arms, one about each of the feverish youths who vied for her favours.

In the downstairs kitchen to where he was attracted by the mouth-watering odour of frying rashers Florry Mullanney was surprised to see his father, freshly shaven, seated at the head of the table. At the bottom sat the Rector, none the worse after the alcoholic excesses of the night before.

A somewhat bleary-eyed Monsignor Binge sat at one side with Henry Sullivan while Florry's brother Jay sat alone at the other. Presiding over the entire proceedings was the immaculately-dressed Lily Carabim who immediately placed a motherly hand around the shoulder of Florry Mullanney and directed him to a place at the table next to his brother Jay.

Florry guessed rightly that his hostess had been comprehensively accommodated by both Jay and his accomplice Henry Sullivan.

Daisy Popple spent the night in the Trallock Arms. Her car remained outside the Durango. The others of the Ballybo contingent spent the night at Fizz Moran's where they were also at breakfast. All were astonished to hear that Sandy Hassett, who decided to go to the dance after all, had left the hall with a buxom woman in tow, a widow of several years standing who attached herself to Sandy the moment he set his foot inside the dance-hall door and without as much as a by-your-leave took him straight to her cottage on the outskirts of the town lest he be lured from her side by some unattached doxie of evil intent. The widow, a decent poor soul, who had reluctantly abandoned her lonely hearth to accompany a female friend to the annual ball felt that she had no reason to look a second time at the soldierly-looking man with so little to say for himself. Here, she sensed, without doubt, is the makings of a partner with whom I wouldn't mind sharing my hearth. It won't be accomplished tonight and it won't be accomplished tomorrow but by the grace of God, accomplished it will be.

For his part Sandy Hassett was impressed and remained in her kitchen till the very crack of dawn, drinking tea and, aided by her subtle prompting, slowly but surely finding his speech.

From the beginning it had been agreed that all would re-group at the Durango at eleven o'clock. After a farewell drink, and it would be no more, by common consent they would set out on the return journey to the hill country. It was agreed that they would travel together with the exception of Sandy Hassett who requested and was granted permission from Daisy Popple for a few days holiday which would be spent at the abode of his newly-acquired girlfriend. Indeed Daisy had intimated that he might avail himself of an ancient cottage on the Popple estate should he commit himself to a lasting relationship with the widow. Since this was the highest notion in the big man's head and since he was a fellow of few words he expressed his appreciation of his mistress' generosity by lifting her bodily into the air and implanting a kiss on her forehead before placing her gently on the ground.

Dell Carabim preceded her bedroom guests downstairs. Haybags Mullanney remarked upon her vivacity and cheerfulness as she prepared breakfast places for his son Tom and a yawning Will Sullivan. Later in the bar they were joined by Fizz Moran and his wife Gertie. The latter never frequented public houses but so taken was she by the kindness and good manners of her overnight guests that she decided to accompany her husband on this particular occasion. Discreetly she handed over a substantial Mass offering to Monsignor Binge and she felt compelled to bestow a similar amount on the reluctant Rector.

'Since,' said she, 'I could not very well make fish of one and fowl of the other.'

When the apothecary and his wife were invited by Mattie Holligan to spend a summer weekend in Ballybo they readily accepted and when the all-conquering Haybags Mullanney presented Gertie and the sisters Carabim with large boxes of chocolates there were tears in Gertie Moran's eyes.

During the final drink at the Durango it was decided that the main party would leave Trallock together at the chiming of the Angelus bell. There was always the danger that the Long Gobberleys might stage another attack if the Ballybo party became fragmented. Had the hill men but known, the Gobberleys were in no condition to resume the battle. Not only were they ashamed to come out-of-doors but they were also afraid for their lives since word was abroad that the giant who had demoralised them the night before was still on the warpath except that this time he was looking for blood. The fearful tidings had been conveyed by their retainers who themselves had little stomach for a resumption of the fray. At five to twelve Danny Dooley arrived with the mare and rail. He tethered the spanking ten year old to an adjacent telephone pole while he rounded up his companions. There was no sign of Mark Doran but it was Danny's guess that he was in the company of Jacko Flannery.

At the first peal of the noonday bell the hill men recited the Angelus. Then they gathered themselves. There were fond farewells and tender embraces but then, manfully, they marched out of doors. It was decided that they would proceed without stop, on foot, to Mattie Holligan's of Ballybo, a distance of twenty-three miles. Because of their great ages the Badger and Philly Hinds travelled in the rail with the guide Danny Dooley and whosoever of the walking party might require a respite over the long journey. It was decided that they would return the way they had come.

Haybags Mullanney with a powerful sweeping movement hoisted the protesting pensioners into the rail. Danny Dooley flicked the reins and the mare, anxious for the pastures of home, lunged against her harness before Danny steadied her into a gait which might be matched by those following behind. These were the Mullanney brothers Tom, Jay and Florry, the Sullivans, Henry and Will, and Mattie Holligan.

'By all rights,' Mattie looked at his watch, 'we should arrive at Holligan's of Ballybo around the same time as the evening star unless I'm very much mistaken but one thing is certain and that is the drinks will be on me.'

They proceeded past the Cunnackawneen where they recalled the rout of the donkey herders. All made the sign of the cross on bent foreheads as a mark of respect to the youth who, they heard, died shortly after the rout. The young fellow had been living on borrowed time because of a dickey heart which had already exceeded its allotted number of beats and they blamed themselves not in the least for his demise. Was he not marked for death anyway! At Crabapple Hill they playfully pelted the occupants of the rail with the plentiful produce of the stunted crab trees. As they put the hill behind them they savoured their first bite since breakfast, succulent crubeens washed down by bottled stout without a moment's stay.

Alas, for all their good intentions the chicks they purchased for Bessie-Lie-Down would never lay an egg in her coop because she expired when she was overcome by a seizure before dawn not long after they had left her.

'All she ever did,' the Badger told his listeners when he heard the news, 'was accommodate a few lonely souls that had no place else to turn'.

In Trallock Daisy Popple availed of Haybags Mullanney's sojourn in the Durango to get her hair done. The hero of the previous evening's hostilities sat modestly in a corner of the bar surrounded by admirers, many of them farmers like himself who prized the company of a celebrity as much as the next man. It would be something to tell their grandchildren in the winter evenings by the firelight's glow. The Rector of Tubberlick sat with Haybags Mullanney while he waited for Monsignor Binge who had retired to an upstairs room so that he might hear the general Confessions of the sisters Cara-bim.

'Bless me father for I have sinned,' Dell had opened in a trembling voice. 'I haven't made a confession for years.' Tears followed.

The Monsignor wished that he could reach out and touch her in order to reassure her. Instead he led her through the commandments, from first to last, asking ever so gently after each one if there had been failure to observe the law of God enshrined in every step of the sacred Decalogue. At the end when she expressed the view that the commandments had their limitations in her particular case he urged her to elaborate. After a moment's hesitation she told of her many iniquitous de-baucheries over the years while the Monsignor listened in wonder. He never ceased to be surprised at the many unanticipated revelations to which he had been sub-jected in the Confessional since his ordination to the priesthood. At the end of Dell's recital he was forced to concede that he had just listened to the outstanding re-pentance of his career. He sent her back into the living world shrived and purified. He knew from experience that her promise never to sin again was one that could well be maintained unbroken till the end of her days. Some time later, after he had absolved Lily Carabim of all her transgressions and listened to her promise that she would indeed sin no more, he knew in his heart that the sisters were on the threshold of a truly devotional phase and would never again relapse into their old ways. It was not for him to question or endeavour to un-ravel the paradox which saw such benign and charitable spirits involved in such contrary excesses. It was for him to forgive and to accept the will of God.

The Badger Doran put it somewhat differently as he and Florry Mullanney walked behind the plodding mare and her rail full of exhausted passengers. Mattie Hollig-an and Philly Hinds followed, a hundred yards behind.

The evening star was in place as expected and the lights of Ballybo beckoned less than a mile ahead. In the rail Danny Dooley was the only occupant standing upright. The others who had only a few short miles before exchanged places with Philly Hinds and the Badger lay huddled together on the floor of the car. Jay and Tom Mullanney slept with their mouths open. The Sullivans, Will and Henry, dozed with their heads resting on their knees.

'It was a great outing,' the Badger declared to Florry his step light, his heart uplifted as he drew nearer Ballybo.

'The best ever,' his young companion replied.

'There is one great thing which don't occur to you just now,' the Badger assumed a philosophical role, 'and that is there will be a flavour to your cud when the time comes for chewing it. There's many a poor man with no cud to chew. You're a lucky lad Florry. You swallowed more material for cud in a day and a night than most men swallow in a lifetime.'

'That's all right,' Florry Mullanney sounded worried, 'but I'll have to go to confession between now and Christmas if I'm to receive the sacred host on Christmas morning with the family.'

'Don't be too hard on yourself,' the Badger placed a hand on his shoulder, 'and try to remember that it's the nature of man to wish women upon themselves.' The Badger stopped in his tracks and pointed his ashplant upwards towards the shining moon and then to every corner of the heavens so that he might include the stars that twinkled in the cloud-free sky.

'Up there is God or so we're told,' the Badger lowered his ashplant as Mattie Holligan and Philly Hinds stopped to hear what he had to say.

'That same God,' the Badger laid a hand for the second time on the shoulder of Florry Mullanney, 'gave man dominion over the fowl and the brute, over every corner of the land and sea but man has no dominion at all over his own flute and the strange tunes it's likely to play, no dominion at all my friend and that's a thing all men must remember when shame reddens the cheek.'

Philly Hinds and Mattie Holligan nodded in silent agreement and proceeded upon their way.

Shortly after Archie Scuttard and Danny Binge made their goodbyes to the Carabims the Monsignor took a turn for the worse. Firstly, there was the most excruciating pain followed by an appalling nausea. He was quick to don his goggles and helmet in order to conceal the anguish on his face. For a moment he was tempted to request the Rector to forego for an hour their trip to Ballybo but already the BSA was in motion. As they moved out of the square Fizz Moran and a tearful Gertie raised their arms in fond farewell. As they gathered speed for their long journey the Rector was astonished and shocked to see a snarling canine leaping for his face. He raised a gloved hand to protect himself but already the bike was out of control and the pillion passenger dislodged. Before he could regain control the Rector was sent tumbling over the handle-bars, helmeted head first. The bike careered across the square dragging the dog still snarling in its wake, its body caught between the wheels, the snarling now reduced to whining and this too ceased when the bike collided with a passing truck. The dog, and Dango it undoubtedly was, had been abandoned by the Drover Mooleys but the pack leader found no difficulty in fending for himself. He had dined on a mixture of easily purloined chops, liver, sausages and assorted scraps. Fending for himself was nothing new. It was well-known that the Drover Mooleys seldom fed their pack and when they did the fare was inferior and there was never enough. The pack leader did pine, however, as any other disowned canine might do. The moment he heard the first distant purrings of the familiar and frightening engine he alerted himself for attack. When he saw the hated figure who had dispatched his pack-mates he coiled himself for onslaught. As the bike neared him Dango slunk in its direction behind a passing ass-cart. As it gathered speed he made his move. The timing was perfect. The hated figure in the saddle was caught completely off-guard. Dango might have spared his own life had he been willing to settle for the paralysis which left his arch-enemy suddenly powerless but his thirst for blood was his undoing. First his tail and then his legs became entangled with the spinning wheel-spikes. If he had not died at the moment of collision with the truck he would certainly have died from loss of blood resulting from the multiple lacerations inflicted by the pedals and spikes. He died instead from decapitation as had the bitch Queenie at the causeway between Bessie Lie-Downs's and Crabapple Hill. Dango's head was severed from his body at the instant of impact. Immediately afterwards the spikes which had been the instruments of decapitation stopped spinning as the red blood spurted from the headless trunk. Nearby lay the body of Monsignor Daniel Binge. At some stage between Dango's leap at the Rector and his collision with the truck the Monsignor lost his helmet. He died instantly from severe head injuries. The Rector lay on his back after he had somersaulted over the handle-bars of his beloved BSA. Concussed and shaken he struggled to his feet. His only concern was for the welfare of his friend. Seating himself with his back to a house-front he took the dead priest's head in his hands and looked around piteously for an explanation of the terrible events which had so mercilessly overtaken them. Daisy Popple was first on the scene. She was followed by Haybags Mullanney who gently lifted the dead Monsignor's body into his arms and bore him back to the Durango. Daisy Popple ministered to the Rector. She helped him to his feet and led him slowly to the Carabim sanctuary. He suffered from no more than mild concussion but the hospital authorities decided, nevertheless, to keep him under observation for a few days. Daisy Popple remained by his side during his waking hours attending to his every need. Surprisingly he did not ask for whiskey.

'I have only one real request Daisy,' he whispered as he took her hand away from his brow.

'And what would that be?' Daisy Popple asked indulgently.

'Your hand in marriage my dear. What else?' the Rector returned.

'Oh Archie do you really mean it?' an elated Daisy Popple asked.

'I should have asked you years ago my love,' Archie Scuttard took her hand in his and fell into a deep sleep.

Monnie the Badger waited for her husband in Holligan's kitchen in Ballybo. He told her before his departure that they would return just before dark on the day after the fair. She never revealed to any person what she had seen at the bottom of her teacup in the Holligan kitchen, not even to the Badger. She had physically recoiled and allowed the cup to smash onto the floor at her feet.

'What did the leaves say?' Maud Holligan asked anxiously, vowing there and then never to allow her beloved Mattie out of her sight again.

'I saw a boy and a girl on a snorting black steed riding into wonderland,' Monnie the Badger spoke truthfully for earlier, after her first cup of tea, she had indeed seen such a vision at the bottom of her cup and she rejoiced for she had recognised the faces of the happy pair. Never, however, would she tell of the other horrific spectacle nor could she, even if she had wanted to, for the man had worn white shining neck-wear above a flowing black robe and she deduced that a priest was at the centre of her dire presentiments. Even if she had wished, it would not have been in her power to tell for

Monnie the Badger had been brought up to believe that to speak of priests in whatever manner was sinful in the extreme.

When the weary travellers arrived at Holligan's of Ballybo they were surprised to see a giant bonfire burning brightly in front of the Holligan premises. As the nine adventurers assembled before entering the pub a cheer went up from the large crowd who had gathered for their homecoming. Moses Madigan, his hand resting on a stout holly cudgel, upraised his sole support in recognition of their achievements.

'I say to you,' he issued a warning to all enemies of Ballybo, 'beware after this day for the might of the five parishes is a match for the world.'

A rousing cheer followed.

'And I say to you,' Moses Madigan went on, his ninety year old frame trembling with rage, 'that the Long Gobberleys and their minions will shake in their boots at the mention of Ballybo from this day forth!'

Much later in the night after every man, woman and child present had commented on the inexplicable absence of Mark, word reached the hostelry of Mattie Holligan that Annie Mullanney was also missing and that search parties were being organised.

'Spare ye'erselves the trouble,' Monnie the Badger took the centre of the premises, 'for I will tell you all this now and after that I'll tell ye no more. Wherever ye'll find Mark Doran ye will also find Annie Mullanney.'

Suddenly it dawned on the assembly that the pair had eloped, and so they had, on the late passenger train from Trallock the night before without a solitary word to a living soul.

After the fight on the previous afternoon Mark had his cut stitched by a local doctor. Then by arrangement he stepped into a waiting car and was borne via the main Trallock to Killarney road and sundry diversions to the crossroads less than a mile from his home and no more than two from the home of Annie Mullanney. There, behind the trunk of a sycamore tree she waited with her suitcase as arranged. When the car stopped and Mark alighted she stepped boldly into his out-stretched arms. The hackney driver, aware for the first time that he was party to an elopement, drove silently along the cattle-cluttered roads until he reached the entrance to the passenger platform at Trallock railway station. There after pocketing his fare he told his passengers that he was taking a vow of silence until they were safely out of the country. It was he who purchased the tickets on their behalf and found for them an empty carriage at the very rear of the train. They crossed the Irish Sea shortly after midnight and married at once upon their arrival at Portsmouth where Annie's sisters acted as witnesses. Before reaching Limerick the train stopped unexpectedly for several minutes before the journey was resumed.

'A man dead on the line,' the ticket-collector explained. 'Must have been drunk, only a drunken man would walk the line on a stormy night.'

When the news of the elopement was broken to Haybags Mullanney he struggled in vain to express himself coherently and after several minutes of apoplectic expostulation he ran through the countryside bellowing like an enraged bull. His roars were heard for miles around. His passion did not abate for days and when it finally did he vowed he would dismember Mark Doran, son-in-law or no, after he had first broken every bone in his body.

Wherever Haybags went in the days that followed he heard mention of his son-in-law. In the combined parishes of Tubberlick, Tubberlee, Ballybo, Kilshunnig and Boherlahan, there was no derogatory word about the young man who had stolen his daughter. After Mass on the second Sunday after the elopement, men and women pressed forward to shake the hand of Haybags Mullanney and his wife on the acquisition of such a distinguished addition to his family. When Ballybo could only manage a fortuitous draw in the final of the district football league the Ballybo supporters bemoaned the loss of Mark Doran. In the Widow Hegarty's after the game Mick Malone brazenly enquired off Haybags Mullanney if his son-in-law would be available for the replay the Sunday before Christmas.

'Yes,' Haybags replied authoritatively after a pause. 'I'll be writing to my daughter tomorrow with instructions that they are to return home without delay.'

Nobody was surprised when word spread that Vester McCarthy's premises was empty of customers after the game. Indeed Vester might have remained a pariah until the end of his days had not his daughter Sally set her cap for Henry Sullivan. Their courtship and subsequent marriage transformed the public attitude to the McCarthy dynasty. Vester was forgiven because of Henry Sullivan's standing in the five parishes but his involvement in the attempts to disrupt the drive would never be forgotten. He continued to parade through the fields and by the river banks with gun or fishing rod as though nothing had happened but always he came and went in fear of his life despite outward appearances.

Father Frank Tapley went on his knees before his Bishop and earnestly beseeched him for a transfer to any other parish in the diocese no matter how isolated. He became convinced after listening to the pre-Christmas confessions of the Mullanney and Sullivan brothers that he was the victim of the most obscene conspiracy. His wish was granted and his confessionals were thereafter to become sanctuaries for the damned and the despairing.

Eventually word filtered through about the death of their dear friend Algie Clawhammer. The body was transferred to Sarsfield Barracks in Limerick and the next of kin notified. He was buried in his family's plot before his erstwhile companions heard of his accidental demise. They mourned him as befitted a trusted and loyal companion, short as had been their acquaintance. Some time after the military burial, with full honours, Private Patrick Desmond Conway, known affectionately and forever in the five villages as Algie Clawhammer, Sergeant Greg Rowley underwent a mental transformation which aged him prematurely and left him subject to bouts of severe depression. He was discharged from the army. He ended his days shortly after his committal, by his own hands, in a mental institution.

Writing in his records the Rector of Tubberlick recalled that the great October cattle drive was, in many ways, similar to a ceremony of purification in that it satisfied a variety of yearnings among a sedentary people unused to debauch or high adventure.

'The casualties,' he wrote, 'and they were many, brought their quota of grief but there was no lasting hardship. Three men and one woman died directly or indirectly. We lost one Shorthorn bull, past his prime, and two Roscreas. Our enemies lost seven canines and suffered several humiliating defeats. They have learned that if you trifle with the livelihood of farmers you must be prepared for dire consequences. My friend Mark Doran has rightly been accorded a hero's status and his return from exile bodes well for the future of farming in the United Parishes. His wife Annie is due to have her baby in mid-August and his mother Nonie will marry Danny Dooley when the harvest is secured. My own marriage has brought me nothing but contentment and joy. My wife is pregnant and we expect the new arrival in late October. Needless to say I am overjoyed and pray daily for a successful confinement so that the name of Scuttard will be preserved, for a time at least, in this part of the world.'

IRISH SHORT STORIES

John B. Keane

There are more shades to John B. Keane's humour than there are colours in the rainbow. Wit, pathos, compassion, shrewdness and a glorious sense of fun and roguery are seen in this book. This fascinating exploration of the striking yet intangible Irish characteristics show us Keane's sensitivity and deep understanding of everyday life in a rural community.

John B. Keane draws our attention to both the comic and tragic effects of small town gossip in 'The Hanging' – a tale of accusation by silence in a small village – and 'The Change' – a carefully etched comment on a town waking up to undiscovered sexuality. With his natural sense of character, a gift for observing and capturing traits he gives us an hilarious, mischievous and accurate portrait of the balance of justice in 'You're on Next Sunday' and 'A Tale of Two Furs'. We see his uncommon gift for creating characters and atmosphere in 'Death be not Proud' and 'The Fort Field'.

Keane's magic, authentic language and recurrent humour weave their spells over the reader making this exciting book a 'must' for all Keane fans.

MORE IRISH SHORT STORIES

John B. Keane

In this excellent collection of *More Irish Short Stories* John B. Keane is as entertaining as ever with his humorous insights into the lives of his fellow countrymen. Few will be able to resist a chuckle at the innocence of bachelor Willie Ramley seeking a 'Guaranteed Pure' bride in Ireland; the preoccupations of the corpse dresser Dousie O'Dea who felt that 'her life's work was complete. For one man she had brought the dead to life. For this, in itself, she would be remembered beyond the grave'; at the concern of Timmy Binn and his friends for 'the custom to exhaust every other topic before asking the reason behind any visit': the intriguing birth of Fred Rimble and 'the man who killed the best friend'.

LETTERS OF A MATCHMAKER

John B. Keane

The letters of a country matchmaker faithfully recorded by John B. Keane, whose knowledge of matchmaking is second to none.

In these letters is revealed the unquenchable, insatiable longing that smoulders unseen under the mute, impassive faces of our bachelor brethren.

Comparisons may be odious but readers will find it fascinating to contrast the Irish matchmaking system with that of the 'Cumangettum Love Parlour' in Philadelphia. They will meet many unique characters from the Judas Jennies of New York to Fionnula Crust of Coomasahara who buried two giant-sized, sexless husbands but eventually found happiness with a pint-sized jockey from North Cork

LETTERS OF A SUCCESSFUL T.D.

John B. Keane

A humorous peep at the correspondence of Tull Mac-Adoo, a rural Irish parliamentary backbencher. Keane's eyes have fastened on the human weaknesses of a man who secured power through the ballot box, and uses it to ensure the comfort of his family and friends.

LETTERS OF AN IRISH PARISH PRIEST

John B. Keane

There is laughter on every page of the correspondence between a country parish priest and his nephew who is studying for the priesthood. Fr O'Mora has been referred to by one of his parishioners as one who 'is suffering from an overdose of racial memory aggravated by religious bigotry'. Keane's humour is neatly pointed, racy of the soil and never forced. This book gives a picture of a way of life which though in great part is vanishing is still familiar to many of our countrymen who still believe 'that priests could turn them into goats'. *Letters of an Irish Parish Priest* brings out all the humour and pathos of Irish life.

LETTERS OF A LOVE-HUNGRY FARMER

John B. Keane

John B. Keane has introduced a new word into the English language – *chastitute*. This is the story of a chastitute, i.e. a man who has never lain with a woman for reasons which are fully disclosed in this book.

THE GENTLE ART OF MATCHMAKING
and other important things

John B. Keane

This book offers a feast of Keane. The title essay reminds us that while some marriages are proverbially made in Heaven others have been made in the back parlour of a celebrated pub in Listowel – and none the worse for that!

But John B. Keane has other interests besides matchmaking and these essays mirror many moods and attitudes. Who could ignore Keane on Potato-Cakes? Keane on Skinless Sausages, on Half-Doors? Is there a husband alive who will not recognise some one near and dear to him when he reads, with a mixture of affection and horror, the essay on 'Female Painters'? And, more seriously, there are other essays that reflect this writer's deep love of tradition; his nostalgic re-creation of an Irish way of life that is gone forever.

LOVE BITES
and other stories

John B. Keane

John B. introduces us to 'Corner Boys', 'Window Peepers', 'Human Gooseberries', 'Fortune-Tellers', 'Funeral Lovers', 'Female Corpses', 'The Girls who came with the Band' and many more fascinating characters.

THREE PLAYS
Sive, The Field, Big Maggie

John B. Keane

SIVE is a powerful folk-drama set in the south-west of Ireland which concerns itself with the attempt of a scheming matchmaker and a bitter woman to sell an innocent young girl to a lecherous old man.

THE FIELD is John B. Keane's fierce and tender study of the love a man can have for land and the ruthless lengths he will go to in order to obtain the object of his desire. *Now a major film.*

BIG MAGGIE: On the death of her husband Maggie is determined to create a better life for herself and her children. The problems arise when her vision of the future begins to sit with increasing discomfort on the shoulders of her surly offspring. John B. Keane's wonderful creation of a rural Irish matriarch ranks with Juno, Mommo and Molly Bloom as one of the great female creations of twentieth-century Irish literature.

THE RED-HAIRED WOMAN
and Other Stories

Sigerson Clifford

'He blamed Red Ellie for his failure to sell. She stood before him on the road that morning, shook her splendid mane of foxy hair at him, and laughed. He should have returned to his house straightaway and waited 'till she left the road. It was what the fishermen always did when they met her. It meant bad luck to meet a red-haired woman when you went fishing or selling. Everyone knew that ...'

'This collection of stories has humour, shrewd obser-vation, sharp wit at times, and the calm sure touch of an accomplished storyteller ... '

From the Introduction by Brendan Kennelly

Each of 'Sigerson Clifford's delicious tales ... in *The Red-Haired Woman and Other Stories* is a quick, often pro-found glimpse of Irish life, mostly in the countryside. The characters appear, fall into a bit of trouble and get wherever they're going without a lot of palaver. The simple plots glisten with semi-precious gems of lang-uage ...'

James F. Clarity, **The New York Times Book Review**

'Flavoured by the wit and sweetness of the Irish lang-uage, this slender volume presents brief affectionate glimpses of Irish country life.'

Leone McDermott, **Booklist**

THE WALK OF A QUEEN

Annie M. P. Smithson

The scene is set in Dublin during the War of Independence and it is a fascinating story of passion and intrigue which holds the reader's interest from start to finish.

THE MARRIAGE OF NURSE HARDING

Annie M. P. Smithson

The Marriage of Nurse Harding is a story of love, bigotry and heroism.

HER IRISH HERITAGE

Annie M. P. Smithson

Her Irish Heritage is an exciting tale of love and courage.

NORA CONNOR
A Romance of Yesterday

Annie M. P. Smithson

Annie M. P. Smithson was one of the most successful of all Irish romantic novelists and all of her books were bestsellers.